The Havana Room

COLIN HARRISON

THE HAVANA ROOM

FARRAR, STRAUS AND GIROUX ■ NEW YORK

Farrar, Straus and Giroux
19 Union Square West, New York 10003

Copyright © 2004 by Colin Harrison
All rights reserved
Distributed in Canada by Douglas & McIntyre Ltd.
Printed in the United States of America
First edition, 2004

The epigraph is taken from
The Will to Live: Selected Writings of Arthur Schopenhauer
(New York: Frederick Ungar Publishing Co.).

Library of Congress Cataloging-in-Publication Data
Harrison, Colin, 1960–
    The Havana room / Colin Harrison.— 1st ed.
        p.   cm.
    ISBN 0-374-29986-2 (alk. paper)
    1. Bars (Drinking establishments)—Fiction.   2. Real estate
lawyers—Fiction.   3. Loss (Psychology)—Fiction.   4. New York
(N.Y.)—Fiction.   5. Unemployed—Fiction.   I. Title.
PS3558.A6655H38 2004
813'.54—dc21   2003009238

Designed by Abby Kagan
Napkin art on page 361 by Lynn Buckley

www.fsgbooks.com

1   3   5   7   9   10   8   6   4   2

FOR DANA

Awakened to life out of the night of unconsciousness, the will finds itself an individual, in an endless and boundless world, among innumerable individuals, all striving, suffering, erring; the desires of the will are limitless, its claims inexhaustible, and every satisfied desire gives rise to a new one. No possible satisfaction in the world could suffice to still its longings, set a goal to its infinite cravings, and fill the bottomless abyss of its heart . . .

—SCHOPENHAUER

The Havana Room

one

BEGIN ON THE NIGHT that my old life ended. Begin on a warm April evening with a rumpled thirty-nine-year-old man stepping out of his cab at Park Avenue and Seventy-seventh. Manhattan steams and rumbles around him. He needs food, he wants sex, he must have sleep, and he'd prefer them in that order. The cab speeds off. The time is 1 a.m., and he looks up at his apartment building with a heavy, encyclopedic exhalation, which in its lung depth and audible *huh* can be found his whole life—wish and dream, sadness and joy, victory and loss. Yes, his whole life swirls in that one wet breath—as it does in everyone's.

The idea was for him to get home in time for his son's birthday party, as a surprise. Even his wife isn't expecting him. But his plane was delayed leaving San Francisco, circled LaGuardia endlessly, and then the traffic into the city was slow, even at that hour, the Brooklyn-Queens Expressway full of bumping badboys in smoked-glass SUVs, off-peak tractor-trailers, limos from hell. Now, planted on the pavement with his suitcase, our man loosens his red silk tie and top shirt button. He's tired of such constriction, though addicted to its rewards. And has he not been rewarded? Why, yes, of course—bonuses and dividends and compound interest and three-for-one splits. And does he not expect many more such rewards—semiannual wifely blow jobs, prompt service at the dry cleaner's, his secretary's unhesitating agreement to do whatever he asks? Yes, how could he not? He's *worked* for all these things.

He's a successful lawyer, our lawyer. *My* lawyer. My own lost self. He's been with his firm for fourteen years, made partner long ago. His client list includes a major *major* bank (run by dragons in suits, minority-owned by the House of Saud, accountable to no one), several real estate developers (testicle-munching madmen), a television network (puppets dangled by puppets), and various high-net-worth individuals (inheritors, connivers, marriage-flippers). He can handle these people. He's a man of brisk phone calls and efficient business lunches and clean paperwork. Dependable, but not a killer. Or rather, *apparently* not a killer. Not a screamer or a power-drinker or a deal-popper—no doors get blown off when he goes by, the secretaries don't look up. In fact, he should be a little flashier, but probably couldn't quite pull it off. His hair is too thin, his waist one Sunday *Times* too thick. On the third hand, the world runs on dependable, unflashy people like him and he knows it. People feel *comfortable* with him. The law firm feels *comfortable*. So he feels only somewhat uncomfortable, only a bit replaceable. He understands that it's going to be a slow climb. Five years long for every big one up. He sees the middle passage looming, the gray hair, the stiffness in the knees, the cholesterol pills. But not yet, quite. Where the climb ends, he isn't sure, but it probably involves golf and a boat and the urologist, and this is acceptable, almost. If there's a streak of fatalism in him, he keeps it under control. He wishes for many things and knows he'll get only a few. He wishes he were taller, richer, slimmer, and had screwed many more girls before getting married. His wife, Judith, who is five years younger, is quite lovely. He wishes, however, that she was just a little nicer to him. She knows that she's still quite lovely, for a while at least, until—as she has announced many times—she gets her mother's neck. (Will it be a softly bloated horror, or an udder of empty skin? He doesn't know; there's a family history of cosmetic surgery.) Meanwhile, he's been faithful and a good provider and even changed a few diapers when their son was young. Steady—the same guy year in and year out. Judith, however, believes in the reinventability of all things, especially herself, and has cycled through shiatsu, aromatherapy, yoga, Lord knows what.

Wanting something, something *else*. Seems frustrated, even by her own orgasms. Wants, wants *more*. More what? Don't he and Judith have quite enough? Of course not. But such desire is dangerous. Thus the constant reinvention. He doesn't understand how that can be done; you are who you are, he believes, and that's it.

He'd like to reinvent his paycheck, however. He's paid a lot. But he's worth more. The old senior partners, amused and goatish, padding along the hallways, suck out more money than they bring in. Though he and Judith live in one of those apartment buildings where a silver-haired doorman greets every resident by name, he wishes that he were paid better—eighty percent would do—for Judith wants another child soon. And kids in New York City are expensive, totems of major money. The ability to project a couple of children through infancy, doctors' visits, baby-sitters, private school, music lessons, and summer camps while living in Manhattan requires a constant stream of after-tax cash. It's not just the cost of education and supervision; it's the protection, the cushioning. The city's children were traumatized enough by the World Trade Center attack. They don't need to see all the panhandlers with seeping sores, the crazies and subway-shitters. You hope to keep them segregated and supervised. Not loitering or dawdling or drifting, because to linger along the path home is to invite bad possibilities. The child snatcher, the pervert, the mob of taunting adolescents wielding box cutters. In Manhattan all monsters are proximate, if not by geography, then by imagination.

And the contours of the imagination are changed by money. The units of luxury get larger. And this lawyer, this man, my own man, this hairless ape in a size 44 suit, knows it. You eat what you kill, he tells himself. Kill more and you'll eat more. Another child means a new apartment, a bigger car. And keeping Selma, their baby-sitter, on for a few more years. He's paying Selma $48,000 a year, when you figure in the extras and freebies and vacations. That's $100,000 pretax. More than he made as a first-year lawyer! How amazing he can pay this, how terrible that he must! And Judith is expecting a big, shingled summer place on Nantucket someday, just like her friends have. Fifteen rooms, tennis court, heated gunite pool, koi pond. "You'll do it, I *know* you will!" she says brightly. He nods in dull acceptance at the years of work necessary;

he'll be humpbacked with fatigue. Yes, money, he needs more money. He's making a ton, needs more! The law firm's compensation committee is run by a tightfisted bean counter named Larry Kirmer; our lawyer, a sophisticated man who made the review at Yale, has enjoyed fantasies of savagely beating Kirmer; these scenarios are quite pleasurable for him to indulge, and such indulgence results in his ability to appear cheerful and positive when in Kirmer's company. Kirmer has no idea of the imaginary wounds he's received, the eye-gougings, dropkicks to the groin, secret heart-punctures. But if Kirmer doubled his salary, the fantasies of violence and retribution would disappear. Life would be kinda great.

Now our man steps toward the apartment house admiring the cherry trees under the windows, just past their peak, as is our man himself. Passersby at this late hour notice nothing unusual about him; if he was once sleekly handsome, he is no longer; if he had once been a vigorous twenty-year-old, now he is paunched in the gut, a man who tosses a rubber football to his son, Timothy, on weekends. A man whose wife apparently does not mind that when he suggests that they have sex he uses mock-witty metaphors involving speedboats ("get up on my water skis") or professional basketball ("drive the lane"). Yes, apparently Judith likes his conventional masculinity. It does not cause any rearrangements of her femininity. It is part of Judith's life, her life*style*, to be honest, which is not quite the same as a sofa or a minivan, but not utterly divisible from them, either. This is the way she prefers it, too, and any danger to their marriage will come not from a challenge to its conventionality—some rogue element, some dark and potent knight—but from her husband's sudden inability to sustain the marriage's predictable comfort. He, for his part, doesn't yet understand such things, which is to say he doesn't really understand his wife. He understands his law firm and his son and the sports page. He is, in fact, very similar to a sofa or a minivan. He has never lost or gained very much. Just dents and unidentified stains. His griefs are thus far minor, his risks utterly safe, his passions unremarkable, his accomplishments incremental and, when measured against his enormous advantages of class and race and sex, more or less obligatory. If he has the capacity for deep astonishment or genuine brutality, it is as yet undiscovered.

Am I too hard on him, is my description cruel and dismissive? Probably. He was, after all, handsome enough, quite well thought of, dependable in word and deed. A real workhorse in the office. A heck of a guy. Right as rain, a straight shooter, a good dude. His waist really wasn't one Sunday *Times* too thick. He was even reasonably fit. But I *am* allowed to distort this man, to seek indications of weakness and decay, because it makes his fate easier to explain. And because that man—you know this already—that man was me, Bill Wyeth.

I'd last talked to Judith early that afternoon, telling her I'd see her the next day. It was one of those marital conversations full of irritation and subtext. "Timothy really misses you," she'd told me. "He wishes you were *here*."

I'd thought about telling her I was taking an earlier flight. But I wanted Timothy's surprise to be hers, too. I'd been away for four days. My boy was turning eight, and he and his friends were set to go bowling, attend a Knicks practice, and eat at a midtown restaurant featuring waiters dressed like aliens. Then, stuffed with stimulation, they'd all sleep over at our apartment that night. And as I opened the door the signs of their wolf-pack activity met me in the hall: a dozen-odd sport shoes scattered over the floor, a spray of coats and hats, a pile of gift bags, then a finer grade of debris—jelly beans, baseball cards, sneaker-flattened candy, removable vampire teeth, balloons, plastic spoons, streamer paper, chocolate cake, even fake rubber fingers oozing fake rubber blood. With children, one learns to read domestic disorder and its patterns like a forensic investigator sifting the wreckage of a plane. Judith, I concluded, had corralled the boys into bed, then skipped cleaning up after them. A shadowed glimpse into our bedroom confirmed my guess; there Judith lay, exhausted in her sleep, her breasts rising and falling. (She hadn't nursed our son much, and they were still "the franchise," I always told her, which both disgusted and pleased her, and which, we both knew—and were to learn again—was exactly correct; at age thirty-four, her breasts still had market value—more, in fact, than either of us had dreamed.)

I gently closed the door—on this, the night my old life was to end—and peered into our son's bedroom, where all nine boys lay huddled and overlapping in their sleeping bags like puppies. Perhaps one sighed or tossed or addressed a professional athlete in intimate dream-whisper. I kept the hall light on in case of bathroom seekers (who can forget the hot shame of pee, the furtive, groin-clutching pajama-shuffle?) and drifted into our new kitchen, which had cost almost $100,000, and picked up stray plates and pieces of shredded paper tablecloth. The multi-colored chaos of the apartment suggested nothing so much as a hurricane passing over a small coastal town, leaving denuded trees and tossed pickups. No wonder Judith was exhausted.

On the new kitchen counter, a kind of grayish Brazilian marble streaked with purple quartz ("It looks—oh, it looks a foot deep!" our designer had moaned at the prospect of further insertions of our money), lay a list, typed by my secretary, of each boy's full name, his parents and/or stepparents and/or nannies, and the numbers of each (offices, home, cell); in addition, the names of certain boys had been annotated by my wife with pickup times, ear infection medication doses, etc. Innocent enough in its intention, the sheet was sociologically revealing. Here were the sons of some of the most prominent fortyish fathers in the city or, in the case of several second marriages, fiftyish fathers, and likely as not their equally prominent mothers. Every day their corporations and banks appeared in the global financial press. Citibank, Pfizer, IBM. This fact hadn't been lost on me from the beginning. Certain boys in our son's class were favorites of his, others not. But the favorites didn't correspond perfectly with the boys in the class whose parents might be cultivated. Perhaps I had suggested a few certain other boys be invited "for fairness." Perhaps? Of course I had.

Judith had just sighed, tallying the added effort and hypocrisy, the cost of arguing with me, the cost of not. "Okay," she'd breathed heavily, knowing my motivations. That was partly why she married me, no? To eat what I killed? Our son, meanwhile, had clapped his hands in excitement. He was a generous kid and so the party went from five to eight other boys. And here was the list of them, blurred by spilled juice, appended with a smear of chocolate icing.

I set it aside and prowled the refrigerator. Some cold pasta, eight-packs of butterscotch pudding for Timothy's school lunches. But nothing ready-to-eat for a hungry man. I called the Thai takeout place two blocks away and ordered up a hot, greasy mess that came in fifteen minutes, the delivery boy smiling as he took the cash tip, and then Bill Wyeth, yours and mine, spent the last minutes of his former life eating dinner, watching the sports scores, opening bills, and checking his e-mail. There was some consolation in all this multitasking and functionality, the servicing of diverse needs at the same time. Some, but not enough.

Bill Wyeth has one other need, so he steals into the bedroom just to check again. But Judith is miles under, her breath faintly foul, her arm flopped out on the sheet like she's just lobbed a hand grenade against his advance. She is not the kind of woman you can wake up in the middle of the night and jump on. Judith needs preparation—on-ramps and gradual acceleration. They'd had sex before he left for San Francisco, but that was five nights ago, and he never partakes of the hotel porn, out of fear that it *will* somehow appear on the law firm's bill. Every click, every selection stored forever, a string of data trailing behind each of us like a spider's filament. He'd been hoping that getting home early might put her in the mood. But no dice. He needs release, a little shot in the dark. He needs some comfort. Just a little. Besides, he'll sleep better, have more energy tomorrow to deal with the work that's piled up in his absence, to deal with Kirmer.

Judith rolls on her back, breasts shifting, letting go her own wet, capacious breath, and he watches her, his hand idly massaging his groin. Is he frustrated? Hard to say. Bill Wyeth has, sexually speaking, reached the Age of Acceptance. He accepts the fact that he is faithful to his wife. He accepts his desire to plunder any number of younger women and a few older ones who cross his path. He accepts that this will not happen. He accepts that it *could* happen, given sufficient prevarication, rerouting of cash, and subtle adjustment of his schedule. He accepts the fact that his wife has become rather unmotivated in bed—"disinterested" would be clinical yet polite. "Lazy" would be inflammatory but true. He accepts the fact that it might be his fault but that it really might not be, either. He accepts the idea that marriage is the best arrangement for raising children, although it's pretty tough on the parents. He accepts the fact that many, if not most, of the women he desires to plunder are, no doubt, biographically bruised, and that their intriguing neuroses would quickly become tedious, and he accepts the fact that, all things given, Judith is a rather wonderful human being and that he is enormously lucky to be married to her. She is, above all, a devoted mother to their son, still feeling guilty about not nursing, but unconflicted by the outlay of time and energy of mothering. She'd wrecked her career to be a mother, and because she's accepted this, so has he. Also finding his acceptance is the fact that Judith—sweet, loving, busty, good and nervous Judith—has failed to understand exactly what he needs sexually, despite his patient, nonconfrontational description of what that is, and it is not a position or explicit behavior—no, not at all (well, maybe a few behaviors), but rather a kind of emotional largesse on her part, a kind of lingering generosity he has yearned for his whole life it seems and received only rarely. He accepts that she may desire all kinds of lovers who are not him, for it is clear—just walk the streets of New York—that human beings are infinite in their variety. She probably thinks about women, and she *definitely* goes a little weak around older, powerful men with full heads of white hair, and *says* she doesn't find black men attractive (but she has said this a few too many times for him to believe it), and anyway, he accepts this, too. Just as he accepts that out there, in the real world, not just the thin stratum of economic frosting where he resides, people are fucking and boffing and sucking and humping, all shapes and sizes, and putting things into each other—dicks, fingers, tongues, hands, fists, toys, vegetables, viruses, etc.—and that often they are made happy by these activities and often not. He accepts that there are women who require their men to be hairless, and men who desire their women to bench-press three hundred pounds. He accepts that a few radical lesbians actually inject themselves with gray-market testosterone even as certain gay men are stealing estrogen pills from their postmenopausal mothers. He accepts the "classical" feminist critique of men, male hegemony, etc. He accepts the "do me" feminist revision of those critiques. He accepts the terror that women feel at the idea of rape—real, mouth-covering, vagina-tearing rape. He accepts his own occasional, always unplugged desire to do so. He accepts that in certain moments in bed with Judith, he gets close to doing it himself. He accepts that this is a lot of baloney. He accepts that sometimes she loves, loves, *loves* this (his forceful passion! her helplessness!) and other times accepts it dutifully as a necessary chore to be endured, as transcendent as replacing empty toilet-paper rolls. He accepts that the she-males advertised in the back pages of *The Village Voice* often look better than the women. He accepts that he has wondered what it would be like to give a blow job or get fucked up the ass. He accepts that he will never know. He accepts that each one of us wants, wants *so* much, yards and miles and continents of affection and sensation and release, and that mostly we do our best to get it and our best not to get it, depending. We deal with disappointment, we sublimate, we masturbate, we accessorize, we fantasize, we sprinkle psychosexual condiments onto our gruel. Yes, he accepts this, he accepts all of it.

And what he accepts most, now anyway, is that his wife is asleep and unavailable, if not unwilling. He's not getting any action, not tonight anyway—and he accepts *that*, yes, he does.

So, mouth still full of Thai food, nutty and chickeny and hot, he returns to his den and flicks through the cable channels, hoping for some T&A. He'll take anything. Television's standards of indecency rise quickly after midnight, the networks desperate to grab anyone not snagged by the Internet's pornucopia. Anything will do. He's not particular. He's generic. He's a minivan, remember! He has a face full of Thai food, grease on his hands and face and shirt, and is sort of nudging himself, who cares if he gets grease on his pants, just to get the feedback loop started, penis-to-head, head-to-penis. He flicks through two dozen channels with genius reflexes, identifying each show's whack-off potential in perhaps a second before moving on—and *yes!* Here's some kind of spring-break concert, girls in bikinis, dudes in hats spinning turntables, the girls lewdly greased up with suntan lotion, white girls, black girls, dancing around, tits jiggling, fine, this is sufficient, not porn exactly, but sufficient, he'll pay his bills afterward, just get it done with, and he unbuckles his belt, mouth burning a bit from the food, and then— then he hears footsteps in the hall.

"Yeah?" he calls anxiously, pulling out his shirt to cover his groin.

"I'm thirsty."

"Okay," he calls heartily, filled with relief he hasn't been seen.

It's one of the boys, which one he doesn't know, standing in the doorway, blinking sleepily, warmly rumpled in pajamas that recapitulate the uniform of the Jets' starting quarterback.

"I'm Timmy's dad. You want something to drink?"

"Okay. Yes, please."

The old Bill Wyeth now jumps up and hurries to the kitchen to pour the boy some milk. Skim? Regular? He chooses regular, which will be a little heavier in the boy's stomach and perhaps help him sleep better. He hurries back to the hall. The boy is so sleep-slumpy that Bill has to help him hold the glass, greasy from Bill's hands. The boy lifts the glass slowly. The milk is just what he wants. A darling kid, long lashes, hair fuzzed up by his pillow. He swallows the last of the milk, leaving a white mustache over his lip. "Thanks," he says, drifting toward the bedroom. Bill follows, stepping carefully over the other boys, and helps him settle into his sleeping bag, with a few fatherly pats on the back.

Then he retreats to the den, locks the door, finds his dancing sluts on the television, and whacks off—very economically, using the greasy Thai food carton as a receptacle. Then he pays bills for half an hour, also making a donation to an environmental group that's fighting global warming. Oceans on the rise, deserts spreading, apocalypse guaranteed. Having done this, he puts the boy's glass in the dishwasher and tidies up the kitchen. This will please Judith. Always good to please the wife a bit. At one point he is on his knees scraping green bubble gum from the slate floor that the designer insisted was low maintenance. Next he gets a garbage bag and fills it with party debris, bill notices, junk mail, the dual-purpose Thai food carton, and whatever other refuse he can find and drops it all into the building's trash chute. Then he pokes his head into the boys' room again. One of them is snoring thickly, gurgling with a stuffed nose. Then Bill Wyeth undresses and slips into bed next to his wife. The tip of his penis has a dab of residual wetness on it, a tickle, a stickum of memory, as if he and Judith have actually just had sex. He shifts his limbs, he grinds against the sheets, he eases joints and releases breath, he pushes away the work worries that quickly grow frondlike on the walls of sleep. He has done nothing wrong, he is loyal and true. He pays his taxes and doesn't sit in the handicapped seating on the subway. He has earned his rest, and now, dropping into sleep, feels something close to happiness.

Bill Wyeth is safe.

In the morning the boys rushed one by one into the dining room. Judith, up early, had arranged perhaps ten different brands of cereal in the middle of the table.

"Did Wilson get up?" she said after a few minutes.

"He was asleep," answered our son, reading the back of a cereal box.

Judith walked out of the kitchen. I returned my attention to the paper.

"Bill?" came her voice from the hall. "Come here."

I didn't worry until I saw Judith kneeling next to the boy to whom I'd given the milk. She gently rubbed his back, trying to wake him. "Wilson?" she said. "Wilson, sweetie?" She stopped rubbing his back and waited for a reaction, for him to stir. But nothing happened.

"Wilson? We've got breakfast ready," Judith cooed.

"I don't like the way he's just lying there," I said.

"Wilson?" Judith tried again.

I thought the boy's face looked oddly puffy, his fingers pale.

"Wilson? Wilson?" Judith turned to me. "I can't wake him up!"

And neither could I. I knelt down and shook him. He was cold, his head too floppy. "We need an ambulance!"

As Judith raced to the phone, I rolled Wilson to his side, releasing pizza-lumpy vomit from his mouth. One of his eyes, nearly closed, showed only a slit of white; the other studied a poster of the great Yankee shortstop Derek Jeter. The surfaces of both eyes were dry. The boy looked *dead*. But he couldn't be. I felt hot, stupid, sickish.

My wife returned, closing the door behind her, phone to her ear. "We have a problem," she announced, trying to stay calm, "we need an ambulance . . . we have an eight-year-old boy who isn't breathing . . . What? I don't know! We just woke up! No, no, *we* just woke up, he didn't! Oh, please, come—I don't know *how* long—" And then our address and phone number. "Please, please hurry!"

"He was fine last night."

The door opened. Timothy poked his head in, eyes panicked. "Mom?"

"I want you to close the door, Timmy."

"*Mom.*"

"Do as I say."

He glanced at me. "The other boys—"

Judith growled, "Close . . . the *door.*"

He did. He did what his mother told him, and would in the future. Now Judith knelt next to Wilson. "What did you say? He was fine?"

"Yes."

"You checked on all the boys?"

"Wilson woke up."

"What did you *do?*" Something twisted in Judith's voice.

"I gave him a glass of milk and put him back to bed."

She seemed to be searching around him, lifting up the other boys' sleeping bags and pillows. "Not peanut butter?"

"I gave him milk," I repeated.

Judith shook her head violently, in anger or frustration. "He has a severe peanut allergy, it's this crazy, crazy thing!" She grabbed Wilson's backpack and frantically pulled out underwear adorned by Jets insignias, a fresh shirt, and socks. "His mother made me swear not to give him *anything* with peanuts in it. Not the tiniest bit. Even *molecules.* It sets off a chain reaction in his immune system. She had to call the restaurant ahead of time to explain, and he carries a shot just in case." She looked at her watch. "It's too late, it's—I threw away all the peanut butter in the house! I threw away the eggs and the cashews! I looked at all the candy!"

"Judith, I gave him *milk.*"

She unzipped the boy's sleeping bag and pulled it back, finding a plastic case marked EPINEPHRINE INJECTION—FOR USE IN ANA-PHYLACTIC EMERGENCY. "It's empty!" she cried. She pulled the sleeping bag open further. Next to the boy's limp hand lay a yellow plastic injector device with a short needle sticking out of it. "There it is!" she said. "He was trying to—he knew . . . oh, he *knew!*" Weeping, she bent down to kiss the boy, as if trying to bring him back to life. "Oh God, I *promised . . .* I promised his mother—" She looked up and faced me savagely. "Was *anything* on the glass?"

"Like what?"

"Like peanut butter!"

"No. There was some grease on my fingers from dinner, maybe."

"What did you have for dinner?"

"I ordered in some Thai food, sweetie, it wasn't—"

"Oh God!" Judith stood rapidly, hand to her mouth. She rushed from the room in horror, and as our lives fell away minute by minute— the arriving EMTs, the police, the call to Wilson's parents, the other boys, now traumatized, crying or chattering nervously, the retrieval of the murderous empty glass (the peanut oil still on its lip, still smellable as the intensified essence of peanuts), the arrival of the other parents— as all that we had known about ourselves crumbled into oblivion, I could not help but recall that drink of milk—the cool glass beaded with condensation, the surface of the milk itself curved upward where it clung to the glass, the satisfying incarnation of liquid love, almost tasteable from arm's length, ample and full, safe and clean. Who would have thought it, who would've thought that I, Bill Wyeth, dependable, taxpaying minivan-man, respected partner in a top law firm, would kill an eight-year-old boy with a glass of milk?

Then I recalled that Wilson was one of the boys I'd wanted invited, for his father was Wilson Doan Sr., a managing partner in one of the city's major investment banks, itself one of my firm's largest clients, a company with offices in 126 countries. His boy had choked to death on my ambition—you could see it that way, you really could.

And an hour later Wilson Doan Sr. stood before me in the hallway of New York Hospital, his only son and namesake still and forever dead. He was a large, strange-looking man in a black coat. His wife had rushed into the hospital screaming, and when the aides explained that her son was *not* in the emergency room, that he was "downstairs now," she'd collapsed to the floor, growling with grief, writhing as hope left her body. Wilson Doan had seen this. Worse still, he had seen me see this. Now, with his wife sedated, he held his hairy fists at his sides, looking at me directly, and I realized I'd shaken his hand once, years ago, at some function—at Parents' Night at our boys' school, perhaps.

"They said you gave him a glass of milk with peanut oil on it."

"Yes," I said, anxious to apologize. "It was a tragic accident—I'm so sorry."

Wilson Doan was a big man, but what was most noticeable about him were his eyes; slightly crooked, one higher and larger than the other, they gave his face a disturbing complexity; half his expression was public and confrontational, the other private and detached in its scrutiny, the smaller eye coldly noncommittal. This was probably the secret of his success.

"We gave your wife absolutely *explicit* instructions."

"Yes. She followed them."

"And you didn't?"

"I didn't know."

"Why not?"

"Judith didn't tell me."

"Why not?"

"She didn't expect me home."

He said nothing, his eyes upon me, murderous.

"I flew home as a surprise," I added. "To be with my family."

"I see."

He was trying to retain the skin of civility, yet yearned, I could tell, to hit me, to pound and punch me until I was broken or until, years from now, his rage was extinguished. And I wanted him to do it. Yes, I did. I wanted to be released from my guilt; I wanted the intimacy of his hot fists upon me, for in making my pain I would feel his, and he would know this. He could have hit and kicked me for a long time, and I would have taken the beating as a warm rain. Welcomed, purifying.

But that did not happen. Instead we stood there tensely, he hating me, and me fearing his hatred. Two men dressed in clothes identical in quality and style and even point of purchase for all I knew; two men with wives and real estate and reputations and secretaries and ever longer ears and portfolios and aging parents. He knew too much about me, finally, for him to strike. If he struck me, then he struck at himself, or the idea of himself, for we were that interchangeable, and the fate of it, what had befallen us, was reversible in an instant. My son, his greasy glass of milk. He knew he could've done the same thing.

But there was another reason Wilson Doan Sr. didn't attack me then. It wouldn't have been good for him. Construable as an unseemly display. He was a banker, after all. If he was unable to control his emotions in public, what happened in private? People would talk. (They always do.) The *Daily News* might run an item. And that was bad for business. But his restraint terrified me all the more because I knew that his impulse must have release sometime, somewhere, and that the further away Wilson Doan's reaction was—the more remote and delayed the detonation—the worse it would be for me. Every minute that he hated me without satisfaction would be another minute in which he gathered his resolve and refined his stratagems. No doubt, too, he understood this, staying his hand with a promise to himself that my eventual punishment would far surpass a mere beating.

Which it did.

I wonder now how Wilson Doan proceeded. Was it by malicious forethought or by organic intuition? Or both, an alternation of ambiguous anger resolving into clear moments of joyfully bitter fulfillment? I don't know. I never asked the man. What is clear, though, is that Wilson Doan did destroy me. Piece by piece, pound by pound, dollar by dollar. And in the end, though not much was left, the result was not disproportionate to the intention, for the intention was great, his grief having no bottom.

People find it difficult to be with a man who killed an eight-year-old boy. Who can blame them? Even though they know it was "a freak accident, one in a million," they wonder, why didn't the wife tell him about the peanut allergy? That just "molecules" would do it? Or *did* she tell him, and he forgot? After all, husbands always forget things like that. Even I started to wonder if Judith had told me. She could have, on the phone to San Francisco. But she didn't. I was almost sure of it. But I *was* tired, a thousand details in my head. What if she *had* told me, in an incidental sort of way? She never claimed she'd told me, but what if she herself didn't remember? How could one forget a phrase like "a chain re-action in the immune system"? Didn't everyone know Thai food often contained peanut oil? (From the article on the death of Wilson Doan Jr. in the metro section of the *Times*: "Several owners of Thai restaurants contacted by a reporter each confirmed that they used peanut oil in many of their dishes, and each stated they would soon include dis-claimers on their menus in an attempt to avoid this increasingly preva-lent and occasionally serious malady.") Maybe, people thought to themselves, *He'd been drinking*. That would explain it. Or maybe *He and his wife had been fighting*. Maybe *anything*. And why hadn't I heard? Af-ter all, the boy was suffocating! He must have made *some* noise, no? Hadn't I heard it? Maybe they'd been having sex and didn't hear it for that reason. *The wife still has a great rack*, the men would think silently to themselves, eyes squinting with wolfish savvy. Or maybe I, the killer, was flat on my back with an empty heroin needle hanging out of my arm. (A surprising number of lawyers are addicted to heroin.) Maybe I was tweezering hairs out of my nose and listening to Louis Armstrong—it didn't matter. The death of little Wilson Doan happened on my watch, in loco parentis. I was responsible. *Bill Wyeth, you did it*. Yes. *You're the bad guy*. Yes. *You did it, you fucker*. Yes. Just me and no one else.

And I was sorry, terribly sorry, though that didn't matter, either. I imagined little Wilson Doan's mother staring disconsolately at her breakfast. Toast, cold eggs. She was said to be dangerously depressed. Losing weight and losing touch. A few years into the future, parents would clone their lost children. Society would decide it was acceptable and let them do it. But not yet. Maybe the Doans would have another baby, but even if they had buckets more kids, there'd always be an ache, a shadow. I had only to think of losing Timothy to imagine their agony. I'd wrecked half a dozen lives, I had not read the list of instructions for each boy, I had sought satiation in the form of Thai takeout and danc-ing babes, I had somehow not been as vigilant as I could have been. This I told myself. You idiot, look what you did. You and your stupid billable hours and retirement accounts and receding gums. You are revealed as a clown—no, a monster-clown. It doesn't matter if absurdity ravished un-likelihood. There are no complete accidents. All effects have causes. You did it. You suggested the boy be invited. You deserve to die instead. But you won't and you can't; you have a family to care for.

Yes, people find it *difficult*. They don't want you around their own children. They don't want the taint, the stain. The best of them smile blankly and find scheduling conflicts. The worst of them sport a certain anthropological curiosity and examine you for proof of remorse— teeth-gnashing perhaps, a sudden onset of Tourette's syndrome, the eating of glass, a burning tire placed around one's own neck, maybe. But if you are trying to live anything close to a normal day, if you still have responsibilities for such things as buying apples and paying your electric bill and kissing your own boy good night ("Everything's going to be fine, pal, I promise . . ."), then you are scraping by, dealing as best you can. And they, those scrutinizing the tightness of your tie knot, don't like what they see. They see you sigh and say, "We're just going to have to get through this." They don't like that because it's confusing. It's *unpunished*. They want to know if there are "legal ramifications." So what if it was an accident, a stray fingernail clipping of God falling in the wrong place? This is America. If you don't get convicted, you do get sued. O. J. Simpson escaped prison—even though he cut off his wife's head—but was successfully sued. They want to know how it's "affecting the marriage." *How do you think?* I wanted to scream, but didn't. *We're dying.*

Judith fell away from me almost instantly. She stopped having sex with me, and my idiotic banter about water skis and basketball disappeared like so much else. There was one night a month or so afterward when I felt her turn in her sleep and hold me from behind, like she used to do, her hands wrapped around my chest, and even as I felt a deep balm go through me she stiffened with a sudden inhalation of breath, pulled her hands back to herself, and turned the other way.

I could stand the loss of Judith, perhaps, but I could not stand the loss of my son. He didn't understand why people said bad things about his father. I explained what had happened, but the kids at school called him names, said his dad killed children. Said he was going to the electric chair. "It's not true," Timothy said hotly, repeating the conversation. "It's not *true*." But his eyes searched mine for some explanation as to how everything would go back to the way it had been before—*Please, Daddy,* his eyes begged, *make it better*—and when I couldn't do that, then his faith was diminished. The idea of dad, of father, shrank and curled inside him. He hated me, I knew, for I had destroyed his universe.

Yes, everyone finds it difficult. The school required counseling for Timothy and for us and suggested we seek "an alternative placement." We had to pull him out of the school, because of the tension, and again and again he asked why his friends didn't have him over for play dates anymore. The other families in the apartment house seemed less interested in taking him out to the park with their kids, as if a blond eight-year-old boy might somehow be a menace, might conduct lightning on a clear day. This was unfair, but expectable. We're still superstitious, all of us. Monkey-men clutching magic feathers and sniffing the wind. The secretaries in my firm, usually cackling and amicably rude, spoke to me with formality, especially after the firm kept me out of its biggest deal of the year, a $400 million office building finance-and-rent-back in midtown Manhattan. I lost eye contact with people. My accountant didn't return my calls. The grocery boy examined the bills in his hand as if they were soaked with plague. Our elevator man, who'd carried the EMTs up and the body of the boy down, whistled silently and looked away.

Meanwhile, Wilson Doan Sr. attacked. He was powerful enough at his bank to force a renegotiation of the bank's of-counsel relationship with my firm. Our performance had been excellent, largely, but I made sure to absent myself from the discussion, which occurred in their offices. We sent my colleague, a senior partner named Dan Tuthill. A good guy, Tuthill, a pal. He was perfection in the law firm, self-destruction everywhere else: he ate sludge for lunch (veal, German chocolate cake), went on extramarital dates with hookerish, raccoon-eyed women he met in bars, and always bought stocks at their top. But he was loyal and determined and righteous on my behalf. By prearrangement, he called my office on his cell phone as he was entering the bank's conference room and placed the phone on the table among his papers. I shut my door and put the call on my speakerphone. This is done all the time, by the way. Sometimes the conversation is secretly taped on the other end or transcribed simultaneously. I could hear the room start to fill, the warm-up chatter, the briefcases clicked open. Donuts and bagels on the side. The coffee-stirring of commerce. I realized that Wilson Doan was not in the room. The conversation went smoothly enough without him, though, and the bankers outlined how they would need the firm's assistance in the coming year. There were a couple of staffing issues, half a dozen technology questions, and a few minor grievances. Very typical. Then Amanda Jenks, the bank's negotiator, said, "Our last area of our concern involves Mr. Wyeth."

"Please explain," Dan Tuthill said.

"We feel that Mr. Wyeth presents genuine difficulties."

A long pause. I stared at my speakerphone.

"It's a matter of confidence," she said.

"Mr. Wyeth is an extraordinary lawyer," came the voice of Dan Tuthill. "You yourself have said as much in the past, I believe."

The room was silent.

"He's a hell of a vicious negotiator."

More nothingness.

"This is nuts. We're talking about a good guy."

"The circumstances are unusual, I would agree," said Amanda Jenks.

"Yes, and everybody is genuinely sensitive to that," answered Dan Tuthill.

"It's *very* problematic."

"Yes, but am I not correct that Mr. Doan is *not* intimately involved with the day-to-day legal matters of the bank?"

"Mr. Doan is extremely valuable to this bank," Amanda Jenks said evenly. "I think you know that. Let's speak plainly, Dan, okay? We can't conclude this agreement if Mr. Wyeth is involved."

"Involved?"

"On the account, yes."

"Your bank has a successful eighteen-year relationship with this firm, one that includes dozens of personnel on both sides, and you're willing to cancel that because of Bill's presence on the account?"

Amanda Jenks did not reply. Someone coughed, as if to emphasize the silence. "What are you guys billing us?" she finally said. "Twenty, twenty-one million a year?"

Thus did I hear the gunshot of my own execution.

Dan Tuthill then gave a very nice speech, but they wouldn't budge. Later I learned that Wilson Doan and a few of my firm's most senior partners had played a round of golf a week earlier at the Blind Brook Country Club north of the city and whatever needed to be said had been uttered by about the fourth hole so that they could enjoy the game. They hadn't bothered to tell Dan Tuthill, either.

I was taken off the bank account, which cut my hours at the firm by more than a third, but Wilson Doan was not done, not by any means. As predicted, he and his wife filed a $40 million personal injury negligence suit against me. How did they arrive at the sum of $40 million? Certainly we didn't have money anywhere close to that. The suit was handled by Adolphus Clay III, the famous trial lawyer, a balding, droopy-eyed fox who stood before the television cameras and explained that the Doans were not in any way vindictive but were concerned with getting the message "out there" about the dangers of peanut products. "This is their sole motivation," he said. "I assure you."

Clay, it may be remembered, was the man who won a $700 million class-action suit against the cigarette companies, so naturally he had an additional motivation to take this case—as a precursor to another class-action suit against the prepared-food manufacturers who used nut oil in their goods without explicit warnings on the packaging. The day he announced the suit, the stock price of the country's largest peanut oil manufacturer dropped by ten points and the major peanut allergy Web site had an additional 320,000 hits. I had stepped from the safety of my own small private life into the serrating edge of American mass culture. On our first consultation, my lawyer put Clay's chances of winning a large verdict at four out of five, and said that even an unsuccessful defense would cost me perhaps $1 million, with a $100,000 retainer, payable immediately, now, right here, in his hand.

When I reported these details to Judith she nodded and said she was going out to have her hair done.

I was not present when Judith first met Wilson Doan Sr., privately, at her suggestion, for only much later was I told, but I know her well enough to bet that her desire to sleep with him probably began at the funeral, which she attended alone—though dressed rather well, her black silk blouse not as loose as it could have been. Doan was massive in his sorrow, and this would have quietly appealed to her. She would have found an enormous, distinguished man heaving in grief unbearably sexy. And the strange violence in his face surely thrilled her. She met Doan somewhere discreetly and let him know, with a touch on the hand, or perhaps even a frank lowering of herself against his thick wool pants, that she wanted him. For Doan's part, Judith's quivered offering of herself would have been an unexpected pleasure that only improved his fury at me, not diluted it. Men are quite able to separate their lusts from their angers, or to mix them, as necessary.

I do not hate Judith for this. Not so much, anymore. She was doing what she thought was best for Timothy. I think she and Wilson spent parts of six or seven days in one of the smaller hotels on the Upper East Side. Long lunches, lost afternoons. I imagine Judith was quite vigorous in her exertions, quite multiple in her enthusiasms. He was probably a good lover, old Wilson Doan, probably gave my wife a hell of a good fucking, certainly of the weird large-eye/small-eye variety, and that would have rattled her on a whole other level. I have no doubt that Judith surrendered to him completely, abandoned herself to the moment, breasts bouncing, mouth agape, eyes rolling. And why not? Sex gets more explicit as you get older. It has to. The clock is running. I imagine she told him he could put it wherever he pleased. Wilson Doan would not have smiled or joked or been relaxed, for the sex was a way for him to strike at me, and being an intelligent man, he would feel the hatred in his own pleasure.

The danger of the interaction undoubtedly excited Judith beyond her usual capacity, and she would have seen this contrast as further proof of her problems with her husband. Somewhere in the talk afterward she let Doan understand that she was going to divorce me and move away. She is a planner, Judith. She paid for these encounters with our family credit card, not bothering in any way to conceal them from me. But this wasn't quite as cruel as it seems. The human dynamic here is quite complicated, in fact, and you have to hand it to Judith, for she is extremely intelligent when it comes to the human dynamic; by giving herself to Wilson Doan, she allowed him, as I said, a measure of retribution against me, indulged her own anger at me, and even found comfort from her own alienation. But that is not all. She probably wanted to make some sort of symbolic atonement and hoped, too, that sleeping with Doan might soften his wrath. Or perhaps she knew his wrath was coming anyway and wished to get on the other side of it before it fell. Or maybe sleeping with Wilson Doan was, paradoxically, an act of sisterly support of his wife, who, tomahawked by grief after the funeral, had retreated to a very nice room in the psych ward of New York Hospital— the logic being that she, Judith, understood the wife's incapacity and wished to take up some of her wifely duties during her infirmity. Or, quite the opposite, maybe Judith was striking directly at Doan's wife, warning her *not* to endanger Timothy, lest she risk losing her marriage as well. It may have been any of these things, or a bit of all of them. Yet I think it was something else, too, and in a perverse sort of way, I could have warned Wilson, man to man, that Judith was more than his equal.

By appealing to his lust as well as to his fury, Judith neatly separated Wilson from his rational awareness of what behaviors most supported his civil suit against Mr. and Mrs. William Wyeth and the hope of collecting damages and penalties from their various holdings. As soon as old Wilson slipped his stiff decision-maker into my wife, he lost his lawyer's interest in the claim, his wife's undiluted righteousness, and a jury's potential sympathies. For, of course, Judith had *documented*. And not just with the credit card and phone records and a couple of friendly, damn near incriminating notes to Wilson *not* marked PRIVATE sent to his office (duly opened, date-stamped, triplicated, and filed by his secretary, thus becoming the instant legal property of the bank), but also in the particulars: seven pairs of sexy new silk underwear, cut high on the leg, worn only once, or rather *afterward*, still possessing not only the occasional gray pubic hair of old Wilson Doan but leavings of the same stuff that had helped launch his doomed son: his semen, in dried form, and protected forever and ever in clear Ziploc bags. (So much in life comes down to what happens to the semen, where it ends up—inside, outside, high or low, lost or found.) If Wilson Doan continued his suit, then it might well come out—it *definitely* would come out—that one of the plaintiffs was banging one of the defendants, which would be very smudgy indeed, and not pleasing to Mrs. Doan or the officers of the bank. Adolphus Clay III, wiser than most and foxier than all, caught wind of his client's afternoon diversions and soon the Doans had quietly dropped their $40 million complaint.

Not yet knowing the reason, however, I thought this development was a victory, a chance to get our old life back.

"Great news!" I said when I came home that night. Judith was kneeling in her bedroom closet. "It's over!"

Judith just smiled blankly, as one does when listening to the terminally ill describe a miracle treatment.

"What are you doing?" I asked.

"Cleaning out." She dove back into the closet and I watched pumps and flats and running shoes fly over her head. They fell on the bedspread, at the foot of the dresser, across the carpet. I didn't know much about women's shoes, but they looked perfectly good to me.

I'll finish this quickly—if only for my own sake.

Larry Kirmer took me to lunch and told me I'd become "ineffective in the office." He was not wrong, but he was not kind, either. He spoke with the full authority of the firm's executive committee. There would be no leave of absence, no half-time arrangement, no face-saving explanation. I was a partner, but in the end that made no difference. According to the agreement I'd signed long ago, I'd be paid the value of my partnership over a period of seven years. They stretched it out to keep you quiet. If I contended the arrangement, the firm could cease payment. I was to be gone in two weeks, Kirmer concluded, and why don't you take your unused vacation now?

Thus began the sudden stutter of our financial engine. We'd been happily driving a huge domestic V-8 that burned tankloads of American currency—hundreds of thousands a year, fuel efficiency very poor. But who had cared? Who had cared when we'd tossed our extra cash into a new kitchen that we didn't need? My first severance check was in hand, already trickling away, but beyond that exactly no new dollars and cents were being pumped into the engine, and over the next six months I took us down to five miles an hour. Doing nothing, barely breathing, cost thousands of dollars a week. I liquidated the Schwab money market account ($246,745). I stared at the monthly mortgage bill ($8,780), in shock now. The monthly apartment maintenance fee ($3,945) was outright theft. We fired Selma, our baby-sitter, who had remained loyal and true and who kissed Timothy over and over and wept on her way out the door. Private health care coverage was $2,165 a month. I stopped getting haircuts ($62) and shoeshines ($4), I turned off the lights (0.03 cent/hour), I bought pasta ($5.90/lb.) instead of fish ($13.99/lb.), I reused the disposable razors (twenty for $9.95). Judith fired the piano teacher ($75 per lesson). I canceled the credit cards. The units of luxury got smaller, then disappeared. I ungaraged the car ($585/month). We owed some taxes ($43,876) from the previous year. I had them take away the rented piano ($259/month). I canceled the paper ($48/month) and the cell phone ($69/month). Our hubcaps were stolen and I didn't bother replacing them with the authentic manufacturer's caps ($316) or the cheap Pep Boys version ($48.99). We were going two miles an hour, the needle on empty.

"*Are* you going to find a job?" Judith finally asked one night.

"Of course."

"No, I really mean it, Bill."

"I will find a job, okay?"

Judith had lost a few pounds, five perhaps. There had been some long, unexplained lunches, and she'd lost a few pounds.

"I understand that you may *subconsciously* need to do this to yourself, because you feel so bad. But you don't have to do it to *us*."

My son had taken down his Derek Jeter posters and given them to me, saying I could sell them if I wanted. *There's nothing subconscious about any of this*, I thought.

"I've contacted twenty-something law firms in the city, Judith. I've been to six search firms, I've been through the alumni directory, I've lunched with everyone I know." But I was damaged goods. The word had gone out. It was in my face, my eyes, my posture. Even though I tried to hide it and wore nice ties and talked about needing "new challenges." When you're desperate they can tell, and they pity you and hire someone else. It's monkey-logic, it's human nature.

"You were *Yale Law Review*, you were top-drawer!" Judith cried. "What's going to happen?"

"I'm waiting for the bounce," I confessed.

She almost laughed. "The bounce?"

"I won't break," I promised. "I'll bounce."

"When?"

"I don't know." It was the truth.

Judith's voice was nakedly bitter, dismissive. "How far down do you *go* before you do this bounce thing?"

I didn't answer.

"It's pretty far, isn't it?" she said, her own voice bouncing off the white ceiling.

I thought I knew you, I muttered to myself.

"And what makes this so-called bounce happen, anyway?" she cried. "What do you *hit* that makes you come back *up*?"

I loved Timothy. This is what I wanted to say. He had a nice motion with a baseball, he was sloppy eating his cereal, he brushed his teeth haphazardly, he was learning script and made funny errors with his capital K's, he could listen to an entire Yankees game on the radio and tell me how every run scored, he never picked up his towels or his underwear or dirty socks, he donated his allowance to the World Trade Center charity, he got carsick in taxis, he loved Bart Simpson, he practiced holding his breath in the tub, he was a boy. He was a boy I loved, every last molecule, and there had been another boy who was loved just as much, and I had caused his death. The bounce would come when I had forgiven myself as best I could, had earned some fragment of peace, but not before then. That was what I knew, deep in my own lost boy-self, but I could not tell Judith that.

"Listen," I said, "we'll sell the apartment. I'll do whatever I can. You know that. I can work for the government. I'll sell real estate. I'll drive a cab, I'll teach high school. We can move to another city and I'll work as a lawyer there. You know I'll do anything to support this family."

Judith didn't reply. Instead she tilted her head, adjusted her angle of perspective. What she did next scared me. She blinked. She was thinking. Understanding something—if not about me, then about herself. "I don't know, Bill."

"What don't you know?"

"I don't know if I can do this."

I nodded supportively, I thought. "It's a tough time. But we'll make it through."

Judith crossed her arms. "I feel very uncomfortable about everything. We're becoming *poor*." She waited for me to react. I didn't. "Poor!" she screamed.

"I would say we've dropped down no farther than what's politely called the upper middle class, Judith. I don't think you or I have the first goddamn idea what real poverty is."

"Well, I *feel* poor."

"That's a perception, not a fact."

"I also don't feel good about us, Bill, I don't feel good about *you*." Her voice was shrill, fearful. "Because I don't think that you can fix everything. I know how much you blame yourself. But it was a fucking accident! But you believe you have to *suffer* because of it! That's what's in your head. And I don't *want* to suffer with you! And I don't want Timmy to have to suffer! Why can't you just shake this off, why can't you just sort of pretend it didn't happen?"

Pretend that Wilson Doan Jr. hadn't died in our son's bedroom? I didn't have an answer. I could only watch Judith's gaze dart around the apartment—as if all we owned were burning before her—and then back at me, her expression furious, her beautiful eyes filled with resolve, even hatred. Yes, she hated me now, and wanted me to know it.

"You're not going to stick around and find out, is that it?"

"I don't think you under—"

"I understand that you're embarrassed by the fact that I'm not making any money right now. I understand that your sense of security has been assaulted—"

"Shattered—fucking *shattered*, Bill."

"And I understand, Judith, that you have withdrawn all spousal affections until such time as money has returned to your hot little hand."

"Oh, fuck you!"

"Well, that's my point. You won't."

"That's right, and why would I want to?"

"Because you used to like it."

"Yeah, well, I used to do a lot of things and now I do other things," she said, coldly. "And you might as well understand that."

Judith moved out less than a month later, after badgering me into letting her sell the apartment. Yes, she moved out—to San Francisco. We didn't know anyone there, so far as I knew. The giant yellow moving van came while I was out buying coffee, and the two of them left that evening, Timothy holding his empty baseball glove. No fight, no tears, even. As if it wasn't really happening. The real estate agent will be here in the morning, Judith said, everything is taken care of. All you have to do is leave. I nodded dumbly. You'll have to find yourself a place to live, Bill, okay? Her arms were folded in front of her. Lips rigid. Voice firm. You understand why this has to happen. I think she had Timothy on some kind of tranquilizers, because he didn't protest or cry, not at that point anyway, and when they were gone, when they had actually left me, forever and ever, I—

—well, I fell apart.

I *know* this is ugly, I know this is sad. If you see a minivan crash off the highway, engine smoking, windshield a bloody mess, rear wheels in the air, you slow down for a good look and then stomp on the gas to get the hell out of there. I do, too. After all, there are so many *pleasant* entertainments. The sitcoms and the cyberfrolic. It's all *great*. Go to it if you must. Flick and click and disappear. You won't get that here. This goes somewhere else. This is about waiting for the bounce.

For a time I rented a two-bedroom apartment in one of the anonymous new towers on the West Side of Manhattan, bright and clean and charmless, faced with pink granite—a bakery confection of an apartment building. The real estate agent, a man who carried three cell phones, sensed my aloneness and distraction and announced that the place was "a guaranteed babe magnet, let me tell you." But that didn't interest me so much as the fact that the building seemed far removed from my old circles. No one I knew would imagine that I'd moved to such a place. The apartment, which faced west toward New Jersey, as well as California, where Judith and Timothy now lived, was large enough that Timothy would have his own room, and I duplicated as many of his possessions as I could remember—clothes, shoes, video games, Yankees posters—keeping alive the dream that my boy might soon be sleeping in the bed or flipping through his baseball cards while listening on the radio to Derek Jeter foul off curveballs. But I quickly found that I was unable to step foot into the room, that doing so filled me with dread, as if Timothy himself had perished, the room merely a shrine to his memory.

A few months into my time there, one of the residents, a woman of about forty with bluish lipstick, frowned as I passed through the lobby. "Excuse me?" she called.

"Yes?" I said.

She stared at me, mouth set.

"Something wrong?" I said.

"I don't know," she answered. "I heard something."

"Heard something?"

"About you, yes."

"What did you hear?"

She looked at my feet and at the expanse of floor between us, then back at me. "I heard that you killed a child and got away with it. That there wasn't enough proof to send you to the electric chair." She waited for my response, her hands on her hips, alert to her own bravery. "There are a lot of kids in this building, mine included, so—"

"So you wanted to know."

"Yes. That's right. Someone knew someone who knew you. They didn't tell me the exact connection."

I said nothing.

"Well?" her voice came back, more righteous now.

I took a step toward her so as not to raise my voice.

"Stay there!"

I stopped. "There was a terrible accident," I said.

"That's not what I heard."

"That's what happened. Believe me, I was there."

"I *don't* believe you. I think there's more to it than that."

I resented this lipsticked woman, whose name I did not know, I hated her nosy instincts, her ferocious willingness to make accusations on the flimsiest of information. She was a dangerous kind of person, but she was also trying to protect her children and the children of other parents, and I doubted that I'd have acted much differently if the tables had been turned. "It was a terrible accident," I repeated. "That's all I can tell you. It destroyed two families."

"It just can*not* have been that simple."

I started to move on.

"Wait a minute! I think you're going to have to explain yourself to the tenants' association."

"Oh?" I remembered their fliers in the lobby, concerning trash removal and where children's bicycles could be stored. "And what if they don't find my explanation satisfactory?"

"Then I guess you'll have to leave."

"My lease is with the building owners, not with the tenants' association," I noted.

At this the woman gave a tight ratlike smile. She was happy that I'd resisted. It meant that now there was an issue, something to pull at, to get the flesh to tear. "We'll see," she threatened. "We will most definitely *see*."

A flier appeared on the bulletin board the next day announcing "a meeting of tenants concerned about family safety issues." Two days later, the minutes of that meeting were posted, announcing that "there was unanimous agreement that there is an urgent need to alert building management about issues relating to the character and criminal histories of specific tenants."

This was an inquisition and a witch-hunt and a vampire-chase, conducted in daylight by people who meant well, and it was coming to get me. I donated the entire contents of my apartment—toys, furniture, kitchen things—to the Catholic church ten blocks to the north and moved out.

Yes, I hurriedly moved out, and I also moved down, where I hoped no one would know me, to a small third-story walk-up on Thirty-sixth Street between Eighth and Ninth Avenues in the garment district. It's a lousy area, one of the city's many pockets of dirty, congested nowhereness, a few blocks from the rump ends of Pennsylvania Station and Macy's. I rather liked its hulking, paint-peeling anonymity. You don't want to go there. It'd be a waste of energy—a neighborhood with no neighbors to speak of, just offset-printing shops squatting in looming ten-floor factories where long fluorescent tubes stay on all night and smoke vents elbow from opaque windows. A place where you can get an industrial sewing machine repaired in an hour, or a greasy breakfast for $1.50. Where tired men push racks of sequined blouses on rolling flat dollies or pile five dozen cellophaned office chairs on the street. At night, there's no interesting decadence, no glammy intrigue, just drifting, muttering shadows, many wandering to and from the Hotel Barbadour around the corner, one of the city's few remaining single-room residences. Sad, unsoaped people—tooth-pickers and flagellomaniacs. Hummers and have-nevers. My building, in the middle of the block, looked out on a parking garage where a tired woman in red pants gave blow jobs from inside her van to the clerks on their lunch hours. When they came out afterward into the sunlight, they paused to tug at their pants, look left and right, then went on. Sometimes the woman's children played outside the van while she was inside. Ninth Avenue provided a Laundromat, a deli, a newspaper shop, and a daily encounter with a big-armed Puerto Rican guy who appeared each morning, always with a White Castle coffee cup and often a black eye, singing off his drunk as he staggered in the sunlight. "I took on the Cubans," he'd cough, "I took on the Haitians. I'ma gonna kill everybody."

Yes, quite a comedown for old Bill Wyeth, someone who'd slept in twenty or thirty of the world's swankiest hotels (the Conrad in Hong Kong, the Connaught in London, the Ritz in Paris, etc.), yes sir, a fellow who'd even been to a White House dinner during the Clinton administration. (The forty-second president himself had come over to me, looming and squinty-eyed, red-nosed, and shaken my hand and said something in his moist, scratchy voice, *Good to see you, we 'preciate your support,* or some such as the White House staff photographers clicked away, but that was enough for me—as he knew. When the president shook Judith's hand, her ability to speak devolved into breathy, near-coital word-bits: "Yes, oh, I—! Thank you! Yes!" The cameras clicked, as they did with everyone whose hand he shook. The pictures of both of us with the president, grinning like maniacs, arrived in a large, crisp, unsmudged envelope exactly two days later, having been borne aloft on some special private presidential postal service, the return address on the envelope simply THE WHITE HOUSE in raised gray letters. Judith spent $600 having the photos framed and she took the one of her with Bill C. with her to San Francisco, and what happened to the other one, with me, was anyone's guess.)

I don't remember much from my first few weeks in the walk-up on Thirty-sixth Street, and the reason is simple: I discovered a bottle of Judith's old sleeping pills tucked into my running shoes and swallowed three or four of them a day. You don't kill yourself on that, not even close, not that I actually wanted to. The changes are subtle. You float as you sink. You watch television while sleeping. You actually feel your eyes roll back into your head and it is in no way objectionable. You forget to take off your socks before stepping into the bath. At some point I bought a mattress, a table, and a chair from a guy on the street. I ordered Chinese food every twenty hours or so. I didn't mind the cold ginger chicken, the ants. I shaved irregularly, I used a T-shirt as a pillowcase, I read the news backward.

In time the divorce papers came; I signed the red-flagged pages without reading them. No custody, arranged visitation. Our old apartment sold quickly, the money went straight to her lawyer. I didn't care. I thought Judith and Timothy should get every cent possible. My retirement savings, so carefully tended and weeded and worshipped, were subject to the division of property, and perhaps already knowing that I was incapable of labor, I agreed to the complete liquidation of all my accounts, subject, of course, to the resulting penalties and retroactive taxes. And after the division of this sum, I was left with enough money to squeak along for a while, a few years anyway.

This noble destruction of wealth soon proved to have been unnecessary; Judith's sudden and rather expeditious remarriage to a young technology entrepreneur relieved me (sadly, for it might have been a source of dignity) of the obligation of child support. I was left to live off my future. I preferred not to know anything about the new husband, but one day, while flipping through the financial-celebrity magazines at a newsstand, I came upon a portrait of him. It was a shock. The article, titled "Young Wizards on the Verge," explained why his new company was so sought after. It held the patent to some laser-data storage technology I didn't understand. Data storage, the country was obsessed with it, a new way to avoid death. The article included a glossy photo of the new husband. He was young. Surprisingly dopey-looking, even, neck too long, eyes too close together, maybe even a little cross-eyed, but decked out in a good suit that I'm sure Judith selected. The text said he was twenty-eight years old, had three advanced computer engineering degrees. Stanford, Caltech. A kid, almost. Another picture: wide-hipped and duck-footed. If I was a wrecked minivan, then he was a new laundry truck. Somehow Judith had smelled him out from across the country, and teased him with some of the good stuff. A wink and a wet smile and he's stump-staggering toward her on his knees. I hated his youth, his brain that understood obscure, fantastically valuable things. Did she suckle him, I wondered miserably, did she press that geeky, appreciative face into her buoyant breasts knowing that the rest of things would take care of themselves? Knowing he didn't have a hundredth of the danger or poisonous power of Wilson Doan, but not caring, and, for his part, did he feel that deep, peaceful slowing of the pulse, as *I* had once felt, Judith's large soft nipples touching the roof of my/his mouth, and did he then know, *know*, that he was home again, parked, garage door down, safe as he had not been since he was two years old, and that this woman, this mother-woman, would take care of him, force these lovely soft things against his face, for him to suck, if only he did what she wished, which was to hand over the money? Well, maybe. Or maybe Judith really loved him.

The joke had one more gruesome laugh. When Judith's new husband took his company public a week later, he was suddenly worth some $852 million, and my obliteration was complete. My knees actually buckled—ever so subtly—as I read the newspaper article on the way up the stairs to my apartment. You had to shake your head, even smile at the thing! I had been well paid, had worked like a sled dog for that pay, but the pile of security I had amassed for my family had been rendered meaningless, reduced to a rounding error in the new husband's countinghouse.

That Timothy now lacked for nothing—except for his father—and never would, was bitter solace. He was still young enough that he'd be blinded by his new stepfather's supernova of wealth—the nineteen-thousand-square-foot house in Marin County, the skybox seats to the '49ers, the beach house in Hawaii. I, his father, who issued the seed of him from my loins, was reduced to a dead moon in a lost galaxy, a small voice of a shrinking, uncle-like presence. For a time, I wrote him letters and sent him e-mail and small gifts. But these activities seemed to make me cry. Yes, I wept at the loss of my son. My wife, too. Oh, I missed Judith, too, everything about her. Would have taken her back, in a minute, forgiven all. I tried to keep up my end. But Timothy's letters and calls became less frequent. We didn't have much to talk about. I didn't know anything about his school or friends. I think he and his mother were happy. She was successful, Judith. She made the transition. She saved her son, she saved him from me, from what I had done.

Days flicked by, months drifted along. I was silting my way to the bottom. One could rightly ask how it was that I failed to find another job or rebuild my life to some minimal degree. Or even talk to someone. What friends remained suggested that I should move to Seattle or gobble antidepressants or practice exercise regimes banned in China. And as for my loneliness, certainly Manhattan is filled with an abundance of intelligent, forbearing women, some of whom might have been patient with my despair, but I was unequal to the task of finding one. Surely a better man would have resisted, argued, fought, asserted his rights and achievements and responsibilities. But as we always learn too late, the world doesn't care who we used to be, not particularly. My identity proved as removable as one of the tailored suits I used to wear, and I must confess that as I witnessed each piece of my life flutter away—job, marriage, child, home, money, friends, I entertained a perverse curiosity as to what might remain. Certain small lifelong habits, such as cracking my knuckles and double-knotting my shoelaces, gave me unnatural satisfaction, and seemed increasingly important proof that I had in fact come from somewhere and not plummeted out of the sky, wet and blinking and alone, a newborn forty-year-old man.

In time, I got used to life in my damp apartment on West Thirty-sixth Street, miserable as the building was. The place included a living room, a small but newish kitchen, a bedroom perhaps eight feet across, and a small bathroom. I kept the apartment reasonably clean, considering no one visited me. I tended my accounts at a small desk, sat in one small sofa, ate at a simple table with one chair, owned ten or eleven dishes, slept in a single bed. Outside, the hallway carpeting was worn thin like a path through the weeds, the windows hadn't been cleaned in at least a decade, and who knew if the fire escapes actually worked? The super, a retired and kindly Latino man with dozens of keys on his belt, was occasionally seen escorting an exterminator inside or changing lightbulbs in the hallway, but in general he remained in the basement, where he ran an unlicensed air-conditioner repair shop and looked after several young grandchildren. The building housed perhaps fifty souls, and at first I told my fellow neighbors almost nothing about myself, for I regarded my stay as quite temporary. Within a few months, however, I began to study them with more curiosity, to engage in harmless conversations in the hallways and lobby that allowed me to patch together a mental map of the building. It became clear that about a quarter of the building's inhabitants were happy and on the way up—young girls with good office jobs, say, or the thirtyish Pakistani couple who'd soon have enough money to buy a small apart-ment—while the rest were moving along various angles of descent, each an example of the grotesque nature of normality: the divorced woman of fifty suffering from cancer, abandoned by her children, painfully climbing the stairs to her apartment, her torso shrunken hideously by her disease, her hair so thinned by the chemo that I could see the shimmering curve of her scalp; the ruined day trader who had high-quality pot delivered three times a week; the would-be dancer with bad skin whose inability to get work was gradually pushing her toward prostitution; the manic sales-man who ran an illegal oyster-exporting business; the fat man with no visible form of income who waddled out each day with his Pekinese and a red cane, and returned a few hours later clutching a greasy bag of fried chicken in one hand and an X-rated gay video from the shop around the corner in the other; the chain-smoking ex-magazine writer (author of lengthy and once important new journalism features in *Sports Illustrated*, *Esquire, Look, Harper's, McCall's*, and the old *Life*), formerly almost-famous and now in his late sixties, coughing softly all day behind his door as he pounded out wads of filler for obscure sports-junkie Web sites; the Russian couple whose fighting and fucking was indistinguishable; the older Italian woman who lived on the income generated by her late husband's ownership of two New York City taxi medallions, now rented to a Bengali taxi company in Queens, and so on.

Yes, and so on. The mood of the hallways was undifferentiated loneliness, the smell a mixture of air freshener and cigarettes, the sound the chatter of television sitcoms—including the famously popular ones about clever young professionals living in Manhattan apartment buildings. We, the people who stayed, regarded each other warily, for the presence of each other's failure and misery confirmed our own.

Judith sent me a postcard saying that she and Timothy and her husband would be spending the summer and fall in Tuscany, perhaps with a few weeks in Nice when it got hot, and that, if necessary, I could contact her through her attorney. Timothy would have private tutors in each city, she added. I studied the postcard carefully. Judith's lettering was precise and orderly, showing no wild emotional looping up and down, no leftward-slanting overcontrol. I could tell from her handwriting that she'd written the postcard in a mood of upbeat functionality, ticking items off her things-to-do list. *Hire house-sitter, pay lawn service, get mail forwarded, drop postcard to sad-sack ex-husband.* The happy wife doing happy things.

I slipped down another notch after that. Life, I understood now, was not ever as it seemed; the windowpane of assumption is shattered, the real view revealed, then shattered again. Yes, I slipped a bit—nothing dramatic, exactly. I was depixillating, becoming invisible, emptying. I let my health insurance lapse, I forgot to pay my bar association dues, I quit checking my e-mail, skipped the latest movies, met no one for lunch, spoke rarely, forgot what I read, dreamed nothing.

You may live emptily in Manhattan and be well entertained, however. It doesn't matter if you're unemployed and emotionally disoriented. The city—mysterious, indifferent, ever-changing—remains available for inspection. It also helps if you wear good suits from your old job, for people won't bother you and you can slide into places and use the men's room. Yes, it helps to look respectable. Which, absurdly, I did—each day dressed in coat and tie, carrying my briefcase on the way to nowhere. The city doesn't mind if you spend too much time on a park bench or street corner; the city invites you to stand anonymously, windy grit swirling by. The buildings and shadows and faces practically beg you to fall into a walking dream, a speculative fugue. I did not quite become one of those chattering philosophers with matted hair and blackened fingernails but I was patrolling the perimeter of sanity. If you'd passed me on the street you'd have seen a man just standing, clearly in no hurry, making private studies of things that busy people don't have time for. The patterns of taxi movement on the widest avenues. The afternoon strobing of shadow and sunlight on Broadway. The way water moved.

Yes, one rainy November morning it was water that interested me, how it arrived in the city and how it left, having touched the people I no longer knew. The waterways of Manhattan begin as bubbling streams one hundred miles north, and become enormous aqueducts roaring through bedrock ninety feet below street level that divide upward into a jungle of pipes that telescope ever narrower as water is pushed hundreds of feet into the air, captured in rooftop tanks, then released through iron to brass, chromed steel, even gold plate. Water, pure as rain, but for the fluoride added upstream, and maintained at relatively constant upward and downward pressure but certain always to be recaptured by pipes and fall earthward—flushed, emptied, drained, trickling from spigots and immediately mixed with coffee grounds, urine, food parts, hair, menstrual blood, including, I imagined, that of Wilson Doan's wife, toothpaste rinse, dirt, vomit, the cold semen of Wilson Doan himself (were they trying to have another child?), cigarette butts, Adolphus Clay III's salt-and-peppery whiskers, the soap scum left from Larry Kirmer's 5 a.m. prework shower, Dan Tuthill's confettied credit card receipts and other small documents of compromising information, and the skin cells from Selma's sweet but disappointed face. This muddy stew, this broth of humanity, joined the rain when it came in sheets across the glassy facades of the skyscrapers, running down copper roofs, tar paper, asphalt shingles, aluminum gutters, the windows my son used to gaze through, downspouts, gargoyles, granite facing, bricks of every shape and color, marble, brownstone, painted clapboard, vinyl siding, rusting fire escapes, air-conditioning units, including those that had cooled my wife's skin after she'd screwed Wilson Doan, furnace exhaust vents, the vacuum-sealed double-paned windows illuminating my former law firm office (a new partner in there now, on the phone, safe as a man could be), the rain rattling the leaded colored glass of the church windows where young Wilson Doan was mourned, the penthouse cedar decking where his father drank martinis in the summer . . . down all these, passing rivets, screws, nails, bolts, mortar joints, caulking, television antenna wire, security cameras either swiveling or of fixed position, including the ones outside our former apartment house that recorded the removal of young Wilson's motionless body to an ambulance, the billioned drops of this vertical floodplain carrying leaves, incinerator soot, a dusting of lead and heavy metals, pigeon and rodent matter, paint chips, rust, volumes of dead and dying insects, the whole mingled sedimentary waterfall plummeting back below street level, sewered and forgotten . . .

. . . yes, you may do nothing in Manhattan but tramp around in a suit and tie and study the rainfall, but you still need to watch out where the hell you're going. Which, that soggy November day, as I descended the subway steps at Sixth Avenue and Thirty-fourth Street, I didn't do. The sky had broken open, and everywhere the streets were flooded, taxis splashing sidewalks, oily runoff gurgling into storm drains. I'd completed my idiot disguise that morning with an umbrella, a raincoat, and a week-old copy of *The Wall Street Journal*. But I failed to notice the muddy waterfall pouring over the header above the subway stairs, and when I felt the cold shower upon me—and leapt sideways—I ran headlong into a younger man in a studded leather jacket as he hurried up the stairs.

"Fucking business *freak*." He squared his shoulders and I noticed the rings in each nostril, the tattooed tiger coiled around his neck.

"Accident," I sputtered. "Sorry."

"I guess you *are*." He swung his fist, hitting me once in the jaw, squarely and with authority, as if he'd done it many times before. I fell back onto the slippery stairs, holding my mouth.

"You keep running into people, they're going to fuck up your executive *shit*, man." He glared, then continued up the steps.

I slumped to one knee, then both, pain ricocheting around my head. Finally I steadied myself and looked up. Had anyone seen the assault? A gaggle of teenage Chinese girls swept down the stairs past me, all colored raincoats and gossiping happiness. In the sluicing downfall they barely noticed me. I spat out a broken molar and staggered back upward, tonguing the throbbing place in my jaw and wanting nothing so much as a drink and a dry place to sit down. Any goddamn place would do. Any place where civilization was still intact. My head hurt as much as my jaw. In front of me a group of young businessmen sporting blue umbrellas with identical corporate logos jostled merrily along Sixth Avenue. I followed them, a lurching figure with a hand to his cheek. The men turned at Thirty-third Street, then disappeared through a big door flanked by potted evergreens. EST. 1847, claimed the gold lettering on the glass. It was an old-time Manhattan steakhouse. I'd passed the place a hundred times before, but never gone inside. Now I did, pulling open the heavy door.

And that—the greasy glass of milk, the long fall from grace, the sudden punch to the head—was how I discovered the Havana Room.

two

FROM THE OUTSIDE, you saw only the gold script and the heavy door—nothing that suggested how big the place really was, nor what went on inside, and with whom. You stepped down to the main floor, a vault of mahogany hung with nineteenth-century oils (railroads, western expansion, warships under sail), and there you submitted to the aroma of steak. The maître d' greeted every arrival from his station, and once you penetrated his skepticism, two blond assistants conveyed you to a table. One could order oysters Rockefeller or Scottish smoked salmon as an appetizer, but these were merely prelude to the fifteen-ounce filet mignon au poivre, the incomparable New York sirloin, or, say, the sixteen-ounce Kobe. Real gut-droppers and heart-stoppers. The cost? Too much, of course, and washed down with liquor marked up five times from wholesale. But no one cared. Each day the place moved four hundred lunches, mostly to office dwellers along Sixth Avenue and Broadway, as well as to a smattering of midwestern and Japanese tourists who believed, incorrectly, that the restaurant represented no more than a quaint exercise in nostalgia and American history. After the lunch rush, however, in the lingering long afternoons and swelling nights, the joint filled with its real customers—space-peddlers and debt-dealers, sex-biters and lie-eaters—the very people, in other words, who've always made New York City so grand.

As soon as I stumbled inside on that rainy winter day, I was seized by the dark, agreeable gravity of the place—the chair-rubbed wainscoting, the ceiling smudged by lamp smoke. Nothing was dingy but all was broken in, softened by the centuries. Within a few minutes I'd sipped a shot of whiskey, which eased the pain in my jaw, and had tasted a bowl of steaming chowder—my first real pleasure, I realized, in quite some time. On the wall next to me hung a map of Manhattan that showed the coastal contours of the island before they were filled in, the inlets and streams and swamps now gone. Next to it hung a framed newspaper account of the great fire of 1835 that specified the tragedy's death count, as well as the lost value of incinerated shops, saddle manufacturers, and apothecaries. Dry rot crept over the yellowed paper into the columns, turning the crisp, type-struck letters into blank, unreadable clouds. Even great catastrophe, it seemed, would be forgotten in time. And this was a comfort. No one knew me here, I realized, no one suspected me of failure or accidental murder, no one begrudged me my soup, my heavy spoon.

I came back that same night, wearing a fresh shirt, and the next day, and the day after that, ten of the next ten nights. I ate, I drank, I chatted with whomever. Screw the cost. Why had no one told me of the place? Where had I been? In those first few weeks I spied newborn movie stars and living-dead politicians, rappers in ghetto-fab white furs, the nation's most prominent feminist theorist (a heavy napkin tucked into her shirt as she chewed her meat savagely), the mayor and his bickering entourage, the city's most famous call girl (a Russian woman, she dined alone, with reading glasses and a book), and members of all New York's professional teams. Presidents and prizefighters had also eaten there, long ago, but no one really cared, because new action was available every night, pounding heavily, cigar in hand, up the stairs that led to the Churchill and Roosevelt Rooms (reserved for private parties six months in advance, piano for hire, strippers allowed), or sitting too mysteriously at the junior bar, smoking with impunity and waiting—perhaps for you. They came exactly because the place was not new, not suddenly famous for its piquant sauces or artful arrangement of vegetables; no, the terms of the transaction had nothing to do with recent discovery, but rather with what was long proven: that you and I and all of us were doomed. The paintings and lithographs on the walls featured only the far departed, and to eat beneath their unchanging gaze was thus to understand—no matter how lovely her smile, no matter how handsome his wallet—that it did not matter if you polluted your lungs or liver or gut with the good stuff being served, because a man or a woman's life was itself just a short meal at the table, so to speak, and one had an obligation to live well and live now, to dine heartily by the logic of the flesh.

Each night the tables filled by six-thirty, and soon I noticed the clientele mostly comprised men eating on business, seven out of ten, anyway. The women could be divided into two groups: the younger ones making their first or second or eighth time around, walking stiffly and with only half-hidden anticipation, and the not-so-younger ones, who by the very fact of their presence had stopped counting just about everything, including tonight's drinks. The men came in more ages and gradations, or so it seemed to me, perhaps because there were many more of them, or because I studied their variety in search of my old self—that optimistic fellow, that happy minivan—as well as versions of my former *future* self, the Bill Wyeth I would now never be: fifty, settled into the law firm, drinking coffee with Judith each morning, perhaps taking a second or even third child to school, richer every year, each August spent in the shingled house on Nantucket. And those former selves, future and past, were there—by the dozen in truth, sweating through their oxford cloth shirts after the second drink, fiddling with their handheld devices and cell phones, young enough to fear their hairlines more than their hearts, old enough to have seen pals get knocked off the high end of the seesaw. Always drilling for the hidden streams of cash running through the city. Sexed up with ambition, but worried that their penises, like a volatile tech stock, might be subject to sudden performance downgrades. I heard a lot of jokes and saw plenty of smiles, but mostly the talk was reducible to money, the laughter mortgaged, the ambition presold. These were men who were prosperous and in demand, loved by women and children, men who possessed life insurance and clean underwear. Mostly Republicans except when they agreed with the Democrats. Knowledgeable about the interest rate cycle. Oil changes every three thousand miles. Retirement plan well funded. Irony well funded. Safe—just as I had been.

The manager of the restaurant, a tall dark-haired woman in glasses named Allison Sparks, tolerated me at first because I was a minor yet constant revenue stream, always willing to sit at Table 17, the worst one in the place, a two-seater against the far wall, almost touching the clanking plate-warmer. Within the smoky stage of the steakhouse, Table 17 lay in the deepest shadows, and if the patron sitting there added nothing to the frisson of the atmosphere, he couldn't detract from it, either. Allison Sparks, who I estimated to be about thirty-five, had managed the place for a long time, and knew all its slow zones and dead spots. I liked her and I watched her from afar, and I confess that she was another reason I returned each day, usually in a suit and tie. Yes, I might as well confess from the start that had I not found Allison's manner so alluring—her rustling, long-legged efficiency as she went by, her perfumed busyness— things would have been very different—for me, and for others, in some ways worse, perhaps, and in many ways better.

How and why a woman is beautiful keeps changing as I get older, for I tend to notice aspects of women that I didn't as a younger man, and in my twenties, say, I wouldn't have described Allison as beautiful. But she was. Not in her separate parts, perhaps, but in the whole of her. What I felt most was her confidence, her relentlessness, her drive to have things her way and no other. She seemed full of humor and fury and sexual need. She arranged people, fixed problems, came to decisions. She checked her watch and kept her back straight and made sure no lipstick was smeared on her teeth. The steakhouse had hundreds of regular patrons who returned at varying intervals, and she knew all of them, often remembering their favorite drink and how they liked their steak done; the place was her stage, and she, not the chef, its true star. Dressed in a conservative blue suit and often carrying a clipboard affixed with wholesalers' wine lists or vendors' bills, she ran the place with absolute authority over everyone, including the owner, a sunken, liver-faced man in his eighties named Lipper who came around once a week in a wheelchair, shook hands indiscriminately with the staff, fondled a waitress or two, drank a glass of Merlot, and was wheeled away by his nurse. He trusted Allison to wring every last cent of profit out of the joint, and she did.

She also welcomed me because I was agreeable with the staff, tipping always and well. When a new waitress or busboy was hired, Allison pointed out the diner at Table 17, explaining that I was a regular, a *regular* regular, often eating lunch and dinner there over six hours, and missing only one or two meals a week, not including the Monday lunch, when the restaurant was closed for cleaning after the weekend. My pile of newspapers and obscure volumes were to be tolerated, they were told, and within a few months my presence at Table 17 became one of the invisible verities of the place. Even when I was not there, I filled the space with my absence. Waitresses and busboys came and went, were hired and fired, but always I was present at Table 17 for lunch and often dinner, appearing to anyone glancing in my direction for the first time as a reasonably prosperous lawyer or businessman, not someone with little better to do. Indeed, I knew how odd it was that I ate there so often, and from time to time I forced myself to miss a meal, if only to appear not to be utterly rooted to the place.

But I was, and beyond my uncomfortable interest in Allison and my enjoyment of the surroundings, I wonder what pressure kept returning me through the heavy front door. Nothing that I later found, nothing that would both make and undo me, was yet perceptible. So I am describing, I suppose, my progress into the heart of things—the incremental movement from newcomer to insider, from observer to actor. In the beginning, however, all I did was sit at Table 17 and make affable chitchat as necessary, watch Allison march past, swinging her clipboard. I found that after a drink or two I was able to forget how much I missed my son and wife—a mercy. I didn't intend to get to know anyone or become involved. I just wanted to be around people. Each day, sitting at my very own Table 17, I'd start with a Coke-no-ice and the soup du jour. There were times when the restaurant quieted and for an hour in the late afternoon I was the only patron. But so regular was my appearance that I disappeared, forgotten while the waitresses sat down and gossiped and the busboys changed the tablecloths. I found these moments peaceful. I had achieved privacy but I wasn't alone. With the merest indication of my eye someone would hurry over to inquire what I wanted, but otherwise I was left alone. Did I make use of this time? Did I read the history of civilization or compose a symphony? No, no, and all no. Yet I was content, in a miserable way; I was not whole, but a collection of fragments, waiting, you could say, for the unexpectable, for something to happen.

Sunk in the shadows, then, I watched, and there was a lot to see. The secret flirtations of the waitresses—with the clientele, the waiters, and each other. I saw a man wolfing down his dinner jump as if struck in the back by a spear, then topple, already dying, facedown onto his plate; I watched a saucy little woman lean forward and slip the watch from the wrist of her date, a drunken fellow whose tongue hung out in anticipation; I heard any number of men being fired over lunch, and when the actual phrase arrived into the conversation ("need to go in a new direction" was popular, as it suggested noble quest and brilliant navigation) the man being let go cut his eyes away or slumped in dejection, and always I felt sick for him. One night I noticed a woman of fifty quietly scissor a man's shirt to ribbons; I saw the denture-worriers and potato-droppers, the bone-gaggers and spoon-inspectors, the toothpick-suckers and pill-arrangers. I saw a rat-sized dog leap out of a woman's purse and lick her fried calamari, I saw a man dab a napkin in his gin and tonic to clean off his hearing aid. And passing around and through them all were the food runners, short squat men, most of them Mexican, who didn't talk or smile, just toted tray after heavy tray to the tables with faces of stoic resignation, like laborers in a mine digging gold they didn't get to keep.

And there was this: If you sat there night upon night, as I did, you noticed that on particular evenings—perhaps once a week—Allison Sparks made a subtle pass through the dining room, stopping for a few words with certain of her regular male patrons. Very few words, to be sure, followed by a nearly imperceptible nod or knowing gleam in her eye. Each fellow appeared pleased to have been selected. At most Allison would speak with fifteen men in one evening, spacing out her contacts over an hour or more so that it'd be difficult to notice a pattern. Unless, like me, you dined alone and made a point of watching for it. I confess my jealousy when Allison bent to whisper in the men's ears, her red lips close to their cheeks, her dark eyes glancing up to check the room and then back into theirs, as if she'd never looked away, crinkling her warmth, privately sealing the deal, whatever it was.

These same patrons tended to linger at their tables as midnight drew near, long past signing the credit card receipt, and after a furtive glance at their watches, perhaps followed by a last swallow of dessert wine, they stood up and eased almost secretively over the creaking boards toward a small, unmarked door to the extreme left of the foyer, quite mistakable as leading to a coatrack or service closet, and kept closed. Affixed to the door was a tiny brass plate, and on particular nights a yellowed card appeared in this plate; on the card was typed a modest instruction: PLEASE KEEP DOOR CLOSED. When the card appeared, the room was found to be unlocked, and the men entered, pulling the door shut behind them. Table 17, so far to one side of the dining room, afforded me a direct if distant vantage on this quiet transit, and on the infrequent nights when the door opened, I saw that no unusual noise or light escaped. The patrons appeared to step down and to the left, and whatever brightness reached their faces came from below, finding only the undersides of their jaws and noses while so darkening their eye sockets that it was as if each man had just pulled on a mask of his own face. Naturally I wondered what went on down there. Were the persons entering any different from the others who stayed in the main dining room or at the bar? Not at first glance. Not necessarily.

But over time I could say with reasonable certainty that the men passing toward the doorway were undeniably prosperous, as I myself had once been, and in particular understood themselves to be still on the upside of the evening. Despite ample food and drink, there was more to learn or wager or steal. During my now wrecked law career, I'd spent quite a bit of time with such men. Their eyes seemed dilated with the conviction that Manhattan was an existentially transactional machine—one person's fate went in and another's came out. Well dressed, rocking on their heels perhaps, tapping a finger against a pant leg, they were eager, these men, they possessed unspent energies and wanted something new, something more. Something *dangerous*, perhaps. And it was not about sex, not directly, or not primarily. The city was full of call girls and strippers and escorts and bar-stalkers, there for the buying and the flying, and anyway, many of the men passing through the doorway kissed their wives or girlfriends goodbye at the foyer, promising to be home in a few hours. But I could not be completely certain of their fidelity, for several times I saw a lovely, unattended black woman carrying a blue suitcase enter the restaurant and proceed directly to this same wooden door, as if acting on previous instructions, and after Allison nodded wordlessly at the maître d', she was always let in.

"What's down there?" I asked a waitress one night when the card appeared on the door.

"The Havana Room?" she said. "It's sort of a special arrangement."

"You mean by reservation?"

"Not exactly. Almost, kind of."

This made no sense to me. Perhaps she didn't actually know. "What do they do in this room?"

She shrugged. "I've heard some things, but I don't believe them."

"Have you ever gone down there?"

"No."

"No?"

"Only a few members of the staff are allowed. Ha, mostly."

"Ha?"

"He's the old Chinese guy? You've seen him. Bald? The handyman?"

Yes, I had seen him, I realized, slender and stooped with a big Adam's apple and bloodshot eyes, somewhere between sixty and eighty years old. Usually he went by holding a wrench or a piece of tubing. But still I didn't understand. "Is there any reason I can't go into this Havana Room?"

The waitress looked around to see if anyone was watching. "It's sort of *restricted*," she said quietly.

"So I can't just stand up right now and walk in?"

"They'd ask you to leave."

"Why?"

"Because it's totally private." She looked at me, perhaps with pity, then lowered her voice further. "You're supposed to, like, *know* somebody."

I nodded. Of course. After all, I didn't know anyone. I had no business, I had no connections, I lacked even a decent operative lie—the one we all need.

Was it inevitable that Allison Sparks and I would fall into conversation? No. Or yes, definitely. She felt me looking at her as she passed back and forth through the restaurant, I'm sure, just as I felt her awareness of my arrival each day, her sidelong contemplation of my books, my solitude. We didn't smile at each other; rather we nodded, as if in silent agreement that although the interest was mutual, the moment was not yet ripe. Of course, I tried to hide my attraction to her, for I had no reason to hope that she felt any toward me. Yet I noticed that she made sure I received very good service at Table 17, and I made a point of never sitting anywhere else. People have such ways of communicating, of course. It was simply a matter of who would speak first, and when.

In the meantime I quietly studied Allison Sparks, and, having encountered many people in my work, imagined that I knew something about her. New York has many avenues to success, but there's a particular kind of young woman who sails upward through businesses (ad agencies, weekly magazines, real estate offices, big restaurants) that are naturally frenzied and unstable. Because she is well organized, industrious, and initially modest, such a young woman reassures those around her; other women feel she is attractive because of her personality, and older men—older than fifty-five, say—see in her a respectful and attentive daughter. So she prospers—at first. And she dates, although often the men are too weak for her and she discards them. Within a year or two her title changes and she has more responsibility, only to find that the parameters of her job now include conflict and neurotic personalities. For a while she tries to deal with these challenges with kindness and tact, yet finds that these strategies often don't work. By now she has identified superiors whom she considers allies and those she does not. She becomes more interested in the end, as opposed to the sweet-voiced means. Is she ready to admit this to herself? Not quite. Meanwhile she becomes adept at all the forms of workplace intimacy, with older men, younger women, people on the phone, and so on. She learns to use her voice, to be playful, teasing, affectionate. She can manufacture energy or humor as necessary, as well as disinterest or rank fury. These qualities of manipulation begin to help her score important successes. She makes money for the operation, she solves problems. The younger women in the business look up to her, but the men of the same age have started to realize that they must compete with her. Her natural ability is intimidating, especially as it seems she is often one step ahead of them in anticipating some small, essential detail. About twenty-nine now, she is at a crucial developmental moment; she is about to plateau or become extremely successful. If she has been working very long hours, the years of toil and loneliness have started to harden her. Men have come and gone; there'll always be another, she thinks. Like a good movie—sooner or later. A year goes by. She senses that the younger women could *fear* her. Another year passes. She has learned to negotiate aggressively for her raises. She begins to change the stores where she shops and to spend money on luxuries and services that make her feel better, that soften her private suffering. She starts to travel alone, not minding that she will appear available—because she is. The spectrum of men with whom she spends time lengthens on one end. She will see older men, in part because they are more patient listeners, but even more so because they have secrets of survival, invisible techniques of power that she wants to master. Is she ready to admit this to herself? Of course not. But she is no longer ashamed to say she is interested in men for their position, their connection to the greater ganglia of wealth and influence and information. The available males now fall into three rough categories for her: handsome boys who are poor, often less intelligent, and surely self involved; barracuda-men in their early forties, usually divorced, who might already be lying about their ages by a year or two; and, lastly, the moguls, small and large, who are now rich enough to die. They are ever more grateful for basic things: untroubled digestion, hair in most of the expectable places. They know they have only ten or twelve good years left. Our woman, nearing thirty-five, sees that the few remaining husband-types are having a rather good time with women ten years her junior. She tells herself she doesn't hate them. She tells herself she needs no one.

This was Allison, so far as I yet understood. And then one day, after I was done with my lunch, she simply walked over to me with a cup of coffee, her footsteps brisk and without hesitation, and said, "So, Mr. Wyeth, you would appear to have a lot of time on your hands."

I checked her dark eyes. "That's true."

"You strike one as unencumbered."

"Unencumbered, yes. Unburdened, no."

"Well, you do seem to like it here," she said after a moment's consideration. She bent close to me and poured sugar and milk into my coffee without being asked. "Assuming you don't mind," she added as she gave the coffee a stir with the spoon.

"Not at all. Perfect. Thanks."

"Well—" She stopped stirring. "I know how you like it."

"You do?"

"Yes, Mr. Wyeth. I notice things."

"You can call me Bill."

"So, where were we?" She tilted her head. "Oh, right, 'Unencumbered, yes. Unburdened, no.' "

"Yes," I said. "But that's no secret."

She blinked, perhaps purposefully. "And what is?"

That stopped me. "You probably know better than I do."

She shifted her weight, one hip to the next. "I just wondered why you come here *each* day." There it was—the point of insertion into the other's life. Once that happens, you can't go back. "Of course, we're glad to see you," she added.

"I hope I'm not your only conspicuous patron."

"Oh, please," Allison sighed. "You should see how many different crazy people come in here."

I made some small noise of concurrence, noting at the same time Allison's nervous red fingernail digging against the wool of her trousers.

"There's one kind of person we need more of, though."

"What's that?"

"Flirters."

"Flirters?"

She looked at me deadpan. "Even though you would *think*."

"What would I think?"

"You would just *think* that in New York City there would be more people who could actually *flirt*." Allison cocked her head, mouth open, daring me for a response.

"Terrible," I agreed.

"Worse. It's unbearable!" she answered. "One feels so *abandoned*."

I could only smile down into my plate.

"You still haven't answered my *implicit* question."

I lifted my eyes. "Which was?"

"We know you are *unencumbered*, but we don't know if you are a *flirter*."

"True," I said, "but we do know the exact opposite of that."

Allison appeared pleasantly confused. "The opposite—?"

"We know," I began, keeping her eye now, "that *you* are a flirter, but we *don't* know if you are unencumbered."

"Well, yes," Allison said, catching up, shrugging away my cleverness, "but that's as it should be."

"Oh?"

"But thank you, anyway."

"For—?"

She bent over the table close. "It was very nice *wordplay*."

"It was all right," I agreed.

"Are you usually so good at—*wordplay*?"

I just stared into her eyes. "All right, I give up," I said.

"Oh, don't. Not *yet*, Mr. Wyeth."

I offered her my hand. "As I said before, I'm Bill."

"Very pleased," Allison said, shaking it lightly, her hand cool and small and experienced, "by the chance encounter."

And with that, Allison excused herself and whirled away to deal with a presumptive crisis in the kitchen. It had been, I reflected happily, a silly little chat, a witty suggestion of what might follow. Oh, I liked her. She liked me, we both knew it, but who knew what it meant? Maybe it was friendship, maybe it was benign, maybe it was prelude to great pounding sex. Maybe it was a lot of things. The city offers you possibilities. Whether you accept them is another matter.

So we began to talk, or mostly Allison did, telling me each day in a low, amused voice as she marched by that "the straight busboys are fighting the gay waiters," or "I have to go fire my druggie waitress," or "a woman vomited in the ladies' room and won't come out." Occasionally she pointed out the celebrities who'd arrived that night, or the woman with two limos waiting outside, one for her, the other for her dogs, or the man who could eat three steaks. It was a huge show, and she was running it. Dozens of employees, hundreds of patrons, money flowing everywhere. But although each night at the restaurant constituted a unique surge of calamity and exhaustion, the place was notable for what was constant, too, and I could see that Allison pondered its larger theatricality. As in any human drama, foolishness announced itself to the room, probity slept peacefully at night, weakness beckoned to strength, and lust bought drinks for loneliness. Night after night, Allison, perched near the maître d' stand, say, or turning the corner to the carpeted stairs leading to the party rooms, would notice one woman or another, or in groups of two or three, arrive late at the bar with only one intention—to find a man. Some would be successful, while a few looked like they might end up in a trombone case by the morning. Many nights Allison tilted her head toward one man or woman or couple like a handicapper at the race-track, and whispered to me, "Watch this one, Bill. Give him about an hour, I'm telling you." Her suspicion rarely went unrewarded. The waiters had to separate men and women who fell upon each other in the rooms upstairs, or they asked a woman to rebutton her blouse, or they lifted a drinker to his feet after he had somehow fallen to the floor.

Allison would have to attend to these little disasters, and as I became witness to her work, saw what she did all day, this put us in a kind of intimate proximity. She felt known by me, and I began to understand that despite dealing with dozens of people, and behind those efficient-looking eyeglasses, she herself was lonely. She lived, she confessed, in an opulent apartment, her living room windows opening north on Eighty-sixth Street, directly at another apartment house, but from her westerly dining room she could look down on the rolling meadows of Central Park. The place had been left to her by her long-widowed father, a banking executive, and she'd moved in after he died with a sense of foreboding, because who really wanted to live in the huge apartment of one's deceased father? "Especially the wallpaper, and the smells and everything," she told me. "*So depressing*." But in time she'd come to love the spaciousness of the place, as well as the attentions of her father's old neighbors, many of whom took a parental interest in her. The rooms were comfortable, and in Manhattan the body craves comfort against the hard edges of curbs and cars and faces, and Allison was no exception.

Within a few weeks we were talking daily, usually after the lunch rush. She'd sit down and tell me about one or the other men in her life, and in general they were confident, intellectual types, witty and accomplished in all the right places, yet somehow insufficient. Something about them was *minor*, she confessed to me—never their achievements or romantic attentions or wallets—but something else, something hard for her to describe. Finally, of course, we are *all* minor, every one of us, but there was something in Allison that discovered this in men. If I hadn't liked her so much, I might have said she was peevish, a bit particular, streaked with a dark skepticism, even. Either she was overpowering the men or undermatching herself, I thought. But I saw a few of her dates when they met her at the restaurant and they seemed decent enough guys, even to me. In time I wondered if I saw a pattern in which Allison met a respectable man, let herself be taken to dinner or the theater, then quickly slept with him—once. *Only* once. As if by design. Soon she was on to the next one. What did this mean? "It would appear you're not a husband-hunter," I said.

"Nope." Allison shrugged. "I don't think I'd be very good at marriage. I mean, I did try it once." She'd had a short, disastrous union in her early twenties, she confessed. "I'd like to have a *baby*, though, if I found the right man. Or maybe I could adopt . . . there are all these *beautiful* Chinese babies with no mothers." And there she left it, her face a little sad, wary of even thinking about the idea. Truth to be told, Allison knew time was running against her. She'd taken good care of herself, as the phrase goes, but she was one of those women whose face brightly masks a deeper disappointment. She had not been satisfied yet. Her body did not seem girlish so much as *unused*, especially by maternity. Motherhood consumes the bodies of women, if not from pregnancy and nursing itself, then by the years of too little sleep. The mothers I've known don't seem to mind this, for in trading away themselves they have been rewarded with children.

Allison's problem, of course, was the restaurant. Running it was an enormous, addictive job, requiring very long days. The customers, the waitstaff, the cooks, the suppliers—each population was distinct in its demands. Allison arrived at 8 a.m. and, except for a few hours off after lunch, rarely left before 9 p.m., or until the dinner shift was running smoothly, a moment that often never came, for what was happening in the dining room was only part of the larger spectacle. On a slow afternoon she invited me through the swinging kitchen doors and into the labyrinth beyond. The restaurant had two enormous kitchens, one for meals, the second for pastries. The steaks arrived on rolling steel platforms from the butcher's room, where they had been trimmed and sized, and were forked onto long flaming grills by sweating, hassled chefs who addressed the waiters and busboys as "fuckhead" and "Mexico." The waitresses were called "kittycat," or "lovelips," which they hated. But it went with the territory.

Below the kitchen lay supply rooms and prep stations. The hallways were narrow, as on a ship, and pipes ran low overhead, red for fire, yellow for gas. Allison swung open a thick, insulated door—and I was surprised; it was the meat room, where dozens of sides of raw beef hung on hooks under a blue light, dated and stamped with wholesalers' marks.

"Don't want to spend the night in *here*," I muttered.

"I guess I'm used to it."

The room was cool but not cold, and we stepped inside. The enormous red carcasses—marbled with fat, headless, halved, rib cages sawed through, legs severed above the hoof—seemed aware of us through some essential mammalian affinity. The dead meat, soon to be transubstantiated into money and laughter, would also be revivified, of course, would become warm flesh again, this time human.

The room was controlled for temperature and humidity, Allison explained, so the steaks would dry-age to perfection.

"Who decides when it's time?" I asked, studying the back of her neck, so close that I could easily lean forward and kiss it.

"I do."

The room was small, the ceiling low, and we were alone.

"It's quiet in here," Allison said, turning, keeping my eye.

I nodded. Take her in your arms, I thought, do it now.

"Bill, something happened to you, didn't it?"

I wasn't ready for this, and the strangeness of the room amplified the power of the question. "Something happens to everyone, I think."

"Of course," Allison said softly. "I just wondered."

I took a breath, let it go. "I was a pretty high-powered real estate attorney, in one of the city's best firms. I was married, had a son. Then something happened, yes. Now I'm alone. I'm the guy you see every day."

Allison nodded, as if I'd confirmed something. "You want to tell me—?"

"Do we really know each other?"

"You see me almost every day."

I thought about it. "I don't usually talk about it much, Allison."

"I'm sorry. Shouldn't have asked."

But I had liked the intimacy of the moment. "I remain conversant on other topics," I said with more energy. "Okay?"

Her playfulness returned. "I'll get it out of you, somehow."

"You will?"

"Even if I have to go to extreme measures."

"That doesn't sound so bad."

"It isn't."

I asked her to continue the tour, so she did. Next came the produce walk-ins, filled with chopped vegetables ready for salads and quail eggs stacked by the dozen. All the supplies came in through sidewalk doors. I couldn't tell where we stood in respect to the Havana Room, whether it was above us or beside us, or if its location was what somehow made the room restricted. But I saw nothing unusual, just pipes and ceiling tiles and rough wiring. I was eager to ask Allison about the Havana Room, but suspected I'd learn more if I didn't.

"Then there's upstairs," she said.

"Oh?"

She meant the second floor, which housed three big private party rooms. The largest had a piano and seating for sixty, and was often used for corporate gatherings, wedding dinners, and the like. The second, also large, was furnished with better sofas and favored by married, middle-aged women for social events. The third room, considerably smaller, was rented almost exclusively by Wall Street men at night. This was where the strippers worked. The limit was twenty-five men. The more men, Allison told me, the more problems they had, and sometimes the stripper would run out of the room having been bitten or plundered in some indecorous way. "What does she expect?" Allison asked.

I followed her to the third and fourth floors, which contained furniture storage, an accountant's office, a main office where Allison worked, and employee locker rooms. Along the way I counted three dozen security cameras, and when we paused in the main office, I watched six black-and-white television screens cycle through their respective views of all that I had just toured, as well as views of the main dining rooms, the bar, every cash register, and even the street outside. I realized that Allison could watch people from her office, including me. Was the Havana Room similarly monitored? I studied the cycling screens but didn't spot any room I hadn't seen before.

"Well, that's it!" said Allison, perhaps noticing my interest. "Except for Ha's penthouse, which we can't see."

"Ha?"

"Yes," said Allison. "Ha. You know Ha."

"The handyman."

"Yes. The only man I completely trust." Perched above the bright inferno of the restaurant, Ha lived in a tiny room on the top floor. No one knew exactly where he came from or just how old he was, she said, and no one who depended on him insisted on being informed. He may have jumped off a ship in Seattle, he may have walked over the Mexican border. What was known about Ha was that he could fix anything— broilers, air conditioners, meat slicers, any of the restaurant's twenty-six refrigerators, the freight elevator, the washing machines, fire alarms. "He's quite brave, too," Allison added.

"Brave?"

"Absolutely." At night, she said, Ha navigated the dim catacombs of the restaurant by touch; one evening years back, after the night porter had left, a thief jimmied the sidewalk doors and crept in. Ha, lying on the kitchen floor wiggling a gas line, heard the intruder and surmised his route toward the kitchens. Immediately he darkened the narrow hallways, turned on the lights in the liquor walk-in, and waited. The intruder lurched along the hallways, drawn to the brightness like an insect, and when he scurried into the cave of expensive booze, Ha swung the door shut, secured it with a length of metal pipe, and called the police. Allison adored him, and believed, I think, that he was more spirit than man.

"He's the only one who has my cell number," she joked. "The rest of them can't have it."

"How do your sad supplicants call you, then?"

"They can look me up in the book." We took the stairs down to the dining room. "Actually, there's a new guy these days," she admitted. "Not that it's *necessarily* going anywhere."

I watched her bounce down the steps in front of me, and felt better for having not declared my affections for her in the meat room. "Go ahead and tell me, just to make me jealous."

"Well, you know I don't eat breakfast at home." Allison sat down at one of the back tables and I joined her. Two busboys were vacuuming at the other end. "I have breakfast at this little place on the corner near my apartment. You'd think I wouldn't want to be in a restaurant, *any* kind of restaurant, but I like this place—and my apartment is kind of big and drafty, you know, kind of empty, even though I love my kitchen, so I go to this little place, and have an egg and toast, something to get started." Her voice was animated, excited by the story, and she'd already forgotten our intimate moment in the meat room. "So I was minding my own business, just sitting in my booth, reading the newspaper, when this big man sat down next to me with his newspaper, and he was wearing this beautiful suit, very conservative, and I said to myself, Well, okay, I might be having a little bit of a problem."

"I know where this is going," I said, secretly miserable.

"I looked at his hand and saw no wedding ring, although you can't always be sure. But I didn't say anything or look at him, I just kept reading, sort of *hoping*, and then I watched him order and eat his meal and he had perfect manners." She sighed, remembering. "I see a lot of people eat, I know what perfect table manners are. And then the waitress brought my check because she wanted the table. And I kind of kept sort of looking at him but he didn't see me and I had to go."

"Which you didn't like."

"No, I didn't. And he wasn't there the next day. But the day after that he was, he was sitting behind me, back to back, and I could smell him, and that—I admit it, I was having a little *problem*. Then he pulls out a phone and he calls someone up and I'm trying to listen as much as I can, you know." Allison smiled guiltily. "I want desperately to hear him, I want to know who he's talking to! It could be some *woman*, of course. And I hear him say, 'Two-point-six million, I'm willing to do that.' That was all he said. And then he just listened and nodded and hung up. And I thought, All right, this guy is for real, you know?"

"You smelled the big money."

"I guess. I mean, I can't *tell* you how many fakers and braggers and jerks are out there, Bill, with their little gold pinkie rings and rented Jaguars. So now I was even more interested, I admit it. A girl has to watch out for herself, right? So I twisted around to see what he was reading. It was the *Financial Times* of London, which is the sexiest newspaper there is to read. Don't ask me why. Those pink pages. It's so European. So I liked that, too. I was trying to think of something to say and then he looked at his watch and got up and left. Afterward the waitresses talked about him. They liked him, too. So I was thinking, Come on, Allison, you're a smart girl, you're a *catch*, you know what to do. So the next day I decided I was—"

She stopped, gave me a devilish smile.

"Go on," I said. "I can take it."

"Oh, Bill, you don't want a woman like *me*."

"How do you know?"

"You just don't. I do terrible things. I even flirt with strange men in *meat* lockers." She pushed at the spoon in front of her. "I really am very, *very* bad, you know. Fickle and irresponsible and manipulative."

"I doubt it." And I did.

"Maybe you'll find out sometime."

"Maybe. God help me if I do. Go on with the story. You decided to—?"

"Yes. I got up early, picked out a good dress, and got down there a little early, trying to match his time of arrival. And I did! He looked up when I came in and gave me a smile. That was *it*. I mean I said hi or something. But I sat down feeling victorious! It's silly, but okay. Then I turned around and asked if I could borrow some of his paper. He said yes and handed it to me. And I said something like it seemed like he was starting to be a regular. Something stupid like that, totally obvious. And he said he'd just been eating there because he had meetings in the neighborhood. But soon would be done. I basically panicked and told him I ran a steakhouse downtown and would love for him to try the place as my guest."

"Very subtle."

"I didn't have a choice! I gave him my card and said please, *puhl-ease* call me ahead of time and—"

"You didn't say it like that."

"No, but almost. I said I'd see that he got a good table. He looked at the card and said that was great and introduced himself and we shook hands and it was all I could do not to put his thumb in my mouth." Allison smiled. "Isn't that awful?"

"Tell me the rest, even though I know what it is."

"Well, he came into the restaurant two days later—he called first and I practically had a heart attack—"

"Did I see him?"

"You weren't in that night."

"And?"

"Well, once I had him in the restaurant, I *had* him." She nodded to herself in satisfaction, and I was touched by her need and vulnerability. Then she saw something in my face. "Come on, I'm not your type. You like *good* women. Virtuous, dependable women."

"You should've met my ex-wife."

"I wish I had."

"You would've liked her."

"Would she have liked me?"

I thought about this. "No."

"Why not?"

Too confident. But I didn't say this aloud. "So, did you see this guy again?"

"Yup," Allison said, "you could say that."

"All the other pretenders are gone, then?"

"Yes." She nodded and recrossed her legs the other way. "Banished."

An hour later I was at Table 17 when I looked up to see the owner, Lipper, in his wheelchair and accompanied by his nurse, an older black woman. He frowned as he passed me and paddled his feet on the floor to stop. "You work for me?"

I shook my head. "Just a loyal customer."

"Ah, good, very good. You like steak?"

"Your hanger steak, especially."

"Good." Lipper edged closer. Hair whirlpooled in his ears, his bottom eyelids sagged forward pinkly. "People still like steak."

"Always will, I think."

He threw a bony finger at me. "I know you. Heard you were a friend of Allison's. Talk with her on my time, too. You're a lawyer, is that it?"

"I suppose."

He showed a lot of old horse teeth at this. "Last I heard, lawyers worked in law offices, but okay. Allison likes to keep her men nearby so she can keep an eye on them, heh! I've seen her over the years . . . she's got all the moves, let me tell—" He looked around the room, as if hearing someone suddenly call his name. "Yeah, anybody can serve a steak! You burn some cow meat and put it on a plate. Plus the city has a bunch of great steakhouses, right? There's Smith and Wollensky, and Keen's— what a beauty *that* place is—and Peter Luger's in Brooklyn. These places make a damn fine steak. But we're a little different, a little special. Sinatra owned this place for a while, back in the sixties. You know that? Lot of girls. Revolving pussy, I always called it. Pussy coming, pussy going." I saw in Lipper the happy mouth-energy of the old, in which all thoughts rise to the surface unrestrained by propriety or forethought. "We went out together a few times, me and Frank. Yeah, he saw this place, said he just had to have a place like that. I guess he might have sung here a few times—" Lipper poked at his testicles excitedly, as if trying to balance one on top of the other. "I was a young man. We never advertise this place, see. Don't have to. We got it just right. Allison's very good. Of course her little room is illegal, her little show in there, I mean. She's very careful, never had a problem. She told you about it, right? She explains the whole story, gets them intrigued. I'm too old but I'd do it, too, if I were younger. Just to experience it. I know it's illegal. Who cares? Half the best part of life is illegal! Sue me, I always say. You going to arrest an old man in a wheelchair? Lock me away? You tell men you got a special room down there and it's like honey to the bees, guy—oh, she doesn't want me to talk about it. What was your name, Rogers? I had a doctor named Rogers, fixed my toes. Wait, I got to take a pill—I got this beeper thing that tells me—"

A black female hand appeared over his shoulder, graceful as a falling leaf, the tiny red pill floating on a soft, milk-chocolate palm. He plucked it up and clapped it into his mouth, where a thick tongue came down and swept it inward like the crushing device in the back of a garbage truck. "I can swallow them dry. Okay, where was—honey and bees . . . Sinatra, oh. Allison knows this. She knows more about men, studied them, I mean we got good selections, good *cuts*, heh. Lots of men. She's had a lot of them, too." He leaned forward, dropped a knuckled paw on my arm and spoke conspiratorially. "Let me give you some advice, son, because I see her paying attention to you. I see what's going on. You got a nice way about you, that's why I'm telling you this. I'm an old man, better listen to me. Don't fall for her. Right? I mean, don't give in, don't make a fool of yourself. She *wants* you to. She'll play with you, she'll find your weakness. Let her stew, let her get frustrated and emotional—*that's* when you put in the sword! Right? It's the guys who *aren't* interested who excite her. I've seen it over and over! The guys that come out and declare themselves, she can't stand them! Plays with them, *tortures* them! She's got some moves on her most men never heard of!" His eyes brightened wickedly and for a moment I glimpsed the charming younger man he'd once been. "I had a rich guy *suicidal* for her once! I tell him, you can buy all the pussy you want, what's the big deal? He took my advice, went to the islands for few weeks with a bunch of little blond fluffy-muffies, heh! Allison, she never blinked. What does she care? I guess he got over it. What's your name again? Woodrow? Never mind, I'll forget, anyway . . . So that's the kind of place I run, simple as that. It's a special. I tell you Sinatra owned this place? Back in the sixties, in fact. Yeah, I bought this place back in the seventies, when you couldn't give it away! That's when I stepped in. Yes, stepped in and stepped *up*. I don't do any of the work anymore, just come and watch my babies eat and drink and have a good time. We had a lot of the greats in here, let me tell you. Wilt Chamberlain when he was in town, he had them lining up, they'd never *seen* someone like him before, Sonny and Cher, Joe Frazier—the boxer, Clint Eastwood, Redford, Billy Crystal, politicians, we had everybody, that guy Puffy Brush, whoever, heh. I just watch now. I don't need the money. I was a good businessman in my time. I did my deals, I signed in *ink*, baby. Not many people like that left these days! Everybody wants the cushion under their asses. Not me. I worked! I'm a fossil. Made of stone, heh. Parts of me still are. Don't look surprised. It still works! Two hundred milligrams of this new stuff they got and watch out. Once a month's all I need. I have a friend. She's very understanding, comes around my apartment. She's a certain age, okay? We like each other. She takes her time. Happy to lie down or just drink jizz." Again the horse teeth, the squinting, amused eyes. "We don't comment too much on human nature here, see. Accept human frailty—that's my philosophy. Shouldn't shock you. You'll be the same, I guarantee. I didn't age gracefully, and that's fine with me. My secret is the omega-three oils. Only the best, made from the littlest fishies! The big ones, tuna and swordfish, too much mercury." He patted my arm urgently. "I know you like Allison, they all do, I can see it in your face, I've seen you in here, fella. You hang on to your mustard, that's my advice. She's smarter than both of us put together. Back in the day I myself could've given her a—"

His old nurse bent close to him and whispered.

"Don't say that to me! You work for me, you—"

Without a word, she rolled Lipper away, and like a child in a stroller he accepted her judgment passively, not bothering to say goodbye, instead eager for his next encounter.

I might have found good reasons to worry in Lipper's monologue—his vague references to the illegality of the Havana Room, to Allison's romantic manipulations—but I didn't, and not just because his words seemed the harmless and even touching ramblings of an old restaurateur edging toward senility. After all, much as I liked Allison, I was not actually involved with her. Having been around awhile, she and I both knew that the other had at least the usual biographical complications. Sure, I was jealous that she'd found a new guy, but I was also just glad to see her each day, satisfied to watch her from a distance as she adjusted her glasses or slipped a bit of hair behind her ear, any of the lovely little things that women do, and if I had been asked if I was getting to know Allison at least passably well, I'd now have answered yes. Moreover, my hours at the steakhouse proved such a pleasant distraction from the rest of my time—in my horrid apartment, feeling guilty about Wilson Doan, missing my son, listening to my similarly doomed neighbors scrape up and down the stairs—that I had no reason to dwell on Lipper's egomaniacal rant.

But that began to change one cold night in late February, long after I'd finished my dinner, when Allison came over to Table 17.

"Going already?" she asked, standing before me, heels together, her voice a little nervy.

"In a minute, maybe."

She looked at her watch. The time was nearly eleven. "Any chance you could stay a while?"

"Stay?"

She smiled. "I'll ply you with coffee or drinks or desserts and anything else we serve."

I told her I was full. "What do you need?"

Allison took a breath. "Remember I told you I met that guy?"

"Sure. You wanted to put his thumb in your mouth."

"Anyway, his name is Jay Rainey, and he called me a few minutes ago, and he needs a lawyer."

"The phone book is full of lawyers, Allison."

She shook her head. "No, no, Bill, he needs one tonight."

"Tonight?"

"He needs one *now*."

"Why? Did he get arrested?"

She sat down at my table, which was unusual, considering the restaurant was full. "It's something to do with—well, Jay's been trying to buy this building downtown and the seller is sort of this jerk, I guess, who's been really hard to deal with, and anyway, now the seller says they have to have a finished sale by midnight *tonight* or the deal's off."

I shook my head. "That's a bluff."

"That's what I thought, too, but Jay says the seller is telling the truth. It's a tax situation or something and—"

"Doesn't Jay have a lawyer?"

"That's the thing. Jay was planning to use his regular lawyer when the papers were ready, but not until then and then this evening the seller just presents him with the contract."

"What's the selling amount?"

Her eyes widened. "It's three million dollars, I think."

Not much. A tiny amount by Manhattan standards. "They've got some kind of deal worked out already?"

"I guess."

"Jay shouldn't sign it, not under this kind of pressure."

"I thought that, too," Allison said, nobody's fool.

"But he wants the building badly, right?"

"Guess so. Also I think the seller is insisting Jay have a lawyer look over the contract."

I tasted my coffee, feeling strangely miserable. "The lawyer's giving Jay no time to have the contract looked over and yet is insisting it be looked over?"

"I know, it's crazy. But will you do it?"

"I can't."

"Why?"

"Lot of reasons. He needs a title search and a survey. Usually there's a tax adjustment to be made. Some of these larger co-op buildings have very complicated tax situations, too. Abatements, escrowed reserve funds, all kinds of stuff. I haven't talked with the seller's lawyer, I haven't seen a title report, I don't have time to do any of the calculations, I don't have a legal secretary to file documents—c'mon, it's crazy."

"Would you at least look at the documents?"

"I can look at them, but that doesn't mean anything, Allison."

She started to stand up. "But you'll look?"

"I repeat. This is crazy."

"I'll set you up in the Havana Room."

I wasn't expecting this. "The room you didn't tell me about?"

"Yes."

"It's going to be open tonight?"

"Ha says he's ready."

"For what?"

She shook her head. She wasn't telling me. Not yet, anyway.

"You better watch out, I might like it in there."

"Yes, you might," Allison said. "Most do."

A few minutes later I followed Allison through the door with the brass plate and yellowed card down a curved marble stairwell—nineteen steps by my count—and was not disappointed when I reached the bottom and entered a long, dark space lit by yellowy sconces. Groups of men sat quietly at the mahogany bar and in booths. The decor hadn't changed much in a hundred years or so. They'd left the old hat racks, the brass spittoon filled with lost umbrellas, the chipped black-and-white tile floor. Allison set me up at one of the end booths, most private of all, and told the waiter to bring whatever I liked.

"Back in a bit," she said.

Now I eagerly inspected the space. True to the room's name, the far wall was shelved with hundreds of small boxes of quality cigars—Cohiba, Montecristo, Bolivar—and under the pressed-tin ceiling each booth was graced with a painting of prerevolutionary Cuba, below which stood a small lamp, in case an item needed close inspection. A supply of pens, pads of paper, and ashtrays, each embossed with the steakhouse's gold script, was provided as well. The napkins, however, were imprinted HAVANA ROOM in small blue letters. The booths were less comfortable than the bar yet superior, for there were only eight of them, each so high-backed that you couldn't overhear adjacent conversation. Well, that's not quite true. I did catch a few lines of dialogue next to me that involved $200 million worth of new Malaysian bonds and how, tonight, guys, *right here, right now*, their credit rating was going to be improved. And I spotted two large fiftyish men in beautiful suits who sat examining the X ray of someone's knee with great interest. One of the men wore a huge championship ring on his hand.

Meanwhile, shuffling through the smoky gloom, came the waiter, ancient and aloof, who passed my order to the barman, himself a tired, unimpeachable fellow who worked without comment or, it seemed, awareness of the enormous, black-eyed nude stretched out behind him. You could not help but stare at the painting; imprisoned within her heavy gilt frame, the naked woman appeared both demure and illicit in her expression, beckoning in brush-stroked stillness across time and fleshly impossibility to all comers—a one-hundred-and-fifty-year selection of souls that now included me. *I know what you want,* her eyes said, and I felt embarrassed to be staring at her, so I stood and examined the dusty bookshelf that ran along the wall opposite the bar; on it sat a complete copy of the 1966 New York State Legal Code, a small volume of Irish poetry, a birds of North America reference work, a heavily marked environmental impact study commissioned prior to the creation of a coastal resort village in Florida, several of Teddy Roosevelt's naval histories, a King James Bible, tidal charts for New York Harbor for the years 1936–41, an owner's manual for a 1967 Corvette, and a series of pornographic novels set in 1970s Hong Kong involving a British banker. These random, brittle-paged leavings confirmed the impression that the room was so crowded with the shards and shadows of lost lives that one was rendered anonymous there; but for an occasional mop over the cigar butts and dead flies, it appeared no one cared what went on, so long as you paid your bill and remained civil. The men's room at the back was a surprisingly ill-kept green coffin, bordering on foul.

Yet all this obvious inattention seemed to appeal to the clientele, for the world has too many clean well-lit places to do business, including the conference room, the golf course, and the hotel suite. Each has its advantages. But there are certain deals that are harmed by sunlight, a printed agenda, and juice and muffins on the buffet. Like insect colonies and creeping plants, these intrigues need a bit of moisture and darkness to thrive. The men in the Havana Room, I noticed, generally only made eye contact with the others in their own party, and didn't display the occupational gregariousness of salesmen and deal makers. Instead they hunched and glared, rotating their heads toward passersby with furtive irritation. I didn't see a phone or laptop in use, and if these items were not expressly prohibited, then I supposed that they were looked upon with disdain. The room's ascendant technologies, I guessed, were the bluff, the grimace, and the long silence. In a man's shrug, millions might appear, or a lifetime's labor turn to ash.

Allison came back into the room a few minutes after eleven, followed by an outsized man with a large head of dark hair and wide shoulders. He turned his head as he walked, swinging his gaze around like a sledgehammer, taking in the whole room.

"Bill?" Allison said. "This is Jay Rainey."

He offered me one of his ample hands, and I found myself looking into a genial, unknowably handsome face.

Allison turned to me, eyes a little crazy, I thought, and said, "Bill's ready to look everything over."

"Great, great," said Jay. "The seller's attorney and the title guy will be here at eleven-thirty."

"I'll see what I can do. I'm not promising anything."

He nodded, somewhat casually, considering I was the one helping him, then excused himself to the bar. He was, I saw, at that point when a young man starts to become an older man. Perhaps a vigorous thirty-five, with a deep chest, not in the exaggerated way of bodybuilders, but as a natural example of superior proportion. Later I learned he forced himself to do three hundred push-ups each morning, less for fitness than as a daily test of will. As a bulwark against despair. He looked heavy—not fat but *heavy*, made of denser, more difficult stuff. You couldn't imagine knocking him over very easily. His strength came up from the ground in him, the kind of slow-mule power that is good for lifting and climbing and other activities—as Allison no doubt already knew.

"Tell me about yourself, Jay," I said when he returned.

"I'm basically a—well, I buy a little, sell a little." He smiled. "Nothing very big, just things as they come along. This is a good building. It's got a couple of tenants—small companies paying decent rents, it's got good systems and I think I can add a floor on the roof, add some kind of pent-house apartment."

A man can talk himself into anything, of course. "Three million, Allison said."

"Yes."

"You have a regular lawyer?"

Jay nodded. "I do, I do, but he's traveling and the seller insists on closing the deal tonight. Threatened to pull his offer."

"Has your lawyer seen the contract?"

"No."

"Couldn't the seller fax the contract to him?"

He nodded at the reasonableness of the question. "I asked his office if I could do that but my guy is in Asia, asleep, and by the time he wakes up, it'll be too late."

I hummed a small agreeable noise as if this explanation made perfect sense, although it didn't, for few lawyers involved in deals in Asia also handle small-time Manhattan real estate transfers—where three million dollars is, as I said, minuscule, and unless somebody had changed the time zones, it was now late morning in the Far East.

"What about the title search?" I asked. "You can't buy property without clear title."

"I ordered it myself. As I said, the title man should be here tonight."

"How about a survey?" I asked, meaning the official drawing of the property's lot lines and location.

"Got it."

"You had the building inspected?"

"Sure."

"You got a written report?"

He opened his briefcase and took out an engineer's report. I flipped through it. According to the write-up the building was lucky to be standing, and would be rubble the next time someone slammed a door. But that's the way they're always written on old buildings.

"So we need a contract, a title, some tax and transfer forms, and some money. Which brings up the question of how you're doing this. Is there a bank involved?"

"No."

"All cash?"

"No, it's a little creative, actually."

I waited, saying nothing.

"Four hundred thousand and a property swap," he said.

"Who is paying the four hundred?"

"They are."

Three million dollars minus four hundred thousand equaled Allison's thumb-suckable two-point-six million dollars.

"What's the other property?"

"Acreage on Long Island, way out, ninety miles out there on the North Fork, looking over Long Island Sound. Beautiful property. They're putting in vineyards and golf courses out there, you know."

I nodded. "I better look at the contract."

"Allison said you'd worry about the small stuff."

"Sure."

"You come in every day?" asked Jay.

"Just about."

"I guess you're retired?"

"I guess I am. Okay, so, Jay, I feel it's in your best interest if you know the following things." I looked straight into his eyes. "First, walking into a steakhouse at night is not a good way to find a lawyer. For all you know, I might not even *be* a lawyer. I am, but the point is I might not be. Second, you don't know anything about me. I haven't practiced law in a while, Jay. I've had a setback or two, okay? Also, I haven't maintained relations with any title company people, I don't know anyone in the city departments anymore, okay? I haven't been watching the little language changes, I don't know how the tax forms might've changed. I'm out of practice, is what I'm saying. What I'm telling you, Jay, is that I'm not competent to be your attorney for this transaction. If it were a little ranch house out on Long Island, I'm sure I could handle it. But this deal involves two big, valuable properties and a—"

"How much do you want?" Jay asked. He was stirring, moving his shoulders around.

"I'm not trying to drive the fee up, Jay." I stared at him. "I'm trying to be honest here."

His brow fell angrily. "Oh, bullshit."

"Excuse me?"

"I said this is bullshit."

"What do you mean?"

He lifted his hands, palms up. "Allison told me you managed some big real estate transactions, the sale of that bank building up on Forty-eighth Street. What was that, like three hundred million? With all sorts of complicated syndication of ownership?"

This was true, but I hadn't told Allison the first word about the deal, though it was easy enough to look it up on the Internet.

"Right?"

Allison had checked me out, I realized. "Well—"

"Well what? C'mon, I'm in a fucking *jam* here, Bill. And you're telling me you're not qualified?" He leaned forward. "Look, really, if it's about the money, I can pay you a good fee." He pulled a checkbook out of his suit pocket. "I'm putting money down, right here, for your services and you don't want it?"

I put my hands up to slow him down. "Let me ask you a couple of questions."

He sat back. "Shoot."

"Who owns the building you're buying?"

"Some Chilean wine company."

"Why did the deal drag out so long?"

"I don't know. They didn't offer enough at first."

"They're buying up empty acreage out on Long Island?"

"Sure, why not? It's beautiful oceanfront property." Jay grinned expansively. "God's not making any more of it. They're going to put it into vines."

"Plant grapes, you mean."

"Right."

"How did you arrive at the price?"

"I had a price in mind for the land. They found me, see. We dicked around, got the deal worked out."

"You didn't just want all the cash out from the property?"

"No."

"Why?"

"Aah, well. I thought this was better."

He thought I shouldn't know, in other words. "You could have taken all cash and you didn't? That's weird."

He bit his drink straw and said, "I wanted the building. It's in good shape. I'm walking away with four hundred thousand in cash, so life can't be too bad."

"Who negotiated for you?"

"I did."

"Ever do a deal this big?"

He stared at me. More straw action.

"Sounds to me like they're getting a nice break on the land value," I noted.

"Yeah," Jay said miserably. "In a hot market it's got to be worth four million, but it's going here for three."

"Why the low figure?"

He drew a deep slow breath.

"You really didn't have anybody negotiate this for you?"

"Like I said, no."

I looked into his big handsome face. "Sounds like they're eating your liver."

"It's enough money," he sighed. "It's okay."

"You have a copy of the proposed contract I can look at?"

"No, actually. The seller's bringing it."

"So you *do* need a lawyer."

"I guess." He dipped his head forward. "I know this is unusual, Bill. You can just charge me extra, whatever seems right."

I wasn't really interested in a fee yet. But before I could tell him how risky it was to sign a contract he'd never seen, Allison walked into the Havana Room with two men in suits.

"Hi guys." She introduced the older man as Gerzon, the seller's attorney. He carried two briefcases, and was decorous and smooth as he shook my hand and introduced the second fellow as Barrett, from the title company. Title men in New York City don't do much except flip through city records, some of them going back three hundred years, to be sure there are no claims, liens, or encumbrances on the title, and that the chain of ownership is clear and unbroken. Most of the time it's straightforward, and the title man just collects his fee for the service and for title insurance.

Gerzon turned to Jay. "Where's your lawyer?"

He waved at me. "This is him."

Gerzon smiled at my wrinkled shirt, my subprofessional appearance. "Pardon me." He was one of those men who are detailed in their instructions to their tailors. But the suit was just the foundation of his vanity. His watch was unapologetically vulgar. The ring and the cuff links matched, and the shirt collar was heavily starched, the silk knot of his tie a confection of soft edges. His toupee was also very good— though they are never good enough.

Yet the inspection was mutual. "Where'd you work?" he asked.

"Private practice."

A cool nod. "I haven't heard of you."

"Big city. Many lawyers."

"I see."

I didn't want him to think he had an advantage. "So," I asked as we all sat down, "why are you selling your client's building in the back room of a steakhouse and not in a law office?"

"It's a time problem." He shrugged. "We're out of it." He looked at Jay. "I was told there would be a lawyer to assist Mr. Rainey. So we came here. We're being accommodating."

I looked at my watch. Twenty-five after eleven. "If you have to get this building sold by midnight, I'd say that Mr. Rainey is the one who's being accommodating."

Gerzon turned to Jay. "Should we discuss who is accommodating whom? I told you, midnight or no deal."

The title man, Barrett, professionally alert to lawyerly tones, interrupted. "Hey listen, if there's not going be a deal, then tell me now, because I could be—"

"It's all right," Jay said. "We're okay. Let's just be cool here." He looked at me, raised his eyebrows to tell me to relax. "There's a lot of expertise at the table. We'll hammer any problem out and get it done."

Gerzon produced copies of the contract and unfolded an oversized pair of tortoiseshell glasses. He seemed to be the kind of man who was acquainted with people everywhere, pointedly remembering the details of their lives, but who himself was genuinely known by almost no one, except perhaps by a former wife or the people who had sued him with righteousness. "What is it?" he asked, uneasy with my attention.

"Is real estate your primary practice?"

"Oh, no, *no*," said Gerzon. "I'm involved in a variety of endeavors." He smiled in such a way that I was to infer that the transaction at hand was a trifle, that larger matters awaited his attention, nine-digit wire transfers from foreign banks, dozens of important phone calls, imminent IPOs—a cyclone of gold and greatness.

Barrett handed around copies of the title report on the oceanfront land. Gerzon turned his attention to it, but I have seen hundreds of lawyers read thousands of documents and if they are reading, actually reading, even under pressurized circumstances, a stillness comes over them, the energies of their personality dropping onto the document at hand. Gerzon wasn't reading. His blink rate wasn't right. He was faking it, and this meant, I suspected, that he felt very good indeed about the deal.

"You have a card?" I said.

He looked up. "Yes, of course." He slipped one from out of a gold case and handed it to me. "You?"

"I don't have any new ones currently printed," I replied.

"Ah," he said, pointedly asking no more.

I fingered his card. It had two addresses, both telling. The first was on lower Fifth Avenue, where the old buildings are chopped up into small offices on the top floors, full of marginal businesses. Someone from out of town might think it was a prestigious address, but those in the city would know better. The second address specified one of Long Island's uncountable small office complexes. I've been to these places. The offices aren't particularly plush, all rent-a-painting decor and wall-to-wall carpeting. The secretaries are young, mean, and well compensated. The lawyers, usually local boys, some of whom have done stints in the city, prefer to handle cases that involve real estate transactions or estate work—generally simple procedures that guarantee a prompt fee. Eviction, tenant-complaint, pro bono work, constitutional defenses of immigrants and minorities, slip-and-fall work, etc., are strictly avoided. In this world the real estate men know the lawyers and the lawyers know the title people, who know the bankers, who are all known by the big-time contractors, who themselves maintain clear, constant, and affectionate relations with the politically appointed members of the county water authority as well as the elected members of the town board, who approve zoning changes and code exemptions. In sum, the second address on Gerzon's card conjured a long-settled, wealthy suburban civilization whose foremost institutions had achieved world-class standing in only certain areas of human endeavor: the luxury-car tune-up, the nerve-sparing removal of the prostate gland; the emergency resodding of a lawn. He probably lived there.

"So, gentlemen," I began, my voice slipping into tones I hadn't used in several years, "we have a deal value of three million dollars. It's a property swap, with four hundred thousand dollars going to Mr. Rainey. Because of the cash outlay, we'll call Mr. Gerzon the buyer and we'll call Mr. Rainey the seller."

"Fine," said Gerzon.

"Who is paying the recording fees, the transfer taxes, the Suffolk County surcharges, the title search, any back taxes owed on either property, and whatever else I haven't been told about?"

"We are," said Gerzon.

I leaned over to Jay. "You negotiated this?"

"It came out of the price, man."

"So there's nothing left to negotiate?"

Both men shook their heads.

I turned to Jay. "You don't need me."

"Yes he does," said Gerzon. "He needs to have legal representation so he can't come back and say the contract was no good, that he didn't understand it."

"And he finds some joker in the back of a steakhouse who happens to have a law degree and that's all right with you?" But then I thought of something. I pointed at the copies of the contract. "Jay, you realize you haven't yet signed these?"

"Not yet," Jay said. He was, I saw, one of those big men who need to keep moving, unable to rest upon the details of such things as contracts, which require stillness and attention. Apparently he knew this about himself, for something in his hopeful glance suggested he was delivering himself into my hands.

"You realize you can still negotiate the price, I mean."

"No he fucking can't!" said Gerzon.

"Of course he can. Nothing's signed here. There is no price. He can walk out of here, go to the movies."

Gerzon looked at Rainey. "I said get a lawyer, not a junkyard dog."

"It's okay—" Jay began.

"We're covering all the fees, we're being totally accommodating," said Gerzon.

I didn't like him and I didn't like the situation but I pulled the chain on the small lamp on the table and slid the contract beneath it, trying to get a better sense of the deal. Jay was acquiring a six-story loft building in lower Manhattan at 162 Reade Street, not far from City Hall, where the streets run according to the obsolete logic of cow paths and farmers' lanes. When the World Trade Center went down, real estate values in the area got strange. Some people panicked over more terrorism or contamination by the chemical soup that wafted from the burning site and sold for nothing, while others stood firm. If I'd had even a day's notice, I'd have checked the city records downtown to see how long Gerzon's client had owned the property, what the cost-basis was. The building was being exchanged by one Voodoo LLC, a limited-liability company, for ownership of eighty-six acres of real estate on the North Fork of Long Island. Survey documents of the land parcel were attached to the proposed contract and showed a deep strip of land running almost half a mile along Long Island Sound.

I looked up at Gerzon. "You're dumping a marginal downtown property with unprofitable long-term leases and possibly contaminated by the World Trade Center disaster for a huge piece of oceanfront acreage," I told him. "My client is short on cash to cover his closing costs and you've squeezed him way down on the price as a result. You're coughing up four hundred thousand dollars, which is nothing, nothing at all!" I turned to Jay. "You understand that once you sign this contract—"

"Let's do the deal, Mr. Wyeth," growled Gerzon. "Let's do the damn deal and go home."

The waiter drifted past, nearly mistakable as a configuration of cigar smoke. Allison signaled him. "Guys," she announced nervously, "anyone want a late dinner, drink, dessert before we begin?"

Barrett laid his pink hands on the table and ordered the largest steak the place sold.

"Mr. Gerzon?"

"Nothing for me."

"Bill?"

"I'll have some of that chocolate cake."

Allison nodded at the waiter to induce action and then glanced at me, her face tense behind her smile. Something about Jay unnerved her, I thought, even though his big hand had already smoothed its way up the small of her back.

"Get me one of those cigars," he said to her, and when she did he inspected it for a moment, ran it under his nose, nodded his satisfaction, and slipped it into the breast pocket of his suit.

"Okay," I told everyone. "I'm going to insist I have a chance to look at the contract privately. Just get me a quiet room where I can read this for"—I checked my watch—"the next twenty-nine minutes."

"Great," said Jay. "Then we—"

"Twenty-four minutes," coughed out Barrett. "I need five minutes for myself, start to end, no more, but no less."

"Twenty-four, then."

Gerzon pulled more papers from his briefcase. "We also have the transfer and tax forms, all the Suffolk County forms, too. That takes five minutes, too."

Jay was nervous. "Can we really do this in nineteen minutes? I could just—"

"No," I said. "Don't sign anything while I'm gone."

Allison led me back up the stairs, through the dining room and kitchen, then down a hallway lined with sacks of onions and potatoes. "That's the only way out of the Havana Room?" I asked.

"Yes," she called over her shoulder. "Now, the night-shift bookkeeper is in my office so I can't put you there, the adding machine drives everyone nuts." I watched the curve of muscle in each of her calves as we climbed a back stairway. What had Lipper said? *She's got some moves on her most men never heard of.* We passed waiters and a tray of canapés and three flights up she opened a small windowless door. "This is the quietest spot we have."

It was the restaurant's laundry room, which I hadn't seen on my earlier tour. Inside, a woman bent over an ancient Singer sewing machine, tapping rhythmically at the electric foot pedal as she fed torn fabric under its jabbing needle, while behind her, in three industrial-size washing machines, cotton tablecloths and napkins and chef's aprons tumbled in a bleachy storm.

"Mrs. Cordelli, we need the room for a little while," Allison said. The woman stood and left. Allison cleared off a small wooden table. "I'm going to knock on the door in fifteen minutes."

I set myself to the pages and soon, my attention sharpened by the room's strong smell of bleach, I had the sense of the contract. It was a perfectly legal funhouse of riders, amendments, powers of attorney, and escrow arrangements. It had passages of vagueness and extreme paranoia. To the best of my understanding, Jay Rainey had made various representations, "subject to the buyer's inspection," the deadline for which had passed, that the land being exchanged was indeed subdividable, free of buried gasoline tanks, had received Department of Health approval for multiple large-scale septic systems, had well water that contained acceptably low levels of perchlorate, a residue from chemical fertilizers used for years by Long Island's potato farmers, did not overlap with any Native American burial grounds, was not the nesting area of the spotted salamander, or any other endangered, threatened, or rare species, and carried various covenants and restrictions pertaining to federally protected marshland, drainage easements, minimum building setbacks, clustered housing arrangements, and so on. The bigger the piece of land, generally, the more complicated its transfer. The buyer, Voodoo LLC, for its part, as represented by Gerzon, had checked off on all of these conditions, not changing any of them. Which was strange—usually in a large real estate transaction there's a last-minute struggle over a number of residual issues as the two parties try to gain some final advantage before everything is signed.

It appeared, moreover, that Voodoo LLC, so eager to dump the Reade Street property, did not particularly care to inspect the nature of the ownership of the Long Island property. I saw no disclosure form regarding debts, liens, or judgments. Plus, in receiving the Reade Street property, Jay was requiring no improvements, consideration of certain conditions, or contingencies for conditions hereinafter discovered. And Gerzon had slipped in some slick language that prohibited Jay from seeking "any claim or reversal of indemnity" of Voodoo should problems arise.

That no bank was directly involved, financing the actual transaction, was unusual, too. Companies usually like to leverage real estate transactions, conserving precious cash where possible. Then again, the transaction was a swap, which might have positive tax consequences . . . clearly, I needed more time. In the old days, a contract like the one in front of me would have required several days of analysis. That no mortgage was being paid off or created might be a bad thing, too. Banks, for all of their excesses, act as a corrective to some of the most foolish or illegal practices, for they usually employ independent inspectors to examine the property proposed for mortgage. Not the case here. As contracts went, this was a one-night stand, and I bet that the reason Jay didn't have a lawyer was that no decent lawyer would be party to such a transaction without insisting that the contract be rewritten from top to bottom. Probably both parties were legally vulnerable. One of them was making a killing and I didn't know which.

The door eased open and there was Allison.

"All set?" she asked brightly.

"I can't be party to this."

"Why?"

"It's a mess."

"Please, Bill."

"I'm trying to *protect* him, Allison."

"He knows the risks, I think."

"I doubt that."

"It means a lot to him, Bill."

"That's great, Allison. I just met the guy."

"It means a lot to *me*."

I flipped over the contract. "Someone's getting screwed here, and I'm going to tell him that, Allison."

Less than a minute later we had returned to the Havana Room.

Jay checked his watch. "It's tight."

An enormous steaming steak was waiting at my place, which I had not ordered, as well as the cake, which I had, and Barrett already had butter on his tie. Jay, I could see, had tossed back a drink or two while I'd been gone.

"Okay?" he asked. "Do we have liftoff?"

"I think we should talk a moment, Jay."

Gerzon pointed to his oversized watch. "Damn it, I've got eleven fifty-three. I'm not turning my watch back, either."

I leaned into Jay's ear. "I'm assuming that you'll sign this thing no matter how rotten it is, no matter my advice to the contrary."

His eyes met mine, and he nodded subtly.

"You're close to desperate."

Again a silent yes.

"You realize," I went on, "that Gerzon is bluffing, either on the deadline or the price, and probably has authority to negotiate one of them."

Jay shook his head no.

"I'm going to show you, okay?" I looked Gerzon in the eye and guessed price. "My client is not going to sign this document until you come up with another three hundred thousand dollars."

Gerzon's face creased backward, like he had suddenly stepped into a wind-tunnel. "What?"

"Yes, we'll scratch out the four hundred thousand dollars and write in seven hundred thousand dollars. Initial every figure. No big deal."

"You're fucking crazy!"

"It's done all the time. Just ask Donald Trump."

"You ask him."

"I don't need to, I've seen him do it."

"You're out of your—"

"Barrett, you ever see initialed sums?" I interrupted, feeling good now. "Yeah, sure."

Jay turned to me. "Bill, the thing is—"

I put my hand on his arm. "Say nothing, pal. Let your lawyer handle it."

Allison watched this exchange, eyes large.

"What's it going to be, Gerzon?"

He already had his cell phone out. He stood up, his face a bitter knot, and stalked out of the room.

"I'm going to lose the deal!" Jay complained, furious now. "I can't believe it!"

"Well, maybe—" Allison began.

Jay confronted me in disbelief. "Bill, I'm going to fucking lose the deal!"

"I don't think so."

We sat a moment, the title man shoveling cake into his mouth.

"He's coming back!"

Gerzon returned, closing his cell phone. "One-fifty," he announced, sitting down again. "That's all I can do."

I'd guessed correctly. "Three hundred."

"*Two.*"

"Two seventy-five," I said. "We won't require a bank check."

"Two *twenty*-five."

"Two-seventy."

"Come on!"

"Two-seventy," I repeated.

"Two-fucking-*fifty*."

I didn't answer.

"I said two-fifty."

I turned to Jay. "Did you know that in the second half of the twentieth century prime waterfront property on Long Island returned close to a six thousand percent profit?"

"No."

"You could sit on this property another five years and double your money easily."

"Well—"

"I said two-fifty!" screamed Gerzon.

I leaned toward him and spoke softly. "Two-seventy."

"Two fifty-five, final."

I watched the second hand on my watch tick away ten seconds. "Two-seventy."

"Two-sixty, final."

"Two sixty-five, final," I replied.

"Two sixty-five. *Done*."

"All right," I said. "Shake my hand."

"You fuck," said Gerzon.

"I know you hate me. Shake it anyway."

He did. I turned to Jay. "You're getting an additional two hundred and sixty-five thousand dollars cash for this property."

He nodded, stunned.

"Wow," breathed Allison. "That was kind of—" She just stared at me. *Sexy*, I think she might have said, but didn't.

"You'll take cash, I assume," said Gerzon, lifting his second briefcase to the table.

"*Cash*-cash? Bills?" asked Jay.

"Yes."

"I guess so. Why?"

"This was my instruction." Gerzon was keeping his briefcase open, hiding its total contents. I probably could have asked for more. He counted stacks of bank-banded bills. Ten thousand a stack. "You'll sign a receipt for it."

"Laundering anything, Gerzon?" I said.

"Screw you," he muttered, peeling off the last five thousand. "This is clean. It's real."

Jay turned to Allison. "Do you have a bag or something?"

"Sure. I guess." She retreated behind the bar.

"That's it," said Gerzon. "You can count it."

"I will," I said, and I did, stack by stack. It was correct. Allison returned with a cardboard box that originally held seltzer water. I stacked the cash in it.

"I can sign now?" asked Jay.

I amended the contracts. "Yes."

Then the paperwork began. We had four minutes. "I've got the bank check for the four hundred—" narrated Gerzon, moving the forms around quickly. "Mr. Barrett has his check, thank you . . . I can sign this . . . the title report, your copy . . . you sign here, the receipt for the *blood* your lawyer took out of my client's arm . . . And here's the deed, yes, the state transfer form . . ."

In a minute or so we had completed all the documents. Gerzon neatened his stack of papers, withdrew a date stamp from his briefcase, checked the day, adjusted the hour and minute, and stamped each sheet, bang, bang, bang. "And . . . that's it, *done.*"

Jay coughed lightly, the box of cash by his side. "Eleven fifty-nine . . . and *midnight*, gentlemen."

"Bye guys." Barrett stood to leave. "The deed will be recorded tomorrow downtown."

Gerzon pulled a chain of keys from his pocket and dropped it on the table. "All yours," he said to Jay, not looking at me.

Jay picked up the keys with an odd caution. But then he pulled a single key from his own pocket and gave it to Gerzon. "This is for the lock on the chain at the end of the dirt road."

And that was it—the moment, the consummation. Did each man think he had swindled the other? Gerzon shook hands with Jay and, surprisingly, again with me as well, his grip a painful warning. And then his eyes slid away from each of us, and he left.

Allison made her way back over the tiled floor with a bottle and three glasses. She gave Jay a kiss and searched his eyes for gladness. "It's exciting!" she cried, and I understood that she was only passingly referring to the property deal and the miraculous appearance of a box of money. Jay smiled at her, but when they embraced, her head and breasts lost within his large chest and arms, his eyes looked away, as if through the very walls of the building, and with no discernible excitement or satisfaction, more like sadness, the resolution of someone burdened with a long and complicated journey toward a destination known only to him. I was not supposed to see this on Jay's face, but I did.

"Let's all go out and celebrate." Jay's mood seemed to lift. "I know a little place. I've got to find a way to thank you, Bill."

He was being kind and I waved them off.

"We'll work out some payment tomorrow, okay?"

"Sure," I said. "You two go on. It's all terrific. I enjoyed myself a great deal. Hang on to that box. Congratulations, Jay. You and the rest of the crooks own a piece of the island of Manhattan."

"You want to see it?" he said, his voice energetic now. "I'll be down there tomorrow morning." Then he caught up his coat and nodded to the waiter with a flashing smile and looked down into Allison's face. Her head hung back, neck exposed, eyes dreaming. She was ready for him and didn't mind if anyone knew it. They were desperate, I would see, in their own ways, but desperate people have a way of matching frequencies and finding each other before the end comes. For now something magical had happened, and the Havana Room seemed to whirlpool in a density of money and smoke and lamplight. I watched them go, Allison leaning heavily against Jay, the box under his arm, cigar in his pocket. Despite myself, my affection for Allison, I liked him. Sometimes you just like people right away. This, on the face of it, was another reason that things went further. It was the explanation I'd have offered myself or anyone else. But the truth is more complicated; somehow I sensed a steep angle to Jay's trajectory, if not its direction up or down, then an absolute velocity toward an outcome I wanted to witness. This is the same loaded attraction that creates politicians and football coaches and movie directors. Their believers believe. You don't just like the person, you want to find out something about him, something terribly important and true—you want to see if he wins or loses, lives or dies.

three

NOW, I ASSUMED, the evening would taper painlessly into oblivion. I ordered another drink to go with my chocolate cake. The Havana Room was dark and comfortable, and the men moved to and from the bar or toilet slowly, enjoying, it seemed, their own gravity. The talk was measured. You could hear money in the murmur, you could hear problems being unbolted and taken apart. I listened hungrily, for of course I used to do these things, used to like being in the big messy heart of the action, shaving away complication, splicing in the fix, watching for the nod of group assent. In big law firms like my former one, there are basically two kinds of lawyers; the first is the glad-handing, business-grabbing opportunist, who accepts that men and women are fallen, wingless creatures, and is in it for the game and the money and the dense structures of connectivity that build up over a career; the second type, rarer, is the emotionally aloof scholar, more interested in the purity of the law than in the impurity of human beings. These same men (and they are usually men) could easily have been priests or research scientists, and might be disappointed not to be sitting on the U.S. Supreme Court. They are paid to compose legal structures (trusts, corporate ownerships, mergers) that open like tulips in the sun for the right person or entity but remain otherwise hidden, impermeable, indestructible. Both types of lawyers can be dangerous politically, and both have their flaws. The back-slappers and group-grinners tend to drink too much, fuck around on out-of-town trips, attract marginal clients with the wrong kind of legal problems, and die suddenly on the tennis court. The legal priests abhor the messy, repetitive work that is the firm's bread and butter. They can't be counted on to chat amiably at social events or conceal their fringy political opinions. They don't let profits stand in the way of righteousness. They tend to fall out of touch with the younger partners and live forever. I'd been the first type of lawyer of course, and let me admit that when a client came to me with the words "Bill, I need a little advice," or the like, I felt happy—grateful to be wanted, eager to be of use. This is, in part, why men enjoy hunching over papers and agendas—it makes them feel useful, or at least not useless; it lets them bounce in the net over the void. I'd enjoyed my little skirmish with Gerzon, the tangle over large sums, the unexpected sprint down overgrown thoughtpaths. I'd tasted a little of the old professional meanness, the venom of cleverness—it had tasted good, too.

In this better mood, I inspected the room, which had started to fill up, despite the late hour. A few men checked their watches, expecting something. But what? In the city of earthly delights, what could actually be new and unusual? And would it start without Allison?

Ha, the Chinese handyman, now stepped into the room, moving with such stooped humility that the men barely glanced at him as he made his way behind the bar. I waited to see if the waiter or bartender paid him any attention. They didn't. Nor did Ha appear to care; his face was a serene mask of wrinkles. Allison had said something about him being ready, and so here he was, in the room, fussing behind the bar, apparently right on schedule.

But I wasn't the only one watching Ha; he'd drawn the interest of a distinguished-looking man at the bar whom I recognized as one of the city's great literary figures of the past era. A youngish entourage accompanied the man, and each fame-licker had arranged himself in a posture he thought most advantageous to receiving the great one's attention. Had Allison invited them? I'd once admired the man; he'd been a brilliant skeptic and an energetic personality around town but widely dissolute in his personal habits, and with each year his original literary accomplishments became harder to remember.

"You sir!" he called loudly to Ha. "I'm here to see if you are a fraud!"

Ha made no response, not a blink.

"Which I suspect you are!"

The man had drawn the room's recognition, and he enjoyed it, nodding gravely at the others who saluted him from their seats. He was perhaps now most famously the author of his own self-destruction, known for his appearances at the city's watering holes, where, curled over his drink, he was to be seen telling forty-year-old tales to twenty-year-old wits. But he still looked good in a tailored suit, and spent heavily to maintain his teeth.

"It's a complete fabrication," he announced wetly, "a parlor trick, a circus act." He swept his hand threateningly at the room. "Which one of you dupes are in on it? Which of you are the ringers?"

The men in the booths, not unworldly themselves, heard hostility and saw alchoholism, and after they looked away, he directed his comments back to the smirking youngsters gathered around him, who no doubt delighted in their secret power over him, for he needed them far more than they did him. "Yes, yes, we will see!" came his voice in response to an unheard question. "We will witness the delusion of the human appetite!" He pounded his fist on the bar, as if to summon the hounds of inquisition, but in this action he was vigor mummified, he was satiation lost. And, in the deep and hideously thick coughing that resulted, he was also death, lingeringly foretold. But not yet. A fresh drink arrived into his hands and soon he was again waiting brightly, like the others.

Then I heard a commotion coming down the stairs.

"I invited myself!" came an angry voice. "Where is he?"

The figures in the room glanced up expectantly. A little man in a wool jacket appeared in the doorway, squinting through the cigar smoke. Snow dusted his watchman's cap. The men turned away in disappointment. Whoever they expected wasn't this person, and he was already arguing with the waiter, who pointed at me.

The man lurched stiffly forward, and then I was looking up into a red face of about sixty, but a tough sixty—battered and doggish.

"Good evening," I said in a mood of full-bellied indulgence, the night having provided already far more entertainment than expected.

"Where's Jay?" the man asked.

I put down my fork. "Not here."

The man stared accusingly at the plates on the table, the empty glasses. "*Was* he here?"

I told him yes.

"When? Just now?"

"Maybe half an hour ago," I said.

"Who're you?" he demanded.

"I come here a lot, I just met him tonight."

The man winced. "Come on, guy!" he said. "I got to find him!"

"I don't know where he is. He went out on the town."

The man examined my face, apparently concluded I was truthful, and, to my surprise, dropped down across from me in the booth.

"I'm just going to sit here a minute, need to rest. I was on the road for two hours." He pulled off his gloves, revealing enormous hands, their fingers crooked and swollen, almost painful to look at, nails packed with grime. "Jesum, I'm tired. Had to park on the sidewalk. Snow's coming out of the northeast, be bad soon." He pushed the dishes to the side, although not without eyeing a few soggy fries. "You got *any* idea where he is?"

"Not really."

He pulled off his cap. His hair appeared to be styled with motor oil. "How about where he's gonna be later tonight—" His face puckered to a leer. "You know what I mean?"

Probably Allison's apartment. "I might see him tomorrow, downtown."

"No, that's too late." He thumbed one of his teeth, as if it might be loose.

"You a friend of his?"

"Friend?" He shook his head. "Everybody calls me Poppy." He didn't offer me his hand, but instead glanced around the Havana Room. "Pretty swank, this place, full of assholes. Wouldn't let me in at first."

"You try to call him?" I asked, assuming Jay didn't want to be contacted.

"'Course I did." Poppy noticed my uneaten cake. "You want that?"

I waved it toward him. He pulled the plate close and chewed diligently for a minute, then drained one of the water glasses.

At that moment, the barman approached. He nodded at me apologetically and addressed Poppy.

"Sir, this is a private room."

"The door was unlocked."

"The door was closed, sir."

"I opened it."

"Sir, they're telling me that there's a big truck full of potatoes parked on our sidewalk."

Poppy nodded. "That's mine."

"Sir, they're asking you to move it."

"I will." He smiled at me, teeth smeared with dark cake. "When I'm ready."

"Sir, it's very inconvenient for—"

Poppy swiveled. "It'll be very inconvenient if I dump those potatoes in front of this place, don't you think?"

"Sir, I expect that we'll need to call the police."

"Fine, call them."

"Sir?"

"But don't expect them to pick up something like nine thousand frozen potatoes."

The barman eased away.

"You got a pen?"

I did. He slid an embossed HAVANA ROOM napkin in front of himself and tried to write. "All right, I'll—" The napkin tore.

I handed him another. He tried again.

"What's wrong?"

"Circulation's gone. This one"—he held up his right hand, wiggled the fingers stiffly—"got run over by a loader sixteen years ago, which lemme tell you hurt like the devil." He lifted the left. "And this one—I got the repeating motion thing. Tendons all gummed up. Got no power, no grip."

With the second napkin, Poppy was successful, moving the pen slowly, like a boy carving his initials into a tree. His eyebrows lifted with each finished letter. "Here. Give this to him."

"Can I read it?" I asked.

"I ain't stopping you."

The napkin said:

JAY—We got a probelm w/Hershul & the cat. Its not my faullt. Get out there quick. I cant do nothing. I'll wate all night.

Poppy

He pulled his cap back on, stood up. "I can trust you to get it to him?" he asked.

I slipped the note into my pocket. "I'll see what I can do."

He swiped a handful of cold french fries and slipped them into his coat pocket. "You'll try, right?"

It was then that I noticed the beautiful black woman I'd seen before in a blue evening gown at the other end of the room. The men looked alert now. Was she the one they'd been waiting for?

"You'll try, right?" Poppy repeated.

I looked back at him. "Sure."

"I mean *tonight*, fella," he coughed. "As soon as goddamn possible."

"Yes, sure," I mumbled. The black woman, so tall and elegant, was greeting each patron with a handshake and warm smile. The literary man had slipped forward off his stool in anticipation.

"Hey, hey, I'm talking to you!" said Poppy. "I got this feeling you can find him, see, like you know his girl, where she can be found. They told me she ran this place." He pointed at the napkin. "Jay'll understand that, he's got to."

I nodded. "Okay."

He was wary. "I can't explain it all to you. It's one hundred percent confidential."

"I get that, yes."

"Tell him I had to go back."

The woman listened to the literary man's banter. He felt himself to be very drunkenly clever, I could see, but he fumbled his cigarette onto her shoes and she glided away, ready to greet others.

"I have to get back," I said."

"Right."

"Because of the snow." Poppy zippered his coat, eyeing me, and seemed already hunched against the cold outside. "If you don't tell him, it's all on you. He'll know. He'll find out."

I didn't like the sound of this.

"And tell him I don't know how it happened."

"Okay." Ha, I noticed, had set a rolled white cloth on the bar. He unrolled the bundle and lifted a flap. Something gleamed from within the folded cloth.

"I still got coffee in my truck."

"Okay, Poppy," I said.

"You got to get the message to him."

Now Ha was filling a plastic bucket with water in the sink behind the bar. "I *will*."

"You tell him it involves Herschel."

The elegant black woman knew almost every man in the room, I realized. "I said I would."

Poppy saw my distraction. "I had to go *back*, he has to understand that. When he sees what happened, he'll understand."

"Right."

"He's probably going to need to bring someone to help. My hands are no good. It's a big problem, you got to say that, too."

"Okay."

"You look like a decent guy. I'm trusting you."

Poppy stood and left, but not before noticing the bowl of nuts on the bar, which he sampled liberally. I read the subliterate napkin message again, unable to make sense of it. How could I get it to Jay? If he and Allison had gone out to celebrate, they could be anywhere. Both probably had cell phones, but I had neither number. But I could call information. She'd said her home number was listed. She had to be, when you thought about it, needed to be reachable if the restaurant burned down in the middle of the night.

"Listen," I said to the waiter, "I'll be right back. I need to use the pay phone upstairs. Hold my table here, okay?"

He shrugged. "I'd make it real quick, pal."

The comment seemed unnecessarily rude, but I ignored it and hurried toward the Havana Room's hunched doorway, past the literary man, who had just been forcibly presented with his check by the bartender. I climbed the worn marble stairs, my shadow rising in front of me. In the foyer, while calling information, I noticed Tom Brokaw arrive for a late bite. Impressive man, Brokaw. Smooth, articulate, reassuring, deeply American in his persona. Bet he never killed anybody with a glass of milk, either. Allison was listed, and I left a perfunctory message about Poppy and hung up. The phone rang back almost instantly.

"Oh hell-o-*ho*, Bill," came Allison's voice—amused, silky, relaxed.

"That was fast. You know the pay phone number?"

"Of course. Got it on speed-dial, too."

"You're at home?"

"No. I have this fancy phone thing that rings me wherever I am."

"I called your apartment."

"I know."

"But you're not there?"

"Oh, no. I'm with Jay. In his big, masculine SUV. You can pronounce that *suv*, which is provocative, don't you think?"

"I need to tell Jay—"

"Like, let's *suv*. Or maybe you'd like to come up for a quick *suv*. Or, like this, all they did was *suv*, just *constantly*."

"You a bit inebriated, Allison?"

"Sort of. We're headed back there right now. I'm running late. But the men will wait. We just went for a *spin*."

"Things seem about ready to start."

"Not without me," she said. "We'll be there in three minutes. Here's Jay."

He came on the line. "Hey guy," he breathed. "I want you to come to my office tomorrow so I can settle up, show you—"

"That's not why I'm calling."

I told him about Poppy, and the potatoes as well. He asked me to read him the message.

"Oh, shit," he muttered, then muffled the phone. I thought I heard a tone of female argumentation. Then the open static returned, the sound of traffic. As I listened I noticed an elderly woman in a long fur waiting to use the phone.

"I don't own a cell phone," she told the maître d'. "My sister had one, gave her brain cancer."

The maître d' nodded at her good sense.

I kept listening. "Thanks a lot," came Allison's voice away from Jay's phone.

"Bill?"

"Jay, I think I should have a look at some of that paperwork tomorrow. At the deed history in particular."

"Sure." He wasn't listening.

"Good night, Jay." I wanted to get back into the Havana Room. "Congratulations again."

"Bill, you got plans tonight?" Jay said.

"I plan to sleep, eventually."

"I've got some kind of a problem. I need a hand."

"I'm a tired guy, Jay. Really. It's almost one."

"Wait, wait, hold on—"

I heard muffled noises, Allison saying something, arguing perhaps, rushing static. Around me people were still arriving at the steakhouse, despite the hour. The great old literary man, however, was being escorted with his entourage from the Havana Room by the waiter. "But the night is still young!" His knees buckled with each step. "Everything's about to begin! I saw the knives!"

"Bill," came Jay's watery cellular voice in my ear again, "I really need a guy to go out to Long Island with me and help with something. It's like three or four hours . . . I might need a guy to help hold stuff, a pair of hands, is what it is."

I'd yanked an extra quarter million bucks from the universe for him only hours before and now he needed me to be a farmworker? But I was polite. "A pair of hands?"

"Yeah, Poppy's are no good."

I saw the door to the Havana Room closing. "Give me the number, I'll call you back."

I walked the nine or ten steps across the foyer. The door was shut now. I tried the old porcelain handle. Nothing. The yellow card had been removed from the brass plate.

"Closed," announced the maître d'.

I felt cheated. "Hey, but it was open a second ago."

"Yes," he said, not looking up from his reservation book. "It was."

I tried the handle, shook the door. It was surprisingly firm, with no vibration to it, as if the handle were merely bolted to a wall.

"Sir!" he called sharply.

"I was just in there, I have food on the table!"

"I'm sorry," he said, with no sympathy.

"I was taken in there by Allison Sparks," I said.

"Yes," he responded, "but you left. And the door is closed."

"I don't get it," I protested.

"I must ask you to move away from the door," he said.

"It's not busy, it's not—"

"Please, sir," he said, his voice ominous.

Now the woman in the fur coat had the pay phone in both hands.

I retrieved my coat and stepped outside into the cold, irritated and disappointed, watching the snow fall. Allison had said she'd be there in three minutes, but it was longer, more like ten. I noticed several potatoes in the gutter. The winter wind off Sixth Avenue slaps you around, sticks a cold finger down your collar, wakes you up. But it doesn't remind you that you are fallible and foolish. Finally a green sport utility truck pulled to the curb, flashing its lights, wipers pushing away the swirling snow. Allison jumped out wearing a big hooded coat and ran up to me in the snowy light outside the door. Her hair was not quite combed, her makeup smudged and forgotten, cheeks flushed.

"I don't get this guy sometimes, I really don't."

I glanced at Jay's shadow behind the snowy window of the truck cab. "I thought the evening was going so well, the real estate deal and every-thing."

"It was. We were having a great time. He was fine ten minutes ago, *fine.*"

She didn't seem as drunk as she'd been on the phone and I wondered if it had been an advertisement of happiness. "What happened?"

Allison leaned close to me, hunched in her coat. "Your phone call, Bill."

"Did he say what the problem was?"

"No, but he got upset after you called. I could see it."

A blast of snow cut down the street and we huddled closer. "He wants me to drive out to the East End of Long Island with him."

"Will you help him?" she asked. "I'm worried about him driving alone."

"I was hoping you'd get me back into the Havana Room, see the cir-cus trick or whatever goes on."

She blinked at the snow in her eyes. "Who says it's a circus trick?"

"What happens? Ha and the black woman do something?"

Allison frowned in disgust. "It's real kinky, Bill, yeah." She checked her watch. "They must have started without me. Ha must have gone first."

"I want to go back in."

"If you've missed Ha's first part, then it won't be any good."

"I don't understand."

She nodded. "I'll get you back in, don't worry."

"When?"

"Another night. Soon." She glanced back at Jay's truck, its hazard lights blinking, as if waiting for me. "He says he's driving out there no matter what."

She was appealing to me to help Jay for the second time that evening, and I could not help but hope that this commended me to her. I looked into Allison's face with frustration and unexpectedly sensed her own. The whole evening was a piece of unfinished sexual business to her. With the snow pattering softly on her hood, there she was, lungs and lips, eyes and breasts, and she *wanted*, she wanted very badly, she wanted him or me or it or everything, and that desire made me want her, too. "Please, Bill?" she whispered. "Will you help him?"

"I should go home to bed. I'm tired."

She studied me a moment. "You don't *look* tired."

"I am. Tired and old."

"Girls have been known to like old men," Allison said. "They find their wrinkles interesting."

I thought of Judith and Wilson Doan, his strange eyes, standing in a black coat at his son's funeral. I thought of this and it reminded me of other things and I found myself thinking of Timothy in a Tuscan villa, kicking a soccer ball against an old stone wall by himself. I hoped that his stepfather was good to him, loved him, wasn't too caught up in how to spend three quarters of a billion dollars. I needed not to think about this, however, anything but this, and the prospect of a late night errand to Long Island had new diversionary value.

"Okay," I muttered. "I'll do it."

"Thank you."

"But you'll get me back into the Havana Room?"

"Promise."

"I really want to see what—"

"I know, yes. I promise, Bill."

"Then it's a deal."

"Please drive safely," she said. "For both of you." She leaned up and kissed me on the cheek. "You'll come by tomorrow?"

"Sure," I said.

"Good. I'd like that."

And then Allison was gone, swirling through the door, the snow following her.

There was still time for me to open the truck's door and make awkward apologies to Jay, but I didn't. Instead I just stood there under the steakhouse's awning feeling the wind slap my cheeks. I've had reason since then to wonder why I resisted the correcting action, the prudent retreat.

I was tired, and I should have gone to bed. Certainly I'd responded to Allison, sensed something genuine in her voice, some muted distress call perhaps. But the reason I walked through the gathering snow to Jay's truck is more than that, and it doesn't reflect well on me: I sensed animal weakness in Jay, and I wanted to find out what it was. To be more precise, I sensed a problem, and not necessarily the one that was worrying Poppy. I sensed edges and change and conflict. A real problem wanting a solution. A solution requires a stratagem, and a stratagem means a game. I'd once been good with problems and stratagems, as I'd proven earlier in the night, and something in me welcomed another challenge.

In this I was a fool. I'd forgotten that any true game is played versus an opponent, or even two simultaneously, against the indifferent backdrop of chance. Who has won and who has lost is often difficult to know, or undecided, or, at the last, reversible. As Wilson Doan Sr. himself had learned, for one. Yes, I'd forgotten all this, and so I walked around to the passenger side of the truck and opened the door. Jay had on the same good coat and suit he'd been wearing a few hours earlier. He looked up at me, his eyes a little dull, I thought, his hands hanging on the steering wheel.

"Really appreciate this," he breathed.

I settled in, and noticed a baseball on the dash. I picked it up. A baseball always feels good in the hands. "Not what I expected to be doing tonight."

"That makes both of us."

The box of cash was behind his seat. "Sounded like you were having kind of a great drive with Allison. Sorry I interrupted."

Most men would have smiled in reply, either in embarrassment or pride. But Jay blinked at the thought of it, lips closed. I had the distinct impression that Allison was not the kind of woman he preferred. He pointed to the glove compartment. "There's a little thing of pills in there. Would you hand it to me?"

I opened the compartment, found an unmarked container.

"Thanks." He shook out three pills and swallowed them. Then he slipped the container into his breast pocket.

"You want me to drive?"

"No, it's all right."

And it was. By the time we'd crossed through the tunnel into Queens, he was sitting up straight and driving with crisp aggression.

"Those pills are pretty good," I noted.

"They are."

"You all right?" I asked.

"I'm fine, man, just tired."

He wasn't interested in talking, so I let it rest. The Long Island Expressway, always a dragway of insane drivers, becomes genuinely otherworldly on a snowy night, and to stay with the traffic we popped up to eighty, flying east past the billboards and shopping centers and exit signs, Jay seemingly noticing none of them. His eyes showed no sign, in fact, that he'd inked a real estate deal that evening or had to break his celebration with Allison, and I found myself remembering the oddly deadened sadness I'd seen in his face when he'd embraced her. In the pin-light darkness of the truck, his mouth was set, his gaze fixed on the road, and I thought I recognized in him a certain kind of man, a man who is damaged and yet unflinching. I've met a few. Because he has taken pain, such a man knows he can take more. In fact, he expects it; suffering, so far as he sees, is in the order of things, the logic of the universe. Usually such men are hard, even self-punishing workers, capable of long periods of isolation or aloneness, and suffer bouts of crippling melancholy. They refuse to take antidepressants, they refuse to talk too much; instead they wait and wait, with the patience of a cat, for the mood to turn. They drink coffee alone in the morning, they smoke cigarettes on the porch. Jay was like this. Such men believe in luck, they watch for signs, and they conduct private rituals that structure their despair and mark their waiting. They are relatively easy to recognize but hard to know, especially during the years when a man is most dangerous to himself, which begins at about age thirty-five, when he starts to tally his losses as well as his wins, and ends at about fifty, when, if he has not destroyed himself, he has learned that the force of time is better caught softly, and in small pieces. Between those points, however, he'd better watch out, better guard against the dangerous journey that beckons to him—the siege, the quest, the grandiosity, the dream. Yes, let me say it again. Quiet men with dreams can be dangerous.

The highway became more desolate as we passed the edge of Long Island's suburban sprawl and into the last thirty miles of farmland. Although far outside the eastern edge of Queens, we were still well within the city's dominion. The money on Long Island, tip to tip, is always, in some measure, New York City money, either coming from or going to. It has to be that way, because, except for potatoes and power boats and fresh fish, everything appearing on the island—every washing machine, every stick of lumber, every carton of orange juice—comes through the city on the way east. Eighty miles out, the island forks north and south, and with the South Fork already filled up with vacation houses and Hamptony attitudes, the North Fork was next; once off the highway we passed signs announcing new golf courses, condo construction, and wineries. I knew a bit about the land game. The idea, of course, is to get hold of an enormous piece of property, preferably with as little cash down as possible, subdivide it "tastefully," which is to say in such a way that it attracts wealthy buyers, and then sell out the whole thing. If the buyer plays cleverly, his leverage can be extraordinary.

"You see what's going on out here," Jay muttered. "It's a gold rush."

"Why did you decide to get rid of the land now?"

"The time was right," he said cryptically.

If able to be subdivided, a big piece of land like Jay's could be worth quite a bit more than he'd exchanged it for. Zoned at an acre per lot with greenbelt set-asides, a developer could still get perhaps seventy lots out of it, with twenty of them on the water. You'd have to drop in a million for water, roads, zoning applications, and sending the politicians to Bermuda, but even so, someone smart and energetic might be able to triple his money in five years. "You try to subdivide?" I asked.

He shook his head silently, made a series of turns, then stopped in the darkness at a chained dirt road that headed directly toward Long Island Sound. He got out and left the chain on the ground. I noticed a real estate broker's sign: HALLOCK PROPERTIES. Jay pulled it up and flung it into the grass.

"This the land?"

"Yeah."

"No longer yours, now."

"Not technically, counselor," he said, sitting down again.

"You gave Gerzon the key, I thought."

"I kept a copy." He nosed the truck ahead. "Always keep a copy, you know?"

The road passed through a stand of spruce trees, then opened up, wide to either side.

Jay hunched close to the windshield. "Where is he?"

I could see in the snowy dark that we were passing through an old farming operation. Massive outbuildings, a couple of abandoned tractors. Jay maneuvered around ruts and holes. "They haven't been keeping the road up."

"You know this land?"

"I grew up here, man."

"Right here, on this land?"

"Exactly," he said. "Hey, look for tracks."

But I saw nothing. The land lay to either side of the road in wide flats. We passed irrigation engine sheds, piles of piping, three ancient trees in a line, leafless yet magestic. The snow slapped against the car.

"The water is close?" I said.

"Quarter mile."

At the end of the road, a deep-bellied farm truck had pulled to the side, beyond which I could see the phosphorescent expanse of Long Island Sound. The truck was a big one, double sets of wheels on the rear, and about the size of a municipal garbage truck except that the container end was a steel trough filled high with potatoes. The truck also appeared to be missing its driver's door. At our approach a figure stepped out. He pulled his hat low and came straight up to Jay's side. It was Poppy, drinking coffee.

"Where's Herschel?" yelled Jay.

Poppy shook his head at the futility of the question. "Come on, it's bad."

I felt sick at the sound of this. We got out and followed Poppy directly to the edge of the sea cliff.

"Watch it there," said Jay, holding my shoulder. "It goes down two hundred feet."

The wind was coming hard off the ocean and pushed up the face of the cliff, so that where we stood snow flew into our faces even as we looked down. Poppy pointed his light at two wide tracks that dropped straight off the cliff. "Went right over."

Jay peered over as best he could. "Is he dead?"

Poppy shrugged. "If he was working in daylight, then he's been there eight hours anyway." He kicked at the sand. "Fucking snow made it hard to see the edge, I guess."

"When'd you find him?" Jay asked.

"Maybe ten o'clock tonight."

This made sense to me, for Poppy hadn't appeared in the Havana Room until after midnight.

"Was he alive?" I asked in terror.

"I don't know," snarled Poppy. "He could have been. But he wasn't moving."

"You didn't go down there?"

"No, no way. Not with my hands."

"You call the police?" I said, shivering now.

Poppy looked at Jay in fury, and despite Poppy's small size I took a step backward.

"Bill, hang on," said Jay. He nodded at Poppy. "All right, so you didn't go down."

"No way."

I peered over, couldn't see much.

"Don't get too close. The sand is shifty, there's no clean line."

Contrary to my expectation, the drop was not sheer but gradual. I edged forward. "There!"

Forty feet down the slope sat a bulldozer, treads right side down, held in place by a stand of leafless trees. A man lay sprawled in the cab. He didn't move. The machine appeared to have slid backward down the irregular slope and come to a stop undamaged. The big bucket on its front rested in the sand, and the hinged arm of the backhoe was tucked in behind the cab.

Jay squinted into the snowing darkness. "Hey Bill, I got a legal question."

"Yeah."

"How easy is it to undo a real estate deal?"

"If both parties agree, and the deed hasn't been recorded, easy."

"If the guys from Voodoo saw a dead guy on their property tomorrow morning, could they undo the deal?"

I thought for a moment. "Yes. They could say a crime may have been committed, that they bought under false pretenses. They could tie it up with a court order. They could try to stop payment, freeze accounts. They could do stuff."

"I wouldn't get my building."

"No," I said.

He studied the bulldozer. "I think we can pull it up."

"You're crazy," said Poppy.

Jay shook his head. "We got to get him out of there."

"How?"

"Drive that thing up. Slope's not too bad. It's made it up grades sharper than that."

"Oh, you pecker!" spat Poppy. "You'll kill us."

"You're moving a dead body?" I asked. "You can't do that."

"And if the slope's okay," insisted Poppy, "why didn't he drive it up himself?"

"I don't know, because he had a heart attack, maybe."

"You don't know that," said Poppy.

Jay ignored him. "You still have that big cable in the barn?"

"Yeah, but so goddamn what?"

I listened to their conversation with mounting fear.

"I saw the forty-five hundred is loaded."

"Won't work," Poppy announced.

"Yes it will, if I can get the Cat started."

"You'll kill somebody. Not me, but somebody. Probably yourself. Cable will snap and whip back and cut off your head."

"Thank you, Poppy, thank you very fucking much."

"Then your girlfriend won't have nobody to suck on her tit."

"You're a gentleman, Poppy. Always have been."

"Guys, you can't do this," I insisted. "Call the police. It's their business."

Poppy pointed at me menacingly. "Why did you bring *him*, anyway?"

"You got somebody else for me at three in the morning?"

Poppy shook his head, no fight left. "I been waiting, Jay, is all."

"You did a lot already," Jay said in a softer voice. "Now we've got just one more thing to do. Go get the cable."

Poppy grunted, climbed in his battered truck, and drove off.

Jay headed down the slope, and despite my misgivings, I followed him, slipping my way down the crusty sand. The bulldozer looked like a yellow toy tossed carelessly within a giant sandbox, but up close it was enormous and in notably poor repair. Its yellow body paint was pocked with rust, its hydraulic lines wrapped with duct tape. The driver, Herschel, was a heavyset black man in a plaid work shirt who sat in the seat fallen backward, feet spread wide, chin up and eyes upon the heavens. He might have been fifty, he might have been seventy. The storm had iced his head and body. He was quite dead.

Jay scrambled alongside the bulldozer. "Oh, Herschel," he moaned. "What're you doing out here?" He climbed up the side of the machine and knelt next to the dead man, his forehead touching the man's hand. "You told me you were done last week! Why did you come out here?" He slumped against the giant treads of the dozer, head down. "Oh, Herschel, oh, man . . ."

I was intruding, so I retreated into the darkness, wondering what Herschel had meant to Jay. The two figures were a study in contrasts—white and black, young and old, alive and dead—but Jay's ease next to the dead man suggested an intimate history. Finally he stood and climbed into the cab. He wiped one of the gauges, examined it, then turned the key in the ignition. Nothing happened. He gave the frozen body a firm push but it didn't move. The dead man's gloveless hand was draped on the shifter knob, not clutching it but making incidental contact.

He pushed and pulled but the hand was stuck fast. "Frozen."

"Don't tear the skin," I called.

"Yes, fuck it, I know!" roared Jay into the snow, his long coat whipping behind him. "Bill, come up here!"

"What?"

"Get up here, I need you."

"For what?"

"Come on!"

I climbed awkwardly to the cab, feeling bad about everything. "Christ, Jay, I'm supposed to be in bed. Not standing here!"

The dead man's face gazed upward into the storm. Snow had crusted over the surface of his eyes. He wore a digital watch, the tiny red seconds-light blinking as if its owner would consult it at any moment. I noticed he was not wearing socks and that his shoes were low carpet-paddlers, not work boots high over the ankle.

"Just put your hands on his, try to start warming it."

"You crazy?"

"Yeah, I am."

"I'm not holding hands with a dead man."

"I can't move this thing otherwise."

"Why not just call the police?"

"I can't, counselor," he said in a low, determined voice. "I just can't do that."

It occurred to me that I could hike up the sandy cliff, get in Jay's truck, check to see if he left the keys in it, take out the box of cash and put it on the ground, then drive away. Back to Manhattan, drop the vehicle in a lot, walk straight to my apartment. Up the stairs, key in the door, jump in bed, good night moon, and dream about Salma Hayek. I could do that. I could do that *now*.

But I didn't. Instead I placed my two warm hands around the large cold one, which was frozen solid. I counted to thirty, then clapped my hands together for warmth and tried again. After several tries, my hands were numb and Herschel's hand was unchanged. Holding hands with a dead man was not why I went to Yale Law School, not why I worked seventy-hour weeks for ten years in my twenties and thirties, not why I said yes to Allison. It was crazy. But despite myself, my mind was working on the problem, figuring it. "Poppy has coffee," I remembered. "In his truck."

"Right!" Jay shouted.

A moment later he had scrambled up and down the slope and was pouring coffee from Poppy's large Thermos onto Herschel's hand. Steam lifted through the glare of the flashlight. "This is going to work," he said, shaking the gearshift violently. He poured more coffee out. "It's—*there.*"

Jay moved the shifter to the side and now the hand stuck straight into space. "Let's see if we can get this started."

There wasn't much room between Herschel's frozen gut and the steering wheel. Jay wriggled into a crouched, half-standing position, his rear against the dead man's groin. "Herschel, man, I'm sorry about this," he muttered. "'Course if you weren't so *fat . . .*" He turned the key. Nothing happened. He tried again. I heard a faint clicking.

Jay climbed down from the cab and lifted the toolbox lid incorporated into the bulldozer's bottom step. "Probably left the lights on. Battery's almost drained." He pulled out what looked like a can of spray paint, leaned up onto the engine hood, and sprayed into the chimney-shaped metallic funnel protruding from it. "Ether," he said. "Right on the starter. Get a hell of a spark."

Jay tossed the can back into the toolbox, then fished inside and pulled out another, smaller can, and staggered through the soft sand around the front of the bulldozer, keeping his hand on the toothed top edge of the huge bucket. Despite his youth and clear physical vitality, he seemed to be laboring. He unscrewed the fuel cap that protruded through the steps on the other side of the cab and upended the can against it, banging it. Then he fingered out a glob of something that looked like blue butter and wiped it into the fuel pipe.

"What's that?" I called.

"Gel." He wiped more of it into the pipe. "Warms diesel fuel."

He threw the can away into the gloom and climbed atop the cab. The controls for the backhoe and the hydraulic pads sat at the rear, downhill side of the cab, and the controls for the bucket and for the bulldozer itself on the uphill side.

"Get me a stick," Jay hollered. "With a Y on the end."

My feet were cold and I had sand in my shoes but I looked around and saw a dead tree a few yards off. I broke off a three-foot branch and lurched back to Jay. He took the stick from me. "Usually you can swing around in the seat here."

This time he sat down on Herschel's lap. Instinctively I looked at the man's face to see what it felt like to have Jay sitting on him. But his stony mask didn't change, of course. Jay turned the key. The engine clicked, turned over, and caught. The bulldozer vibrated loudly. I felt a sort of worried joy. Sand started trickling from behind the dozer. Jay twisted backward and pushed at the hand controls with the stick. One of the huge hydraulic pads descended slowly, settling into the sand. Jay switched off the engine.

We climbed up the slope. Poppy had returned with the cable and was sitting in the large truck. A work glove was taped to its steering wheel like a disembodied hand, and I assumed that Poppy slipped his ruined fingers into it for a better grip. He hopped down to the ground and he and Jay pinned both ends of the thick cable to a tow ring on the rear of the truck. They dragged the loop end of the cable down to the bulldozer, where Jay attached it to a ring in the top of the bucket. I could follow his movements by the swinging arc of his flashlight. Meanwhile Poppy dragged a thick log out of the bramble and set this parallel to the cliff edge and draped the cable over it, so that the cable would ride smoothly across the log and not cut into the sand. They knew what they were doing, and moved with very little communication. When they were done the doubled cable from bulldozer to truck lay lightly on the log.

"Guys, this is fucking crazy," I called. "You're about to break the law, okay? Jay, you should just leave it there, let the police deal with it. Look, I'm a lawyer, take my advice!"

"This is how I want to do it," Jay said. "Poppy, you start the truck. Keep the emergency brake on. I'll start the Cat. When I hit the horn, I'm ready.

Then I'll shift forward easy and you do too. Keep it in low. I'll be going very slowly, if I go at all. I don't want to snap the cable—I'll fall backward. But don't let the cable get slack, either. Tight. Bill, I want you standing right here with the flashlight. Poppy won't be able to see anything and neither will I, but I can see you and so can Poppy in the rearview mirror."

"This is crazy. I don't—"

"Bill, I'm doing this whether you help or not."

"I'm not helping—I'm not."

"Then stand back, okay?" He stuck out his hand. "Thanks for everything earlier tonight. If something happens to me, it was nice to know you."

"What?"

"Hey, if the dozer falls backwards, I'm fish bait, man. Hundred and fifty feet, rolling over and over, then right down into the ocean. It's high tide down there. Like I said, fish bait."

And with that he scrambled down the sea cliff in his good shoes. "Hey!" called Poppy after him. "Don't run around so much."

But before I could ask why, Poppy retreated to the truck. I was miserable but shined the light up to the cab as instructed. Poppy gave a slow wave. From my position on the edge of the sea cliff, I could see both men. I signaled to Jay. He'd climbed atop Herschel and started the bulldozer again. He lifted the stabilizing pad and then the big front bucket so it wouldn't catch on the upward slope. A short blast on the horn followed. I signaled Poppy, and the truck lurched forward two feet. The cable snapped tight. The dozer didn't move. Then the treads shuddered and rotated a foot, sand crumbling behind the dozer. I signaled Poppy to pull ahead hard. Jay was shifting the gears with one hand, steering with the other. The dozer began to climb, one foot, then two, the snow shaking off it, the treads biting the frozen dune grass. Diesel smoke filled my nose. I could hear the truck engine grinding. The cable was tight. Now the truck was throwing back ice and mud, tires spinning. But Jay moved upward anyway. The cable slackened. Then the truck kicked forward four or five feet, delivering a jolt to the bulldozer. Both machines moved in sync then, and the dozer reached the top edge of the sea cliff, dragging a couple of small branches with it, and instead of breaking up and over the crest, the dozer crushed the crest beneath it, nearly throwing Jay forward, spinning a thirty-foot rooster tail of dirt and sand and snow backward until the thing was safely ten feet from the edge. I swung the light back and forth, and the truck stopped.

Poppy jumped down and came running back. "It worked!"

"Damn right!" said Jay, sitting atop the dead man. He let the dozer idle and climbed down.

Poppy stood before the corpse, getting his first good look. The stiff hand extending into nothingness seemed to fascinate him most. "Getting too old for this shit," he muttered. Then his natural poison flowed through him again. "I don't want to fucking drive into New York City every time there's a problem, you know?"

"There aren't going to be any more problems," Jay said. "We got rid of the only problem tonight." He reached into his pocket, pulled out a wad of bills, peeled off five fifties. "Here, Poppy, for your time and everything."

Poppy held the money. It was more than he expected. He pointed at the truck. "I think the drive train just got fucked, though."

"Will the truck move?"

"First gear, ten, fifteen miles an hour maybe."

"Take it back to the barn."

"I will. What you going to do with him?" He jerked his thumb at the corpse.

"I want you to move the Cat over to the blue barn."

"Onto the *old* property, you mean."

"That's what I mean, Poppy, yes. And park it."

Across a property line. Why, I wondered. "Hey, wait—"

Poppy understood the plan. "Like he was just kind of parking the dozer near the barn when—right?"

Jay breathed heavily. "Sure. Make sure the shifter is back under his hand, too, make sure it's *perfect*. Let a little snow accumulate on the dozer tracks. Maybe go up and down the road in the car a few times. Say you just got home."

"I was out, I was doing something."

"Then call nine-one-one and say you found him."

"Okay."

"I'm not part of this," I told them. "You're way out of bounds here. Way out. Jay, either drive me back to the city now or take me to a train station. Get me out of here."

But he was still instructing Poppy. "You're going to have to take the fence down and put it back up."

"I know."

"We got that straight?"

"I mean, Herschel died already," said Poppy, running through the logic again.

"That's what I'm saying. You just found him out there on the Cat, and you called nine-one-one."

"That's true. He looks the same, nobody moved *him*."

"I'm not part of this."

"Nobody is asking you to be." Jay turned to Poppy again. "Once you go through the fence, take the dozer down straight to the east road—you have to watch out for the drainage gully on that piece where we used to put in cabbages, and then cut over on that dirt road until you pick up the main driveway to the blue barn. Keep it on the main driveway, be-cause we'll get a lot of drifting. Snow'll pretty much cover the tracks in half an—"

"Also anybody coming in and out of there, ambulance, whatever, is going to go right over anything that's left. Tracks'll be covered up *that* way, too."

"Yes," Jay said quietly.

Poppy rubbed his hands against each other vigorously.

"Guys," I began. "You're—"

"Hey!" Jay interrupted me. "He was already dead, okay? Herschel had a terrible heart. I asked him if he was up to it. He was supposed to be done with his grading a week ago! When it was still warm! I told him I'd do it myself."

I stood there then, snow in my face, feet cold, dumbfounded by the arc of the evening.

"It's just bad luck," Jay explained. "Okay? He was supposed to do a little grading to get the property ready. Smooth out the old ditches, as a courtesy." He stared at me, mouth open and eyes unblinking, and I wondered if there was violence in the man. "He called me and said he was done, but I guess he wasn't, I guess he lied to me."

"So, Poppy, why did *you* find him?" I asked. "Were you going for a stroll?"

"I saw the dozer. Wondered what was going on."

"Hey, it doesn't change anything for Herschel," Jay said. "Also, you've got people walking the beach in the morning. Get a couple of kids climbing on that thing, who knows what happens? Poppy is calling the police. I can't lose the deal, man. I mean what fucking difference does it make whether Herschel died over here or over there?"

I could have said that clearly it made a large difference to Jay himself, since he'd driven out of the city in the middle of the night and a snowstorm to move the body, but I saw nothing to be gained by the comment. I wanted out of there, plain and simple.

"Look," said Poppy. He pointed toward the main road. Car lights were coming our way.

"Take the truck," Jay ordered Poppy. "I changed my mind. Go without your lights to the barn. I'll take the Cat myself."

They hurried to their respective vehicles. Poppy unhooked the cable from the back of the big potato truck, leapt into the cab where the door used to be, and rumbled slowly down the road. Jay, meanwhile, unhooked the cable from the dozer, pulled it hand over hand into the bucket, climbed up, again sitting atop the frozen belly of Herschel, and, wind whipping his hair and coat, turned the dozer parallel to the shoreline, keeping the lights off, and rumbled into the dark, the dozer pitching sideways across the uneven ground.

Which left me there with Jay's truck. The lights continued toward me. Across the field lay only darkness, both vehicles having already disappeared. I hurried over the snow, knowing the truck would be spotted. Twenty yards away I hopped over the edge of the sea cliff and lay down, pressing my chest against the snowy sand, the wind raw against my legs.

The car approached, slowed. A police cruiser, its flasher bar off. It turned in a slow circle, lights catching Jay's truck, then stopped. If they found a cardboard box with two hundred and sixty-five thousand dollars in it, then things would get interesting. A handheld flashlight beam shot directly at the driver's window, illuminating the falling snow, moved to the passenger side, found nothing, rubbed over the ground, rested on the license plate. I expected a figure to emerge and inspect the vehicle, but instead the police car crunched forward in its turn, wheels biting the road again, and disappeared the way it had come, red lights getting smaller.

I stood up anxiously, wanting to escape. Where were Poppy and Jay? Maybe the police car had encountered them along the road. I considered stumbling my way down the sea cliff then walking along the shore. But it was bitter cold, the wind from the sound whipping upward behind me. Jay's truck would be warmer, and maybe he'd left the keys in it. I ran over the frozen ground to the driver's door and threw myself inside. Drag your ass out of here, Billy-boy. The keys weren't in the ignition. I checked under the seat. Nothing. In the glove compartment I found an owner's manual, another heavily scuffed baseball, an insurance document (which showed that Jay's coverage had lapsed), an empty ammunition box, and, strangely, a schedule of winter sporting events at one of Manhattan's private schools, with every Thursday night girls' basketball game circled. Random, useless things. I put them all back and huddled miserably in my seat.

Then a figure emerged out of the darkness. Jay in his long coat. I opened the driver's door.

"You see the car?" he asked.

"Yeah, Jay, it was the police."

He sat down in the driver's seat, his face pinched by the cold.

"Why would the police roll up, Jay?"

Instead of answering he closed his eyes and seemed to be pulling deep breaths into himself. "Okay . . . just a second here."

"You all right?"

He nodded and pulled the keys from his pocket.

"Should I drive?"

"I'll be fine."

"You need more of those pills?" I suggested.

"Let me just—" He got out of the truck, opened the rear door, then lay down.

"Jay?"

"I'm fine," he said. "I got this under control . . . Do me a favor and don't tell Allison."

I reached back and grabbed the keys from him. "I'm taking us out of here."

I guided the truck back the way we'd come, away from the water. The snow had already started to obscure the police car's tracks, and was piling in drifts on the westerly side of the road in fragile crests and valleys. As we passed the large barns, I noticed something I'd missed before, a modest farmhouse set back from the road, a snowy mirage almost, windows unlit, front porch drifted with snow. Someone had lived there once.

At the gate to the main road, the police car was waiting for us, parked craftily so that any escape attempt would land the truck in the drainage ditch. I pulled to a stop and cut the engine, keeping the lights on.

"What's happening?" asked Jay.

"Cops."

He groaned and fell back into the seat.

The policemen opened their doors and walked toward the car, hands on guns, flashlights held up like spears.

"Who's that?" demanded one.

I lowered the window. "Hi guys," I said, worrying about the box of cash behind my seat.

"You taking a little drive?" One of the cops shined the light into the backseat. "Who you got there?"

"This is my friend," I said.

"This ain't lovers' lane, buddy," the cop said. "This is private property."

"It's not like that."

He smiled with a happy sadism. "What's it like, then? I always wanted to know."

"Hey, hey, is that Dougie?" Jay called from the darkness of the rear seat.

"Who you got in there?"

"Dougie," bellowed Jay, "you married that girl yet?"

"Who's that? Jay? Jay Rainey?"

Jay sat up and opened his door, and practically fell into the snow. "Who do you think?"

The cop shook his head, laughing. "Jay, we thought you was the big-city boy now." He shook hands with Jay, then motioned at me. "Who's this?"

"This?" Jay answered sloppily. "This is my lawyer, boys."

"Lawyer?"

"Up*town*, man. The best money can buy."

The cop shoved his light at my face, making me blink. "You been drinking, too?"

I shook my head. Snow was blowing into the truck.

"You don't mind if I check you?"

"Nope."

He came over, gave me a perfunctory sniff. "You *were* drinking but it was hours ago, and you had dinner and somebody was smoking cigars or something."

"That's right," I said. "Pretty good."

The other cop laughed. "He can fucking smell pussy in a swimming pool."

"I gotta get back in the car," Jay announced.

Dougie helped him and closed the door. Then he held out his hand. "You got some ID?"

I showed him my license.

"You got something that tells me who you *are*, I mean?"

I fumbled with my wallet. "This is my old business card."

The cop pinched it from my fingers. "Hey, I even heard of this law firm. You don't work there no more?"

"Uh, no."

"Disbarred?"

"What?"

"Only joking."

"I wasn't disbarred."

"Just want to make sure that you're giving Jay here proper representation, Mr. William Wyeth." He nodded at his partner. "Okay, since the car is not stolen, and since you are not drinking and since the owner of the property is with you, although apparently rather incapacitated, then I don't think we have a problem." He slipped my card into his pocket, however. "We saw lights from the main road, thought people was messing around." He looked at me. "What you guys doing out here this late, anyway?"

"He was showing me the land," I said. "He had kind of a big night and wanted me to see it."

"I heard Jay was selling it." He bent and addressed the backseat of the truck. "Jay, you come back here before the city eats you up, hear?"

No answer came. "Get the local boy home safe, okay?" he said softly to me. "Jay and I go way back. Played some ball together before—" He stopped.

"Before—?" I prompted.

But he'd turned away. "Just take care of him, okay?"

"You got it," I said, eager to get going.

The cop car backed over the snow, then pulled away in front of us. I let the truck roll forward. "Jay?"

He didn't say anything.

"Jay," I announced anyway, "you need another lawyer." I waited for an answer. I remembered to hang the chain back up behind us and close the lock. I turned the truck onto the main road and watched for oncoming traffic. Ninety minutes back to the city. "I mean, this is not what I do, not what I *used* to do, not what I *want* to be doing." I looked over to see his response.

He had none. He was gone, curled asleep against the seat like—well, like a boy.

It was late now, past 4 a.m. The evening seemed impossible, scenes in a strange, cold dream. From the moment I'd stepped into the Havana Room five hours earlier, nothing had made sense. I drove west, toward the lights of Manhattan, running the heater and wishing the cop hadn't kept my business card. He hadn't needed it, right? I glanced back over the seat. Jay was completely gone, his breath entering and leaving his nostrils noisily, coughing thickly now and then. From time to time he muttered in his sleep. I didn't like what had happened, I didn't like my complicity. Certainly Jay had enjoyed the right to move the bulldozer up over the sea cliff because it constituted a danger to anyone below. That much was justifiable. The rights of the living trump the rights of the dead. And my own assistance in this discrete action seemed more or less defensible. But moving the body farther from its absolute point of true death was loaded with problems. Of course, Herschel, being deceased, never knew that his body was being transported over the frozen farmland a few hundred yards away. But his very unknowingness constituted part of my objection. Surely the dead have the right to be properly discovered by the living—that is, to be preserved in the circumstances of death so that their families may reckon with death, may complete the narrative, compose an ending. The principle of the undisturbed body derives from the basic needs of society and tribe. Moreover, I'd not told the policemen what we'd done. I'd lied to his face, despite the fact that policemen are often quite interested in lies, especially as they pertain to bodies moved in the night.

All this gave me a bad feeling that I was falling, *again*, falling even further from my old life, further from Timothy. And I missed him so, missed the soft flop of his head against my chest when he was a baby in my arms, lips pooching and puckering in his sleep, missed the errant burps and innocent fartings, the blond duckling softness of his hair after his bath, drowsing, the soft breathing weight of him on my chest. Years removed, as I drove through the night, this memory pierced me again and again. Where was he? In misery I almost said it aloud. Where was my son? The boy who sat on my shoulders and steered me by pulling on one ear or the other, the boy who was reading the sports page when he was five years old, the boy who left streaks of toothpaste all over the bathroom, the towels thrown across the floor, wet footprints stamping down the hall? The boy I kissed good night each evening at nine sharp. *My boy, where are you?* In another land, in the arms of another man, in a place far away and waiting for your father to come and get you.

I pressed forward through the snow. Given the hour, we moved quickly. Arriving from the east, New York City is a sequence of subtraction and addition. First comes dark, pine-barren nothingness that gives way to exurb tract housing and new office buildings, and they in turn fill into traditional suburban sprawl. Soon the yards shrink as the borough of Queens approaches and the buildings become squat and dense, crowding each other, semidetached houses changing to row homes. Meanwhile the road surface becomes worse, the exits more frequent, the drivers more insane, and then you are in Queens proper, facing the sheer wall of Manhattan, a thousand-foot stone tapestry hung from the sky, and then you're whizzing downward under the East River into the halogen-mad tunnel, daring and dared by the other vehicles to pass at eighty miles an hour, then up onto the island proper, the city that night a muffled village of snow. Behind me Jay slept. At the first stoplight I glanced back at him; his face was slack, almost as if he were the second dead man of the evening, but then he gave a grunty cough and lifted his head.

"You konked out," I said.

"Yeah."

"I'm driving to my place and then you can go on."

"Sure. That's great."

"I'll check on your deed tomorrow, like I promised." I let a snowplow rumble past me. "But then I'm *out*, Jay. Don't consider me your lawyer."

I turned on Thirty-sixth Street. The sky was starting to lighten, and in an hour the sun would start to drop along the eastern face of the buildings. "We're here."

Jay didn't seem to notice my miserable neighborhood.

"I've got to go upstairs and sleep," I told Jay. "Can you drive? I can call Allison."

"No, no," he said, pulling himself up. "I can drive." He opened his door. "Cold out there."

I didn't like the way he looked, but I got out anyway, leaving the driver's door open for him. "You all right? Remember you got a box of cash with you."

"Sure, sure."

I waited for some kind of thanks, or recognition of the extremity of the evening. But none came. I hopped up the steps into my building and let the door swing shut. Then, perhaps out of worry, I lingered behind the glass and watched him.

For a moment nothing happened, and I considered going back outside to insist that I drive him home. He looked barely able to stand. But then he pulled himself out of the truck and made his way unsteadily to the rear hatch. He popped it open, looked up and down the street, then bent over into the rear. I couldn't see what he was doing but he was busy with his hands. I glanced at what looked like a thick plastic tube, but it disappeared. He stood bent over for a minute or so, a vulnerable position given the hour and the location, and I remembered the Puerto Rican guy who prowled the neighborhood looking for a fight. But Jay stood up and shut the back of the truck. It took him two tries. How could such a big guy be so weak? He shuffled toward the driver's side, almost slipping once, and reached the door. Then he stood with his arms on the roof, like a winded runner.

I was just about to go outside when he slid in his seat. The driver's door closed, the truck rolled forward. I stepped out to see if he made the left-hand turn onto Eighth Avenue, which would be the logical action if he was headed to Allison's. He didn't turn, and instead continued east on Thirty-sixth Street. Maybe he was going crosstown and then up to her neighborhood. I stepped out into the street and watched Jay's taillights two blocks away. At Seventh Avenue, he turned south. He definitely wasn't headed to Allison's apartment. No, Jay Rainey, whoever he was and whatever his condition, was on his way somewhere else.

four

HEREWITH, an abbreviated history of Manhattan real estate: a mountain range of stone, ancient as the moon; twelve thousand years of pulverizing glaciers, which, receding as recorded time began, left behind an island of bedrock buried over with gravel and sand, as well as a wide river flowing into a protected bay; unbroken expanses of oak, maple, elm, and chestnut; infinities of oysters, clams, fish, deer, beaver, rabbit, and fox; Algonquin Indians and their leafy footpaths; Henrik Hudson and the Dutch East India Company; Peter Stuyvesant and his *bowerie*; improvements in the construction of sailing vessels; King Charles II and his kid brother, the Duke of York; the 1720 riot by black slaves, which accelerated the segregation of their housing; the 1763 Treaty of Paris, in which all of North America was ceded to England; the adoption of the largest Algonquin trail as a "broad way" north and south; a lovely buttonwood tree on Wall Street under which men in beaver hats traded securities; Robert Fulton and his spluttering steamboat, which improved trade upriver; the great fire of 1835, which destroyed the business district; the Erie Canal, which connected Manhattan to the continental interior and allowed immeasurable amounts of lumber, rye whiskey, livestock, and farm produce to float downstream into the digestive maw of the new city; further extension of Broadway up the length of the island; the potato famine of 1846, which flooded the city with cheap Irish labor; the failed Revolution of 1848, which flooded the city with cheap German labor; the shantytowns in the center of the island, which contained such pestilence, crime, and shocking immorality that the city fathers decided to clear the land for a central park; the willingness to fill in coves along the banks of the Hudson River with oyster shells, bottles, dead horses, cannonballs, leather shoes, and anything else; the Civil War, which made merchants rich; improvements in the manufacture of iron; Cornelius Vanderbilt and his Pennsylvania Railroad; the aforementioned purity and ample supply of the watershed north of the city, which could support a mighty population; the construction of great docks along both sides of the island; the discovery of oil in western Pennsylvania; banker J. P. Morgan and his enormous, florid nose, so ugly it scared people who might otherwise have opposed him; Thomas Edison's 1878 invention of the lightbulb, which became instantly irresistible and led to the wiring of the city; the conversion of trains from steam to electric; the Lower East Side's houses of prostitution, which ignited the sexual appetites of innumerable young men; "Boss" Tweed, who, although he stole $160 million, accelerated the naturalization of aliens, including hundreds of thousands of Italians and Jews from Eastern Europe, many of whom crowded into the Lower East Side and frequented the houses of prostitution; the invention of the electrified elevated train to move these masses; the booming stock market; the documentation, by photographer Jacob Riis, of the Lower East Side's pestilence, crime, and shocking immorality; the arrival of "patent" medicines, often little more than opium and so pleasurable that their customers forgot they were dying of dysentery; the stock market crash of 1894; the obsolescence of the wooden sailing ship; the development of cast-iron architecture; improvements in the refining of crude oil; the invention of the internal combustion engine; the new and irresistible telephone, which led to the wiring of the city; improvements in the manufacture of structural steel; World War I, which flooded the city with cheap black labor from the South and made merchants rich; the destruction of Europe; the new and irresistible radio; the obsolescence of the horse; the rise of Harlem as the center of black culture, much of it from the South; Prohibition and the appearance of speakeasies; the presence or absence of bedrock upon which high office buildings might now be erected; the booming stock market; the com-modification of a certain well-dollared, ironic smugness, which sup-ported various purveyors of this consciousness, among them dozens of celebrated bars, hotels, and clubs; the smoky burlesque theaters, which ignited the sexual appetites of innumerable young men; the new and irresistible ocean liners; the stock market crash of 1929; the Great De-pression, during which time the Chrysler Building, the Empire State Building, the Waldorf-Astoria, and Rockefeller Center were completed; the new and irresistible moving pictures; World War II, which made merchants rich; the conversion of the old Times Square burlesque the-aters to movie houses; the 1943 riots by blacks in Harlem; the destruc-tion of Europe; the building of the United Nations complex, which introduced the glass-curtain-walled skyscraper to the city; rising Puerto Rican immigration, much of which packed into the Lower East Side as Jews and Italians left; improvements in the refining of crude oil to create a new product called "jet" fuel; the new and irresistible television; the falling cost of domestic airplane travel; the 1960s riots by blacks in Harlem; the booming stock market; the construction of the American interstate highway system, which helped the trucking industry; the bankruptcy of railroads and the 1966 demolition of the old Pennsylva-nia Station (looming, neoclassically magnificent, *civitas* captured in stone), prompting a storm of protest; the arrival of heroin, so pleasura-ble that addicts would commit daily felonies to support their habits; the conversion of Times Square movie houses to porno theaters, which ig-nited the sexual appetites of innumerable young men; the collapse and removal of the rotting, obsolete docks on both sides of the island; white flight out of the city; the depressed stock market; the erection of the 110-floor twin towers of the World Trade Center; the suburbs as haven; the Stonewall riots by gay men in the Village; the suburbs as wasteland; the arrival of high-quality cocaine, so pleasurable that people did not mind burning holes inside their heads with it; the booming stock market; population explosions in Haiti, India, and Pakistan; the falling cost of international travel by jumbo jet; the arrival of crack cocaine, so plea-surable it could make men suck happily on the leg of a chair; the dissolution of the USSR; white flight back into the city for the purposes of real estate speculation and convivial association; the soaring, gaudily crenellated edifice of Donald Trump's ego; the stock market crash of 1987; the obsolescence of ocean liners; the 1994 riot by blacks in Howard Beach; the shantytowns in Tompkins Square Park, which contained such pestilence, crime, and shocking immorality that the city fathers decided to clear the land; the commodification of a certain well-dollared, ironic smugness, which supported various purveyors of this consciousness, among them dozens of celebrated bars, hotels, and clubs; a post-Communist wave of stamping, ginseng-chewing Chinese immigration; the new popularity of the Internet, which led to the wiring of the city and ignited the sexual appetites of innumerable young men; the conversion of Times Square porno theaters to tourist hotels; the booming stock market, borne aloft by the Internet; coffee bars filled with people discussing the Internet and the stock market; the postmillenial stock market implosion; and, of course, the crashing of two jumbo jets into the World Trade Center towers, which—some would say—marked the true beginning of the twenty-first century.

Hidden within this metamorphosis has always been the legal antwork of individual humans and corporations, repeatedly buying, selling, leasing, mortgaging, and reparceling every square inch of the island, and even the rights to the smoggy air above it, in greedy pursuit of their own interests. And although the particulars of that greed—the piled and papered secrets of who owns the island's thirty or forty thousand buildings and how much they paid for them—would seem almost infinite, nearly all are contained within just one place: Room 205, Surrogate Court, 31 Chambers Street, in lower Manhattan.

And that was where I stood the next morning, outside the court under a threatening sky, stamping my feet and nibbling from a warm bag of caramel peanuts bought from a vendor. The building, erected in 1901, was a magnificent beaux arts pile, with giant bronze Puritans guarding its doors. I'd slept poorly, almost not at all, and when the gray light of day crept down the airshaft next to my window, I'd jolted awake, hoping that the events of the previous night might somehow be remembered as benign. Many mornings I woke in my grimy cell on Thirty-sixth Street hoping in the half-second blink to consciousness that I might discover that I was still living in my eight-room apartment on the Upper East Side, with Timothy asleep in his pajamas and Judith involved in her coffee rituals, available for a cottony, dorsal grope in the kitchen, but on this morning a simple return to my lonely, cracked-plaster innocence of the day before would have filled me with relief, even a kind of refracted happiness.

No such luck. The vision of Herschel's frozen, snow-covered grimace—conjurable and godlike as an Easter Island totem—had chased me along Broadway's snowy, shadowed facades as I'd walked the long blocks toward Chambers Street. You don't move dead bodies, I cursed myself, not in the middle of the night when no one's looking. White lawyers, *especially*, even ones down on their luck, don't move dead black bodies, no matter how plausible the explanation. *And then lie to the cops about it.* I could only hope that a few days would go by, Poppy and Jay would smooth over any questions from Herschel's family, the man would be buried in peace, and that would be that. If Jay was smart, he'd pay for the funeral.

And if I was smart, I'd have nothing further to do with him, no matter what Allison might say or promise. The problem was that my name had been hijacked onto his documents of sale, forever and ever, and even as his quickie, one-night-stand lawyer, I was obliged, if only to myself, to see that the deal was sound. Having had no opportunity to examine the documents beforehand, and given the dubious activities of the previous night, I wanted a look at the recorded deeds of the building at 162 Reade Street. The word "recorded" is the key term. A deed has to be executed, tendered, and received, but it's not official until recorded. Only then is the pile of bricks, the box of timbers, *possessed.* The change in ownership of any property is mysterious, when you think about it; the tangible thing remains unaltered but the description of it, the name attached to it, changes in an instant. Three hundred years ago, under English common law, the sale of real estate used to be marked by the snapping of a stick, which symbolized the specificity and permanence of the moment.

Now the courthouse's brass doors opened and I followed the others up the steps. I'd been to the building years ago, and the place hadn't changed much. Inside, past the posted notices for sheriff's auctions of confiscated cars, you skate across yellowy marbled floors to wide staircases that convey you magnificently into the various rooms of the city's Department of Finance. Here the illusion of grandeur abruptly ceases. Room 205, where paint hangs from the ceiling like peeling sycamore bark, is divided into a records section and an area where those records may be examined on microfiche readers. The room is frequented by two distinct populations: lawyers in good suits and everyone else; the everyone else generally look like drug addicts, drunks, felons, and crazies—the usual shank-shovers and shape-shifters. Derelict as they appear, though, these men and women play a crucial role in the economic life of the city; they are the freelance deed-pullers who work for the title companies and law firms. They know each other in a friendly fuck-you sort of way, and compete for use of the microfiche readers, the computer-record generators, and the attention of the garrulous Russian man who dispenses the microfiche cassettes that are so valuable. (That the definitive records of private property ownership in the capital of global commerce are overseen by a man who grew up under Soviet Communism goes unnoted.) The process is this: You submit the address to the clerk. He gives you the building's block and lot numbers, which are then fed into computers in the adjacent room, which in turn produce mortgage and deed record numbers and their respective microfiche reel and page numbers. This information is resubmitted to the clerk with a small voucher (purchased in the cashier's office down the hall from middle-aged black women discussing their love lives on the taxpayers' time) and the clerk returns a microfiche cassette, which may then be examined, page by blurring page. All help is given grudgingly, and you are under suspicion of stupidity, by definition.

The arcana of the tax stamps on the documents is never explained, but if you know what to look for, which I did, then a wealth of information reveals itself, not least of which is the ever-rocketing value of Manhattan real estate. From the ancient annum of 1697 until April 1983, the great city of New York imposed a real estate transfer tax of $1.10 per thousand dollars of assessed value. In 1983, owing to the booming value of condominiums, the city raised the transfer tax to $4 per thousand of assessed value, which is where it stands today and probably far into the future. Thus could I calculate that 162 Reade Street, the building Jay Rainey had purchased by exchange the night before in the Havana Room, had a value of $9,000 in 1912, $56,000 in 1946, $112,000 in 1964, $212,000 in 1967, $402,000 in 1972, $875,000 in 1988, $1.5 million in 1996, and $2.2 million in 1998, this last the sum paid by an entity calling itself Bongo Partners. Voodoo LLC, the company listed as the owner on the contract for sale the night before, was *not* on the deed history.

I sat awhile, as irritated as I was confused, and not unaware of the tentacle of legal abstraction quietly encircling my leg. Of course there was a problem with the deed. Why would it be simple or easy? This was a real estate transaction that had started in a steakhouse and ended up with a dead guy on a bulldozer! So screw you, Bill Wyeth! You blew it! So far as the city of New York was concerned, Bongo Partners was—today, right now—the owner of record of 162 Reade Street. If Voodoo LLC was not the legitimate seller, then Jay might have traded his precious ocean-front acreage for nothing—might have been defrauded. And if this was the case, then Jay could easily sue me for malpractice! The title man was supposed to make sure the title was clear, that the property was in fact owned by Voodoo LLC. In the hurry of events I hadn't asked him any questions. Why hadn't he told us that Bongo Partners were the owners of record? I could invent several explanatory scenarios, none of which was reassuring. The irreverence of the names of both corporations was probably connected, of course. Voodoo drums, bongo drums—something like that. I was not free of Jay Rainey, not yet anyway. I copied the records and slipped them into my briefcase.

I was on my way out when I remembered Lipper's claim that his steakhouse had once been owned by Frank Sinatra. Maybe that was true, which would be a smile, as they say, and so, in a mood for distraction, I pulled the deed on the restaurant's West Thirty-third Street address. The provenance of the property constituted a pocket history of New York; as two unimproved lots it had originally been owned by the First Presby-terian Church; fifteen years later the first and narrower lot was sold still unimproved to the Pennsylvania Railroad, which, having train tracks all over that part of town, erected a "below-grade iron-ribbed train shed" on the western edge of the property; this long, narrow rectangle, I realized, constituted the footprint of the Havana Room, and explained why its elevation was so different from that of the steakhouse's first floor. Then, in 1845, the larger lot was sold by the church to an Englishman, who built the first version of the restaurant, a "steaks and ale house," in 1847. He bought the train shed in 1851 and, it appeared, remodeled and connected the structure to his existing building. The merged property changed hands several times in the period 1877–79, perhaps because of the crash that occurred that year, and was merged with an adjacent brownstone to the east in 1921, as the twenties roared and people ate out, and sold again. The transfer tax indicated an enormous leap in value, which suggested to me that three buildings had successfully been remodeled into one and enjoyed great popularity. But not for long; the restaurant had been seized by the city for unpaid taxes during the Depression, then sold soon after. The configuration of the lot had been stable since then and the owners changed once a decade or so from the thirties until the sixties, the restaurant business being as difficult then as it is today, and then settled into a long continuous ownership by an evolving entity: from 1972 until 1984, City Partners, Ltd.; from 1984 until 1988, City Partners & Co.; from 1988 to the present, City Partners Real Estate Investment Trust—a publicly traded real estate holding company. The ownership of the restaurant could not be more generic, more ho-hum. Frank Sinatra, the mobster-hangin', whore-bangin', egomaniacal crooner, was nowhere to be found on record. More surprising, neither was Old Man Lipper.

But who owned the steakhouse wasn't my concern. I needed to find Jay and tell him about Bongo Partners and his maybe-rotten deed.

His building in TriBeCa wasn't far from City Hall, a crosstown walk of five minutes, so I set out, finding no comfort in the honk-and-go of Broadway. It was just another wintry Thursday. The snow from the night before was already filthy, and the sky looked like rain. Which would melt not only the snow in the city but all the snow out on Jay's farm. Our tire tracks and footprints from the night before would be lost. But maybe that meant that any bulldozer tracks in the soil would be revealed—the earlier record of Herschel's activity the day before. Was that good? Would it corroborate Poppy's description of events? Something was bothering me about that description, I realized. What was it? Go back to what you were taught, I thought. Which was this: one of the summers I was in law school, I worked in the Brooklyn D.A.'s office, and there was an older career prosecutor named Coover who refused promotion to management and instead—in addition to ruining his teeth by chewing on plastic coffee swizzle sticks—simply banged out one conviction after another. He was a quiet legend. He'd seen any number of slick law students come and go—mostly go, on to lucrative corporate jobs—and wasn't much impressed. I was no exception, nor should I have been, flummoxed as I was trying to square the rules of evidence with the jargon of police write-ups. But early in my time, Coover had seen me puzzling over a simple arrest report for a misdemeanor drug charge and muttered as he passed by, "Worship Chronos, kid." I puzzled over the statement until I remembered that Chronos was the god of time, which led me to understand the invincible truth of simple chronology. I never forgot the lesson, and here it was, essential to understanding what had happened the day before.

But I had already turned the corner to Reade Street and needed now to follow the street numbers. There was number 162, set in a row of similar buildings, with high windows fronting the street, architecturally utilitarian but elegant in its simplicity and impressive in its size. The windows were double-paned and glazed, the facade cleaned and repointed, the enclosed foyer up to date, the brasswork polished. I cupped my hand against the glass of the lobby. Men have gotten very comfortable owning such structures, and I could see Jay desiring this building, knowing that it would provide him a steady stream of rental income for the rest of his life, if he so wished. Across the street stood a nearly finished apartment house, a straggler from the recent boom. Around the corner hunched the kind of bar where European tourists hoping to ogle movie stars rub shoulders with fluffed-up girls from Jersey hoping to be ogled as movie stars.

"Bill!" came a voice. "You beat me to it!"

I turned to see Jay pull up in his truck. He hopped out, dressed in a fine suit and blue tie, shaved and shined, ready for business, a big and bouncy man who looked nothing like the stooped wretch I'd seen only seven hours before. *Here* was the man I'd first met in the Havana Room, large and confident. He looked up and stretched out his arms. "Well, this is it! And the check is in the bank, man."

I let him shake my hand but warned, "We need to talk."

His smile froze. "Sure, I know we do, but first, c'mon, we'll have a look."

He pulled out the key ring he'd received from Gerzon the night before and opened the main door. The foyer was dusty and someone had shoved a thick wad of takeout menus through the mail slot. He moved toward the wide staircase that led to the first floor.

"Wait a minute, Jay," I began, putting a hand on the shoulder of his overcoat. "What happened after we left? Did Herschel's body get found? Did the police deal with it?"

He turned. "I called Poppy this morning—he said the ambulance guys came and declared Herschel dead. They had a little trouble getting him off the tractor." He winced appreciatively. "Had to use an air blower."

"Then?"

"He got taken to Riverhead Hospital and his body was going to be picked up this afternoon. I sent flowers to the family this morning. There's a big funeral home in downtown Riverhead, handles a lot of the black funerals."

I watched Jay's face for worry. He seemed untroubled. Then again, he might be an adept liar. "You know, Poppy said he noticed Herschel out there at ten at night."

"Yes?"

"Kind of weird to be out there on a bulldozer, in the cold."

Jay shrugged. "He was running late."

I was figuring this out as I spoke. "Poppy also said he saw the bulldozer."

"So?"

"At ten at night? A half mile or more away?"

"The bulldozer has lights, good ones."

"But if the dozer had gone over the cliff, how did Poppy see it from the road?"

Jay stared at me. "You got me on that."

"In fact, remember he said something like if Herschel had been working there during the day, then his body had been out there about eight hours. He said that."

"He did?"

"That means Poppy *didn't* see him working in the night."

Jay held up his hands. "Poppy's always gotten stuff screwed up, Bill. He got hit in the head by a sledgehammer when he was a kid. Never finished fourth grade."

I wasn't convinced. "You notice that Herschel wasn't wearing any socks?"

"No."

"Makes you sort of wonder what a guy is doing working out in the cold on a bulldozer with no socks," I said.

"He was a pretty tough old guy."

Tough old guys usually keep their feet warm, in my experience, but I didn't press it. "This whole deal is fucked up," I muttered. "From top to bottom. I help you with a real estate transaction and end up moving a dead black guy? *Your* dead black guy, okay? That pisses me off, Jay." A fleck of my spit hit his face. "Then the police find us? I don't like it."

Jay held up his hands. "I didn't know Herschel had gone off the edge. Poppy's note didn't say that, right? I know you're worried about it. Don't be. It's fine. Poppy worked it out. He told me this morning. He's known Herschel's family a long time."

"What was going on out there, anyway?"

He nodded, anticipating the question. "I asked Herschel to do some grading for me a week ago. The road was all washed out, and we had a lot of gravel on the other side of the property. He and his family rent an old house on the adjacent property. I still have some trucks and that bulldozer in the barn there."

"What about the police?"

"I called them this morning," Jay said. "I've known these guys my whole life. It's all right. Herschel obviously had a heart attack."

"Why is it obvious?"

"He's sitting there, dead on the tractor. Not a scratch on him. Long history of heart trouble, pericarditis, pulmonary edema. Working in the cold often gives—"

I didn't want to hear a lot of medical jargon from a layman. "Did they ask you why you were out there on the same night that Herschel died?"

"Yeah, they did."

"What did you say?"

"I told them I'd just finished the deal and I wanted to be sure some grading had gotten done."

"Which is pretty close to the truth."

"The first part of that *is* the truth, Bill. What else could it be? Herschel didn't do his grading on time and then was in a hurry to get started before the snow came too heavy, and then went out there in the cold on the bulldozer and had a goddamn fucking heart attack."

"And if they come to me with the same question?"

Here Jay's face went slack and he stared through me, eyes seemingly focused on his own imaginings. He was, I felt, reminding himself of an idea or belief. "I doubt they'll ask you," he said.

I went on to the question of the deed. "I checked on the records of the building and I think you've got a problem."

"You do, huh?" Jay scooped up the menus and dropped them into the trash. "I don't."

"Voodoo LLC is not the current listed owner of the building."

"Oh, hell, I know *that*, guy," Jay answered as he examined the building directory. "It's not so complicated. It's just paperwork. You didn't need to check on that." He turned toward me. "But I do need you to talk to a guy for me tonight, actually."

"Jay, did you hear me? I don't think you own this building."

"Of course I own this building!" He jabbed his fist against the staircase's newel post, making it shudder.

"You better explain."

But that held no interest for him—he was already on his way up the stairs, making them creak under his weight. "It's a corporate shell thing, Bill, no big deal. They do this all the time." His voice bounced off the pressed-tin ceiling high above us. "Really. You should know that, a guy with your experience. I do want you to talk to this other guy this evening, though, be my lawyer again, hold his hand, whatever. Go have dinner with him."

"Forget it."

"What?"

"I'm out." I turned to go. And I should have gone, too, right then, should have stamped my way back down to the snowy sidewalk and not stopped until I had crossed back into some safer country of probability, but Jay came after me and pulled a slip of paper from his breast pocket. "This is for last night, for the whole deal."

"I never gave you a fee."

"I estimated."

It was a check for twenty-five thousand dollars. Very generous. Too generous, in fact. Shut-your-mouth money. I handed the check back. "I don't want it. I want *out*."

"All right," he nodded. "Fine."

"But what do I have to do to understand, legally, what happened last night? It seems the title man didn't—"

"Just go have dinner with this guy for me tonight, and everything will be explained."

"Who is it?"

"The seller."

"The guy who owned this building?"

"Yeah."

"So also the guy who now owns your old farm."

"Right."

"Why are you set to have dinner?"

"We weren't. He called me half an hour ago, said he had to hand over a couple more papers. Insisted. I just deposited his check, so I want to be polite. I didn't tell him I couldn't make it. Tonight is impossible for me. You can ask him whatever you want about the paperwork, Bill. He'll explain. Okay?"

"Just have dinner with him?"

"Yeah. Ask him anything."

I shrugged. That was enough for Jay. He stood up. "Let me at least show you the place. We can start in the basement."

And so we did, then worked our way up. "It's got eight office spaces. I've got several leases to renegotiate and you can help me with that, if you're interested," Jay said.

"Nope."

"All right. Anyway, it's a good location. People like the funky downtown locations. Good restaurants nearby, art galleries." He pointed to a line of ancient screw holes that ran up the center of the wide stairs. They'd been sanded over and filled in with wood putty. "See that?" he said. "There used to be a long metal slide that went down the middle."

"For finished goods."

"Right. In the nineteenth century, beaver hats, then chairs. In the early twentieth, it was baseball gloves for a while."

Now the building housed companies that manipulated symbols.

We knocked on the door of one small company named RetroTech, and a young Indian man opened it.

"Is Mr. Cowles around?" Jay asked.

"He's on the phone," said the man, his accent British.

"My name's Jay Rainey. I'm the new owner. This is Bill Wyeth, my lawyer. Thought I'd introduce myself."

He showed us in. It was a small but obviously prosperous operation. Green carpeting, brass desk lamps, oak filing cabinets, major league coffee machine. Information dripped brightly down a handful of screens.

"You did a nice job designing it," said Jay, looking around.

"We like it, thank you."

"Mr. Cowles free?"

"I'll check."

He disappeared down a hallway and a moment later returned, followed by a large, well-dressed man who looked like he might have played a little rugby twenty years earlier. "Hello, hello," came a booming British voice. "David Cowles." His eyes passed me and landed on Jay. "You must be the new owner?"

Both men appeared surprised by the other's size. They shook hands.

"Glad to meet you," said Jay. "You have a great shop."

"We try, yes," said Cowles.

"What do you do?" I asked.

"Oh, a little of this and a lot of that." Cowles smiled at this oblique answer. "Basically, we build proprietary financial software, we do a little momentum trading in securities, we play the field, we try to jump on and off the train at the right time."

"Been here long?" asked Jay.

"Little more than a year."

"Moved from London?"

"Yes, in fact." Cowles looked at Jay. "You've checked on us, it would seem?"

"Nope," said Jay agreeably, "just a hunch."

"Want to have a look around?"

"Sure. I did see the office once, with the seller," said Jay. "But I don't think you were here."

The tour took a few minutes. Behind a desk of family photos, Cowles's office had a good view to the west, filled with the irregular brick buildings of the neighborhood, stovepipes poking over slanting rooftops.

"Reminds me a little of London," Cowles laughed. "Just a little, just enough to miss it."

I noticed chewed pen tops on the desk, several calculators, stacks of newspaper clippings, an ashtray filled with butts. Cowles was a worrier, a figurer, and a smoker.

"You've got, what, a year left on your lease?" asked Jay.

"Indeed. It's been a good location for us. Even in this economy, we're growing."

"You want more space in the building?"

"I don't know." Cowles smiled at me. "Let's see how accommodating my landlord is."

"The adjacent offices are empty."

"I know."

"Though I have one possible tenant."

"Better fire away then," said Cowles. "We have enough room here." Jay studied Cowles's office wall. "You might hear a bit of construction."

"A lot of noise?"

"Some noise. I can ask them to minimize it, work on the weekends."

"We'll appreciate that."

"Not to worry," said Jay. He pointed at the photos. "Nice family."

"Yes . . . thank you," said Cowles, and his eyes fell upon them. There was a shot of a darling girl with dark hair sitting with a baby boy. And separate photos of two women, one older, the other younger and blonde, each posed with Cowles himself. "I know that's odd," he said, seeing me frown. "I lost my first wife some years ago." He picked up the photo of the older woman. "She's—she was my daughter's mum, and so I feel it's all right to keep her picture." His grief was still on his face. "I remarried as soon as I could, for my daughter, really." He turned to me. "You have kids?"

"Yes, well—yes, I do," I stammered, feeling clubbed in the head. "A son."

We stood there awkwardly for a moment, three men hanging in separate cocoons of thought.

"All right then," announced Cowles. "I need to get to work."

"Did you ever meet the previous owners?" I asked. "They had kind of a funny name?"

"You mean Bongo Partners," said Cowles. "Oh sure. Bunch of fish-and-chippers, too. They set up their New York City leases in their London office. Helps with the dollars and pounds thing. Decent enough chaps, didn't rob me too badly."

I was about to ask if he knew of Voodoo LLC but we heard a loud banging at the door downstairs.

"Maybe someone forgot his key," said Jay. "Better go look."

We said goodbye to Cowles, and I followed Jay down the wide stairs. At the bottom we could see a figure outside in the winter sun—a short black woman of about sixty in a sensible coat, gloves, and red woolen cap.

"Hell's bells," Jay muttered. He opened the door. "Mrs. Jones? You came all the way into the city?"

"Yes, Jay Rainey, I did."

He held the door open for her. "You want to come in?"

She frowned at him and didn't step inside.

"How did you—"

"Poppy told me you might be here, so I kept banging."

"You try the buzzer?"

"Didn't see no buzzer."

"You want to come in where it's warm?"

"No, I don't. I'm going to say my piece and then be done. I don't need much of your time where that is concerned, Jay Rainey, not much time at all."

So we stepped outside into the cold.

"This is my lawyer, Bill Wyeth."

The old woman nodded at me, but it was a disgusted and wary nod, too. "All right then. You've got your lawyer with you. You expecting me?"

"No," said Jay. "Why?"

"Funny, 'cause you got a lawyer with you."

"We were just looking at the building," I said.

"You knowed I was coming?" she demanded. "Poppy tell you?"

Jay shook his head. "What can I do for you, Mrs. Jones? I'm sorry about Herschel. I sent some—"

She waved her hand in his face bitterly. "Jay Rainey, don't start all that with me. I come down here to tell you that you got to do something."

"Like what?"

"Something for the *family*." Her eyes, yellowed and old, didn't blink. "Herschel, he work for your family almost forty years."

"I know that," said Jay.

"He kept that farm going all those years things was so bad for your family and when your daddy get sick and then after he die! You was gone most of that time, you don't *know* how it was."

"Yes."

"So now you got to do *something*."

"You mean money."

"That's what I mean, yes. I mean money! Herschel was all we had." She looked disapprovingly at me, a stranger hearing her business. "You know my boys, the two of them, Robert and Tyree, they settled now with families, they the ones who worked with Herschel, but you don't know Tommy and his cousin Harold."

Jay was silent.

"They *upset*."

"Okay—" Jay glanced at me, trying to sound reasonable.

"I said they *upset* and that ain't good!" Mrs. Jones stamped her foot. "They call me this morning and they say they hear about it from Tyree's wife, who say some kind of foolishness about her husband's daddy being left way out there *frozen* and all, and they pretty angry about that! Something about how the ambulance man had to blow hot air all over him to get him out of that tractor seat." She lifted her chin defiantly at Jay. "That's *disrespectful*, see, that's saying the man was dying and no one helped him! He was sitting there calling out to heaven in the cold and no one in this world *knew nothing*! No one cared he was dying alone, *dying with no comfort*! He dying of his bad heart right there, so bad he couldn't move! Tyree's wife told them all that. She was angry and she was crying and she was mad. Yes, she was! And it made *them* mad, too, yes, it did. I ain't going to lie about that, not where that is concerned, no I ain't. Them boys is *dangerous*, Jay Rainey, and they got a *reason* to be mad, is all I'm saying. Nobody was thinking about *him*, nobody was worrying about some old black man! Just *assuming* Herschel was always going to do what he was told no matter *how* cold it be outside! And your father, he never pay Herschel his Social Security. That's why he still working! And that's why he end up dead! Seventy-three-year-old man have no *business* being out there in that kind of cold, and the family—we is *up-*

set! You hearing me? We is *upset*! Now Harold, you know he always look up to Herschel. And now Harold, he gotten *big*, he got some kind of club or something here in the city, he got all kinds of money, and people working for him, and you don't want to cross that boy. He heard about this and I *know* he ain't happy. That boy has some kind of temper! The things he done, *hoo*! Don't get me started on that! He come out of prison five years ago and I suspect it *was* his fault, too. I don't like to think about what *gets in his mind*. Uh-uh, no! That boy is *dangerous*, I always said." She tightened her lips, and her cheap theatrics were both utterly obvious and entirely convincing.

"Now then," she went on, sensing her advantage, "you was good to Herschel, Jay Rainey, so I think I owe you a warning in that respect." She waited to see if he understood. Then she addressed me, as if I were implicated, too. "I mean, I can't *control* them boys. They ain't boys no more, neither. I lost them when they was fourteen or fifteen. They men now. They live here in the city most times." She looked away a moment. I wondered if she might be glancing down the street. "Harold, they say he was *lucky* to get the time he did, that he beat a man so *bad* he—"

"Please tell them we'll work out a fair settlement," said Jay.

"Huh. They want one hundred thousand dollars."

"That's a lot of money, Mrs. Jones."

She looked at me, eyes dark. "So, Mr. Wyeth, tell him."

I glanced at Jay. "Tell him what?"

"Tell him it *ain't* a lot of money. Even a *old* woman know that! Lots of other things cost more. Lots of *problems* cost more."

"Mrs. Jones," Jay said. "Herschel had a terrible heart. How many heart attacks did he already have? Four? I drove him to the hospital once myself. I paid for his doctor, I don't know how many times."

She pressed her mouth tight and shook her head. "You also asked him to go out there in the cold, do that farmwork."

"I asked him a week *earlier*, when it was still plenty warm," answered Jay, his voice tight. "It was maybe four hours of work. I guess he put it off and then the weather got cold."

She was already shaking her head. "Naw, he *was* out there five or six days before. He *was* finished, because Herschel was making applesauce that day. He go picking up the grass apples in November and put them in the cellar and he always start making his sauce after the fieldwork done for the winter. That Herschel, see, I know him my whole life. I *know* the man. He had habits. He was *done* in the field! He had five bushels of apples on the kitchen counter in the morning, he had his paring knife and board, he turned on the sports, he wasn't planning on doing no bulldozing in no snowstorm."

Jay shook his head, ready to disagree. "But I guess he wasn't through, not if he was on the bulldozer. I hadn't been out there in a week or—"

"I *talked* to him about that!" Mrs. Jones shrieked. "He said you kept calling him and saying it was important it get done by such and such a time, and he was sick one of those days and he took himself out there anyway, even though I *told* him he was sick. But that was almost a week ago, Jay Rainey! He *was* all done with his work! Yesterday he wash his apples and then go down in the cellar and say I need me some more jars and then he goes out driving and then the next thing I know he ain't coming home. And it gets later and later and we is worried *sick*! Then we get a call at four in the morning that he's *dead*! On a bulldozer! I don't know why he was out there. But the way I look at it, if he was on that thing, he was working for *you*."

"But if he'd already—" Jay began, then stopped, knowing he was arguing against the memory of a dead man. "All that's done. We'll find an acceptable settlement."

It was a standoff. "Mrs. Jones," I asked, "just out of curiosity, what game was on the TV? The Knicks?"

She looked at Jay. "You better get yourself a new lawyer."

"What? Why?"

"He's putting things in my mouth."

"What?"

"Herschel always watching that Tiger Woods hit the ball *far*."

One of the winter golf tournaments, in the early rounds. "I see my mistake."

"You do?"

"I thought this was happening at night," I said.

"Herschel ain't going out to bulldoze at night! You think he's crazy? This was after lunch." Mrs. Jones looked from Jay to me and back again in frustration. "Why we talking about this? I'm going tell those boys you said you'd pay the family that money, Jay Rainey. I'm going tell them you said you was *happy* to pay it! I'm going tell them you thought that was a *good* number, that was a *fair* number! How you feel real *bad* about Herschel. Yes, that's what I'm do! They expecting a call this morning. They watching closely! They know this is your new building, 'cause I told them. Poppy told me the number and I told them. So you see? I'm going tell them you said you'd pay! I think they'll take it. But I can't be sure. I can't control them boys no more, Jay Rainey. They *wild* now! They go around with their girls and cars and whatnot, it's out of my hands." She rebuttoned the top button of her coat and yanked her gloves tight. "I'll be going, then."

She said nothing more, turned briskly, and picked her way along the snowy sidewalk. I turned back to Jay. "That little old lady just shook you *down*."

Jay watched her go. "I've got to do something for them. But I can't pay off Herschel's whole life. He was just supposed to grade the roadbed, maybe dump some gravel in the holes. I paid him ahead of time, I told him to do it when the weather was warm, because the bulldozer works better then, anyway. I was sure he was done. It wasn't a big job."

"What was he doing too close to the edge?"

"Don't know. I couldn't tell what he was doing because it was all covered with snow. And hell, why was the dozer left in reverse? Don't worry about it, okay? It's my problem."

I was glad to hear this.

Jay asked, "What did you think of Cowles, the guy upstairs?"

"Good guy, I guess."

"You see the family pictures? The first wife was beautiful," he said. "I think he loved her very much."

It was a strangely sympathetic thing for him to say, and we stood there in a sudden, not uncomfortable silence. Men sometimes make friends this way, I think. They decide quickly. Jay gazed into his hands, then looked away. There was something vulnerable and temporary about the moment, and I was attentive to it, for a man, let us agree, is a kind of shelled animal. There is the hardened surface he presents to the world, the face and the words and the behavior, but very often these do not correlate very well with the being inside the shell. By hardened I mean coherent, deflective of attack, and capable of being recognized by others; I don't mean unchangeable—quite the opposite, in fact. But the shell is always there, growing outward from within, flaking and breaking away, and the quivering wet stuff inside remains largely hidden. Appearances are not deceiving so much as incomplete. What you see is what you get, but what you don't see is also what you get. For a moment Jay seemed unshelled, disinterested in protecting himself from my scrutiny or judgment.

"Yeah, I think he was crazy about her," he repeated. "You have one like that, a woman who just haunts you?"

"I was married."

"Yeah?"

"She left."

"You said you had a son."

"Yes. I haven't seen him in—" I couldn't finish the sentence.

Jay opened his mouth but said nothing. In contrast to his behavior thirty minutes earlier, he seemed tired or discouraged, deflated really, and it occurred to me that this was now the third time I'd seen such a cycle in less than a day; the first had been in the Havana Room, when he was up, then outside the steakhouse, when he was down; the second had been while he was recovering the bulldozer, up, and the drive back into the city, down.

"You all right?" I asked.

"Sure." He rose to his feet. "Here." He handed me a slip of paper with an uptown address on it. "This is the place for dinner."

"For what?"

"To meet with this guy for me tonight. Six p.m. The wine guy from Chile."

"What's his name?"

"Marceno, something like that."

"Why can't you do it, anyway?" I asked. "This sounds pretty important."

"I have another engagement."

"More important than this?"

Jay didn't meet my eyes. "Yes, actually."

Maybe I would do it, maybe not. Maybe it would be wise to talk to Allison first. And maybe I wanted to talk with her anyway. I found a cab going uptown, told the driver the address of the steakhouse, slinging it at him through the news radio chatter. He grunted, and clunked the car into drive. Outside, rain began to slather against the windows, a sudden dark wintry emptying of the sky, and I settled back in my seat as lower Manhattan blurred past; it was as if I were taxiing through the torrent of meaningless data from everywhere, able to discern every info-droplet but removed from their collective chill. The thought provoked me to inspect the piece of paper Jay had given me. He'd written the restaurant address in slanting box letters, but this was not what intrigued me. The slip had apparently been torn from some kind of business stationery, for on the reverse was printed SAFETY, RELIABILITY, AND PROMPT DE— What did Jay need or use that was safe, reliable, and required prompt delivery?

Fifteen minutes later I was sitting at Table 17 and looking at the daily soup specials.

Allison came over after I'd been served, carrying her clipboard. "Hey, mister backroom lawyer." She let her finger touch my shoulder and stood close to me. "So, what did you boys do last night?" she asked.

"Didn't Jay call you today?"

"Not yet." She shrugged. "So—?"

"It's his business, actually," I said.

"Come on, you can tell *me*."

"We went out and looked at his land."

"That's all?"

I lifted my hands. "That's it."

Allison didn't like my terse answer. "When did you get home?"

"He dropped me off at my place close to five," I said. "Now, listen, I want you to sign me up for the Havana Room. Or whatever you do. Get me in there."

She looked around to see that no one was listening. "I will. I told you I will."

"When's the next time?"

"It's irregular. You know that by now."

"Once every week or two, I've noticed."

"Whenever Ha is ready."

"Why does it depend on Ha?"

"Why? Because Ha, unbeknownst to the likes of you, is an artist."

"An artist? Doing what?"

"You'll find out, okay?"

I remembered him unrolling the folded white cloth, the gleaming instrument inside. "By the way, Frank Sinatra never owned this place, not in his name, anyway."

"Oh, I know. Lipper just says that. You looked it up?"

"I did, yes."

"Lipper is one of the great old liars, really."

"You know, he doesn't own the building, either."

"Sure he does," Allison said.

"No, actually, he doesn't."

"He owns the building, Bill. I *know* it."

"No, it's some public company. I'm sure he has a long-term lease with them."

"So Lipper *rents* the place?"

"Looks that way."

She sighed. "You know, I've asked him to give me a percentage of the restaurant's profits and he won't. And you know what?" She leaned forward, her teeth tight against her bottom lip. "This is *my* restaurant. I run it, I make it work. It really is mine, Bill. I *possess* it, you know? Lipper doesn't do anything. The bookkeeper sends him some papers a few times a month, and he comes in here with his nurse. I'm the one who is *killing* myself for him."

One of the waiters beckoned her.

"I think we might have a fish problem," she said. "I'll be back."

I watched her go. The question of who owns property is always interesting; here was a situation in which a building had a legal owner, a company, and someone else, Lipper, who claimed to be its public owner, and yet another person, Allison, who claimed to be its moral owner. Things often work this way, though; anyone who has practiced real estate law is soon conveyed into a realm of human affairs where the pressures behind decisions are often enormous, and include death, divorce, illness, stupidity, greed, sexual indiscretion, grief—everything. Whatever is in the human spirit becomes expressed through bricks and mortar, which is also to say there's always a story. I remember in my first year in the practice a short Puerto Rican man came to me. He looked ill used by life, yet had been able to find a decent shirt, though no tie. He'd been shunted off to me by the partners and senior associates as not worth their billable time; I made the same assumption. But within a minute I knew myself to be wrong. He was coming to me, he said, and not a local lawyer in Queens, because he wanted his affairs handled quietly and correctly. He wanted, it remained unsaid, the cultural protection of a midtown law firm loaded with Jews and WASPs. He was dying of prostate cancer and had to proceed expeditiously. He owned three apartment buildings, a car-painting business, a garage, a septic tank–cleaning company on Long Island, a half interest in a gasoline station, and a number of lesser properties. He had come to the United States in 1962 and gotten a job as a union painter. "Three years I was here and then I ask my friend who owns a delicatessen what do you do with your money, and he say I buy bricks. I say why? And he say because bricks, they always grow. Bricks grow. Money, it does not grow like bricks."

Now that he was dying, he had to dispose of his properties before his family started to argue over them, which would lead to the erosion of their value. Equally important, he had fathered four children by three women outside his marriage. His wife didn't know of any of the women, and none of the women knew of each other. One of these liaisons, he confessed between coughs, "back when I was young—you know, *guapo*—with good hair," had been with a Rockette showgirl thirty years prior who had since been married and divorced twice and was living in a tiny apartment in Brooklyn. "Oh, man," he smiled, eyes suddenly bright with the memory, "could that girl fuck. She practically broke my penises." Another woman had involved a longer relationship. Their child had been born with a heart problem and had to avoid strenuous activity. She'd uncomplainingly taken care of him for fifteen years, my client said. Then he started to cry. "He never threw a ball, never swam at the beach." He'd arranged, he said, for a cousin of his to marry the woman and be a father for the boy. Surprisingly, it had worked out. "That was the best thing I ever do in my life," he said. He wanted to sell off his properties to provide for his love children. The properties, he thought, might total ten or twelve million dollars. I sat there, a smug twenty-five-year-old who still thought law was what they taught you in law school, and said I'd look into it. Which I did. The properties were worth nineteen million dollars, and my client died two weeks after the papers were finished. He signed them while on a respirator and between morphine doses.

Or there was the case of the billionaire real estate developer who bought one of the fancy old hotels near the Public Library and spent $116 million rehabilitating it so that he could wheel his mother inside and tell her that it belonged to him. His whole career, successful as it was, had been to prove himself to his mother. All this was conveyed to me by his statuesque wife, on a party boat cruising Long Island Sound. Her breasts were perfect nose-cones of flesh yet suspiciously real-looking, too. She was his third wife, and she knew she had a couple of years to go before she was traded in. I saw in her a good but weak person whose beauty had been debilitating, for it had attracted only men who wished to conquer her. Finishing her drink, she suddenly tossed her ice and lime wedge into the ocean, then the glass too, and turned to me, face beautiful, eyes bitter, and said, "All because of his mother, whom he *hates!*" I'd just nodded. "Why doesn't he want some children?" she asked. "That's all *I* want." She was removed and replaced within a year, and when the hotel's renovation was complete, I attended the ribbon-cutting ceremony and noticed—how could I not—that the developer's mother was asleep in her padded armchair, mouth open, dentures dry in the air, cane nestled between her bony knees.

Now Allison came back to me, her hips swaying. "Fish," she said. "You'd think they'd be easy! Somebody catches them, somebody buys them, somebody cooks them." She slumped in the chair. "Maybe Ha should look at them for me."

"Why should Ha look at the fish?"

"He knows a lot about them."

But this wasn't of interest; I was worried about the night before. "Allison, what else can you tell me about Jay? Where does he work, that kind of thing?"

She took a breath, let it out. "I don't know where he works."

"He's never discussed it?"

"I think he said he was in the construction business."

"When you call him, during the day, where do you call?"

She smiled a sick little smile. "I *don't* call."

"You don't call him?"

"No. Isn't that funny?"

"He calls you?"

"Yes."

"Have you ever seen his place?"

"No."

"Do you know where he lives?"

"No."

"You have any number for him?"

"No."

"No?"

"It's embarrassing. He won't give it to me."

"No home phone?"

"No."

"No cell phone, or business phone? I'm pretty sure he has a cell phone."

Allison doodled on the edge of her clipboard. "I worry that he doesn't really like me, sometimes."

"Why? Just because he won't tell you anything about himself? You search on the Internet?"

"Of course. Nothing."

"He just calls you up and tells you to meet him?"

"Basically."

"What happened to all your tough single New York woman survival rules?"

"I forgot them."

"What do you two do? I'm trying to get a bead on this guy."

"He calls me here. We meet at my place."

"And then?"

"Well, you know."

"Just tell me."

"Usually we you know, we have fun, and then I make him a bite to eat."

"So this is not at night?"

She wasn't expecting the question. "Not usually."

"When?"

"When it's slow here in the afternoon, maybe three or four."

"You ever go out to dinner?"

"Not much," she admitted. "He says he wants to see me in my apartment."

"And you put up with this because—"

Here Allison bit her lip and looked down and then found a cigarette in her bag. I'd pushed pretty hard. But I pushed some more. "The visits don't last long, do they? I mean, maybe an hour or two."

"Yeah," she said. "So?"

"That's not that long for a date, a romantic arrangement."

"You're telling me?"

"Does he begin with a lot of energy and then end up very tired?"

"Yes! That kind of happened last—" She didn't finish. Instead she looked up at a heavy man in a white uniform who had barged into the room.

It was the restaurant's chef. "I canna have this!" he called. "Again the swordfish!"

"You want me to look?" Allison asked.

"It is garbage! A direct insult! He is not wholesaler, he is a crook! He is saying, Eat my shit, take my delicious shit and press it through your teeth! That is what he is saying!" He turned and left.

Allison stood. "You want to see what I have to deal with today?"

I followed her through the swinging door with the little window and past long preparation tables and swinging steel pots. A Mexican man was hosing down the floor. The chef waited for us, a headless fish three feet long resting on a wet drainboard in front of him. I would have said it was a yellowfin tuna. Someone had started to clean it.

"I will not eat shit!" the chef sputtered. "Look!"

The fish had been slit down the middle and he lifted up one half of the pink meat to reveal a milky, pencil-thick tube that snaked through the flesh. It looked about two feet long and recoiled wetly when touched.

"Yeah, okay," said Allison. "I'll call him." She looked at me. "I have to deal with this."

"Worms! Parasites!" cried the chef as I turned to leave. "I canna have them! No worms!" He took his cleaver and hacked the fish. We stepped back. "No—no worms!" He chopped at the red flesh, pulverizing it. "Get—your—fucking—fish—man—to—deliv—er—fish!"

Among Manhattan's many improbable rooms is what appears from inside to be a Kashmiri houseboat floating fifteen stories above Central Park South. Filled with pillows and fabrics and statues of Ganesh, the room is a mogul's private love-chamber in the sky, every surface decorated, sitar music drifting in and out of consciousness. From this view, the park is a great dark lake, with the taxi headlights tunneling crosstown beneath the trees like miniature submarines bound for the lighted apartment buildings on the far shore. The room's many candles flicker in the windows, creating the odd sense of muted explosions over the park.

The room is in fact a small restaurant, only two tables deep, and it was here that I sat in my one good suit, fondling an ornate brass spoon, waiting for Marceno, the new owner of Jay Rainey's family farm. Across the table, saying nothing, sat a dark-eyed woman with a very small nose, pinched perfect by a surgeon, perfect and pointed and small. The nose accentuated the woman's beautiful and enormous mouth, a mouth that promised everything, promised itself as a cave of pleasure that would accept the most torrid urgencies, if only the mouth's owner were made *comfortable*. I had tried very hard not to look at the mouth as the woman introduced herself as Miss Allana, Mr. Marceno's New York associate. The name sounded like one of those soothingly synthetic names of cars or pharmaceuticals. Miss Allana spoke with a crisp South American accent and did not, I understood, see any reason to make further chitchat, instead sitting and staring into some imagined faraway place where— maid service included—low-rent mouth-oglers like myself were not admitted.

"Ah, Mr. Rainey," came a voice behind me, and it was Marceno himself, a small man with a tanned face and dark eyebrows. As confident as he was rich, I thought. He set down his briefcase and shook my hand.

"I'm afraid that I'm not Jay Rainey," I said, then introduced myself.

Mr. Marceno smiled poisonously, dabbed his fingertips together. "Then you are the man who cost me so much money last night?"

I could see that the sum was a trifle to him. "Yes."

He waggled his eyebrows at Miss Allana, then returned his attention to me. "Perhaps I should have hired *you* instead of Mr. Gerzon."

"I was just trying to protect the interests of my client."

"Of course. And why is your client not coming?"

"He had a sudden interruption."

"I see." He nodded again at the woman. Her disinterest in the conversation was painfully erotic. "Yes, this can happen, yes. I am glad he sent his representative. Do you like the view, Miss Allana?"

This seemed some sort of romantic code, for she nodded and the mouth smiled the slow, wet orifice-dilation of a sea creature that senses nourishment might be near.

"Here is our problem, Mr. Wy-eth," began Marceno after we ordered dinner. "We bought the land that Mr. Rainey sold."

"Well, he mostly swapped his land for your building."

"Let me put it another way. The new owner of his land is a company called Voodoo LLC, yes? Very humorous, *Voodoo*."

"Right."

"We bought Voodoo LLC."

"When?"

"Prior to the exchange of the land."

"Was the exchange one of the conditions of your purchase of Voodoo?"

"Yes."

"Why didn't you wait until the exchange was complete?"

"It was not necessary. We knew the exchange would take place."

I nodded. "So you bought the shell corporation that subsequently swapped its office building for a piece of land?"

"Yes."

I still didn't get it. "What do you know about Bongo Partners, which happens to be the listed owner of the Reade Street property?"

Marceno leaned back. "It is not so complicated. Bongo owned the office building. They deeded the building into a new corporate entity called Voodoo. This happened only three days ago."

"Which is why the deed change hasn't yet shown up downtown in the records."

"Right. I see you checked."

And I could see that he was being patient with me, that he had other matters to discuss. "Let me be sure that I have it right. Bongo Partners, formed by a bunch of British investors, starts out owning the Reade Street property. It's a regular commercial property investment. They deed it into a new corporate ownership called Voodoo, then sell Voodoo to your company. Then Voodoo, which you now own, swaps the building for an eighty-six-acre farm on the North Fork of Long Island."

"Yes."

"Pretty ridiculous, isn't it?"

"Why?"

"Why didn't you buy the land outright from Jay?"

Marceno smiled with odd sadism and somehow I knew he thought me the fool. "Because, Mr. Wy-eth, your client would not *sell* it."

"I don't understand."

"He would not *sell* his land, he would only *exchange* it for that building."

I wanted to look at the woman's mouth but it would have distracted me.

"He wouldn't take dollars for the land?"

"No, he had to have the building."

"*That* building in particular?"

"Yes. I frankly do not understand why he did the deal. The building is, well, just a little brick box. The land is forever. Grapevines are forever, Mr. Wy-eth. But then again, I am biased." He looked at Miss Allana. "I am a romantic, it is my flaw."

She smiled and looked away.

"There was probably some tax benefit," I thought aloud. "If he sold the land first, he would have triggered a capital gains tax—"

"We looked into that," interrupted Marceno. "We figured that. We were even willing to make some kind of compensation for that."

"What was the order of events?"

"Pardon me?"

"Who found whom first?"

"We were looking to buy acreage," answered Marceno. "We found Mr. Rainey's land. Then our sales agent told us the land was not for sale, not exactly. That Mr. Rainey would only swap it for a certain building. This was very unusual. We were told to approach the owner of the building, which was, as you have determined, Bongo Partners. Of course they had never heard of us or of Mr. Rainey. They were amused. They might have been thinking about selling the building. So, okay, they were willing to sell. Our lawyers advised that they deed it into a new corporation that we would buy. There are certain tax advantages for us that way, as well as liability protections. So we did that as fast as we could. We bought Voodoo contingent on our ability to swap the building for the land. It went through fine."

"There was a hard-ass deadline for this deal."

"We ordered Mr. Gerzon to get this deal finished, I will admit that. I don't know how he dealt with Mr. Rainey."

Gerzon's pressure on Jay, in other words, had been real. "Why the big rush?"

"Because we are very anxious to develop that property, Mr. Wy-eth. Every day counts when you plant grapes."

"Do you have copies of these contracts?"

He reached in his briefcase, flipped me a small stack of documents. "It's all there. Ownership of the Reade Street building passed from Bongo to Voodoo, then a day later to Mr. Rainey."

"All this crazy legal paperwork because Rainey had to own that one particular building?"

"Yes." And then, perhaps seeing my pensiveness, Marceno said, "Now that I have given you an explanation, perhaps you can give me one. But first, let me tell you a little about my family, Mr. Wy-eth. We have been in the wine business for almost two hundred years. We are located in the Llano del Maipo region, near Santiago. We have a very good Cabernet Sauvignon, the Pinot Noir, and the Merlot. We are starting the Syrah, which you would call Shiraz. This is what we do. We practice controlled vineyard management. Extensive pruning to curb vigor." He looked at Miss Allana. She smiled again and looked away. "We want concentration of the fruit. We are careful about how we treat the land and the people. We are very careful with herbicides and pesticides. We are very lucky. In Chile we do not have the phylloxera epidemic. We can use French vines on French roots. Not French vines grafted onto American roots, like you have in California. We have been very successful. But we would like to branch out a bit. My family has maintained several apartments in Manhattan for decades now, it is a city that we love. And now we find the North Fork of Long Island very intriguing. We have started to hear that some very fine Merlots are coming along. The bottles are expensive, but the market is catching up."

"What do you mean?"

"It's still expensive to make wine there, yes. The land costs are high, the vines need three or four years before they can produce, another ten before they produce good wine. In the great historical regions of winemaking, the cost of the land, as well as of the vines, is more or less sunk. All of it was paid for so long ago that it's no longer a cost factor. Same thing happened in Napa and Sonoma. The land is paid for, the vines are in. As you know, great wine is in the grapes. And before that it is in the soil. There is only so much we can do in the winery. So then, where was I?"

"You love to come to New York City," prompted Miss Allana, her voice throaty and moist. "You love to be here."

"Yes. That is right. And I come and am hearing about the North Fork vineyards and naturally I am curious and ask my driver to take me out there and see the land and I come back with mud all over my shoes and maps and—!" He tempered himself. "It is spectacular. It is a special gift we are only just starting to understand. And the farm that we have just purchased or exchanged with Mr. Rainey is excellent, too. The location is very good because we find that, yes, on a statistical basis, there are about four more degree days, four more days of warm weather, in the fall than there are even fifteen miles to the east. This is important to get the grapes ready for harvest. Every extra degree day decreases our risk, increases our potential yield before the first frost. And there are about two inches more rain. Forty-four inches a year instead of forty-two. To make a truly great Merlot, you do not irrigate. You drop your extra fruit and then use what is left. It takes self-discipline. But that is how the French have done it for a thousand years. It is against the law to irrigate grapes in Bordeaux, did you know that?"

He waited for an answer. "Uh, no," I said.

"We looked at all the weather data, too. Only five days a year above ninety degrees Fahrenheit and less than one day per year below zero degrees, on a historical basis. No prolonged heat, no deep freezes that kill the roots. This is very good!" He nodded in excitement. "And the soil data is good. The soil is loam—porous, sandy, and friable. Very, very good. Some of the best in the world for growing grapes, did you know that? We have a soil laboratory in Chile, with eight thousand soil samples. Our soil is volcanic, very different. But we study all soil. We had our agronomist look at the site, and we did our own gradient calculations, yes? If the slope of the land is more than eleven degrees, we find that the water vapor lingers in the low areas and we don't get the drying of the leaves that we like. We can get fungus, we get terrible black rot. So grade of land is very important. We examined the whole area, Mr. Wy-eth. We looked at nine different large properties. Frankly there was one that we liked a little more but a French company bought it before we could. But Mr. Rainey's property was larger and slightly cheaper by the acre and so we decided to acquire his. Our broker, she let us know about it."

"Hallock Properties?" I asked, remembering the sign on the field.

"Yes." Marceno looked at Miss Allana, then smiled at me.

I realized I'd just made a mistake.

But he continued. "When we buy acreage, we like to enter the community on very good terms—that makes sense, yes? We want the local people to be glad that we came. We try to build relationships, we try to have people feel good that the Marceno family has arrived. After all, we hire local labor, rely on local merchants. We need goodwill."

"Sounds reasonable."

He leaned forward. "It *is* reasonable. It is also reasonable to suppose, Mr. Wy-eth, that when we buy a piece of land, yes, we expect that what we see is what we get."

I said nothing, thinking, of course, of Herschel atop the bulldozer.

"Do you understand me?"

"So what did you see?"

"We saw a lovely piece of farmland with good drainage fronting Long Island Sound, the kind of place where you could put in a wonderful winery and have a tasting center looking out over the ocean."

"Isn't that what you got?"

"We don't know what we got, Mr. Wy-eth. We did soil tests, but those are random. Yesterday after we signed the copies of the contract to buy Voodoo LLC, but *before* Mr. Gerzon finalized the deal last night, we took a drive out to look at the land. Somebody had been out there with a bulldozer."

"A bulldozer?"

"Yes, moving topsoil around. It looked to me like he was filling in a low area but it was starting to snow. I couldn't quite tell. But I could see the bulldozer tracks."

"This was yesterday?"

"I told you, yesterday afternoon, Wednesday."

Yes, in the daylight, which matched what Mrs. Jones had said. "What time?"

Marceno twisted his head. "Midafternoon, just after four o'clock. This wasn't just a few tracks, Mr. Wy-eth. I myself worked a bulldozer on our family vineyard when I was young. Someone had spent hours moving the soil around."

The chronology wasn't quite clear, but it sounded as if Herschel had already gone over the cliff when Marceno had inspected the land. Marceno hadn't actually seen a bulldozer.

"Mr. Wy-eth, I know what goes on in an agricultural operation. Soil gets moved around, holes get dug, this kind of thing. But this land had been undisturbed for a while. I myself had been over that property by foot six times already. And then, the day we are finishing the deal, I see bulldozer tracks everywhere. What does this mean, I think. Why are they moving earth? What are they hiding from us?"

I didn't have an answer for him, of course, but it occurred to me then that whoever had moved the soil around might have timed his activity in respect not only to the falling darkness but also to the coming snowstorm. If he—Herschel, it seemed—had begun at, say, 1 p.m., and the snow had started to fall at 3 p.m., with darkness descending about ninety minutes after that, then the discoverability of the bulldozer work prior to the deal being done that night was shrinkingly brief. "What happened then?" I said vaguely.

"It was getting dark and our driver said a bad storm of snow was coming and perhaps we should try to get back to the city soon." He looked at the woman and said something in Spanish quickly. She blushed and turned away, her lips pressed together in amusement. I got part of it. Something along the lines of, *When I'm done with this gringo idiot you and I will* . . . "So I did not get enough time to look around."

Right. He did not get enough time to see Herschel dead and frozen forty feet down the sea cliff.

"Why didn't you stop the deal if you had a question about the land?"

"I tried to call your client, but he was unresponsive. I called the real estate agent and she said if we stopped the deal, then another buyer was ready to step in. I didn't want to risk that. So I let the deal go ahead." He stared at me without blinking, his mouth sucked small with fury. "This morning my foreman tells me he finds *new* tracks and also potatoes in the snow. I am thinking I did not see potatoes in the snow yesterday afternoon, and they are in the snow the next morning?"

I was close to urinating in my pants, but instead I quietly bit the tip of my tongue, as hard as I could stand it.

"I would like to know what is being covered up, Mr. Wy-eth! I would like Jay Rainey to tell us! He knows the land. He grew up on it. It's eighty-six acres, Mr. Wy-eth. Not so big. But we could spend a very long time and lots of money trying to find out. The snow will be gone soon, maybe tomorrow. We want to know what we are dealing with here. Underground gasoline tanks? Buried herbicide? I know that the potato farmers used arsenic for many years and that many of the old barns still have bags and bags of it. It could be many things. Water moves under the ground. Sideways, up and down. I am worried about planting vines and in three years the roots find some kind of poison. The vines die, maybe. Or, worse than that, we find herbicide in our wine, we find trace elements. We use Roundup, this is very good stuff, breaks down to water. We like that. But other farmers in the past used very bad stuff. You can get terrible things in the wine. You have to tear out vines, Mr. Wy-eth! A terrible thing. Expensive, and very painful. So we are careful. We are thorough."

"Yes."

"It looks to me like the bulldozer was trying to add some soil over about a two-acre area, okay? The till depth to establish the vines is twenty-four inches, in your measurements. This is standard out there and is well known. Deeper than potatoes. I suspect, yes, that he was trying to be sure our tillers did not hit anything. You see, when the ground freezes and thaws, things come up. But if you add soil on top of them, they might stay hidden longer. We want to know what the problem is, Mr. Wy-eth. We want to take care of the problem in such a way that it doesn't attract the interest of the local residents. The environmental officials, okay? I have heard that when the New York State Department of Environmental Conservation gets involved, the delays are usually measured in years. *Years!* I am sure you understand that we do not want the publicity of our arrival in any way damaged by bad news, Mr. Wy-eth."

"I'll have to talk to my client."

"Yes. You see, we have to get moving on the construction of our vineyard. We have financing lined up, we have a planting schedule, we are about to build the first two barns. We have to get the land ready. The vines get planted in May, but there's a lot to do before that. The land has to be tilled and raked, graded and fertilized, thousands of posts put in. For the variety we wish to grow, we have a two-week window to plant the vines, so that the roots go deep enough to take the summer heat— otherwise we wait another year, Mr. Wy-eth. So we need Mr. Rainey's help soon, very soon."

"I will talk with him."

"We would like him to take us to the place on the land and tell us just what exactly we may find under the soil. I want him to point to a spot in the ground and say dig *here* and you will find whatever it is that he is hiding from me. We do not want to plant vines and then find out we have to tear them out."

"That's reasonable." I bit my roll, but it might as well have been my fist.

"We know a lot about Mr. Rainey already, we know he grew up there. I have tried to call him, I have been goddamn fucking polite."

I didn't doubt this.

"I would like an answer in one day, please."

"I'll see what I can do."

"Yes," he said. "Or you will see what we can do." He pulled something from his breast pocket. "Here," he said. "I believe this is yours."

He handed me the same old business card I'd given the cop the night before.

"That is yours, no?"

Yes. The lettering, so neat and formal, the name and address, my name, my title, all my old phone numbers, four of them and e-mail, all the signifiers of a former life. The sight of the card made me sick. I'd handed it to the policeman late the night before, a hundred miles away, and here it was again? How? Marceno, like any good businessman, might already have an understanding with the local police department, may even have asked them to keep an eye out for trespassers, and when called and told about the interaction, had one of his minions drive out to retrieve the card.

"I have something else for you, Mr. Wy-eth."

"Yes?"

He looked at Miss Allana. She reached down to her feet—slowly, keeping her back straight and legs crossed—and retrieved a large purse, from which she pulled a legal-size manila envelope. Marceno took the envelope, opened it, and slid out two documents. Even across the table I could tell it was a lawsuit.

"Please deliver this to Jay Rainey." He handed me one of the documents. "And this copy—this copy is for you."

I skipped my eyes over the first page. I was named as a defendant.

"Wait—"

"If he gives us a good answer, we will tear it up."

"Listen, I'm not—"

"You were Mr. Rainey's legal representation in his deal with Voodoo LLC."

"But I'm not involved in—"

"And according to the local police, you accompanied Mr. Rainey out to the land last night. Trespassing, I should add."

Marceno stood, as did Miss Allana, and they left without further word. He was going to take her to a hotel or apartment and spend some time with her beautiful sea-creature mouth and I was going to spend some time with a lawsuit. A great steaming plate of tandori chicken landed in front of me, but I slid it aside and lifted the first page of the document. There it was, Jay and I both named as defendants, allegations of fraud, misconduct, misrepresentation, and whatever else they could dream up, the amount being sought nothing less than ten million dollars. Some junior associate at a third-string law firm had pumped out the language. It's easy; you get an old suit, change the names and addresses, doctor up the wording. It was just a bluff, a device meant to get one's attention. Yes, meant to make the acid creep up your throat, meant to remind you that mistakes are costly and dread very cheap indeed. But even such trumped-up attacks have a way of quietly sucking the sauce out of people; they are expensive to win and disastrous to lose, they become part of your psychic history, they snap your life onto a grid of legal filings and motions and court calendars. But worse than that, I feared the unknown connection between Herschel, his frozen eyes lifted to a dark heaven, and Marceno's orderly wrath. Old black farmhands with sixty years' experience don't end up on bulldozers in the middle of a snowstorm without their socks on.

Was the next part luck? Not quite. Mostly a guess as I stood out on the street, wind against my cheeks, angry with Jay and a little scared, the lawsuit rolled thick as a magazine and jammed in my pocket. It was, after all, a Thursday night in February, and Jay had circled all the Thursday night games on the girls' basketball schedule I'd found in his car the night before. Plus, he'd said that very afternoon that he had an important appointment in the evening. No, it wasn't much of a deduction, but still it took me a while. I flagged down a cab near the Plaza Hotel. The school was only twenty blocks away, and I knew it well, for it was one that Timothy might have gone to when he'd gotten older.

The school's gym stood around the corner from its main entrance and I could hear the cheers roaring out of the high, lighted windows. I stepped past the guard without making eye contact, walked down a corridor of pewter trophies, many of them fifty or eighty years old, and into a small, old-time gym. It was packed with parents. They looked tired and quite prosperous, many of them clearly on the way home from the office, dragging briefcases, caught in the whirling time-squeeze of parenthood and work. These were people with jobs and marriages and lunches scheduled months into the future; I used to be one of them and I hunched a bit, as much out of shame as from the worry I might see someone I knew. You never can tell whom you're going to run into in these places and it was quite possible I'd encounter fathers or mothers of

Timothy's old friends, or even people who knew Wilson Doan. This thought nearly made me turn around, and I was glad to be dressed in a suit, as if that might protect me from something.

The home team was losing by nine points. I found a seat in the bleachers. Time was running out—eight minutes left in the fourth quarter. The girls on the court were sweaty and red-faced and excited; most of them had breasts or the beginning of breasts and they fussed with their hair and uniforms, but by the standards of the world, they were children. I scanned the crowd for Jay, and after a minute spotted him on the far side of the gym, in the section reserved for rooters from the other school. He sat on the top bleacher next to the wall, bent over.

Something in me recoiled. Perhaps it was the avid lean of Jay's big body. He was peering intently through a small pair of binoculars, but not, it seemed, following the game. The ball was passing back and forth in front of him, the girls shrieking, the coach hollering directions. But the binoculars didn't move. Then he put them down and opened a small notebook. He scrawled a few sentences, presumably in the same slanting block letters he'd written on the back of the slip of stationery, closed his eyes, and then wrote a little more. I was watching an act of worship. He folded the notebook into his breast pocket and lifted the binoculars again.

I considered going over to Jay, but realized I might learn more if I watched him from across the court. Maybe he knew one of the girls on the court. Maybe he was a sexual predator stalking one of them. Maybe Allison would be interested to know. The game progressed. The gym was warm and I loosened my coat. The visiting team looked like it would win by about a dozen points. The coach hollered, the crowd cheered. One of the home-team girls fouled out.

"Substitution," called the announcer, a nasally teenage boy in a coat and tie. "Coming in, number five, Sally Cowles."

A girl stepped forward from the scorer's table and ran onto the court to a smattering of polite applause. She was tallish and leggy and a little awkward in her baggy jersey and shorts, but she took her position on the floor quickly. Cowles, Sally Cowles. This had to be the daughter of the Englishman we'd met that morning, no? I had not seen the photo on Cowles's desk well enough to make the match. She looked about fourteen, still very much a girl, breasts not yet developed, her body more up and down than curving. But her large eyes and well-formed face promised beauty. I glanced back at Jay. Now his binoculars followed the action of the game, the action of the girl, I should say, and on the occasion when play stopped at the end of the court near him, when Sally Cowles stood just thirty feet or so from him, her face sweaty and eyes alert, knees bent and waiting for the referee to whistle play to begin, Jay Rainey lowered his binoculars and stared at her.

I glanced from one to the other, trying to understand their connection, but then someone behind me was calling my name. I turned fearfully, and there was Dan Tuthill five bleacher rows up, good old Dan Tuthill, looking a little grayer, and a lot heavier, firing me a big wave. He said something to his wife next to him, then began stepping down the bleachers, his enormous stomach tented in a green sport short.

"Jeez, Bill, you look great!" he said when he reached me, breathing like the wealthy fat man he was. "I told Mindy, I think that's *got* to be Bill Wyeth, can't believe it, just great to see you."

We shook hands with the old conspiratorial intimacy. "You here to see your daughter?" I asked.

"Yeah, she made a layup in the second quarter. Total luck it went in. You?"

"I'm here, well, to meet a client."

He nodded, perhaps impressed. "Anyone I know?"

"Probably not."

He knew I wouldn't tell him.

"How's it going at the firm?" I asked him.

"Ah, don't ask." His face sagged in pain. I'd always liked this about Dan; his emotions were right there for you to see, up or down. "I mean, I'll tell you, but Christ! Nobody knows where the power is anymore. All the young guys are pissed off at the old guys for sucking up all the bonus money. I qualify as an old guy now. The *really* old guys are nervous. They fired two lawyers last week and two more quit. It's a fucking nightmare, Bill. The executive committee is a snake pit."

"I thought you were *on* that committee now," I said, glancing to see that Jay was still in his seat.

"I used to be." He shrugged at the unstoppable flow of time. "Listen, it's good to see you, Bill. See that you're out there, in circulation." He gave me a little affectionate slug in the arm. "You look *good*, you look trim. Been working out?"

I laughed. "I eat mostly steak."

"I've heard about that diet, I should try it. All protein or something. . . . You know, Bill, I'm *still* sorry about—all that stuff that happened . . ."

"Yeah," I said.

"Did you land anywhere, pardon the expression?"

"I landed hard, Dan. Let's put it that way."

"But it looks like you've got a little work?" he asked gently.

"I could always use more."

He stared at me, wheels clicking in his head. I remembered the look. Dan liked deals, he liked speed, he liked action. "We should have lunch." His voice was thoughtful. "We could talk about some things, you know?"

"Name the time, guy."

He pulled an electronic device out of his pocket. "I always say I better not drop this thing . . ." He pushed a button, studied the tiny screen. "Day after tomorrow? One? Harvard Club?"

"You got it."

"I'm really glad to see you. Frankly, there's a lot going on—I can't discuss it here, but we'll kick it around, okay?" He shook my hand as if it was he who needed me, and returned to his wife. I didn't know what to make of the interaction except that it had been surprisingly pleasant and confirmed that you should always keep a decent suit around. I could still fit in. In fact, the parents around me didn't give me a second look at all; I was just another fortyish guy in a tie. It felt good, it felt *possible*.

Then I turned back to look for Jay. He was gone.

But perhaps I could follow him. I bounced down the bleacher steps, making my apologies, and hurried out to the street, hoping to see his large frame ahead of me. I took a chance and walked east toward Lexington Avenue, past the lighted windows of other people's lives.

That was when I felt a hand slide into my armpit.

A hoarse voice: "Easy."

Two tall, well-dressed white guys walked on either side of me.

"Take the wallet," I said. "Just leave me the ID, okay?"

"Relax."

"I don't care about the credit cards, just—"

"Hey, re-*lax*."

They were hustling me toward a double-parked limo. A third man jumped out and opened the back doors.

"Look, I talked with Marceno earlier! I have the lawsuit in my pocket right here, I understand the situation, I know he's serious."

One of the men shrugged at the other. "Not a clue."

A taxi went by, not stopping. They hustled me inside the limo, sat on either side of me. The seat was soft and I sank backward comfortably. Both men sank down next to me as well.

The one on my right said, "Let's go," and the car started to move.

"H.J. said he'd call when."

We were cruising downtown. "Who is H.J.?" I asked.

"He's the gentleman who keeps us in his admirable employ."

The accent was Irish, I guessed. "Hey guys, come on."

"Just taking orders."

"I think you got the wrong man."

The man on my right whispered something under his breath, and instead of shooting me in the head, right there in the car, a mess for someone to clean up, he leaned forward and turned on the television in the console in front of us. It was CNN and we watched a terse summary of the situation in the Middle East.

"They got it wrong, Denny," announced the man on my left. "They left out the part about who really owns the bloody oil."

"My cousin from over here was in the second Gulf War, you know."

"Guys, come on," I tried again. "This is the wrong—"

"He kill anybody? Any wee action with the ragheads?"

"He killed forty-one, by his count," said the one named Denny. "Also he shot at some Iraqi trucks, blew them to shite with a grenade launcher."

"Look, you guys aren't looking for me, you're probably looking for—"

"There's a fellow in Queens who sells those things."

"Get out."

"Swear to it. Eight thousand dollars."

The man on my left nodded. "We could go there now, after we deal with Andrew Wyeth here."

"Bill Wyeth, not Andrew Wyeth."

"He's the great painter, the artist, right?"

"Yes, American archetypes, Maine, all that. Bit of the stony coast and the sea."

"But a great American nonetheless."

"In a manner of speaking, I suppose."

"Hello Billy, are you a great American as well?"

Thugs living a thuggish dream. Yet they seemed to bear me no particular ill will, so I remained quiet. The car cut west on Twenty-third Street, nosed onto the West Side Highway going south, where they turned off the television, and rode it down the tip of Manhattan, around Battery Park, then north up the east side of the island on the FDR, slow in the traffic, then around the top of the island on the Harlem River Drive, then south down the West Side.

"How long are we to do this?" Denny asked.

"However long H.J. says."

"I'll need a bog."

"There's a McDonald's at Thirty-fourth and Ninth."

A few minutes later we pulled in. One by one they went to use the bathroom.

"You?"

I shook my head. Too scared.

We circled the island one more time, and by then, almost midnight, the men were bored.

"Fucking H.J., man."

"This is the job. When you're for hire, this is the job."

"You guys bribable?" I asked. "You can take me to a cash machine, clean out my account, let me walk away with a little pocket money, go buy myself a drink."

The man on my left laughed. "You're all right."

Then a cell phone in the car rang and the three men straightened up. The man on my left answered.

"Okay," he said, lowering his voice, "we'll be right there."

We rolled into the West Twenties, not so far from where I lived. The limo eased along the curb and I was escorted up the steps of an old factory building. The men kept close to me now, urging me along, one tight hand under my arm. I thought about running, knew it would be futile. We approached an unmarked black metal door.

"This is where *we* get off," one of the men said.

"What do you mean?" I asked.

"The likes of us are not welcome in there." He looked at me, eyes mirthful. "Not that you will find us complaining, though."

The door opened. Four black guys in good suits stepped out. I was passed to their firm control. The door shut quickly behind me. Inside I heard rap music pounding, and it became louder as I was hurried through a dark hallway constructed of painted plywood. We passed several young black girls giggling outside a door marked PRIVATE and I knew that the sight of a middle-aged white man there was shocking to them, anomalous, as impossible as a reindeer. Next the hallway became tinted with red lights, the smell of pot lingering. We passed a stairwell where two black men were casually beating a third. They turned in surprise when they saw us.

"Chill," murmured one of my escorts.

"He's a cop?"

They pushed me along, up a set of stairs. At the landing we came upon a crowd of black teenagers watching a pit bull hanging three feet in the air from a thick, knotted rope. The dog had the rope in his jaws.

"Yo," said one of my escorts. "How long?"

"Nine minutes."

The dog's eyeballs rolled around and he shook his head savagely, a froth at the edges of his teeth.

"What's the record?"

"Twenty-six."

We climbed another flight of stairs, passing promotional fliers, pictures of rap artists, and framed album covers. A large black woman in gold lamé and sunglasses passed. "Hi baby," she murmured. We came to a glass door with HANDJOB PRODUCTIONS stenciled on it.

"Inside, yo."

Inside was a small office with a black glass window overlooking the club's dance floor. The men followed me, pulling the door shut behind them. To one side lay a panel of unused mixing equipment, turntables and tape decks, and to the other sat an enormously fat black man in a red silken robe and security headset. He had on gold sunglasses, the lenses coated with some sort of shimmery hologramic stuff. His chair was elevated so that he had a bird's-eye view of the dance floor. Next to him stood a two-hundred-gallon oil can with a slit in the lid. Around us, and up through the floor, came the heavy thud of the bass. Occasionally a scream of excitement. Below on the floor, hundreds of bodies moved in an undulant mass, spotlights strobing crazily across them as a rap group spun through its stylized, chain-swinging, crotch-grabbing moves.

"Yo, H.J., this is the dude."

H.J. pointed at a chair for me to sit and waved away the other guys.

"We'll be right outside, bro."

He didn't bother to look at me. Instead he watched the dance floor for a few minutes and talked into his headset. "See what them niggas is doin' over by the red couch." He leaned forward, watching. "No, the dude in the green—yeah, *him*. He bitin' my style. Tell that nigga I'm in his *mind*. All right . . . be cool. Yo, Antwawn? Antwawn, I want that box up here right now. Bring it up."

"Hey," I said. "You want to tell me why I'm here?"

"Don't talk when a man is doin' his business," came the response. "Antwawn, I want to see yo ass in like—" He turned around. "What'd you call me? You call me 'Hey'?"

"I asked you why you had me here."

A giant smile under the sunglasses. "White man, you got an improper education. My name is H.J."

"Pleased to meet you," I said. "Now tell me why I'm here."

The door opened. A young man with dreadlocks and a tattoo of Daffy Duck on his arm carried in a lockbox. This, presumably, was Antwawn. He looked at me. "Who that?"

H.J. ignored the question. "Open it."

Antwawn unlocked the box and tilted it toward H.J. Even from where I sat I could see it was full of cash. "Okay?"

H.J. opened the box, removed a short stack of bills that he put in his pocket, then took a roll of masking tape and wrapped the box about five times. "That's enough," he told himself. He signed his name over the tape with a thick felt marker. "Put it in the safe."

Antwawn knelt under the console, opened a door, placed the box inside, closed the safe.

Down on the dance floor they were screaming. "How many girls you got out there?" H.J. asked.

"Nineteen, plus Serena at the register."

"You got LaQueen on tonight?"

"Yeah." Antwawn smiled. "You want her?"

"Tell her come up here, show me somethin'."

As Antwawn left, another man in a velveteen shirt came in. He had a bad scar across one forearm. He looked at us. "Who this white dude?"

"He just visiting. Let's see it."

The man with the scar pulled out a small silver pistol.

"Good. He fight at all?"

"Not really, boss."

H.J. dropped the gun into the slit in the oil can. He pulled a fistful of bills out of his red robe, gave it to the man. "Here." They tapped their fists together and the man with the scar left.

Now he turned to me. "You work for that Jay Rainey?"

"No."

"That's bullshit."

I shrugged.

"My aunt say she talked with you today."

"With Rainey, mostly. I just happened to be there."

"What she want?"

"Money."

"That's right. But she made one mistake."

"What?"

"She got the number wrong."

I said nothing.

"I said she got the number wrong, she got it too *low*."

"I heard you."

"You disrespectin' my people?" he asked, lights strobing behind his head.

"No."

"You hate black people?"

"No."

"You think they should stay poor and get AIDS and shit?"

"No."

"You think black people stupid?"

"No."

"I think you do. I think you got ideas about black people."

"I'm sure you've got a few ideas about white people."

"You hate the black man."

"No."

"You hate his superiority."

"No."

"You hate his sexual prowess."

"No."

"You hate everything about him."

"You hate white people?" I asked.

He breathed through his nose. "Yes."

"You hate the white man?"

"Yes, indeed I do."

A girl poked her head inside. Her lips were the color of taxis. She was wearing high heels, a thong, and a fringed top. All the color of taxis.

"Come here, LaQueen."

"Oh, I know what you want," she said in a high, happy voice that suggested little pills that gave people high, happy voices. She saw me. "Who this?"

"He just some white dude who don't know what the fuck he doin'."

"You want some fun?"

"Come here. Like my daddy used to say, girl, you look better than a government check."

She glanced at me playfully. "Don't look, mister."

I looked. She knelt down between his huge jellied thighs, spread the red robe. But all I could see was the lovely dark violin of her back, her ankles together, heels sticking out.

"Slow, baby." Then he lifted her face off of him. "You love that thing, don't you? You love my monster."

"I do, baby."

"Say it, say I love your monster."

"I love it, H.J. You my *diesel* nigga."

He pressed her head back onto him. Then he looked up to address me, over her bobbing head. "My auntie tells me you—you sent my Uncle Herschel out into cold weather and he had—a heart attack. Everybody who know Uncle Herschel know he got a bad heart."

"I don't know what happened to him. He was working for Jay Rainey."

H.J.'s feet were tapping a kind of slow rhythm. I saw a gun strapped to his ankle. "You're takin'—money from him, it's the—same thing."

"That's not exactly what—"

H.J. looked at me, showed his gold teeth. "You want my blow job?"

"No thanks," I said, coolly as I could.

"'Cause you *lookin'* like—like it looks *good* to you. I seen your eyes." He glanced at the girl's head. "Looks *tasty*."

"No thanks," I said.

"What—something wrong with my woman?"

"No," I said.

"Not good enough for you?"

"I didn't say that."

"Maybe she *too* black for you."

"No."

"See, the white man like you, he *scared* of the black woman. And the white woman, *she* want the black man. And the black woman, she ain't interested in the white man. They *all* want the black man, see. Same for the Chinese and the Spanish. Once they go *black* they *never* go back!" He let his hand fall on the girl's head, rubbed it, and smiled at me hatefully. "Maybe you need to learn to *appreciate*. You know, I ask LaQueen—

she'll do you, after me. She may not want to but she will. Ain't that right, baby?"

She nodded, made a humming, filled-mouth affirmative.

"So then you could see for—*yourself,* boy."

I said nothing. We were living in different movies, both terrifying. H.J. whispered to the girl, "LaQueen, go easy there." He lifted his freaky sunglasses up to his forehead and stared at me with oddly small and sensitive eyes set on his large cheeks. "My auntie, she say they found Herschel's ass out on the bulldozer, frozen. Frozen! How you let a black man freeze, boy? That don't go down, you know what I'm sayin'? Something *wrong* in all this, and we gonna find that Poppy or Popeye or whatever the fuck he called!" He reached down to his ankle and pulled out his gun, pointed it at me. "That make a man feel murderous! White man never pay Uncle Herschel shit! He work that land for somethin' like thirty years, never saw nothin'!" He let his hand rest on LaQueen's shoulder, holding the tempo. "I want repairation! You got to pay the repairations! We heard that land got sold for fourteen million dollars!"

"You heard wrong."

"Shut up! I want three hundred—"

"You're talking to the wrong guy."

"—thousand dollars. Don't think so, Mr. Wyeth. I think we got exactly the right muthafucka! We watchin' you, we know where you hang out, we know where this guy Rainey's new building is. We got it covered, boy."

Some of this was bluffing, I hoped. "You've got to take all this to Rainey," I said.

He moaned and rolled his head and looked upward in anticipation. "Go, LaQueen, do it, sista!" The girl was working harder, faster. "Give me the booty!" he screamed. He pushed the girl deeply onto himself, holding her head all the way down with both of his hands, making her feet kick a bit in gagging panic, the gun next to her ear, his knees shaking with the pleasure, and when the moment came, he lifted the gun over his head triumphantly—"Oh, you fucka!" he screamed—and fired into the ceiling, then again. I flinched. "Oh, sista!" he cried, collapsing backward and pushing the girl away to reveal a giant wet black penis that leapt from between his thighs. He tipped his head forward, inspected himself, then looked up at me looking at him, at it. The girl lay her head on his thigh, licked his softening size with obligatory reverence, her eyes on mine, coldly dismissive. The room smelled burnt. H.J. grabbed his security headset. "Antwawn, come up here and get this white boy outta my face." He aimed the gun at me. "You get me my money," he said, stroking the girl's head as she sucked him in and out. "Lawyer-man, you get me that goddamn fuckin' money or I'm goin' find you and fuck up whatever shit ain't already in your pants."

five

THE NEXT MORNING was blue-skied and excellent—

—if you weren't freaked out. Which I was, coffee-jittery, anxious, driving a rent-a-wreck too fast away from the city toward Jay Rainey's old farm, my terrorized heart pattering, *It's bad, they're bad, it's bad.* Like anyone, I prefer to *forget* that I am to die, not be reminded, prefer to think of my last breath as a far-off event, the years measurable in, say, the unit of time it takes to discover, test, refine, approve, and market a major new pharmaceutical. Yes, give me two or three of those epochs, a couple of new brain-boosters and cartilage-thickeners, and I'll be fine; the romping American society I die in will be unrecognizable to me. But meanwhile, the passage of days is ominous. I feel the past dropping away an inch behind me, a dark wind sucking coldly at my ears, yanking on the shorthairs of the back of my neck, gurgling like a suffocating eight-year-old boy. Yesterday is *not* yesterday, it is lost and gone forever, collapsed, rotten, moaning in the graveyard. Day by day I see that my future holds far less than does my past—ever fewer pieces of chocolate cake, clean shirts, fresh newspapers, hot cups of coffee, the milk swirling in a beguiling cloud. Yes, I scare much more easily than before. I *freak* more easily. I take threats *very seriously.* I believe, for example, that when an insane black guy with no pants on pulls out a gun and fires it, then that threat is *real*. When that happens, you *run*.

Yes, you run and stumble and have people yell at you and you see the pit bull still hanging from the rope, and you hear kids pointing and laughing and saying *Mister! Yo!* And you stumble whitely out into the cool air of the street and run with no wind and little form as fast and as far as you can before hailing a cab, which is what I did, arriving back at my miserable apartment and high-stepping it up the stairs to my door with great gratitude for the peeling paint and bald carpeting, the half-clogged sink, the soft-sagged bed—my shithole deluxe, the most wonderful place in the world.

And that was where I'd slept not at all, wondering in the dark if I should go to the police. H.J.'s thugsters had kidnapped me and he'd pulled a gun on me, after all. Many beautiful, time-honored laws had been broken. On the other hand, what was my proof, given that I was unharmed? And no doubt H.J. could produce any number of people in his club who'd say that never happened. And then he'd mention his dead Uncle Herschel and that would point any interested policemen toward the question of his body. And that I didn't want.

But was H.J.'s outrage linked to Marceno's complaint? After all, whatever Herschel had been doing with the bulldozer had occurred before he died. And H.J.'s rage stemmed from the fact of Herschel's death on a bulldozer rather than *why* he was on the bulldozer. By this analysis, the two problems were potentially unconnected. But I was troubled. I was troubled in the way that makes you sit up and turn on the cheap light by your bed and pick at your fingernail, wondering why Mrs. Jones had seemed to dispute the reason why Herschel was on the bulldozer in the first place. Or why H.J., while ranting at me, had said that he or his people were looking for Poppy. Which was interesting. And maybe logical, given that Poppy had called the ambulance upon "finding" the body of Herschel. But Mrs. Jones had said she'd been pointed toward Jay's building by Poppy. How was this possible? Why would Poppy know the address of Jay's building unless Jay had told him? And why would Jay do that? Poppy was apparently just a longtime farm laborer with damaged hands. Why would he need to know the address of a specific building in downtown Manhattan? And, for that matter, how did H.J. know that the old Rainey farm had even been sold? Well, maybe because the new owner, Marceno, or his workers, had arrived the day before, the morning after the sale. But H.J. didn't seem like the kind of guy to be messing around on an old farmstead. He had a hip-hop club to run. Which meant that someone, probably Mrs. Jones, had told him. But she'd arrived at Jay's building early enough the morning before, around 10 a.m., that it was likely that she'd left the North Fork too early to see the arrival of the new owners, especially if they were driving out from the city at the same time. Which suggested she'd made a subsequent call to H.J. after threatening Jay in front of his building. Yes, *that* made sense, *that* was how H.J. had known what I looked like so that his men could follow me. Mrs. Jones, one hundred pounds of righteous determination, had described me to him.

But even if they'd had my photo (a Web search of the back copies of New York City legal publications would probably turn up a cheesy five-year-old black-and-white head shot), how had they known where I'd be? Had they tracked me the previous day from Jay's building to the steak house to my apartment to the Indian restaurant to the school? Doubtful. More likely that they'd been following Jay, then lost him—he had disappeared quickly—seen me come out of the basketball game, recognized me, and then moved in.

Now I came to the rump end of the Long Island Expressway for the second time in thirty-six hours, turning onto the country roads leading to the North Fork, wishing my rental, a beaten delivery van with stenciled letters on the door and Jesus decals on the headlights, had a decent heater. I sipped my coffee and jittered up more tangled questions for myself, feeling driven—not crazy, but into the coldly rational, ultraparanoid part of myself. My old, capable, bastardly law-firm self. I began to see that whatever was going on with Marceno, H.J., Poppy, Mrs. Jones, and Jay constituted, in its entirety, a piece of machinery, call it a gear, that was engaged with another smaller gear, this one sprocketed by Jay, and the building on Reade Street he so badly wanted, a building that housed the business owned by David Cowles, whose daughter, Sally

Cowles, apparently so fascinated Jay that he was secretly attending her high school basketball games. Did Jay himself understand these two sets of complications? And where did Allison fit in? Despite her insistence that I help Jay, she'd been pretty vague when describing his real estate deal. The fact that he hadn't explained to me the convoluted purchase of the Reade Street property suggested he was in no hurry for anyone to learn that he'd sought to buy that building *and no other*. And from Marceno's chronology, it appeared Jay had decided to buy the Reade Street building and *then* put the acreage up for sale. Looking back now—from whatever miserably chastened perspective I enjoy—I see that the moment Jay disappeared from the basketball bleachers into the Manhattan night marked his acceleration toward his own long-sought imaginings. What he wanted seemed so close that his natural caution had become a burden to him and had been jettisoned. If he had seen me at the game, then he would have suspected why I was seeking him, which meant of course that others sought him, too. And if, on the other hand, he hadn't seen me, he'd nonetheless made a sudden exit, which suggested he felt a vulnerability as he sat watching Sally Cowles run up and down the court. Perhaps he'd sensed he'd overstayed his opportunity. In either case, my relationship to Jay had changed. I was hunting him now.

The single-lane road winding east toward the Atlantic revealed a charming and classically American dreamscape almost too good to be true—three-hundred-year-old saltwater cottages, steepled churches and clapboard farmhouses, silver barns next to ancient, heavy-limbed maples. My glimpse of Jay's dark frozen fields two nights earlier, I realized now, had been insufficient to understand the forces at work on the value of his property. The rolling land was a heart-yanking time warp to a simpler age. People find such authenticity frighteningly attractive, for it lets them forget terrorism and global warming and genetic counseling, lets them forget that time runs in only one direction, at least for those of us still roped to the mast of Western rationalism. Such places conjure a lost psychic era, pre-Nixonian, when Cadillacs looked like rockets and silicone was used only to caulk windows. Back *then*, when America was the great good place. And people will happily pay for that, they will pay twenty-first century prices. I passed a tractor pulling a wagonload of hay; in the other direction flew three white limousines in sequence, carrying who knows who—corporate executives, pro athletes, movie stars? A few miles farther I swept past two golf courses going in, then half a dozen wineries, each expensively grand structures of shingle and glass centered among precise four-foot-high rows of trellised grapevines that swept backward toward the horizon. In the instances where obsolete farm buildings or modest homes fronted the main road, these were being purchased and demolished. Indeed, the large projects I saw had probably been the result of the consolidation of multiple lots, an expensive and time-consuming way to assemble a land parcel, and typically only done when prices are rising dramatically. But as Jay had said, the prospect of world-class vineyards and wineries within what amounted to a stone's throw of New York City—which, let it be remembered, still holds more wealth than any other city on the globe, even London, even Hong Kong, even Kuwait City—was a surefire bet. Overlay on that proximity various other factors—the cheek-by-jowl development of the Hamptons, the recent local land-use restrictions enacted in an effort to block that very same kind of development, and America's ever-burgeoning retirement-age population—and the surefire bet became a kind of slo-mo bank robbery.

Yet even more proof awaited me when I parked in the quaint town of Southold and found Hallock Properties, one of whose signs, I'd remembered, lay flat in the weeds on Jay's old property. The office's windows were adorned with listings for large pieces of land, complete with aerial photos of woods and field and gorgeous shoreline headlined THE LAST UNCUT JEWEL! and HISTORY DOESN'T REPEAT ITSELF!

I stepped through the agency's door; it was as one might expect, a bustling hive of office cubicles, the walls plastered with house listings. For a moment I mused over the prices. A trailer home on a tenth of an acre? Try $195,000. A clapped-out one-bedroom shack on half an acre? $320,000. Undeveloped mere half-acre oceanfront lots ran $475,000. Two acres of swampy overgrown brush on a brackish inlet? $950,000. A terrific five-bedroom job on the water with gourmet kitchen, "rocking chair porch," tennis court, and "forever views"? At least a million five. Vineyard acreage? Prices started at three million and went to the moon. What had happened to the Hamptons and Martha's Vineyard and Nan-

tucket and Malibu and Pebble Beach and Coral Gables was happening
here. It was America, after all; somebody had to be getting rich.

The brokers stood or sat talking into their headsets, consulting files
or computer screens, the women attractive and tough, in their thirties
and forties, and the few men older and ruined-looking—clutching the
floating logs of their careers.

"Help you?" asked a woman who introduced herself as Pamela. Her
hair reminded me of a bowl of Frosted Flakes.

I told her I wanted to talk with someone about the large property in
Jamesport they'd recently handled. "Acreage up on the Sound," I added.

"I'm not sure which—?" she said, politely inspecting my shoes.

"It was just bought by some Chilean wine people."

Pamela frowned politely. "We didn't handle that."

"I thought you did. I saw your sign out there."

"No."

I stared at her Frosted Flakes hair, which made her nervous. "Who
did then?"

"I don't know."

"Was it listed with multiple brokers?"

She was dodgy, even for a real estate agent. "I couldn't say."

Already I knew enough about the region to see that large properties
with ocean frontage didn't come along too often. "I was told, by the
buyer of the property, that one of your agents specifically told him"—
and here I glanced at some scribbled notes in my hand—"that another
bidder was in the picture and that the second party was prepared to bid
again if the buyer didn't close."

She was still looking at my shoes, blinking rapidly.

"I should also probably mention, Pamela, that I am a New York City
attorney specializing in real estate matters."

Now she looked up at me, a tight smile pinned on her face. "You need
to talk with Martha. But first, understand this. That property, the old
Rainey farm, was never handled by us. It was never *officially* listed by us."
She lowered her voice. "I don't know *what* Martha may have said, or
done. Maybe she stuck one of the agency's signs next to the road—whatever. She's—she could have said—well, I'm sure I don't want to know."

I made a show of writing all this down.

"May I have your name again, Mr.—?"

"Bill Wyeth."

I followed Pamela through the partitioned offices, down a wainscoted hallway.

"Martha?" she called when we reached a closed door.

No answer. Pamela pushed the door open and the room we entered could not have been more different—a vintage realtor's office at least fifty years old, stuffed with files, yellow topographical maps, and curled tax survey volumes. An old, rather heavyset woman sat sleeping in an armchair, despite the early hour. Her housedress had fallen open a little too far and she was holding a spoon. On the table next to her lay a glass of tea and a thick biography of the Duke of Windsor. Propped next to the seat was a cane.

"Martha!" cried Pamela. "Hello-o?"

"Yes?" The elderly woman blinked awake.

"This is Mr. Wyeth," announced Pamela hatefully.

"How do you do?"

"He's come to discuss the old Rainey farm?"

"Has he?"

The women stared at each other. "I'm going to leave you two alone," Pamela said, "so I can have a quick look for my sanity."

She departed, her heels clicking smartly down the hall.

"Get that, would you?" Martha pointed to the door. When I closed it she waved at the chair opposite her for me to sit. "Pammy's a dreadful woman. A shocking hussy. A *tart*, they used to say."

"Oh?"

"Yes, we're lashed together, and neither of us likes it much! I taught her everything she knows but there's no respect, no loyalty anymore."

"This was your agency?" I guessed.

"Still is." She nodded defiantly. "Which my father started in 1906." She noticed her housedress and pulled it closed. "I was the baby of the family. I'm eighty-three, Mr. Wyeth, so you can see how long I've been around."

"Seen a lot of things."

"Oh my," she agreed. "I remember when the potato trucks used to go down the main road by the dozens. We had one doctor, paid him with firewood in the winter and produce in the summer. Nobody knew about this place. Most beautiful spot in the world. Everything's different now. I can't begin to tell you. Everybody was on well water. You could eat oysters at every meal when they were in season. And lobster, too. We had a lovely church community."

Humor her, I thought. "What did farmland go for, Martha, when you were a girl?"

"I'd say three hundred dollars an acre."

"And what is it now out here?"

"With the vineyards coming in, maybe fifty thousand."

Jay had been screwed, I realized. I pointed up at a local map. "And the future?"

"Easy," she sighed. "Million-dollar homes on the water. Million-dollar homes off the water. Vineyards owned by rich people. Wineries owned by even richer people. All the big farms will go to grapes. The fix is in on that, see, because of the water-use problems. Vineyards are low-impact agriculture. Low water use, low pesticide use. Government loves that. Lot of these grape growers are environmentalists, too." She put her spoon in her teacup. "Amazing it took the world so long to find us."

I liked old Martha Hallock. "Want to give me the whole pitch?"

"What else is there to say? Eighty-two beaches mixed with vineyards. Napa Valley doesn't have that. And quaint New England capes and farmhouses? And the longest growing season at this latitude? And two hours from New York City? For years it was the Hamptons. No more. They ruined it and this is still here. And we've got strict land-use zoning."

"People in your business must feel pretty good."

"If I were thirty years younger, I'd be selling fifty houses a year myself, easy. I'd be selling cabbages to kings. But I'm too old, Mr. Wyeth. People are scared of old people. Think death is catching, I guess. Maybe it is. I sold my last house three years ago and that was my neighbor's. Doesn't count. Got old. No one to blame but myself, I suppose. I own half this business but I don't bring anything in anymore. They'll get rid of me any day now. Waiting for me to die, mostly. Put me in the wheelbarrow in the shed."

I didn't believe this. She still had a lot of moxie for an eighty-three-year-old. "How long can you hold out?"

"Me? Maybe a minute or two."

"Pamela want to buy you out?"

"She wants to *live* me out."

"What'll you do?"

"Well, I still have an ace in the hole, as my father used to say."

"Which is?"

"I know the territory." She saw me nodding dutifully. "No, no, I really do. I went out with my father and the surveyors. A lot of things don't turn up on regular surveys, you know. I know the creeks and flood lines. I remembered what happened in 1957, that big flood. I remember what the lot lines used to be." She tapped her head. "That's still worth something, Mr. Wyeth. Less and less every day, but still something."

"And I bet you can talk to the old farm widows."

"Yes, I can. They know me, they trust me. Not these little hussies in their convertibles. Half the girls out there are friendly with the developers and contractors. You know, *friendly*. Long lunches, who knows where! Come back to the office looking like they went through the bush backwards. Pamela hires her own type." She shrugged to herself. "Which is smart, actually. Easier to control."

"Do you have any children, Martha?"

She lifted her face to me and I knew that I had stabbed her with the question. "I made a lot of mistakes, Mr. Wyeth. Most of them involved men's shoes."

"Excuse me?"

"Men's shoes. I saw a lot of empty ones on my rug the next morning, if you know what I mean." Her eyes twinkled devilishly. "I know that seems preposterous, looking at me *now*."

"I'm sure—"

"No, no, I'm an old bag. Anyway, when it came time to settle down—well, it's my great regret. On the other hand, I don't burden anyone." She examined her tea. I had little doubt that every word she'd told me was true, yet said with absolute calculation, too. The lonely old woman act. I didn't quite buy it, either. Subtract thirty years from her, and you'd have a very formidable fifty-three-year-old businesswoman—a negotiator, tough, precise, perceptive. So the woman I was looking at *was* that woman, plus thirty more years' experience.

"Now then," she said. "What can I do for you?"

"What do you know about the Rainey farm?"

"Fine piece. Eighty-something acres. North road frontage, some elevation to the west, very few low areas. Probably could use some regrading in spots. The bluff is not perfectly stable—they've lost a good fifty feet over the last hundred years, probably needs some kind of stabilization. Potatoes for the first part of the twentieth century. Had the blight in '66 and switched to cabbages and flowers, switched crops a few times. Nursery trees for a while, then something else. Russell Rainey was a lovely man. I knew him well. It's a very fine piece of land."

"Was Russell Rainey the father of Jay Rainey?"

She shook her head vehemently. "No, no. *Grandfather.*"

"Where's the father?"

"Somewhere very, very hot," she clucked. "I hope."

"Did you sell the land for Jay Rainey?"

She looked at me. "It was a private sale."

"But didn't you have some kind of contact with the buyer, a Mr. Marceno?" I pressed.

"I'm an old woman, Mr. Wyeth. I fall asleep in my chair. I have one eye that's weak, my feet cramp up at night, and I take a lot of heart pills. It's frankly hard to remember what I've done one day to the next." She stirred her tea. "And you know, even though I'm just a country girl who learned to sell a bit of land here and there, I've met a lot of people in my time. I've met businessmen and movie stars and two senators and three governors and buckets of congressmen on the island, all *kinds* of people. I met the Shah of Iran when he came here for medical treatment. I met Joe DiMaggio and General Westmoreland and Jackie Gleason. So, you see, Mr. Wyeth, I've learned that people who know their business *state* their business. Sooner rather than later. It's a habit of successful people. Here you've let me blather on about so *many* things. And I don't know why you're here."

"I'm Jay Rainey's lawyer, Martha. I live in the city. I examined the contract of sale for him for the farm and told him not to do it. It all

looked funny to me. He did it anyway. Now, Jay is in—he's got a problem and the buyer is putting big pressure on him."

"Wants to undo the deal? He can't. Why? It's a beautiful piece."

"No, there's something buried in the land and Marceno is anxious to
know what it is."

"And he wants to get the soil ready to plant?"

"Exactly. He's putting in Merlot vines and won't be getting any us-
able yield for three years."

"I know the game," she said.

"And I suppose you know Marceno as well?"

She casually retrieved the biography of the Duke of Windsor and
turned a page. Her hair was rather thin on the top of her head.

"I'm on the right team here, Martha, okay? Marceno said he talked
with a broker from this agency saying another buyer had come forward
and would buy the property if Marceno's deal fell through. I'm figuring
he was talking to you."

She flipped another page.

I took a half step forward. "Was there another potential buyer?"

"The world is full of potential buyers."

"You were just pressuring him, then?"

Now she looked up at me. "Yes."

"Why? Why'd you do it?"

"Why'd I do anything?" she cried. "Because it was Jay's chance to be
free! All these wine companies are so big! They can pay to dig up a little
sand and truck it away. There's been enough pain in that family. How is
Jay, Mr. Wyeth?"

"He seems—" She'd changed the topic, I realized. "He seems fine."

"Oh, that's very good. I saw him a few months ago . . . he seemed a
little tired . . . He was the most, *most* beautiful boy. A perfectly beautiful
boy, very good at football and baseball as I remember . . . This was more
than fifteen years ago." She closed her book. "His father farmed that
piece. Didn't do too well. Not a nice man, not in any way. But Jay got his
size from him. Mother was lovely, though, saved him from his father.
She poured herself into him. Taught him everything. Jay was charming
and did very well with the summer girls, you know. Never boastful. Yes,

I knew his mother. Sweet. But sad, you know. Wanted more children. Nervous woman. Tired of terrible fights with her husband. But she had Jay, she was just so proud of him, he was her prize. Consolation for her *husband*."

Mrs. Hallock uttered this last word as if she were unexpectedly tasting a small bitter object on her tongue. "The accident must have just unnerved her, see. That night . . . she lost her bearings. The husband"— that tone again—"was no good, didn't stand up, just drank himself away."

"The accident—?"

Martha looked at me hawkishly. "Known Jay long?" she asked.

"No. Just a short time." Three days, I didn't say.

"Oh, I see."

"You mentioned an accident?"

"I shouldn't have. I'm not the one to discuss that. It's his business." She dropped her hands to the arms of her chair and gripped them. "It was very nice of you to visit me, Mr. Wyeth. And I'm sure things will get resolved smoothly. That piece of land's got nothing but three feet of loam over who knows how many hundred feet of beautiful sand below that. It's perfect acreage and I'll give the new owner a call to remind him of that."

But I wasn't quite ready to evaporate. "You seem to know Jay and his family pretty well, Martha," I said. "And it appears you *were* the agent on the sale of his property. As such, you have a responsibility to the buyer as well as to the seller. I think you know this even better than I do. The buyer has contacted me with the accusation that something was covered up out there, right before the sale went through. *Hours* before, Martha. As it turns out, there's good reason to think that. The buyer is a busy guy. Making frivolous complaints is not worth his time. He's going to pursue this until he has satisfaction. As it is, he's probably going to sue Jay to get compliance. Let's hope you're not named, either."

"Don't be ridiculous, Mr. Wyeth."

"I'm going to call you tomorrow to see if you have more insight into how this problem can get fixed."

"Maybe I'll still be alive to take your call."

I don't like getting mad at old women—generally they have enough problems—but she hadn't been much help. We glared at each other, and then I left.

On the way out of the offices, I saw Pamela. "Thank you," I called behind me.

She glanced over her shoulder. "I doubt you mean that."

"A tough case."

"Anyway, see any properties that interest you?" She pulled off her headset. "But I guess that's not why you're here."

"No." I put my hand on the door to go. "Any advice?"

"You could try finding her nephew, he usually knows what's going on."

This didn't much interest me. But I'd be polite. "Who's that?"

Pamela wrinkled her nose. "A nasty little man. Gives me the creeps. Everybody calls him Poppy."

Back in the city, I returned the van, and on my way to the steakhouse passed some guy hawking cell phone deals. I walked in the shop and signed up for the cheapest deal they had.

"I heard these things give you brain cancer," I joked, fondling the little device.

The clerk, a short black guy with sad eyes, considered the statement. "I believe that's true," he said. "I think they'll find that out, eventually."

"You're probably not supposed to tell me that."

"They want me to lie, they should pay me more."

The steakhouse was slow, the lunch rush done, the staff vacuuming the carpeting. As ever, Table 17 stood empty.

"Allison around?" I asked my waitress.

"She left you a note in case you came."

Which I opened. It said, *Meet me in Havana Room.*

I declined to order some food and instead got up and found the little door next to the foyer unlocked. The curved stairwell was dark.

"Hello?" I called. "Allison?"

The long room was dim, the smell of cigars lingering. No natural light fell upon the paintings, the black-and-white tile floor. A rack of dirty glasses stood on the bar. Allison sat in the farthest booth.

"Hey Bill," came her voice.

A stack of restaurant paperwork lay to one side of her, a shot glass and bottle of Maker's Mark to the other. Allison gave me an uneasy smile, embarrassed at her vulnerability. "You working or drinking?" I said.

"Drinking."

"And in private, too."

"Didn't see you last night," she ventured.

I thought about telling her about the previous evening, about Jay's appearance at the basketball game, about the lawsuit. "I was detained."

Allison smiled. "Against your will?"

"Yes, as a matter of fact."

But she didn't believe me. "Well, I think I've been stupid," she announced. "Silly and stupid."

"Jay?"

"Yes. I mean, I probably hoped too much, you know?" She pushed at her shot glass. "He came over last night—I said I'd make a late dinner, like ten-thirty—have a nice evening. So I left here about nine. And he showed up, just what you'd expect."

This meant, I realized, that Jay had left the basketball game straight for Allison's apartment, and maybe not because he'd seen me or H.J.'s men looking for him.

"He stayed in the living room while I made dinner and I saw he left his briefcase in the kitchen with me, and—" She shrugged. "It had papers in it, you know, interesting stuff."

"You couldn't help yourself."

"I know it was wrong. But I sort of saw his date book in there, his schedule, and I opened it." She lifted the shot glass and knocked back the last half inch of whiskey. "I was just *curious*, hoping to kind of know him better, that's all. He never tells me *anything*."

"Unlike the other guys."

Allison nodded. "They tell me too much."

"Every human relationship has its power structure."

"Well, Jay has too much power."

"You like that?"

"It bugs me."

"And excites you."

"How did you know?"

"How could I not?"

Allison nodded. "Well, it bugs me mostly. *Now*, I mean."

"What does he want from you?"

This stopped her. She looked up. "I have no idea."

"Does Jay ask you questions? Does he want to know things about you?"

"Like what?"

"Well, Allison, if I were romantically involved with you—"

"Which would really *not* be in your best interests."

"—I'd ask why is it that you work so hard when you don't have to, and why you actually live in the same place where your father lived, and why is it that you never mention your mother, or where you grew up, or if your father remarried, or why you are so loyal to Lipper even though you pretend to be annoyed by him, and let's see—those are just the ones off my head—and all right, why are you so chronically dissatisfied when actually it might be that it's *yourself* you are hardest on, and—"

"Stop."

"—and then I'd ask isn't it true that you want to be known and yet are afraid as to what will happen if you are, afraid someone will reject you when they see the truth, so you fill your head with the exhausting swirl of people and work so that you never—"

"Stop! Please. *Please*, Bill!"

"Okay."

"That was a little bit cruel."

I couldn't disagree.

"But it shows something . . ." she mused, pouring another glass.

"It shows I interrupted your story."

"What was I—oh, the date book! I wasn't suspicious or anything. But okay, it was sneaky and wrong. He was watching the news, didn't notice at all. I spent five minutes looking at the thing. Shameless." Allison's eyes brightened wickedly. "Practically *memorized* it."

"Was it busy?"

"Well, it had all the *usual* stuff, like going to the dentist, take car to garage, that kind of thing, plus some other stuff . . ." Allison looked up, eyes brimming. "He's got another woman!"

"Nah, I don't believe that."

"He does! He's got dates with her, *regular* dates." She pressed a fingernail against her eyelashes. "Here I have to *beg* to see him and it's because—of course, *hello!*—he's got a regular girlfriend. He's got dates with her going back months! I flipped through every week, every single one this year!"

"What's her name?"

"I don't know! And that bothers me, too! It starts with O. He doesn't write her whole name down, just O to remind himself. Olivia or Olympia or Orgasmia or something, *fuck.*"

If Jay had a regular girlfriend, then his behavior at the basketball game, his interest in Sally Cowles, seemed even odder yet. A big, good-looking guy with a steady girlfriend plus a little action on the side with a woman like Allison didn't seem like the type of man who would then stalk a teenage girl. I couldn't put it together. "He sees her pretty often?"

"All the time!" Her bitterness sharpened. "Like I'm not going to figure *that* out, if I just happen to *accidentally* see his calendar. Come on, nobody is fooled." But then Allison's voice softened, as if she wished she'd been fooled, would even have preferred it.

"Any chance he left the briefcase there *hoping* you'd have a look?"

"Maybe. He seemed more distracted than anything else. Whatever. It's that O that bothers me, Bill. O is a very sexy letter, if you think about it, right?" She looked at me for commiseration. "It stands for orifice. It opens up and lets stuff in. It means *she* opens up and lets *his* stuff in."

"Guys do things like this," I said.

"I *know* they do, Bill! They just don't do it to *me.* So then I thought I'm going to ask him, I'm going to just be brave and go in there and turn off the TV and straight out ask him. I was making this nice paella. I wanted to throw it in his face!" She smiled now. "I got the hot pad and actually lifted up the dish to see how heavy it was, but then I realized it'd stain the rug."

"He didn't figure out you were mad?"

"No . . . I just took the dinner into the dining room. He wasn't even watching the television, just standing at the window, thinking about Ophelia or whatever her name is."

"You don't know that."

Allison didn't answer, and instead took another sizable sip of whiskey, and when she put down the glass something had changed in her face, her bitter disappointment replaced by the desire beneath it. I was struck by how quiet the room was; all the normal sounds of the restaurant, the vacuuming and chatter, were gone. "Oh, Bill," she whispered, pushing away her hair from her face. "I just don't know." She was, I saw, one of those women whose sexuality didn't embarrass her. That she had discussed one man with another didn't mean she preferred either, or anyone in particular. The man—whoever he was—was temporary, the desire permanent, the emptiness intolerable. The man was something that fit into things for a while—a night, a month, a changeable self-perception. This is a dangerous, attractive thing in a woman. As a man, you see that she is capable of forgetting the last guy quickly. Which is encouraging. She's able to launch into an obliterating passion, a passion capable of forgetting its own depthless nature. Of course this means that you yourself will be forgotten easily too, but that is later, and afterward. I wish I could say that in that moment I held all these things clearly in my head. But I didn't. Instead I watched as Allison cut her eyes back at me, almost daringly, her diffused desire turning to a kind of angry want, which itself might change into anything, her mouth twisted, a little cruel, a little ugly even, but then she closed her eyes and sighed. She opened her lips and breathed heavily. "Bill?" she whispered. Her eyebrows lifted in expectation. "Come here."

I went to her and she lifted a hand, which I took. She squeezed it softly, a smile on her lips. She rolled her head forward, her hair curtaining her face, and this was an invitation for me to touch her, which I did, with one hand, caressing her smooth, firm neck. I let my fingers slip behind her ear. She sighed, then looked up at me, and it was the same gaze she'd given Jay Rainey a few nights earlier, not a copy but the original, wanton and soft and wishing, and in her breath I smelled the whiskey, the sweetness of her intoxication. She did not want me particularly, I knew, she did not want anyone, not Jay, not even necessarily a man, she just wanted. Like all of us. She *wanted* and *needed* and I just happened to be there. She was willing to give in to whatever or whoever wanted her. The requirement was mutual oblivion. She had arrived at that moment of possibility. She had been there before and would certainly be there again, many times, and the true arc of her life was constructed of these points. She closed her eyes and opened her mouth, waiting, and despite myself, despite all that I knew and now worried about, I myself had been lonely a very long time, yes, it had been a sorrowfully long time since a woman had wanted my affection, and so I bent slowly and pressed my mouth to hers.

It was a long and good kiss, wet and whiskey-fumed, but I ended it, gently. Allison smiled and mouthed *Thank you* and then dropped her head and I could see that the moment was done.

"So, do you happen to remember what was on Jay's schedule for to-day?" I said as casually as possible.

"Yes, I *do*. He goes to a place called Red Hook cages, like once or twice a week."

"Red Hook cages—?"

"Doesn't that sound terrible? Like he hangs from a bloody hook or something? I think he's going there this afternoon. Red Hook cages. Which is *fine*, just so long as he isn't going to see O. Miss O, whoever she is, the *bitch*. Red Hook. There are a lot of bars in that part of Brooklyn, whatever, maybe it's some kind of construction business thing."

She was wrong. I knew what the Red Hook cages were, for I'd been there with my son, in fact, on a rainy Saturday. Allison was falling softly back into herself and the right thing to do was to leave her alone. The right thing to do was to leave for Red Hook immediately.

"Wait a minute, Mr. Wyeth."

"What?"

She grabbed my hand, rubbed the knuckles. "I got something to tell you."

If we'd been near a bed, we'd have been in it now, estranged boy-friend or not. "Yeah?"

"But there's a *price*."

"What?"

"You have to promise not to be *judgmental.*"

"Of what?"

"Of something we do."

"Who is we?"

"Don't you want to know the what?"

"Who, what—I'll take either."

"You'll find out."

"When?"

"Tonight." She kept her eyes on mine. "In the Havana Room."

"Tonight?"

"Ha says he's ready again."

"So soon?"

"Sometimes," Allison said slowly, with drunken amusement, "things happen faster than you ex-*pect* them to."

"What time?"

"Come round about midnight. I will have sobered up, I promise. I will be in top form. You'll find me *very* impressive." She wagged a finger at me. "Oh, also."

"Yes?"

"Anyone told you that you are a very fine kisser of women?"

If so, it had been a very long time ago. "You're pretty drunk, Allison. Get some coffee, okay?"

Before I reached the marble stairs, I looked back at Allison once more. In the darkness of the far booth, she hung her head, perhaps despairingly. Perhaps kissing her had been a mistake. Perhaps I had enjoyed it a great deal and wanted to do it again. And perhaps I would. Then I climbed the stairs, turned the door handle, and eased toward the entrance of the restaurant, hoping no one would see me leave.

The waitresses sat at a table at the far end of the main dining room, smoking and chatting, and several busboys were involved with sorting silverware and folding napkins. None of them saw me. Yes, no one saw me save one—it was Ha himself, standing in his baggy overalls on a ladder in the foyer replacing a bulb. He saw me exit the Havana Room and he watched me wait to see if the waitresses or busboys had noticed and he saw me look in surprise, up at him, and when our eyes met, he knew everything about me, it seemed, that I was a lonely, unattached man who ate too often at the steakhouse, in some kind of trouble now, and who had just emerged from within the Havana Room, where Allison, a woman he saw every day, sat drunk and alone in the far booth; that something had happened between us in the room. Yes, gazing into Ha's weathered Chinese face, the folded skin, the wide-set, unblinking eyes, I saw he knew these things about me.

I, on the other hand, knew nothing about him. Especially why it was he who controlled the schedule of the Havana Room's activities.

But I knew something else—I knew that when Robert Moses, the great, bullheaded architect of modern New York, builder of highways and parks and municipal swimming pools, insisted that the Brooklyn-Queens Expressway be constructed to facilitate the traffic flowing around New York City to and from the rapidly growing suburbs in Long Island, Connecticut, and New Jersey, the elevated highway was erected through and over the working-class neighborhoods of short brick row homes that used to house the men who serviced the Brooklyn Navy Yard and the docks on the East River. If any thought was given to what would happen to the buildings beneath the highway, it did not change their fate, which was to be subjected to the noise and pollution of the road, the constant shower of hubcaps, empty 10W40 oil cartons, milk shake cups, bags of vomit from carsick children, lost Yankees hats, used diapers, cigarette butts, beer bottles, discarded cassette tapes, condoms, watermelons, radiator caps, and God knows everything else that falls out of or is thrown from cars and trucks. Squatting within the shadows of this rusting, rushing superstructure are businesses that depend upon such a marginal location, where rents are lower, squalor ignored, parking ample and unpoliced: porn shops, taxi garages, car service offices, and so on. It's a bad zone; it was here, for example that a New York City policeman, drinking for twelve hours after his shift ended, some of that time in a strip joint, ran over a pregnant Latina woman and her two children with his van going seventy miles an hour, an event which, for those who believe in such places, sent four souls to heaven and one to the front page of the tabloids. The city has these fissures, deep crevices in the landscape that bad stuff falls into, and it was here that I went looking for Jay that same afternoon, based upon what Allison had told me.

The building in Red Hook that I wanted sat on Third Avenue. I pushed through the door in a mood of apprehension, because I remembered how much Timothy had liked the place when we'd been there a few years before, and returning now was a measure of my fall since then. But I kept going. The first room, a murky cave of pinball and video games, sold cheap sports memorabilia and junk food. Boys in mismatched Little League uniforms ran pell-mell. I could hear rock music and every few seconds a loud metallic clang. Through a doorway, a much larger room appeared, under this sign:

35 MPH: All Youngsters Under 9

45 MPH: Youngsters 9 and Older

55 MPH: Youngsters 10 and Older

65 MPH: Youngsters 11 and Older

75 MPH: Teenagers 13 and Older

85 MPH: Teenagers 17 and Older

95 MPH: Special Access, Mgt. Approval Required

Behind a high curtain of netting, the pitching machines were firing baseballs at the batters. I stood for a moment behind the 45 mph machine as a lanky boy of about ten swung at pitch after pitch with an aluminum bat. The balls seemed pretty fast, but he made contact with every third pitch or so. A middle-aged man in a green Jets cap stepped in and adjusted the boy's stance, the ball whizzing past his eyebrows. Baseball is still sacred in Brooklyn, in a way it never could be on the East Side of Manhattan, and the Red Hook cages are part of a world where forgotten old men sit in lawn chairs in the lumpy fields of public parks, eating unlit cigars and catching smoking rockets from young hurlers, boys whose mothers bleach the uniforms the night before a game, a game often as not umped by a cop or fireman and which, if played at the Ty Cobb Little League field near Avenue X, will be watched not only by the black residents of the housing project across the street and the mothers and fathers sitting on the cement bleachers, but by the men who run the maintenance train of the subway's N line, men who park the massive yellow-and-black engines on the elevated track that directly overlooks right field; on the rare occasion when a boy clanks a ball off the home run wall, one of the men climbs nonchalantly into the cab of the engine and yanks the horn as the boy circles the bases. That's Brooklyn, Brooklyn baseball.

I moved on. No sign of Jay. A knot of hollering, hot-dog-stuffing boys clustered behind each machine, and the noise was formidable. At the 75 mph cage, I watched one of the boys lean in too close over the plate and take a pitch right on the temple of his batting helmet; his coach reached inside the steel fence, hit the red stop button, and went to pick up his player, who shook off the injury. Of course I thought of Timothy, ten now, quite capable of swinging a bat as hard as many of these kids.

At the far end of the building lay the 95 mph cage and through the many layers of wire mesh I could see a large figure in T-shirt and shorts taking dramatic cuts at the ball. Others were watching him, and as I approached I realized it was Jay, with something made of green plastic sticking out of his mouth. He clanged an enormous shot. I got closer and saw that the device clenched in his mouth was an inhaler; between pitches he squeezed down on it, shooting whatever chemicals it contained into himself.

I melted in among the others, worried and fascinated. I knew Jay was a big man, of course, but his body had always been cloaked by a suit or heavy winter coat; here, now, I plainly saw a man about six foot three, two hundred and forty pounds, powerful in the arms and chest and back, with a little extra in the gut, and, most notably, heavily muscled legs that swelled below the knee into enormous, veined calves, large as a comic book superhero's, three times normal size, and oddly, even disturbingly, compelling—beautiful fruits of muscle that splayed widely from the downward line of his legs—legs that Allison had presumably had between her own. Jay and I were not sexual rivals, but we weren't exactly *not*, either. I wondered if Allison measured our deep but solitary kiss in the Havana Room only a few hours earlier against the ongoing pleasures Jay had provided her. The question was silly but the answer was yes, of course, and seeing Jay's obvious vitality, I thought it was possible that Allison would shrug off our brief intimacy as silly or wrong.

"Fuckin' freak," sniggered one of the teenage boys hanging their fingers through the wire fencing. "Sucking on that thing, fucking cocaine gas or something."

"It's brain steroids, like makes your bat speed faster. Major leaguers use them secretly before they come out of the dugout."

"That's totally fucked, man."

"No it's not! Every major league dugout has like this little bathroom next to it. Guys go in there, toke on that stuff, and come out and hit. Why you think the home run records keep getting broken? It wasn't all the muscle stuff, it was the *brain* stuff."

"You have like no fucking idea what you're talking about."

"Look, he's *hitting* it, you pussy."

Indeed he was, and not just dinging them back or popping them up but swinging his bat parallel to the ground and driving the ball straight back against the mesh at the far end, one after another. Then he missed, and the ball rocketed against the screen in front of me. He let out a muffled roar of frustration, then gave himself two shots of the drug, seemingly swelling up with them before the next pitch came.

Which it did, and Jay got a piece of the ball, clanking it hard against the screen fifteen feet up. He roared again, and slammed the bat into the earth.

"See?" said the boy, stroking what he hoped was a mustache. "Freakman. Steroids in the brain, making him crazy."

Jay dug his cleats in and took a practice swing, then pulled the bat back to the loaded position, knees bent, head up, right elbow high and a little jumpy. The mechanical arm lifted and Jay rocked and cocked, as the coaches say, and when the ball came he was ready and drilled it into the nets.

"Haaa!" came his cry of satisfaction. The sound was sexual, murderous.

"See?" announced one of the boys. "See that?"

"I see your momma."

"*Your* momma fucked my baseball bat."

"Yeah, the one your sister gave her after she was done with it."

"You mean the one you *licked* for three hours."

"Shut up," said a third boy, "he's switch-hitting."

I watched Jay shift from rightie to leftie and swing at another forty pitches or so. Batting from the left, he wasn't nearly as effective, and missed every other pitch. But of course being able to switch-hit well is one of the rarest of skills in baseball, and I was intrigued that he was even trying it, especially with balls coming at major league speed. The back of his shirt grew dark between the shoulder blades, then a red light on the pitching machine popped on, signaling the end of the session.

"No good," Jay snarled to himself. He spat the inhaler out of his mouth, flipping it up in the air before him, and swung at it with the bat. It shattered and its metal canister flew in our direction, skittering over the dirt.

"He always does that, too," said one of the boys, "that's how come I know it's brain steroids."

Jay pushed up his helmet and started to pull off his batting gloves. I slipped back a step, thinking that it might not be right to confront him there, before so many people, while he held a baseball bat and was under the effects of whatever drug he'd been inhaling.

"Yo, mister," cried one of the boys. "What you *got* in that thing?"

"I'm finding out," said the other boy, and he scampered into the cage. Jay watched him with disinterest. The boy scooped up the canister from the dirt and ran back.

"What is it?"

The boys studied the fine print and I edged closer for my own look.

"Ad-ren-o-something."

"Let me see that, you fucking illiterate."

"Hey, yo *mister*," one of the boys hooted.

A heavyset man in his twenties in a Rangers jersey suddenly appeared, bent low to the boy, and spoke harshly to him, glancing up at Jay now and then.

"Okay, *okay*," the boy protested. Then he and the other boys ran off with their prize.

Adrenaline. In aerosol form. Did it really help one's bat speed? The idea made a kind of crazy sense. Jay opened the cage door and lurched forward through the crowd, his Yankees cap down low over his forehead, a coat and sweatpants slung over his shoulder, eyes on the ground, his face angry and determined and oblivious to all, including me. I made sure he couldn't see me, intimidated by his staggering, violent strength, no doubt enhanced by the stuff he'd pumped into his system. He also appeared deeply alone, threatening in his bulk. My planned declarations seemed puny and even imbecile, but I decided to press forward, and followed him from thirty feet back as he disappeared into the front room, saying goodbye to no one, though it had seemed from the boy's comments that Jay was well known there. I fought through a sudden influx of eight-year-old boys, any of whom could have been Timothy a couple of years earlier, and watched Jay plunge out the front door into the cold. When I reached the door he had already crossed the three southbound lanes of Third Avenue and disappeared under the deep shadowed roar of the expressway. Across the street a neon sign promised XXX VIDEOS & BUDDY BOOTHS. I'd missed him again, or rather had found him and then let him go. Impossible, impossibly *stupid*. Or was I just scared of him? Was letting him go smarter?

"Jay!" I called, trying to lift my voice over the river of heavy traffic before me. I stepped into the street, waiting for an opening.

"Yo, man," called a hoarse voice next to me. "Don't mess with that dude."

A face emerged from the doorway behind me, a man a few years younger, his hair brilloed around his head. He might have been white, dressed Latino, talking black. It gets harder and harder to tell these days. I turned back toward Jay, then checked the light.

"Why?" I answered, still watching. "Why shouldn't I mess with him?"

Through the traffic I could see Jay getting into his truck.

"That guy? Lemme tell you about that guy, okay? He's no good. I mean it."

"Come on."

The cab darkened, the headlights went on.

"Jay!" I called again, stepping forward.

"Do I look like I'm messing with you?" the man said.

I watched the traffic slow. "Jay! Jay!"

His truck bumped its way onto the other side of the avenue, heading north, toward Manhattan.

"I'm telling you, don't *fuck* with him!" He jerked his thumb toward the batting cages. "Fucking gorilla, they ought to throw him out of there. Sucking on drugs, scaring those kids. Shit fucks you up, makes you crazy. The polices, they don't do shit, neither."

"What, what?"

"That guy, he's done some stuff, okay? Let's just leave it at that. You ain't from around here, okay? I would of seen you before." The man bobbed his head assertively, as if I had argued the point. "One time some guy got into a argument with him, and it wasn't pretty. You know what I'm saying?" He stepped forward, grabbed my coat, yanked. Instinctively I stepped backward but it was too late. His face was close to mine, breath warmly foul. "Just like that, huh? Like pulling down the fucking zipper on your coat, ha!"

This seemed unlikely to me. Street rumor, false legend. But I was scared anyway. "How often does he come here?"

"All the time, anytime. Maybe like three times a week."

So he probably lived nearby, I thought. "You know anybody wants to make any money?"

He looked at me like I had a dead fish hanging out of my mouth. "What're you talking about?"

I said, "You heard me."

"Tell me that again?"

"I'm saying I'll pay a hundred bucks to know where he lives. Somebody could watch for him, follow him home."

"Come on, what the fuck." He pulled a galvanized roofing nail out of his pocket and began to suck on it.

I wrote down my new phone number. "Here's what the guy does. He follows that guy home. By car, whatever. Doesn't do anything. Nothing. No talking, nothing. Just the address. Then he calls this number"—I handed him the slip—"and leaves the address. Then he tells me how he wants to be paid. I'll come right back out here, if necessary."

"Come on, you kidding me with that shit."

"You're right," I said. "I am. I'm kidding."

The nail bobbed up and down. "Hundred's not much."

"I'll pay three hundred."

"Get out of here, three hundred?"

"Sure. What's your name?"

"Everyone call me Helmo." He smiled with sly pride. "You know, the hair and all."

I nodded. "Okay, Helmo."

"Who are you?"

"Who cares who I am?"

Helmo made scissor fingers and took the slip of paper from me. "Yeah, who cares?"

There was at least a chance that Jay had driven to his new building, so I got off the train at the City Hall stop and walked down Reade Street, past the Mexican guys cutting flowers in the Korean delis, past the delivery trucks and battered cabs. When I got to the building I looked for Jay's truck. Nothing. But a couple of windows were lit in the building. I rang the various doorbells until someone buzzed the main door. Inside I saw new menus and fliers on the floor, as well as a garbage can filled with plaster bits, lathing, trash. Had Jay already started some renovation? The more I thought about him, the stranger he seemed. He'd just bought a three-million-dollar building and here he was whacking baseballs in Brooklyn? A guy with a girlfriend named O and who attended basketball games at a private girls' school? I checked the door to the basement, which was locked, then headed up the high, steep stairs, hoping Jay might somehow be in one of the offices, still in his sweaty baseball clothes. I knocked on the various doors but got no response.

On my way down, the door to RetroTech opened, and David Cowles poked his big head out. "You ring downstairs?"

"I did, yes."

"It's Bill, right?"

"Bill Wyeth."

He said, "I was wondering whom I'd let in."

"Just me. I'm looking for Jay."

Cowles had one eye on a computer screen. "Haven't seen him."

"Has he been around?"

"Yes, in fact he was earlier and we discussed—oh, hell, hold on, that's the phone. Here, come on in while I get that." I followed Cowles back toward his office and when I got there he was standing at the window.

"That's good," he said into the receiver. "All the way through?" He listened and nodded. "Sure, all right." He covered the phone. "This will just take a second, Mr. Wyeth, bear with me. Just here—have a seat. My daughter wants to—" He uncovered the phone. "Yes, yes, okay, I'm putting it on, go ahead."

Then he turned on the speakerphone and I could hear a piano, some sweet and romantic sonata trilling into the room. I might have said it was Beethoven's "Für Elise," but the sound through the phone was poor, as was the quality of the performance. But Cowles was enjoying it, smiling and looking at the phone and nodding his head with the music. Then the playing stopped. "Good, good!" he called heartily, in the way of an encouraging father.

"You liked it?" came a girl's voice. "I only messed up once."

Cowles smiled at me. "Very good, but keep practicing."

"Daddy, I practiced it five times already!"

"How many times did you get it right all the way through?"

"None."

"Do you want to mess it up tomorrow night?"

"No! What do you think?"

"I think you should keep practicing, sweetie."

"Daddy! You're so *mean*."

"It's true," said Cowles affectionately. "Nothing you can do."

"*Daddy!*"

"I have someone in my office, Sally, so I'm going to have to go."

"A pianist," I said after he'd hung up.

"Well, *hardly*. But she likes to play, and she's got a little recital at the Steinway store."

"The Steinway store?"

"On Fifty-seventh Street? Have you ever been? Amazing pianos! Dozens of them. Ebony, mahogany, everything. Even one of John Lennon's. You're not supposed to touch it but everyone does. They have student recitals there, and of course they don't mind if you *buy* a piano while you're there. It's quite the setting."

I nodded but wondered if I should tell him that Jay had gone to his daughter's basketball game. He'd ask me what it meant, and I couldn't tell him. But why hadn't I seen Cowles at the game? Of course, he might have been busy, or his wife could have been in attendance and I wouldn't have known.

"Now then," Cowles said, "you were looking for Mr. Rainey?"

"Have you seen him?"

"He was in this morning. About the lease?"

I searched his face. "The lease?"

"My lease? He said you and I'd go over it the next day or so?"

I made a vague sound of recognition.

"He offered me a better rate."

"He did?"

"I agreed to lengthen the lease, which he wanted, but I got him to bring the rent down a bit—only fair, in this climate."

"Was he accommodating?"

Cowles smiled. "For a rapacious landlord, yes. He seems—is he new to all this?"

"Why do you ask?"

Cowles let his eyes drift over his family pictures and out the window to the rooftops of lower Manhattan. "A sense, that's all."

A minute later, I stepped back out into the street. The cold cloak of evening had dropped. The prudent thing would have been to go home, order in dinner, and write down all I'd learned. Worship Chronos a bit. I used to be pretty good with complex problems but now I was stumped. Too many shards of information. Martha Hallock had handled the real estate transaction between Jay and Marceno, to the dismay of her own business partner. She'd probably lied to Marceno to clinch the deal. She knew a lot about Jay. There'd been an accident. Poppy was her nephew. How did these things connect? Mrs. Jones had described me so well I'd been successfully recognized. Or maybe they had a photo of me. Allison Sparks didn't mind snooping into a man's private business. And didn't mind telling me that, either. What else? Jay hung out in Brooklyn and probably dated a woman named O. He had some kind of weird drug habit that involved inhaled adrenaline. His occasional girlfriend, Allison Sparks, didn't mind getting kissed by an unemployed lawyer who'd been forced to watch some world-class fellatio the night before. She didn't mind having his tongue shoved down her throat and she didn't mind telling him that she'd liked it. Watching the fellatio had probably made him more aggressive, too. Under the momentary behaviors rose the hungers, the looming desires. Jay wanting to kill the baseball, Martha Hallock waiting bitterly for death, Helmo willing to spy on Jay for a few bucks, Allison needing satisfaction. You could drive yourself nuts with these things. Cowles's daughter played the piano. Jay had lowered Cowles's rent, presumably to keep him in the building. Marceno was waiting for his information. H.J. was waiting for his money. Both expected me to get these things for them, both had made their threats well known. What else? What other pieces could I torment myself with? Ha, Allison had basically conceded, controlled the Havana Room—which would be open that night.

Yes, she'd told me that, in her alluring drunkenness. The Havana Room would be open that night. And I was invited.

six

ANOTHER NIGHT IN THE CITY. Showered and shaved, wallet full of cash. How good can you look, pal? Best shoes, best suit, killer silk tie. Worried H.J.'s men had discovered where I lived. You never knew, until you knew for sure. A quick look up and down the street. Then dart past the gold lettering and potted evergreens, through the heavy door. Immediately, the smell of steak. Then Table 17, as always. Hanger steak, as always. Oil paintings and table linen. No Allison yet. Mexican busboys sailing through the room with steaming trays. Worried about Jay, yes. Determined to have a good time, yes. The joint was topped-off full, an ocean liner of steak-eaters, a fleshatorium. Action upstairs in the private rooms, judging from the lipstick and aftershave heading up the stairs, action at the bar, crossing its legs, checking its watch, shooting its cuffs. I looked around, wondering which of the other men would be heading into the Havana Room. And then there was Allison, coming out of the kitchen, eyes right on me, tongue peeking from the corner of the mouth I'd kissed six hours before, marching toward me in a red satiny dress, which showed me more than I'd seen before. Knees, cleavage, firm attitude. She looked good, Allison, and she knew it as she bent close to my ear.

"Bill!" she whispered. "I'm *shocked*."

"Why?"

"You took advantage of me!"

"Might have been the other way around," I said.

Allison looked at me fixedly, thoughts kept in reserve, so close that I could see the mascara on her eyelashes, and I didn't know if she regretted the interlude earlier that day. "Midnight," she said. "Door opens at midnight."

I was there on the dot, of course, stepping casually down the stairs and over the tiled floor to the far booth where I'd sat before, wall sconce and painting next to me. Other men followed and I thought I recognized several from the last time I'd been in the room when it was full, including the two large fellows who'd been examining a set of X rays. My eyes drifted toward the enormous black-eyed nude over the bar. The ancient bartender beneath her, his white hair fuzzed to dissipation, took no notice as he set out drafts and highballs and drinks neat and on the rocks and in shot glasses and the last one tonight, I promise. Within ten minutes, two dozen men had arrived, filling the booths and the barstools.

At that moment the aging literary gentleman I'd seen before came lurching in. Somehow he seemed always to know when the room was open. In his suit and greatcoat he was a pile of elegant ruin, but that night's dosing of booze had torn away his mask of droll amusement at the hopeless strivings of men and revealed something more sinister, more hatefully despairing. He reached out and held my arm, tightly.

"I'ma get in here, I'ma see what's going on."

"And what do you think—?"

"I'ma investigate—" But at that he tilted sideways. "It can't be true, just not possible!" He stumbled about and I steadied him, only to confront a leering face whose brows seemed arched in perpetual humor but whose eyes belied unfathomable despair. "You, mister, don't you *know* what they're doing in here, donya *see*—is absolutely the final, the last—"

The maître d' arrived with three busboys, and the man was taken away.

A minute later Allison appeared, having brushed her hair and put on a bit more lipstick.

"Gentlemen," she announced loudly, settling the room, "this is the moment when we explain the Havana Room to new attenders—there are a few tonight—so I am going to go through my entire presentation, which only takes a minute, and then we'll close the door. Good to see so many of you could make it." She nodded at several men—nodded at them in particular, it seemed—and I felt a shot of jealousy.

At that moment the beautiful black woman I'd seen before entered with her blue suitcase. She shrugged off a long winter coat and hung it behind the bar. She was dressed in a frilly cocktail dress with subtle golden epaulets on the shoulders and matching oversized buttons, a getup somewhat theatrical, I realized. She opened the blue suitcase and lifted out a golden tray with two silken straps attached at the sides. These she lifted over her shoulder, raising the tray in front of her like an old-time cigarette girl.

Allison followed her progress, turned back to the men, and began again. "As you may know, the Havana Room has been open continuously for more than one hundred and fifty years, including as a speakeasy, a betting parlor, and even, for a year in the thirties, as an opium den. These nefarious uses would seem more or less obligatory, given its sunken and protected setting, and the fact that there's only one door in. Anything less unsavory would be a bit of a disappointment, don't you think?" The men smiled, happy to feel themselves included in the city's long history of vice and lawlessness. "In more recent years," Allison continued, "it's mostly served as a spare bar for this marvelous restaurant of ours. And except for the routine intrusions of law enforcement, operation of the Havana Room in one form or another has been interrupted only *three times* in the last century. I know the dates, too. November 23, 1963, the day after the assassination of John F. Kennedy, and then for two days during the 1977 power blackout in New York City, and for a week following the attack on the World Trade Center. And you, gentlemen"— here Allison smiled at the obviously memorized nature of her speech— "are not the only illustrious patrons of this room. We know that souls who have sat in these very booths include Ulysses S. Grant, "Boss" Tweed, and Babe Ruth. Yes, after he was traded by the Boston Red Sox. We know that Charles Dickens was taken here on one of his celebrated visits to

New York City. Mark Twain ate upstairs and was invited downstairs but declined. It was in this room that Franklin Delano Roosevelt first discussed running for governor of New York in 1927. It was also in this room that the details of one of the Joe Lewis title bouts in the old Madison Square Garden were finalized. What else? Billie Holiday met one of her male pals here, and they argued, it is said. Oh, and Eisenhower visited here before he was elevated to power during World War II. The room was opened especially for Jacqueline Kennedy Onassis one morning in the 1980s, when she became faint outside."

"What about Elvis?" came a voice. "I heard that he—"

"Yes, that's true. Elvis rented the room in the 1970s after performing at Madison Square Garden only a few blocks away. I could go on and on, gentlemen, but you get the idea. We are proud of the history of the Havana Room, especially its appeal to important and successful men like yourselves."

The beautiful black cigarette girl, if that's what she was, had now started at the far end of the room, presenting her tray to the men.

"Now then," continued Allison, drawing a breath, hands clasped before her, the model of poise, "we know that our clientele lead busy and harried lives, and so what we offer here is a respite from that. Plain and simple, gentlemen. In a moment or two we will lock the door for no more than sixty minutes. You will be sealed in. Quite comfortably, I might add. We have a full bar menu available. Lastly, please note that all our cigars are, of course, Cuban, and are complimentary. We have the very best brands: Cohiba, Montecristo, Excalibur, all of them. Your waiter is knowledgeable, should you need some help with your choice. And yes, you are allowed, encouraged, and *invited* to smoke here, despite the draconian antismoking laws enforced by the city, which we have managed to elude by way of metaphysical semantics. We hope that you enjoy your brief time in the Havana Room."

I could feel Allison pulling the room of men along a slow logical track, drawing us into an altered frame of reference—changing the rules of perception, perhaps. I didn't mind that she hadn't looked directly at me, for I could feel myself staring in wonderment.

"We do ask that you not discuss the Havana Room outside its confines, for entry is strictly by invitation only, at the discretion of management. This is to ensure an elite clientele and high level of service. Prior to the opening of the doors, Shantelle, our cigarette goddess"—Allison threw a quick glance at Shantelle, who smiled mysteriously—"will come around a second time with a selection of goodies. I'm afraid that she is not one of them. Should you be interested in their purchase, they may be put on your bill but will not be itemized or described in any way. Please enjoy your time with us tonight. Thank you."

And with that the men dropped their heads into momentary conversation. Now Ha entered the room, went behind the bar, and pushed a wheeled glass tank under the bridge and forward into the room. Whereas before I'd always seen him in work clothes, he was dressed in a crisp white uniform and carried a small stainless steel case. A number of the men watched him with curiosity. He whispered something to Allison, then stood back. Meanwhile, Shantelle had set down her tray and stacked a set of porcelain plates on the bar behind Ha.

"Gentlemen!" called Allison. "It looks like we're ready. All right then?" She waited until the room quieted and she had every man's attention. "Each of you is cultured and well traveled, and many of you know of the Japanese fugu fish, a delicacy in Tokyo and rumored to be actually served at one or two places here in New York. The fugu fish, for those who don't know, is famous for being dangerous to eat, if not served by a chef trained in its preparation. Trained ten years, I might add." She smiled playfully. "The next part is a little hard. Let's see if I can get it, okay? The fugu fish is from the family called Tetraondontidae, class Osteichthyes, and order Tetradontiformes. Also known as the puffer fish or globefish or swellfish. Usually it's eaten raw, and when it's prepared in Japan correctly, the diner receives a buzzy, numb feeling around the lips and an interesting light-headedness. If prepared incorrectly, the fish, eaten in significant quantities, will kill you." She nodded vigorously. "Yes, and rather quickly, depending on how much poison you ingest. In Japan, fifty or sixty people die each year from fugu poisoning. The most poisonous parts include the liver, skin, muscles, and the ovaries. These sections of the fish are rich in tetrodotoxin, the principal poison, which is perhaps a thousand times more deadly than cyanide. Tetrodotoxin is heat-stable, so cooking the fish does not make it safer to eat. The lethal dose for an adult would fit on the head of a pin, perhaps one to two milligrams."

"How does it work?" came a voice from the room.

"I'm not a doctor," said Allison, "but my understanding is that the poison blocks the sodium channels in nerve tissue. That means nerves can't fire, can't make muscles contract. There's paralysis, the degrees of which we'll get to in a minute. But full-blown poisoning means respiratory arrest, cardiac dysfunction, central nervous system failure, that kind of thing."

"Do you have the antidote on hand?"

"No."

"Why not?"

"There is none." While the room absorbed this difficult fact, Allison paused, nodded at Ha, then went on. "Where was I? Oh, the deaths. Yes, indeed in the last few decades there've been many hundreds of documented deaths, the great majority of them in Japan. The fish's attraction has always been the genuine chance that it might be one's last meal." She smiled dangerously. "The fugu fish has been generally banned from time to time throughout history, and specifically banned for certain populations at other times. To this day, it remains the only delicacy which cannot, by law, be served to the Japanese emperor and his family."

"I don't see the attraction," muttered someone.

"Oh, I do," came another voice.

"The taste is said to be enslaving," Allison responded. "But beyond the taste there does appear to be a desire in human beings to taste that which is prohibited them." She studied the men before her, as if to see if they possessed such an impulse. "While we appreciate that some people enjoy the Japanese fugu fish, it seems a somewhat tame entertainment, not *particularly* provocative, not particularly *interesting*. It has not caught on here in New York City, and maybe that reflects the genuine scarcity of the fish and the chefs who can prepare it, or it may reflect the fact that New Yorkers are inured to certain dangers, the *regular* dangers, if you will, and are not compelled by the idea of paying four hundred dollars for a piece of fish that may just cause only a little numbness around the mouth."

She paused, and in this interlude each man appeared to privately assess what might represent the regular dangers of life in the city, and whether he had, in fact, become inured to them. No one protested Allison's description, and in this there seemed to be a collective acknowledgment that she was right, and that, moreover, the burden of the usual dangers was itself tiresome and might require diversion.

"When people think of the most dangerous fugu," Allison resumed, "they usually refer to the torafugu, which is caught off the coast of Korea in the winter. But what is not known by many people is that there are more than three hundred varieties of the fugu, with the one served in Japan the most common. Also not generally known is that the delicacy is originally from China, as are many of the fish in the fugu family. In fact the dish has only been eaten in Japan for the last few hundred years, whereas in China the fugu, both in forms still alive and others now extinct, have been eaten for almost three *thousand* years. So, when I said we were interested in history here in the Havana Room, I didn't just mean good old Franklin Roosevelt and his pince-nez."

She waited and swept her eyes across the room. Several men were leaning forward attentively. "Of those three-hundred-odd varieties of the fugu, there is one very rare variety, the Shao-tzou, which comes from the Jiangsu region of China. It's pronounced *show-zoo*." Allison stepped next to the tank that Ha had wheeled out and gazed down into it. "For the last twenty years," she continued, "this fish was understood to be so rare—if not outright extinct—that the occasional specimen never made it out of Jiangsu. This despite the famous willingness of the Japanese to pay nearly any price for a prized fish." Allison looked up. "But somehow Ha discovered a source—a story you'll hear in a moment. Even so, the fish is exceedingly rare and exceptionally expensive. It must be delivered live to the cook, and you can imagine the difficulty of getting living fish from some muddy riverbed in China to this room in New York City. We have a standing order with our supplier, but we never quite know when we'll get a fish. Generally we're able to procure only one or two per month, sometimes none, and when we *do* get a fish, we immediately schedule the event you are about to witness and perhaps participate in." Allison smiled at me directly, and I wondered if she pushed her jaw outward at me ever so subtly in playful aggression. But then she blinked and resumed her presentation. "This month we've been lucky—I think we've gotten two. The Shao-tzou is also only seasonally available, only dependably caught five months out of the year, when it moves in from deeper waters to feed and spawn off the coast of Jiangsu. Sometimes the fish arrive dead or so damaged as to be useless. The cost is close to two thousand dollars wholesale for one fish. I know that's surprising, especially when you consider that the number of culinarily acceptable portions per fish is only two, three, or four. And never more than that. Once above a certain size the flesh of the Shao-tzou becomes almost inedible and the toxins too concentrated to be safe at any dose. But the cost and trouble are worth it, gentlemen. Because to compare the Shao-tzou with regular fugu fish is like—well, it's like comparing one of our Texan long-horn steaks to a burger at McDonald's. There *is* no comparison. Both are extremely dangerous, but the effects are different and various."

Ha now wheeled a butcher-block table forward. A white dinner napkin covered whatever lay on the table. He appeared more erect and dignified than when I'd seen him earlier.

Allison looked about the room. "Any questions so far?"

"I'd like to know what the fish does to you if you actually dare eat it," called a man.

Allison nodded in anticipation of this question. "There are a number of effects, but only one that interests us."

"Which is?"

"Paralytic euphoria."

"What?"

She spoke more slowly this time. "Paralytic euphoria. For a short period of time, less than five minutes, the diner is rendered nearly paralyzed—he can breathe and blink his eyes but not much more—and yet he feels euphoric. It's the very inability to move that intensifies the pleasure."

The room fell silent as the men weighed the probability that Allison's statements were true. Given her poise and intelligence and forthright presentation, they well might be. But if such statements were true, the men seemed to ask themselves privately, what did that mean? How might such an altered state compare to the remembered effects of the various opiates, amphetamines, psychotropics, stimulants, antidepressants, or hallucinogens they might or might not have ingested over the years? Allison said nothing in these long seconds. It appeared that, as the roomful of men shuffled through what was, if taken as a whole, no doubt a voluminous drug-taking experience, there were many remembered experiences that might have been called euphoric, and even a few in which a near-paralytic state was achieved, but there were none that could be recalled as both paralytic *and* euphoric, and so the period of individual contemplation recombined to a collective mood of curiosity.

"Is it *sexual* euphoria?" came a voice. Some laughter followed, most of it worried.

"This is always asked," said Allison solemnly, somewhat like a clinician responding to an overly earnest patient. "My answer is that different diners explain their experience differently, but they do seem to suggest a general effect, a *universal* pleasure." Her eyebrows shot up. "However, I confess I have read accounts that claim that the testes of the fish, if served in hot sake, is an aphrodisiac."

This information seemed unnerving, at best, for none of us knew if it was true, few of us wanted it to be false, and everyone now had to reconsider the notion of paralytic sexual euphoria, a concept that seemed as paradoxical as it did tantalizing. Yet Allison would not indulge further speculation. She shook her head coyly and said, "Chinese culture makes many such claims—for deer, bulls, bears, all sorts of creatures. But we're not interested in wishful thinking. And anyway, we're seeking high *art* here, gentlemen, not low sensationalism."

"Oh, stop that," came a voice again.

"Besides, we don't even know what sex this fish is, assuming it's not obviously pregnant. Ha, isn't that right? Can you tell by just looking?"

He shook his head. "Very messy to find out."

A general murmur followed. The room was becoming impatient. "Gentlemen," Allison called loudly, "there's more I need to tell you. Please listen closely to what follows."

The room quieted.

"Those of you with better short-term memories will recall what I said earlier—that compared to eating regular fugu fish the effects of eating Shao-tzou are different and various. The Shao-tzou offers three recipes for pleasure. The Chinese translation of these are Sun, Moon, and Stars. This is where the skill of the chef is paramount, gentlemen. The Sun effect involves more toxin from the fish's kidneys, the Moon involves more from the liver, and the Stars more from the brain. Now then, what does that mean? With the Sun portion, the diner remains nearly paralyzed and senses great heat, waves of it moving up and down the spinal column. The Moon portion is said to involve a perception of darkness interrupted by a moving luminescence, almost like a moon rising and falling in the night. And the Stars portion, which is always served last, involves a feeling of soaring, spinning, and tumbling, a kind of uncontrolled flying, which probably reflects some kind of disturbance to the nerves traveling from the inner ear to the brain.

"I know this sounds wonderful. It *is*. But I need to tell you a few more things. We only allow our diners one portion of this fish, ever. I keep a list of the names, in fact. There are two reasons. The first is that the toxins have differential rates of clearance from the body, depending on the health and age of the man who has eaten it, especially from the liver. Many of you are in your forties and fifties, and despite the fact—or indeed, *because*—you are, as one and as a whole, successful and charming and sexy and terrific, your livers are not what they used to be. Many of you are taking cholesterol medication, blood pressure pills, and so on, to say nothing of whatever drinking you might be doing."

"Don't say nothing of it," replied one wit, "it's the drinking that keeps me alive."

"And that's what we want to do, too," replied Allison, not missing a beat. "Short of an enzyme liver test, we are in no position to be able to know how fast or slow your liver clears the poison that you might so happily send it. If you ate the fish again, even a few weeks later, it is possible that the disease would cause permanent damage or death. And that we do not want."

"You said there were two reasons. What's the other one?"

Allison nodded. "The other reason is that it is said that eating the Shao-tzou fish is, or can be, for certain individuals, highly addictive. You may remember I used the word *enslaving* earlier."

"Addicted to fish?"

"Addicted either physically to the concentrations of the chemical or psychologically to the experience it creates."

"Which is what, again, exactly?"

"Hard to be exact. Patrons describing the experience say they undergo almost complete paralysis, as I said, and within their euphoria, a heightened consciousness of all things—light, sound, the air against their skin. They feel dead yet paradoxically, and exquisitely, alive. Most diners say this—that they felt both alive and dead *simultaneously*. This seems to be, in retrospect, a very valuable experience for them. A few pass out and wake up with a headache that lasts well into the next day. That could happen to any of you. But those who have a peak experience usually want to repeat it. The problem with being addicted to the fish is that if it doesn't kill you slowly, then it might kill you instantly. Historically, people have been known to eat too large a portion in hopes that the effect will be greater. And it is—they die. There are stories in Chinese literature of nobles stealing each other's portion and falling over dead. Okay, so that's my introduction. It always goes longer than I expect. Now, I'd like to introduce our chef, Mr. Ha, and let him tell you about himself. He will explain how he came to us here in the Havana Room, and then I will come back and say a few things, and then we may begin. Gentlemen, please pay close attention to everything that Mr. Ha has to say."

Ha stepped forward and bowed his head respectfully. I sensed among the men an irritation at this further delay.

"Good evenings every-body. My name is yes, Mr. Ha." He smiled nervously. "I know that sounds like the joke. Ha-ha. Like that. I am from China. I have live here about ten year, so I am not exactly American citizen. But I am very happy here, working for Miss Allison. Now I tell you a story. Before I come to America I live in China all my life and for many of those year I was working for Chinese government. Technically I am working for the People's Republic Army, but that is government in China. I am from the Jiangsu region of China. I was trained in the Jiangsu

Institute of Cooking in 1965 and 1966. At this time I go to work in Mao's kitchen in Beijing. My title is deputy assistant inspector of fish. I am learning then everything we know about fish. We learn how to make fish for the diplomats from Soviet Union and North Korea and Cuba. In 1971 I am getting my star chef's hat, so I am official chef of the Chinese government. I am thirty-eight years old. I study Shao-tzou fish. Chairman Mao like this fish. Even though he become very old, he try to have this fish once a month. Mao very careful with this fish. We never make mistake. We clean fish knife after every slice in seawater and vinegar. Then dry in sun every morning. We do it Japanese style, *sashi*, or *chiri*, *kara-age*, you know, deep-fry, even *hire-zake*, very dangerous put fish into hot sake because alcohol make poison travel fast. Also we cook Chinese style in rice and soup. I am very proud doing this for my country. Chairman Mao like my fish very much, say many nice thing to Ha. At this time I remember when Nixon come to China. We joke that we give him Shao-tzou, make him so happy he must die. But that was big joke of course. Mr. Kissinger, everybody say too much trick.

"Then many big thing happen in China. Mao, he die in 1976, China start to change, People's Republic Army change, too, and soon, I am not chef, I am put in office to cook food for factory in small city in western China called Hua Xing, where air is bad because of nickel smelter. I am sent to this city and my children and my wife, they must come and they get dysentery and sad to say now they die. I am a sad man because my children die and my wife has die and I have no good heart. I lost my heart. I spend too much time watching bird, sleep too much in park even though I have good bed. Then I am getting older and I am tired of China. Maybe I am not so old yet but I feel old. Then Deng Xiaoping come to power and I do not know what China is. I know Communism did not work too good but I also do not know new China. So I come to United States, I do not want to say, okay, I come to this country illegally, that is all I say. I never think I am chef again. I come work for Miss Allison. Sweep, fix electric wire, do that. All this big beef is new to me! I never see it before. We do not have this kind of big beef in China at that time. Only some water buffalo. But I say to Allison I know how to cut the fish if she want me to do it. I show her how fillet is done in China and she like this. But I do not have license to be a chef. Then sometime maybe last year I am in Chinatown buying fish for her. I am looking at Chinese fish all frozen. Big bucket, too dirty. Dead fish and dead crabs. No good for you. Fresh fish best. But I see in the dead fish a Shao-tzou. I say it cannot be, I must make mistake. So many year. Shao-tzou very, very hard to find, even in China! Mostly find in rivers. Ugly fish. Shao-tzou mean little pig. But in New York City everything come to city, even funny people I never see before! So why not Shao-tzou fish? Little-pig fish. So, okay, you know, I buy the fish. I think it was three-dollar seventy-five cent even if it is dead. They do not know what fish it is. The woman say she never have see it before. Outside she is Chinese but inside American. Too long in United State. I take little-pig fish to my home and I take very good photograph and I put it in freezer here. Allison not know." He looked at Allison in embarrassment.

She waved her hand, a flourish of indulgence.

"So I hide fish in freezer with my name on little paper in case they find it. Then I go to library with my photograph of fish and they have very big book on every fish in the world. So I find Shao-tzou fish, I look it up, I see picture in book, I see picture in my hand. Same eye. Same gill. Same mouth. I pay for high-quality Xerox copy. I am a little bit happy, a little feel funny. Why does this fish swim to me now?"

Ha looked down at the butcher-block table, took one corner of the white napkin, and lifted it, revealing an array of gleaming knives. He gazed up again. "Then the big French cook here find the fish I put in freezer. He tell Allison. He is very mad at Ha. I am just man who clean up. I say it is no big deal, a little mistake I make. Allison very busy lady, she is not interested in frozen fish belong to old Chinese man. But I go back to Chinatown fish dealer and I show picture. I say can you get me some of this fish and they say let us see picture and we tell you. They send me little paper one month later. They say yes. I say how much. They say if dead, then one hundred and forty dollar, maybe more. Fish is very hard to catch. I say the first time it cost three dollar, seventy-five cent. They say that was big mistake. They say if I want fish alive I pay maybe two thousand dollar. Very expensive for fish to live on airplane. More than for me or you. So I say send me dead fish, biggest one. They send me fish. Cost me two hundred and sixty dollar, because they lie so much to me. But I don't care. I want to see if I can cut it up, if I remember from Jiangsu Institute of Cooking. I get fish downtown. It is big. Somebody has tear off fin. But I take it and I put it in big beef freezer. This time I get good fish knife."

He held up one of the knives. Curved, thin, maybe fourteen inches long. "I let fish get soft and cut up. Allison find me and I say it is nothing just a mistake I am very sorry. But she say why you freezing these funny fish in my beefs? I tell her the story because I like Miss Allison too much. Maybe like you, heh. She says can you cook the frozen fish and make it do funny thing like fugu fish. I say no, only live fish, frozen no good. So she say get live fish, we will see. She will pay. I say fish is two thousand dollar and she says we will pay, get fish. I say I do not know if it good idea—"

"But of course I was *curious*, gentlemen, very curious," Allison interrupted. "More curious than I have been about *many* things." And what those things were would be left to our imaginations, her expression said. "When I saw Ha handling the live fish, preparing it, I realized how unusual he was! How skilled! As I said before, there are *maybe* one or two Japanese restaurants in this entire city that serve fugu, but no one, and I mean *no one*, serves Chinese Shao-tzou fish. The fish itself may be illegal. Well, yes, it is, technically. But, as I say, I was curious—"

"I am ready," Ha said.

"Gentlemen, if anyone would like to leave now, please feel free. We only want you to stay if you feel comfortable." She looked around. "Everyone is staying? Very good." She nodded at Shantelle, who disappeared up the stairs to close the door.

"Now, a few more words before we begin. This is how the evening works. Ha will kill the fish, clean it, examine it, and then he will tell me how many Sun, Moon, and Stars portions he has. He will have at least one of each. Sometimes he will have an extra Sun or Moon. But only sometimes, depending on the individual fish. The order always goes Sun, Moon, Stars. Those of you who are interested in a certain portion may bid using the slate paddles that Shantelle will provide. Please write your bid with the chalk she will give you, and hold it up. Write in large numerals please. Those of you who are not bidding are asked to remain silent. There is only one round of bidding per portion, which means it's blind bidding, understand? One bid only—except for the last portion, which I will auction off like a conventional live auction, in which bidders bid against each other. Once your bid is accepted, you make a credit card payment. No tipping or gratuity is necessary. As I said earlier, the billing to your card will be the same as any other billing here at the restaurant. It will not say Havana Room, or Shao-tzou fish, or anything else unusual. There's complete confidentiality."

She looked at Ha. He was stirring the water in the fish tank, and a tail slapped the surface. He withdrew his hand, folded back his white sleeve, then pulled from beneath the tank a wide rectangular screen attached to a handle. This he dropped into one end of the tank.

"Okay, what else?" continued Allison. "There will be no splitting of portions between people, and if the diner inexplicably decides *not* to eat his portion, or part of his portion, then it will be thrown away. The fish will be killed and prepared in front of you, gentlemen, cut sushi style. You may use your hands or a fork or chopsticks, but in any case we suggest that you try to consume the entire portion within thirty seconds or so, for maximum effect."

"What do we do after we eat the fish?"

"Good question. Shantelle?"

Shantelle had retreated to the dark back corner, and now she whisked off a heavy blanket, revealing a luxurious, wide-armed leather chair. This she pushed forward into the square of light.

"Before you eat your portion, or certainly just after, we advise that you quickly sit in this very comfortable chair. You will lose most muscle control, and if you are seated, you will not fall or injure yourself. As I said, the total effect lasts only five minutes or so." She looked at her watch. "Let's get started. First, though, does anyone want to see the fish?"

We obligingly crept forward from our chairs and peered in the murky tank to see a brownish fish about twenty inches long, boxy, and scaleless, with a blunted, indistinct face. Its eyes were set high, and seemed oddly intelligent. The body of the fish was unappetizingly soft, its skin gluey, its dorsal fin and tail shredded. Not a fish built for speed or beauty, a bottom-feeder, a garbage fish. It lazily circled the perimeter of the tank, reversing direction, idling—a fish, I mused, without a country or an ocean or a future.

"Doesn't look like much," the fellow next to me whispered.

Back in our chairs, we watched Ha move the screen gently toward the other end of the tank, trapping the fish against its glass wall. There was a splash of water as the fish fought its imprisonment. Keeping pressure on the screen, Ha lifted a long gleaming pick and placed it above the fish. We waited.

"Must be just right," Ha muttered.

He stared into the water, and we saw him take a breath, hold it, then plunge the pick downward. Instantly he let go of the screen and lifted the pick and the wriggling, impaled fish into the air. The pick had gone straight down into the fish's nose, through its mouth, and out the bottom side. Ha inspected the fish. "Very healthy," he noted.

He nailed the fish onto his board, held its back with his other hand, drew a short knife, and quickly severed the fish's spinal column. "Now," he announced with the affability of a television show gourmet, "we make very good Shao-tzou fish."

He bent at the knees, hunched himself toward the fish. "First we see what you eat." He sliced open the belly and picked through some greenish-black gunk. "Maybe some crab, some clam. In China bad boy in my village feed cat meat sometime, when too many cat in the town you know. Very ugly fish. In China they call this fish 'river pig.'"

Working quickly, he removed the organs of the fish and dropped them into small blue ceramic bowls. Then he beheaded the fish, cut out the brain, and deposited it into another bowl. After each operation he dropped his knife into a wide bucket on the floor and withdrew from his gleaming array another identical one, so that the fluids of one part of the fish did not touch any from the others. With the organs and brain segregated, he dropped the remains of the head into another bucket, lifted up his board, wiped it, dropped the towel in the bucket, then flipped over the board. Now he quickly skinned the fish and filleted it.

Meanwhile Shantelle was passing through the room with sets of slate paddles and chalk. She handed each man one and I could see that most, like me, were torn between our desire to study Shantelle and our fascination with Ha's activities. Paddle in hand, I watched him lift the fillets onto a new cutting board, whisk the skin and backbone into the bucket, then remove the old larger cutting board completely.

"How many, Ha?" came Allison's voice.

He bent forward to examine his fillets, made an adjusting trim on one—the fleck of flesh flying instantly into the bucket—then checked the organs in their separate bowls. "I have just one Sun, just one Moon, and always just one Stars," he announced.

"Okay, this is the usual number. Those of you bidding on the Sun portion, please write down your sums," Allison instructed. "Remember, the Sun is a portion that involves great heat." She looked about the room. The men appeared tentative, not sure of what to do. But I saw several men leaning over their paddles.

"Please lift your bids . . . I see $75, that will not do, I see $100, that won't either, $50, you should be ashamed of yourself, sir, this fish came from the other side of the world, I see $250, yes, that's better, I'm ignoring the lesser bids, I see—you may drop your $100 bid, sir—I see $300, I see $600, *he's* the most motivated, clearly, $600, this will be the cheapest portion of the evening I guarantee you, $600, again, and that's it. Sold to the man in the green tie."

Instantly Shantelle was next to him, a balding man of about forty-five, indeed wearing a green tie, and he gave her a credit card.

"Please come forward."

Allison received him, and he stood before us, a bit embarrassed to be the first one, perhaps afraid to be revealed as a fool before the room. Shantelle returned with the credit card slip and a pen. She smiled helpfully as he signed. Ha, meanwhile, was preparing the portion of Shao-tzou sushi, his fingers patting and rolling rice and seaweed and tucking until the tiny delicacy was done.

"Do I get soy sauce?" the man joked.

"I'm afraid not."

"Okay, here I go." He picked up his sushi, held it before his mouth, looked at Ha, looked at Allison, then gently took it into his mouth. He chewed slowly and swallowed.

"How's it taste?" someone called.

"That is rather *good*," he said.

"Please," said Allison, leading him by the hand to the chair.

We studied him.

"I feel okay," he announced. "I feel really pretty normal."

Shantelle had collected the slate paddles from the unsuccessful bidders, erased them, and given them back.

"I'm—okay, okay—there . . . it's—" The first winning bidder gripped the arm of his chair, then tipped his head back. His fingers relaxed, his feet slipped forward, and he eased into the comfortable leather, his eyes still open but blank. He breathed deeply through his nose, as though appreciating a fine wine. Then his mouth sagged open, his eyelids heavy. His eyes fluttered closed, his face still tranquil, attentive to some far pleasure, as if he were listening to exquisitely drifting jazz.

"Is he sick?" asked a worried voice.

Allison held up a hand. "Wait."

The man in the green tie slackened further, his head lolling softly on his shoulder. The muscles around his eyes twitched, as did his lips. These movements suggested surprise and deep internal experience, the pleasurable awareness of light across a sleeping form. His face seemed to set itself within a coma of concentration, eager to receive as much sensation as possible. The fingers on both his hands quivered as if it was all too unbearably good, and he moaned indistinctly, the pleasure forcing its release through his mouth.

"For God's sake!" one of the men called. "Is he dying?"

The room remained hushed, the men looking back and forth at one another, uncertain whether to be worried or outraged or entertained. Allison followed her watch closely.

"This man looks ill!" came a protest. "I insist you call—!"

Allison held up a calm finger, following her watch. "One of the training elements for a Shao-tzou chef is to estimate body weight and size the portion accordingly. Mr. Ha is an *artist*, gentlemen, not a murderer. Please, have a little faith."

Half a minute more went by agonizingly, then the intensity of the man's pleasure began to subside, and we saw the gradual reassertion of consciousness. He blinked, lifted his head, coughed, focused, lost focus, blinked again, munched his mouth dryly, then sat up in his chair, recognizing the room and the rest of us.

"Oh," he said in a low, thoughtful voice. He sighed a noise of contentment. Then he noticed the expectant eyes upon him and nodded. "Yeah, it was unbelievable . . ."

He started to stand.

"Just wait a minute or so, sir," said Allison, gently pushing him back down in the chair. "Just let your body figure it all out."

He looked up at Allison and smiled coyly. "Can we do it again?"

"No," Allison said, rejecting his innuendo.

"Wait, you don't understand," he protested. "Just tell me what to pay! I'm good for it." Despite Allison's insistence, he rose unsteadily, but his halting steps seemed caused by his amazement as much as by any infirmity.

He was pacified by Shantelle and escorted to his seat.

"We have *two* more pieces of Shao-tzou fish," Allison announced. "Next we have the piece of Moon, with the blade wipe coming from the liver. Write your bids, please. Let me remind you that the winning bid in the last round was a mere $600."

This time more men hunched over their slates and I could see a few of them look up, study the other men, then erase whatever had been on the slate and write another figure.

"Bids please," Allison said loudly. "Get the paddles up. Here we go. I see $800, $900, $2,000, $1,000 is it? Yes, very nice, the highest so far is $2,000, please, sir, don't change your bid, ah! $3,316, quite an odd bid, I think we have a winner at $3,316."

This time a younger, heavyset man in a blazer came forward, sporty and confident. He nodded back to the men, stepped forward to Ha, grabbed the piece of sushi, pivoted, faced us, and pushed the whole thing in his mouth.

"No hesitation there," Allison narrated.

He swallowed and stepped forward to the chair.

"Do you have anything to say to us?" Allison inquired. "Any chit or chat?"

"No," he said quietly.

He closed his eyes and tilted his head back. Allison stepped toward him, adjusted his head forward and sideways, then turned to the group. "What you're seeing here is *art*, gentleman. Mr. Ha's art. The poison in the Shao-tzou is so deadly that even a sliver more of the flesh or an accidentally large wipe through the organ—in this case the liver—would kill. But Mr. Ha is a master."

Ha nodded ever so subtly, then inspected one of his knives. Meanwhile the heavyset man in the chair slumped to one side, face slack, his mouth almost closed, a thin line of saliva dripping down one side of his chin. His lips trembled softly, as if privately repeating a liturgy of devotion. This time the group watched with less trepidation. Several men, I saw, timed the process themselves, looking up at the man in the chair and then at their watches. He continued his private prayer, which deteriorated into speechless puffs, a panting of gratification that became winded breathing even as his eyebrows arched upward in appreciation. We were transfixed. No one doubted his transport to realms of unknown sweetness.

And then, just as it crested, that sweetness fell back, fell away, and his legs stilled and his eyebrows dropped. He began to come out of it. He began to remember that he was alive, and opened his eyes in full consciousness, respiration almost normal, his color good.

"Well?" inquired Allison, on behalf of the rest of us.

"Oh God, the light just came up like a giant moon . . ." He turned toward Ha and shot out his arm. "You are a *rock star*, man!" He rose to his feet, pumped the air once or twice, then fell back heavily. "All the time I'm seeing the surface of death, man, the rolling surface of bones or the *moon* or something, just beaming this white death light that feels so good and I can't *move*, man."

He started to stand again, fell back into his seat, then stood successfully. He staggered toward Ha. "Hey man, just make me a *little one* of those, just take some of that stuff you threw away in the bucket, look, look! You got *plenty* of that brown stuff to wipe on there—"

"Excuse me, excuse me!" cried Ha. He brandished the knife. "No, no! You cannot have this fish!"

The young man held up his hands, backed away. "Okay! Right. *Sorry*. I just, let me just congratulate you, you are the artist, the—"

"Bids please, gentlemen," Allison called over him. "We have just *one* portion left, the Stars. The winning bid last time was thirty-three hundred and something dollars. *One* more portion left, everyone, just one, and it may be weeks again, months even, before we can find another Shao-tzou."

Allison reminded the men that it was open bidding, multiple bids accepted, highest bid wins. "Just like Sotheby's," she added. The bids began at $3,400 and three rounds later reached $6,050, two men bidding against each other from either side of the room. The counterbid increments dropped from five hundred dollars to one hundred to fifty until one of the men shook his head in disgust at a bid of $6,750 and gave up. The successful bidder dropped heavily into the chair, loosened his necktie, swigged a glass of water, checked his watch, which appeared to have cost only a little less than his piece of Chinese sushi, and tossed back the morsel.

"Here we go," he said, looking pleased with himself for displaying that he could spend almost seven thousand dollars for a bite of poisonous fish. I didn't like him, I confess, irritated that he was about to have a singular, expensive pleasure and I was not.

Almost a minute went by and the Stars winner looked at Allison in exasperation. "Nothing's happening here."

"Just wait," she said.

"I am. I did wait. I feel fine."

"Just a minute or so," Allison said.

We waited.

"It's a dud," the winner said. "I want my money back."

"Sometimes if you've had a heavy dinner, then—"

But she didn't need to finish. The Stars winner collapsed backward as if he'd caught a pillow filled with sand. His arms retained a sort of sleepwalker's rigidity. The effect of his portion seemed harsher, arriving not only late and not gradually but with a punitive force. Of the three men, this last one appeared to be the closest to pain. His feet paddled a bit, as if he was suffering in silence.

A minute went by; the man displayed none of the behaviors the first two men had showed, and I wondered if he was truly enjoying the experience. Then it seemed *too much* time had gone by. Allison checked her watch, the smile on her lips a little frozen, a little worried, I thought, and I caught her glancing quickly at Ha, who received her anxiety with a slow, reassuring blink. At that same moment the man's body lengthened rigidly in the chair, legs straight, arms at his side, his nervous system conducting a lightning bolt of ecstasy, and he lifted his face upward at some unseen spectacle and completely opened his mouth, issuing a kind of silent scream—most unnerving. And then the scream *came*—a lung-loud hollering that filled the room, a man yelling across a canyon, summoning all of nature's attention, calling the gods down from the sky.

"Holy *fuck*," another man whispered, weirded out.

At that, the man in the chair dropped silent and seized up into the fetal position, having birthed his experience out of himself, and began to wake groggily, apparently exhausted. Allison's posture softened and I saw her exhale.

"It wasn't stars," the man said, opening his eyes.

"No?" Allison came over to be sure he stayed in his seat.

"It was *fireworks*! Touching my face! I could feel them burning against my face. Three of them went right through me." He lifted his hands and examined his fingers, as if they might have been singed as well. "Swear to God. Burning. Right *through* me. Little cinders, sparks. One big one went right in my mouth and down through me, right out of my asshole." He addressed the other men. "I'm lying there, my body is dead and I can see these sparks, red little comets coming at me and going right through me. I'll never forget that. I mean, I've done acid and I've done lots of stuff, you know, but *nothing* like that."

"Was it pleasurable?"

He squinted one eye. "Completely. Total pleasure, yeah."

"And with that admission as to the absolute artistry of Mr. Ha," announced Allison triumphantly, sweeping her arms, "we are done, gentlemen! Those of you who did not have any fish are invited back, and those of you who did we wish well in the future. Remember, please, not to discuss what you saw tonight outside this room. As ever, I will be seeing many of you in the main dining room in the days and weeks to come. Thank you to Mr. Ha, and thank you to our lovely Shantelle. Good night!"

The room broke into polite but ambivalent applause and stayed hushed. The old waiter reappeared, followed by the bartender, and with the prospect of further drinking the room became louder, more relaxed. Several men lit their complimentary cigars. Like some of the others, I wasn't sure I believed what I'd seen, and I studied the faces of the first two men who'd eaten the fish as they described their experiences to the men close to them. I remembered the old literary man's claim that the demonstration was fraudulent, complete with ringers. Could he be right? Short of eating the fish myself, how could I be sure that the whole thing wasn't a charade?

Now the last eater of the fish stood, took a step, steadied himself, then walked to his seat. Shantelle took this opportunity to push the comfortable armchair to its dark corner and I did not mind seeing the back of her, her soft hips going left-right-left. I also did not mind that Allison caught me doing this. She came over and let her fingers fall on my shoulder with a certain proprietary design.

"Was it a good show?"

"Excellent."

"But I hear a tone in your voice."

"You do, yes."

Allison glanced around the room. She still had things to do. "So you may need further proof?"

I was about to answer but she left to talk with Ha as he cleaned up. He worked a bit more on the fish, it seemed, cut something out of it, dipped it in water, wrapped it in a piece of cabbage. I wanted to understand what he was doing and why Allison wanted to watch him, but I was distracted by the arrival of Shantelle next to me, whose golden tray, I saw at last, held a thoughtful selection of minute jars of caviar, premium tickets to Knicks games and Broadway shows, airline bottles of liquor, French cigarettes, ladies' wristwatches, combination condom/Viagra bubble packs, Swiss chocolate, untraceable telephone cards in prepaid amounts, gift certificates to Victoria's Secret in denominations of five hundred dollars, gold coins, and several baseballs signed by prominent members of the Yankees.

"You have Derek Jeter?" I asked, examining the balls.

"I think," came Shantelle's voice. She pointed. "Yes."

I picked the ball up, liking the way the leather felt in my hand. Jeter's signature was tight, not floridly excessive. The ball felt lucky to me, something my son would like. Yes—*something my son would like.* "This is authentic?"

"Oh yes," she purred. "They come through a very reputable dealer."

"I'll take it."

Which I did. The price was ridiculous, but not when measured against Timothy's happy surprise, if I could get the ball to him.

When I looked up again Ha was wiping the counter obsessively. He sprayed it with soap from a bottle, then wiped it again. Everything he touched, I saw, went into the green bucket. Knives, rags, bits of fish, pieces of rice ball, everything. Then he reached under the counter and pulled out a bag of charcoal briquettes. A barbecue? No. Ha ripped open the bag and dumped half of it into the green bucket, adding a bit of water. He took a common toilet plunger, thrashed the contents of the bucket, dropped the plunger in, took off his white coat and hat, dropped them in, followed by his plastic gloves and goggles, then sealed the top on the green container. This he then taped shut.

"Charcoal?" I called to Allison.

"It absorbs all the bad stuff," she explained. "He dumps it safely."

"Diluted by the New York City sewage system."

"Something like that."

"One poison among innumerable poisons?"

Allison nodded. "Like men."

"Men being innumerable or poisonous?"

"Both," she said. "Just like women."

She nodded goodbye to some of the patrons as they left. "Yes," she said to one, "I'll let you know the next time."

Now she came over and sat down across from me. "Well?"

"I don't believe it," I told her. "It's got to be a trick."

"It's not," Allison said. "The stuff works."

"I don't believe that for one minute."

"Oh, you do. You don't want to, but you *do*."

"Nah."

She shrugged. "Try it yourself then, prove me wrong."

"Thanks, but no."

"Afraid?"

"The stuff's poisonous."

"I thought you said you didn't believe it."

"I believe in the poison, but not the brain magic."

"You don't get the brain magic without the poison. If you believe in one, you believe in the other."

"Sorry," I told her.

"You really think it's a fake?"

"It could be a bunch of ringers. Or maybe those bidders were real but Ha did something to the fish, sprinkled LSD on it."

"It's real," Allison said right away.

"I'm just not convinced."

"What *are* you convinced by, then?"

"Other things. I find other things more convincing, Allison."

Allison sighed, pushed a finger along my collar. "Hey Bill?"

"Yes?"

"Can you convince yourself to get your coat and meet me outside?"

She was all over me in the cab, a leg thrown over mine, holding my cheeks in her gloved hands, and I lay back and enjoyed this—although not without worrying that H.J.'s men were somehow cruising along behind us, having waited for me outside. I could just about convince myself that they were capable of that, too. They'd grabbed me once, so maybe they'd grab me again.

Somewhere in the East Eighties Allison told the cabbie to make his turn, and a moment later we were walking through the lobby of her building; Allison's salutation to her uniformed doorman on his stool was as sharp and quick as a flung knife—and nearly had the same effect; his head slumped onto his chest and he said nothing. I was not, I knew, the first man to follow Allison across the marble chess squares of her lobby, but never would I hear that from her doorman.

Upstairs the elevator opened into an enormous apartment, deep as a tennis court.

"Wow, what a great—"

"I'll show you it in the morning," Allison interrupted. "Come *on.*"

So I did, following her directly to the bedroom. The bed was immense, large enough for three people. Allison stared at me, threw her purse on a chair, then took off her clothes. Shoes—flung over the carpet, dress—dropped in the chair, bra—a quick snap and her breasts were before me, panties—down past the knees, flicked away.

"Now you, mister."

In a moment I was naked as well and tasted the saltiness of her skin, her nipples in my mouth. It had been a painfully long time since I'd held a woman, any woman, and I felt grateful to Allison for giving herself to me, or taking me to her, so very grateful when she pushed me onto my back and sucked me with frank abandon. A moment later I was inside of her, and if I was not exactly heroic, then I was serviceable and of sufficient duration, and besides, Allison was easy—she took it in and made use of it for herself. Like mixing batter with a spoon. There is nothing like the velvety wetness of a woman, and my head swam with pleasure.

"Wait," Allison said suddenly. "Pull out a moment!"

"What?"

"It's okay. Hold your fire."

I rolled off of her in the darkness, baffled.

"I'll be right back, folks."

She grabbed something from her purse and ran into the bathroom. The light flashed on just before the door closed. I didn't know whether to be angry or hurt or amused. Then the door opened and Allison's naked shadow flew through the darkness right back into bed.

I wondered if I smelled something in her breath. "Everything okay?"

"A minor adjustment."

"Ah," I said as if I knew, trying to remember the obscure locations of certain forms of birth control.

"Okay," Allison purred, grabbing me. "Where were we?"

We started again and of course the interval created a new ascent of pleasure. I felt her hands pull me close to her, so hard her forehead bumped my nose. "Bill, if I act a little weird," Allison whispered in the dark, her lips against my neck, "just deal with it, okay? Take care of me, okay?"

"Okay." But I'd have said anything.

"Good," Allison breathed. She pulled me closer and suddenly bit my bottom lip so hard that it bled. "Now," she growled in a strange, panting whisper, a voice I'd never heard from her before, "now fuck me hard, go as long as you—"

I did. But it wasn't that long, a minute or two, perhaps, and then, when I was done, had roared my private roar, I understood that she lay limp in my arms.

"Allison?"

Her head dropped back, eyes unseeing—and I suffered a memory of Wilson Doan Jr.

Cold fright now. "Allison? Hey!"

I sat up. She lay collapsed on the bed, arms akimbo. I turned on the table lamp. She breathed slowly, eyes closed, twitching infrequently. I took her hand, worried that I'd done something wrong, had somehow hurt her, that she was dying or in danger.

"Allison?" Nothing. Then a slow blink, tongue on her bottom lip. *If I act a little weird, take care of me.*

"You okay?"

Nothing. A tremor of a smile played strangely at the side of her mouth.

It occurred to me that when she'd gone to the bathroom a few minutes earlier she hadn't flushed the toilet.

I jumped up, entered her bathroom and closed the door, fanned the wall for the switch, and was shocked by the sight of a naked man in front of me. He didn't look too good, either. Eyes wild, hair a mess, a bit of a gut. The mirror. I let my eyes adjust to the light, and then searched the bathroom cupboard. Makeup, birth control pills, Tylenol, the usual. Nothing interesting. I stared into the toilet. Nothing there. Nothing in the pocket of the bathrobe on the back of the door. Maybe I simply had—maybe I'd better look in the trash. I knelt down. Yes, there, dropped into a nest of tissues and dental floss lay a little wide-mouthed jar with a lid screwed on tight. I held it up to the bright light and swished around some flecks of white stuff and a piece of cabbage in some sort of vinegary liquid. I unscrewed the lid and smelled the contents of the jar.

Fishy. Yes, fishy. What was left of a small bit of fish, no doubt. Shao-tzou fish.

If I were a man different from the one I am, I might have taken furious advantage of Allison in some way. She lay insensate on her sheets, deep tremors occasionally playing across her face, utterly undefended, fuckable, murderable. I could have done anything to her, rifled her drawers, shaved her head. And I won't pretend I wasn't angry, either; on the pretense of sexual affection, she'd coldly duped me into being her hospital orderly while she departed on a drug trip. Is this what she did with all her men? Fluffed them up so that she could overlay one pleasure with another? The fish must really be good, I realized, for her to undergo such risk. I rolled Allison on her side, on the off chance she would vomit, and doing this, I saw that she'd urinated a bit in the sheets. This was sad and a little sweet and deeply weird, and my anger toward her melted away. What a lovely, lonely woman. What a waste of her vitality. I covered her with the blanket, made sure that she was warm. She didn't wake. I checked her pulse every few minutes for almost an hour. It was steady. Her respiration held steady, too. How much fish had she eaten? Enough to have a strong effect, much stronger than the effect the men had experienced earlier. But not so much that she was in danger. An amount that was—well, perfect. An art, she'd said, an art.

An hour later I got Allison to sit up once and have a little water, and she muttered something half coherent and told me thank you, she was fine, please forgive her, and fell asleep again, this time holding me tight—as if I mattered to her.

I woke a little after six, bolt upright, and for a moment didn't know where I was. Then I saw Allison next to me, clutching a silk pillow. She breathed easily, and had put on a nightgown. Or had I put it on her? I couldn't remember. I studied her. She was fine now. Warm, breathing easily. I eased out of the bed, feeling a ghost of that old domestic rhythm. Man, woman, bed. Coffee, sunlight, and where are my pants? It had been a weird night, and I wanted to retreat to my apartment, get a shower and shave. In the kitchen I nabbed a few swallows of orange juice in the refrigerator and incidentally perused Allison's books, which seemed to lean toward Catholic mysticism and novels by the tough-chick literary crowd.

I drifted along the bank of windows in the living room, watching the day begin outside, the sun hitting the bricks and rainspouts, the taxis denser on the avenue. I confess my melancholy in this moment. You reach a certain age and you know that jumping into bed isn't as simple as it used to be—not that it ever was. But now reality seeps in more quickly. People grind against each other, expectations limited, patience provisional. She'd lured me back to her apartment so that she could get a fix of her dangerous fish, getting fucked as she dropped off to sleep. Fish-fucked. Did this explain the parade of kindly, ineffectual men she'd seen before Jay Rainey? Guys who could be depended upon not to take advantage of a tripped-out Allison Sparks?

And how much did I mind? I wasn't sure. I dropped my forehead against the cool glass, fogging it a bit, and let my eyes drift to the other side of the street. Across from me I saw a woman in a white robe pouring coffee into a mug. The morning light was such that I could see her rather well. Young, but not that young. She was not my wife. But she might have been, once. The demographics weren't far off. I watched her pour milk into her coffee. She reached into her kitchen cabinet and pulled down four cereal bowls, one after another. Here was a mother, dutifully meeting the day. Not a woman who dragged in lonely fish-fuck partners. Her wholeness saddened me, made me think not only of Judith in the good days but also of little Wilson Doan's mother. I'd killed her son. Who can measure a mother's grief? Who can find its bottom? Now the mother looked at her wall clock and left the kitchen. What had happened to my life? That expected trajectory, the planned vector, was abandoned, a weed-cracked highway to nowhere.

Yes, the domestic tableau across the street filled me with longing and misery—there it was, as close as balcony seats at a Broadway show—and I was about to turn away when I saw the woman enter a room two windows down from her kitchen. She leaned softly over a bed and seemed to be waking someone, who then got up, shrugged on some clothing, and left the bedroom. A light went on in a larger window closer to the park. The figure appeared, wearing a man's oversized plaid flannel shirt, and sat down before a piano. She was a young woman, a girl, really—

—Sally Cowles.

Yes, that was Sally Cowles, sitting down at a piano, in profile to me. The woman—her stepmother, I assumed—appeared again with a glass of juice, encouraging, nodding, pointing to a page of music. Sally Cowles was practicing the piano. Sally Cowles lived across the street from Allison Sparks. Jay Rainey was obsessed with Sally Cowles. I remembered Allison's story about how she'd met Jay in the little breakfast place near her apartment. He'd told her that he was in the neighborhood because of a deal he was doing nearby. But what reason would Jay have to be in this neighborhood, *except for Sally Cowles*? He had no deal, other than the building on Reade Street, no reason to be on the Upper East Side.

Now Allison came out of her bedroom in her silk gown.

"Morning!" she called cheerily.

"Hi."

She came up to me from behind, rubbed her hands across my chest. I turned. Allison smiled up at me, searching for my mood, as if in a kind of penance. Don't be mad at her, I told myself. It's just loneliness. The whole goddamned thing. On her part and on mine.

"Oh, you men are all alike."

"We are?"

"Well, *mostly*."

I made some sound. "And why are we all alike, mostly?"

"Oh, nothing. It's just that Jay used to do this, too."

"What?"

"Stood here and looked right across the street."

Yes, of course, I thought, all my anxieties amping back through my head, of course he did. That's why he let you think you seduced him, so that he could come up to your apartment and watch young Sally Cowles.

seven

I HURRIED OUT of Allison's apartment a few minutes later, wondering which was more disturbing, Allison's calculated seduction, or the fact that Sally Cowles lived directly across the street from her. Allison had seen me stare at the girl, seen it all too well, and after her initial banter about Jay doing the same thing—a naked attempt to reassure herself—I'd said nothing, had only glanced stupidly at her, then stared again across the street. At this, Allison took two shocked steps backward, arms suddenly crossed in front of her, eyes jittery and defensive, as if she'd been struck in the face. Why had the two men who'd recently come to her apartment *both* been fixated on a teenage girl living across the street? For a moment I thought Allison was going to run to the phone and call the police. But she was frozen where she stood. We were both stunned, in fact—revealed as strangers to each other, silhouettes caught in Jay's strange psychic machinery. I almost blurted out that the girl was the daughter of one of his tenants, and that he appeared to be obsessed with her, but I stopped myself.

Allison, however, had seen me nearly tell her. "You *know* who that girl is!" she said. "I can see it in your face!"

I picked up my coat, feeling the Derek Jeter ball in the pocket. "I better go."

Allison didn't like my overly calm tone. "What's going on?"

I didn't tell her, because I couldn't. What *was* going on? On my subway ride home, pressed between commuters headed downtown, I didn't know what to worry about more, H.J., or Marceno, or Sally Cowles. It made for a jangled journey, and only a block away from my apartment, hunched against the morning's cold, did I remember my lunch with Dan Tuthill that day. He was a connection to my old life, one I wanted to keep. I'd take a long shower, pull myself together, and at lunch subtly pump Tuthill for possible job leads. I quickened my pace, and as I did I saw an old man pass by on the sidewalk wearing a spectacular red silk tie that looked a great deal like the one Judith had given to me many Christmases past, back when I didn't move dead men in the night or sleep with women addicted to psychedelic fish flesh. The man lurched along in an army jacket and a wool cap, a certain triumphant energy in his eyes, as if he had stuffed his pockets with contraband, and the incongruity of the red silk tie should have warned me that, indeed, this *was* what had happened.

When I turned the corner I saw a swarm of homeless people, office boys, and garment workers in front of my building, several fighting over a pile of junk in the street. Someone had pulled a car up and was shoveling clothes and other household items into the trunk. I got closer. The stuff looked like—like *my* stuff. I glanced up at my apartment window. It was shattered, frame and all.

I broke into a run and flew into my building and up the stairs. On the third floor, I found my apartment door ajar, ripped off one hinge, the lock splintered. The sight was so improbable that I thought I'd entered the wrong apartment. They—whoever they were—had emptied the place, literally thrown everything I owned out of the two windows: the bed, the tables, the chairs, the clothes, the pots and pans, my old tennis racquet, long unused, the bank account records, the checkbook, the divorce papers, the food in the refrigerator, just *all* of it, the bath towels, the books, pillows, the rug, the CDs, the cleanser under the sink, the stereo, the clean socks, all the cheap junk of an ever cheaper life. I checked the closets. Empty, not a coat hanger. I checked under the sink. Nothing. In the corner the radiator whistled as the steam rose in the building's pipes. Newly naked, the apartment was reduced to its essence: pathetic, dirty, small. A hole.

But wait—they'd left one thing in the living room, with a certain sadistic flourish: a broom, propped casually against the wall. I edged to the window and looked out. My old belongings were strewn twenty yards down the sidewalk, into the gutter. Whatever had carried or bounced into the street proper had been run over many times by the belching delivery trucks that serviced the block.

In the bedroom, on the wall where my bed used to be, red-spray-paint letters looped two feet high: GIVE ME WHAT I WANT. I collapsed to one knee, staggered by my predicament.

"Nobody saw them," came a voice behind me. It was the kindly and ineffectual super. He was holding a handful of envelopes. "Well, they saw it was a couple of guys, that's all."

"White guys? Black guys?"

"Like I said, nobody saw them." He swung his eyes around the bare walls. "I called the police, though who knows when they show up."

He held up the envelopes. "They broke into your mailbox, too. You expecting something?"

I shook my head, dazed by the whole event.

"You, uh—" He studied me with the intent to get to the bottom of the problem. "So you know why they come do this to you? You know who these guys are? The police are going to have a lot of questions." He stared at me meaningfully, in the manner of a man who has already seen far too many things in his time—bodies drained of blood in bathtubs, widows curled stiffly in their beds, kitchens set afire, drunks insensate on the stairs. "I don't know who is in the wrong, don't know if it's them or if it's you. I don't know if you did something to make some peoples mad at you, if they're going to come back, okay?"

"I see what you mean," I said.

"So I brought you your mail, just in case, you know—"

"In case I felt like not being here for a while."

"You got it, yes."

"I'll pay for the door, the window, all that."

He nodded, unmollified, and his voice found his genuine mood:

"Why don't you get out, Mr. Wyeth? I mean *now*. We don't need problems here. This building is full of peaceful people."

"I didn't—"

"The police are coming, Mr. Wyeth. They will have some questions for you."

I took the mail from him, jammed it in my coat pocket, and hit the stairs. Outside, I saw a man holding a picture frame—Timothy in his baseball uniform, bat cocked on his shoulder, a happy grin on his face.

"Give me that," I said. "That's my son."

"Fuck you, Slim."

"This is all my stuff!" I hollered.

"Not no more."

"Give me the picture."

He started to rip apart the frame and I picked up what used to be the leg of my kitchen table. "You can have all this stuff," I announced, sweeping my hands at the clothes and shoes and kitchen chairs, all of it. "Just let me have the picture of my son!"

"Put down the stick."

"No," I said.

"I'm not giving you the fucking—"

Dead Herschel on a tractor, the mysterious Jay Rainey, the disturbing nocturnal activities of Allison—I swung the table leg in frustration at all of them, catching the man in the shoulder. He howled in fury.

"I'm kill you, you fuck!"

"No you're not!" I snarled, foolish beyond any past history of myself. "I'm going to hit you until you give me that picture, okay? Ready?" I swung the table leg like a bat. "Right in the head, ready?"

He flung the photo to the ground, cracking the glass. I snatched it up. I wanted to poke through the trash for my checkbook or more photos of Timothy, but a police car turned the corner of the block. I slipped down the street, not much more than a vagrant now, hunted and alone.

I was a block from the Harvard Club, on my way to lunch in a new shirt, when I figured out who to call. Martha Hallock.

"Not you again?" she said. "The Grand Inquisitor?"

"Jay's in real trouble, Martha. I'm trying to help him."

"This I doubt."

"He's got people breathing down his neck, Martha, and I can't reach him." I tried to drain the fury and fear out of my voice. "You had something to do with the deal, didn't you? These people are putting a lot of pressure on him now. And me. We need to—"

"I'm afraid you're on your own."

"Thank you," I said, adding, "you fucking old witch."

There was no response, just a series of wheezy, shallow breaths. Finally Martha's voice returned, no longer defiant, but rather somehow burdened. "How much trouble is he in?"

"A lot," I said. "And I don't even know where he is."

"Well, neither do I."

"But you could tell me what I'm dealing with here."

"I could—"

"But?"

"— but I don't have my broomstick."

"Broomstick?"

"Yes, the fucking old witch wants to come talk to the rude Manhattan lawyer but doesn't have a broomstick. However, the fucking old witch *could* take the 10 a.m. bus into the city tomorrow, I guess."

"The rude Manhattan lawyer would be honored."

"The old witch is fat and unstable on her feet," Martha continued, "and will need assistance."

"Not to worry. Would she like a nice meal as well?"

"Oh, yes."

"How about lunch in a great old steakhouse?"

"Swell beans, as we used to say when I was young, back in the seventeenth century."

"I guess witches live a long time."

"Too long, Mr. Wyeth, that's the problem." She hung up.

Now I stood outside the Harvard Club, not quite able to step inside. A cold Manhattan rain, the kind that promises you nothing but misery, blew in sheets across the avenue, smattering the building. I saw Dan Tuthill waiting for me in the anteroom near the coat check, rocking on his heels, inspecting the cuffs of his shirt, and impossibly, looking a little fatter than two days before. I stepped inside and he shook my hand. We headed straight to the dining room, where we were shown to a table. After we ordered, I asked, "How's Mindy?"

"She's fine. I mean, you know how it was with me . . ." Dan sighed. "Things are, well, we've got the kids, I always say."

"How's the lawyerly life then?"

"The usual. Pimps and maggots."

"Which are you?"

"I go back and forth—as necessary."

"What about Kirmer, my old pal?"

His smile dropped. "Kirmer? He's running the place, Bill."

"What about—?"

"All those guys? Nah, gone. He mowed down every one of them. Tied them up with phone wire and threw them in the river." He smiled. "Everything's different, Bill, the secretaries, the ways things are organized. I feel like a dinosaur and I'm forty-four!" He smiled up at the waiter. "Scotch on the rocks, double." He looked back at me. "And I don't like the way the wind is blowing. You have to have a thousand attorneys on staff these days to *compete*! The business is so global, so complex. All these Indian kids who passed the bar in New York and Bombay and have a master's degree in computer systems or bioengineering. They're actually smarter than you or me, Bill, that's the honest fucking truth. So the firm is going to go in directions that a lot of the old guys can't go."

"But you're set, right?"

"They have to buy me out if I leave, everything, even buy my shoes." We sat there, Dan paddling his soup with his spoon to make the steam rise. "Heard you weren't doing much," he said softly.

"Me?" I said. "No."

"Not even a little work?"

"A little. But very little."

"You into something else?"

I shook my head.

"What they did to you was fucking criminal, Bill."

I shrugged. "They had good lawyers."

"Yeah." Dan leaned closer. "So, listen," he said, "I'm going to tell Kirmer to take his hand out of my ass."

"Leave?"

"Leave? *Eject*, pal. Let those fuckers rot in their own gravy. I got some bucks set aside, I got my partnership share coming to me, and I've got Mindy's father."

"I don't get it."

Dan sat back and rubbed his chest, which meant, I remembered, that he had a story to tell. "Well, you know I'm a bad guy, I slink around."

"I always figured," I said.

"You, however, always kept your whistle clean."

"I'm a conformist," I said. "Dull as dishwater."

He grunted.

"Anyway, Mindy's dad."

He was eager to talk about it, I could see. "It's a crazy thing, Bill. Something you'd never expect. Mindy's dad calls me up three weeks ago, says he wants to play golf. I say okay, and so we go out to the National in East Hampton. Beautiful. He's a pretty distinguished guy, made a mint in the seventies with the airlines. He's got to be worth like two hundred million bucks. Can live off the interest of the interest."

"Does some of it go to Mindy?"

"Yeah, someday, but this guy's going to live till he's ninety, minimum. His resting pulse is fifty-four, blood pressure ninety-four over seventy."

"Nice guy?"

"No. Not at all. A bastard. A manipulator. Doesn't have enough to do with himself. Wife died ten years ago, and now he has this beautiful Japanese lady who lives with him. There's Japanese stuff all over the house. Bamboo rugs, jade things. Plus fish and rice every night. He looks great, looks *relaxed*. She takes care of everything, is my bet. That whole thing about the compliant Asian woman is a bunch of shit. She's the one in control. He's given up control."

"Well, he still controls two hundred million bucks."

"So we play a couple of holes. I keep waiting. Nothing. He's playing well, me, nothing. I'm all over the place."

"Nervous."

"Totally. So there's a bench near the sixth tee. He says let's have a seat."

"This was it."

"Yep." Dan nodded as the entrée arrived. "We sit down. He takes off his golf glove and puts it on my knee. Says, Listen, I know you're fucking another woman besides my daughter, maybe even more than one."

"He use that word?"

"Yes, *fucking*, which is a bad sign, of course. Because it's angry."

I agreed. "Visceral."

"I'm thinking, Oh no, he's angry, he's going to hit me with his seven iron. He says, Don't ask how I know, but I do. The world's a small place."

"So were you?" I asked.

Dan raised his palm. "I'm going to plead the Fifth Amendment, senator."

"Fine."

"So then he says, I know Mindy is a pain. I *raised* her. I know what she's like. But you can't leave her. I'm just about crapping in my pants at this point. I say, Okay. He says, No, I really mean it. I know she's gotten overweight. Actually he said fat. *He* used that word, about *his* daughter! I sort of waved my hands, you know, it's no big deal. *I'm* fat, too, of course. But she *has* gotten fat. *Really* fat. *Purposefully* fat, even. I mean, Bill, it creates a copulatory *impediment*. A sexual handicap. The only thing that works, frankly, is from behind."

I put my hands up in front of me. "Hey, I'm not asking you to tell me this—not that it's not incredibly fascinating."

"Don't worry, this goes somewhere. It connects to your future, in fact."

"The sexual position you use with your obese wife impinges on my future?"

"Well, in a manner of speaking. Just listen. So, Mindy's father looks at me and says—"

At that moment my phone rang.

"Quick, get it." Dan was irritated. "They don't like that here."

"Martha?" I answered, taking a guess. "You change your mind?"

"Yo, fuckwango!" came a male voice. "You got the wrong number!"

"Excuse me?"

"Hey, I'm looking for this guy, he gave me this number. In Brooklyn."

Dan was watching me.

"Is this Helmo?" I asked.

"Yeah. I got that address for you, the one we was talking about? Rainey shows up again this morning, swung the bat for a hour. I followed him home. I want my three hundred bucks."

"What's the address?"

"Who you think I am?" he hollered in my ear. "Give me the three hundred first!"

"Let's meet," I suggested.

"Half hour in front of the batting cages."

"I can't do that."

"What the fuck?"

I worried Dan could hear the voice in my ear. "How about three this afternoon?"

"Be there. Or I'm telling Rainey about you."

I put the phone away.

"Who was it?" asked Dan.

"Some guy who'll probably double-cross me."

He nodded flatly. "Okay, so where was I? So Mindy's father, right. We're on the bench near the sixth tee. And he says, I know everything that you are or will be thinking right now. *I know it.* So I'm sitting there, I'm shish kabob. I'm cooked son-in-law. Then he says, I understand who you are."

"What?"

Dan nodded vigorously, mouth full of food. "He says I understand who you are. Then he says, But you can't leave her. I say, I have no plans to leave her, it would hurt the kids too much. He's not fooled. He says he's heard twenty or thirty of his friends say the same thing over the years. They always leave their wives anyway, soon as the kids are out of the house. Mindy will never leave *you*, he says. She doesn't have it in her, even if she wanted to. She's *weak*. That's true. Plus, he says, plus she loves you too much, not to mention the kids. I feel like a pig when he says this. He's right, of course, Mindy with her moon eyes, mooning after me, seeing if I'm *happy*, seeing if I have a drink. She'll do *anything* for me, Bill, suck my freaking toes, anything . . . which I *hate*, of course! She's lost all her self-respect, she just wants to be loved, filled *up*, like the new four-hundred-and-fifty-gallon oil tank I got in the basement in case of shortages. Huge, extra capacity! Mindy's like that, she lies there in bed with her fat legs out and calls to me, like, Oh just please come love me, please, *please*, waving her arms and moaning, Oh come tell me everything is okay. And it sort of breaks my heart but *also* sort of makes me *hate* her." Here Dan paused, eyes narrowing, mouth an evil little smile. "I like those thin girls who are tough cases, man—the sly, *mean* ones who you got to *crack* open."

He breathed out heavily, gulped his drink.

"Hey Dan," I said. "We're barely done with the soup."

"Yeah, then he says, I want to make you an offer. I say okay, what? And he says if you don't make the deal now, you will never get this offer again. *Ever*."

"And?"

"He says, two million dollars and you promise you will never leave my daughter."

"Two million?"

"I can't even open my mouth. It's not a lot of money to him, remember. He says, I know you want to know what the catch is, what the conditions are. I say well, sure. I try to be relaxed saying it but it sort of squeaks out. He says, I'd never tell another man he couldn't sleep around. That's unrealistic. You have to let the big dog hunt, and all that. So here're my conditions, he says. Number one, you never leave Mindy. *Never*. Like that. A little scary. Number two, you get a vasectomy. So even though you *do* fuck around, you don't get anyone pregnant, and number three, you use the money in the exact way I tell you, don't just eat it up."

"Don't buy a vineyard."

"A vineyard, a castle in Scotland, whatever."

"So?"

"So he says, Think about it while I tee off. After I hit my ball, he says, I'm going to come back to the bench and get your answer. If you have *no* answer, he says, I'll assume no deal. If you say no, I'll never offer it to you again. *Ever.*"

"And you believe that."

"Totally."

"Is he going to tell you how you have to use the money before you agree to take it?"

"I asked that. The answer was no."

"Tough game."

Dan nodded, though not without some appreciation for the old man. "Then he goes, If you say *yes*, I'll write you a check and assume that you'll be good to your word. Plus, you'll send me a copy of the vasectomy bill." Dan shot his hands in the air, fork above his head. "Bill! He wants *documentation* that they chopped up my nuts! Then he goes over and puts down his golf ball, takes out his driver."

"He's forcing an answer."

"Yeah, and I'm a little pissed off, plus a little shocked."

"It's total guts-ball poker," I agreed.

"Total."

"Pretty emasculating to have the father-in-law insisting on the snip job."

"You're telling *me*." Dan pushed his empty plate away. "So he lines up the ball and gets his grip right, then whacks the hell out of it. The ball disappears. Then he picks up his tee and comes back to me. I'm still sitting on the bench. I haven't moved."

"You've decided to say yes."

"I've decided to say *no*."

"Really?" This didn't seem like the Dan Tuthill I remembered, always looking for the next cash-pipe to suck on.

"Yeah. I mean, I can't be bought like that! Fuck him! Mindy's got an ass like a wrinkled beach ball! She tries to hide it but I see it anyway. Fucking lowers my testosterone, too! So I'm thinking, a few more years, let the kids get out of school, I can split up and go hunting for these cha-chas I see in the bars all the time." He leaned close again, his eyes sleepy-looking. "You have any idea of the fucking *action* that's out there, Bill? Even for a fat old shit like me? Their ovaries are calling to them, like trumpets from the mountains! *Make us pregnant, make us pregnant, do something about all this es-tro-gen!* They can't help themselves, Bill! It's wired in, it's biological. These apartment houses filled with unmarried women? Palaces of estrogen!" He pointed to his chest. "I'm *perfect*, see. I'm well off, physically unattractive, and *in no way* marriageable. It's totally counterintuitive, and most women would never admit it. I'm perfect for the woman who needs sex, *some* kind of sex, but doesn't want to get involved with somebody she might actually get involved with! Do you see that? It's a niche specialty. They all *say* they are looking for the good guys or the husband types, but those are the guys that freak them out! Guys like *me*, they know what to do with. See? A few laughs, a few drinks, fuckle you, fuckle me, see you later, I lost your business card, so what, no harm, no foul. Right?"

"Wow." Somehow this sounded harsh, despite my disastrous exit from Allison's apartment that morning.

"The girls are *desperate,* man! They hate to admit it, and they *won't* admit it, but it's a fact! So I'm figuring, I get to fifty, I'm single again, I drop eighty pounds, I got ten years of cha-cha to look forward to."

"But your kids," I said, thinking of my son. "It'd kill them."

He waved this away. "I'd let them grow up a bit. They know things aren't so great, anyway."

I didn't want to hear any of this.

He smiled. "So now Mindy's father comes over and says, Well? Like that—Well? I'm going to have some guy, some asshole who left *his* wife, chop up my testicles? I'm going to live with this woman who drives me nuts, the whole thing? Forget it! What am I, a monkey on a string? Forget the money! I make plenty of money! Fuck him, I can't be bought, right?"

"Right," I said in solidarity.

Dan settled back, rested his hands on his stomach, the matter seemingly as settled as his soup. "So I look up at him, and I say, 'You said two million?'"

"And he says, 'Yes.'"

"And I say, 'Make it three.'"

"What?"

"And *he* says yes! It's a deal!"

"Wait—*what?*"

"It's a deal! Three mil! We shook hands! I looked him in the eye! Fact, we both got a little moist about it. He hugged me, even. And it *is* a deal. I'm good for it. Felt good, in fact, it felt *very* good, Bill! I know I'm safe now. I'm sort of *dead*, in fact. The gate closed, the train left the station, whatever. It feels *good*, too. I can't fuck things up now, because I took the money! I know this, I accept this, okay? And now I feel really, really *good*."

"So you had the vasectomy?"

"Piece of cake. Sore for a few days, nothing more."

"What about the cha-chas?"

He shrugged. "Whatever. I don't seem as interested."

"Psychological?"

"Probably. Whatever."

I stared at him. Dan's mood was bouncing around so much that I dared not push the conversation much further. "So you asked me to lunch so that you could tell me someone handed you three million dollars on the golf course to get your balls disconnected?"

"No, Bill," he said. "I asked you to lunch because I want to offer you a *job*, you jerk-weed."

I didn't understand.

"Remember, I had to use the money exactly as he specified. And he specified I take it and open my own firm, a boutique firm. He gave me a whole speech, how I was talented and had great energy and the reason I was fucking around was I'd lost my way, I was swallowed up in a large firm and my talents couldn't shine. I was wasting my time with the cha-chas when I could be building something, something big. He said I would use the three million for seed money, that he knew plenty of bankers who would help me out. It was *beautiful*. He's a beautiful *man*, I'm telling you. Wise. Deeply wise. So I'm taking my snip-job money, the partnership buyout, and some other stuff. I've got space on Fifty-third Street, bought out what was left of a dot-com lease. Company crashed and burned, place was empty for a year. The agent practically gave it away, said the original leaseholder was panicked, living off leaves and twigs. So, basically, I *stole* it. Eight of my long-term clients are coming with me, plus some smaller new ones. I've got some young guys from the firm who want to come with me. All of them can make rain. Plus me." He paused, watching me absorb this scenario. "What I need is a guy who'll look at everything coming in and going out. The young guys don't have the overall background. They can't sit tight, they need action. Which is fine. I'm going to run them like dogs. But I need a guy in the center."

"Someone cheap, too."

"Okay, I admit that. I can't pay big-league money. But it'll be decent. We'll be making the big gravy in a couple of years. I mean, how much are you making now?"

I almost smiled. The salesman in Brooks Brothers that morning had frowned when I discarded my dirty shirt in a trash can on the way out. "Not enough," I said.

Dan knocked his tongue around his mouth. "So, listen, this is a step up, a step back. You can help me, I can help you."

"You have staff, secretaries, fax machines, stuff like that?"

"We're good to go."

"When're you starting up?"

"Tuesday. I should have contacted you earlier, I admit."

A few years back I'd have received this information as an insult. But no longer. He knew I was unemployed. "First choice fell through?" I said.

Dan looked into my eyes.

"Just tell me," I said. "I can take it."

"I had a guy, a great guy, and he said yes, but he got another offer last week. I'd sent him the contract but he hadn't signed it. He totally screwed me. Then I saw you at the game."

"Right."

"You're not offended?"

"Nah."

"Good."

"What are you going to pay me, Dan?"

He told me. Considering my experience, it was nickels and dimes.

Considering I was a homeless, unemployed drifter trying not to get arrested for moving a dead body, or worse, it was pretty good.

"You've got to do better than that," I said.

"I'll knock it up twenty-five percent in nine months once we get some cash flow."

"Knock it up twenty now, twenty in nine months, or take your chances with the next guy you meet at a basketball game."

He looked at me. "That's a little rich."

"You're the guy getting three million clams on the sixth tee."

"Fifteen percent now, twenty more in nine."

"Twenty now, fifteen in nine," I said.

"Deal."

"Deal."

We shook hands. He went into the further particulars of the job, the setup, the address, everything, but I only half listened, so happy was I to be back in the world. "This'll get you started," he said, reaching into his briefcase.

"You brought paperwork? You knew I'd say yes?"

He only smiled. I glanced at the materials, eager to familiarize myself with the cases and clients he was bringing with him. I remembered several—in the torpor of litigation they hadn't progressed far in the intervening years—but most were new and reminded me again of the basic conflict built into all human activity; in front of me were torts for nonpayment, breach of contract, nonperformance, illegal competition, copyright infringement, patent infringement, and product failure. The legal language did not really disguise the bile and greed and hatred accumulating in each case, but at least the entities and individuals were fighting through civilized means, not kidnapping and intimidation.

"Wait, I got something else," Dan said, reaching into his briefcase again.

"What?"

"This. I had the guy do it in one day." He handed me a box of business cards. They had my name and new number on them, the address of the firm, everything.

I fanned the cards. Their stiff newness was satisfying. "You know I love this."

"Figured," said Dan. "Makes it feel official." He watched a boat of ice cream float down in front of his place. "Bill, one more thing."

"Sure."

"Just reassure me that—that you're coming to me with no problems."

"What do you mean?"

"I mean with no situations, no bad clients. No *problems*."

"Everybody has problems."

"Sure, sure," he said. "I mean *real* problems. Like funny clients you might be working with, whatever . . ."

"Not to worry," I said, starting to worry.

Sixty minutes later I stood in the doorway of the batting cages building in Brooklyn and spotted Helmo. He saw me right away and gave me that chin-up recognition guys use when they don't want to call out. I followed him across the street under the shadows of the Brooklyn-Queens Expressway. He smelled like Chinese food, but I didn't bring it up.

"So I was thinking," he said.

"About what?"

"I was thinking about your teeth."

"My teeth?"

"Yeah. They're good."

"So?"

"So I think three hundred is too low."

"Why?"

"Your teeth're too good. So're your clothes. Guy that's got good teeth, he can pay more."

I shook my head. Everyone was a chiseler, working the extra percentage, biting off the last dime. Including me.

"You want it or not?"

"How much?" I grumbled.

"Five hundred."

I dug it out of my wallet. Helmo handed me a slip of paper with Jay's address written in block letters. "You gotta go in the back. It's over the garage, up the side. I watched him go in there myself."

"How do you know it's not a friend's house or something?" I thought of Allison's anxiety about another woman. "Maybe a girlfriend?"

Helmo nodded slyly. "You check that place out, you'll see nobody else lives there."

"Which means—?"

"Just check it out. Trust in your common man, dude."

I stared at the address in my hand, it was near Fifth Avenue and Seventeenth Street. "It's only about ten blocks away."

"Deal's a deal, bro."

I was eager to get going.

"What you looking for him for, anyway?" Helmo asked. "He do something bad?"

If Jay came back to the cages, Helmo could tell him of my inquiry, maybe get a round-trip payday.

"No, no, it's not like that," I said. "I'm trying to help the guy."

"Trying-a *save* his ass, like?"

"Something like that."

I set off then, on foot. Along Third Avenue under the BQE, then up the hill on Seventeenth Street. Once an Italian, maybe Irish neighborhood, now drifting Latino and urban mix. That's what everything is now, urban mix. If you're a white guy wearing a great suit in these places, you might as well have a blue-and-white NYPD chopper hovering over your head, announcing your appearance. I bought a Giants cap and a quart of milk at the corner deli, and yanked up my coat collar, hiding my jacket and tie. Cap low, carrying the plastic bag, shuffling along, trying to blend into the neighborhood. You could be somebody else. You aren't necessarily this thing or that. Just some guy. You don't look at people, because you're not interested, and if you're not interested, then it's no problem, we got no problem here.

I reached Seventeenth Street and found the address. Behind the house stood a garage with what looked like an illegal, owner-built addition on top, its shingles crooked, windows off-plumb, the roofing job patched and repatched. Here was the home of a man buying a three-million-dollar commercial building in downtown Manhattan? The idea was absurd. Behind the garage rose a twenty-foot-high chain-link fence grown over with ivy and ribboned with trash. A burglar could climb over it, but it wouldn't be much fun, and if you fell down on the garage side, you landed on a disassembled powerboat and a pile of cement blocks. Thus the apartment over the garage was well protected; the only way in was the exterior wooden staircase up the side. I looked behind me—no one watched. I pushed through the gate. Someone had abandoned a repainting job on the side of the house: Ladder, bucket, and brushes all fallen to the ground. In the weeds lay a rotting pile of freebie newspapers, phone books, shopping fliers, a leaking car battery, and whatever else someone didn't have the time for. I climbed the stairs and peered inside the one small window. The shade was down, nothing. I tried the door—locked. I knocked softly. Nothing. Maybe it was the wrong place; maybe Helmo had ripped me off. Nothing I'd seen proved Jay lived here. Going down the stairs I noticed that the treads were battered and worn. Even the risers were scraped, vertically. And there was a streaked pattern to the wear, suggesting repetition, something heavy going up or down on a regular basis.

Next I tried the garage door; it went up. I ducked beneath and closed it behind me. In the dusty half-light I recognized Jay's truck, a little slush stain on the sidewalls from the trip three nights prior. The truck's doors were locked. I peered into the windows; nothing. But the walls of the garage, I saw, were lined with large tanks, perhaps two dozen. I turned my attention to some boxes set in the back of the garage. They held car stuff, mostly, plus knitting materials and books on collecting dollhouses. Probably not Jay's. What else?

I slipped back under the garage door, picked up one of the paint cans in the weeds, and climbed the stairs. The apartment door was old, with nine panels of glass. I looked around, checked the street. This isn't much of a crime, I told myself, considering what he's already put me through. I swung the paint can against one of the bottom panels, and it cracked the glass enough for me to break out a few pieces. I checked the street again; nobody saw me drop the paint can into the weeds. I reached inside and flipped the dead-bolt lock. The door didn't open. I felt around and found a slide bolt below the doorknob.

Three minutes, I told myself—in and then get the hell out. Here I was breaking into someone's apartment hours after someone had broken into mine. *Nice.* I turned the knob and shut the door behind me. Jay would discover that someone had broken in, but he wouldn't know who.

The room was a monk's cell ten feet by twelve. You entered directly into the bedroom. A simple camp bed, neatly made. Next to it, an answering machine, red message-light blinking. To one side sat an enormous stainless steel box with a small window in its top, not unlike a space-age sarcophagus. It was the biggest thing in the room and a quick inspection of its dials and switches revealed it to be a hyperbolic oxygen chamber.

Oxygen. The man needed oxygen?

Three oxygen tanks identical to the ones in the garage stood next to the chamber. Bottled oxygen is a controlled substance, I remembered, considered a medicine. You need a doctor's prescription to get it. The tanks are heavy when full. They had to be delivered, and were probably carried with some kind of dolly up and down the outside stairs, hence the wear on the treads.

At the foot of the bed stood an oxygen compressor that huffed rhythmically, its sound not unlike that of waves breaking on a beach.

I saw two trunks under the bed and slid them out. Look inside? I'd come this far, so yes. The first trunk contained work tools: hammers, screwdrivers, socket wrenches. The second had socks, jeans, underwear, T-shirts, all neatly folded. Such neatness is depressing, as if one is preparing for death. I closed the trunks and slid them back. In Jay's closet hung ten suits arranged by color, each with matching shirt and tie, including the one he'd worn the night I'd met him in the Havana Room. These were expensive, good-looking clothes, but in the context of the tiny room, they seemed costumes for a theatrical production. Here was a man who lived militarily, who could move out in the amount of time it took to carry his belongings down the stairs. Perhaps four trips, not including the hyperbolic chamber. In the back of the closet, under a raincoat, sat the seltzer-water box Allison had given him the night of the deal. I tipped it toward myself to look inside: the cash was gone, all of it. Two hundred and sixty-five thousand dollars. Where had he stashed it?

Seconds, burning away. I checked my watch. I'd been inside the apartment one minute. The answering machine beckoned. What else? The kitchenette off to one side looked unused. The refrigerator had no food in it, only a carton of orange juice, several bottles of vitamins, and a dozen odd unmarked cardboard boxes. I pulled one out and opened it. Inside clattered bottles labeled UNIVERSITY OF IOWA HOSPITALS PHARMACY, and by hand: Adrenaline, 500 mg. Another marked Dexi-amphetamine. Prednisone in 10 mg pills. Another marked "Andro." Below this were dozens of small inhalers marked Beclomethasone, Ventolin, Serevent, Albuterol. All stuff to open up the airway, get more oxygen in. In a second box was a bottle of white pills marked Singulair. None of the containers carried the name of a prescribing physician.

In the freezer: hot dogs, bread, TV dinners, ice.

The bathroom was spotless. One towel. Shaving kit. I looked inside. Nothing unusual. No pills in the cabinet. No condoms, no electric nose-hair buzzers. Next to the toilet was a stack of reading material, and it was not your usual hodgepodge of glossy magazines and *New Yorker* cartoon collections: here, with some articles dog-eared for reference, lay copies of the *Journal of American Pulmonary Specialists*, *The Report of the Oxygen Therapists Association*, a printout of "Asthma and the Pulsed Administration of Synthetic Adrenaline," *Clinical Tests of Respiratory Function*, the *Research Journal of the New York Hospitals' Endocrinology Association*, and so on. Clearly Jay suffered from some debilitating respiratory problem and was more or less managing his own treatment, depressingly so. I heard myself exhale, out of dread, and put the materials back the way I'd found them. I checked my watch. Six minutes, for God's sake.

I returned to the bedroom and froze there—fascinated, saddened, perplexed. Inasmuch as Jay's life had a physical center, this was it, and what a lonely center it was, too. I saw no television, no personal mail, no sign of indulgent activity or relaxation. No wonder he hadn't told Allison where he lived.

Next to the bed stood a wooden desk and a chair. On top was a give-away calendar from a heating oil company, and this—a full-height

photo of Sally Cowles, taken at great distance. She was in her school uniform, walking on a sidewalk with two friends on a sunny afternoon. From
the trees, I could see that the photo had been shot in the late fall or early
winter. The girls wore coats but not gloves or hats, and the surfaces of the
buildings around them suggested a well-to-do neighborhood in the city.
Upper East Side, perhaps, behind them a flower shop. Was there a flower
shop near Allison's apartment? Around the corner on the avenue? The
girls were walking with unconscious happiness, knapsacks jingling, their
school uniforms rippling, hair caught by the breeze, matching socks different lengths. I tried to picture Jay studying this photo. It was in no way
overtly sexual, at least not to me. But certain men, I knew, were driven into
a frenzy by the sight of a girl in a school uniform. The implied innocence
sent them into spasms of lust, and despite myself, then and there I remembered a business trip to Tokyo almost ten years earlier when I was
dragged by three drunken Japanese businessmen into a strip joint in the
famed Shinjuku district, where along with two hundred more Japanese
businessmen I watched one near-pubescent girl after another shed her
plaid school uniform and bobby socks. The sight had left me cold—I prefer older women with the mark of gravity upon them, with eyes that
smoke with the absolute *lack* of innocence—but the Japanese men were
transfixed by the sight, a few even producing expensive cameras and unapologetically recording the open-thighed displays for later review. Was
Jay such a man? I couldn't believe it, I didn't want to believe it.

What I wanted to do was listen to the answering machine message.
Maybe Allison really did have his number. Instead I slid open the desk
drawer, wondering if Jay perhaps kept his legal papers in there, such as
copies of the contract for the building on Reade Street. But the drawer
was empty, save for a few pens and rubber bands and a paper pad of order slips for Brooklyn Oxygen and Hospital Supplies, adorned with their
motto, SAFETY, RELIABILITY, AND PROMPT DELIVERY. This, I remembered, matched the slip of paper Jay had given me two days earlier
with the restaurant address where I'd met Marceno.

What else? Hurry, I told myself, find the important stuff. I spied a list
tacked to the wall:

Every day:
300 push-ups, no O
500 sit-ups, O afterward okay
Read newspapers (for conversation)
Read one page of the dictionary
Maintain foot hygiene, inspect for infection
Don't obsess about FEV

So here was the O that had upset Allison. O for oxygen, oxygen clearly being delivered to the garage downstairs. This was why the garage door had been left open, so that the empty tanks could be picked up; in all likelihood, I realized, their delivery schedule corresponded to the regularly appearing O's that Allison had seen in Jay's date book. A man who needs oxygen delivered will know when it is coming.

There, a secret revealed, worth a lot more than my investment of five hundred dollars and a couple of subway rides. But what was FEV? And why might Jay obsess about it? Did the letters stand for someone, another young woman he was stalking? Next to the list hung a small framed newspaper clipping with a photograph. It showed a young man in a bulky baseball uniform and batting helmet swinging a bat. The swing is nearly over and he is off balance from the effort. The headline read CLANKS HOMER IN INTERCOUNTY CHAMP DUEL. I checked the date; the clip was fifteen years old.

> John "Jay" Rainey, of Jamesport, hit a towering three-run homer yesterday in the intercounty summer-league play at Bethpage High School, clinching their victory 3–1.
>
> Rainey, who is leading the Bulldogs in slugging this season with sixteen round-trippers in twenty-three games, had every ballplayer's dream come true when he was recently signed to a minor league contract by the New York Yankees, following his second college season. Rainey will report to their double A farm team in three weeks.
>
> His homer came off of Tino Salgado, Bethpage's ace pitcher

who went 6–1 during the regular season. Salgado had been throwing a shutout until the Bulldog's homer.

"I got a good look at it," Rainey said after the game. "I'm just glad we won."

To be signed to a minor league baseball contract is quite an honor, of course, but this is not what caught my attention. The article suggested that Rainey's condition worsened after the date of the article, for no major league team signs up a prospect without giving him a thorough physical first. Martha Hallock had mentioned an accident. Was this the cause of Rainey's trouble?

Time to leave, no matter how much I wanted to stay. But at the door I was drawn back to the oxygen chamber, so sleek and streamlined, a bullet-shaped casket. I touched the spring-loaded door and it rose slowly, revealing a white, body-length cushion. Its spotlessness was depressing. Just about the loneliest place imaginable. Inside was a reading light and a pad of paper and pen. I flipped open the pad: *Dear Mr. David Cowles,* said the first sheet. *This is an extremely difficult letter to write. For many years now—* The letter ended. The next sheet said, *Dear David Cowles, Many years ago, your late wife, Eliza Carmody—* The third sheet said, *Dear David, My left ear has a small bump on the inside of the curl of cartilage. It's not something people usually notice but—*

Now I heard something outside, or perhaps downstairs in the garage. I'd taken too big a chance as it was—on the premises almost twelve minutes. I dropped the pad of unfinished letters back into the chamber, pressed down on the lid until it clicked shut, and glanced around the room to see that nothing had been disturbed. I slipped out the door and locked it from the outside again, not bothering to kick aside the broken glass—

—then pushed back inside the door, cursing myself, and stepped straight to the answering machine. Keeping on my glove, I pressed PLAY.

"Listen, you peckerass!" boomed Poppy's voice through a squall of static, "just pay these guys some fucking blood money, all right? Herschel's family, somebody working for them, are here. They're here! Right here, okay? Found me at the diner this afternoon. Did *you* tell them I eat there? I don't get it, Jay. They got me. They're listening to every word I'm telling you right now. Said they knew something about Herschel, I said I didn't know what. I said okay I called in the ambulance but he was already dead. They think we killed him! They're not going to the police, either. That's what they say, anyway, what—?" The voice became indistinct. "Yeah, they got—I mean, I told them your phone number, Jay, and where your girlfriend at the steakhouse works, okay? I got to give them *something*, that's all I got to give, and I don't know what else to say. I told them that's all I know. Just pay them, Jay, just—"

That was it. End of message. My fingers trembled, but I hit the memory button for old messages. Nothing. Time to go. But I didn't. I did one more thing; I dialed my new cell phone from Jay's phone. His number popped up on the display, and I saved it.

This done, I shot out of the room, pulled the door behind me, and scooted down the stairs. I kept my cap low and turned downhill on the street. Had anyone seen me? I caught a getaway taxi on Third Avenue, and the driver flicked on some kind of Indian or Bangladeshi stand-up comedy show. *Urmatta-eshi-ohvalindi-halaloo,* came a man's voice. *Heh-heh,* came the response. *Durmeshala-burmatta-valnahnah-galod-pulurshindaloo!* And then, *Heh-heh.*

I settled into my seat—Brooklyn to midtown Manhattan would take a while. I didn't want to keep thinking of Jay as an adversary, for clearly he was living under desperate circumstances, to a degree I hadn't realized before. But that same desperation worried me; a man who needs oxygen tanks at night is not as scared of lawsuits and other threats as is another man. It was also true that my illegal entry of Jay's premises hadn't resulted in any information that would help me deal with Marceno. What, then, had I learned? H.J.'s men were threatening Poppy. I needed to tell Allison to watch out, didn't I? And Jay, involved with Sally Cowles, was trying to draft a strange letter to her father. Had he bought the Reade Street building for some reason involving them? What else? The cartilage in his ear was related to the problem. He had a refrigerator full of black-market pharmaceuticals. He was obsessed with someone or something named FEV.

I leaned across the taxi's partition. The driver glanced in his rearview. "Take me to the New York Public Library," I said.

Varanasi-amattagobi-halapur-geshura-nanaloo!
Heh-heh.

Two hours later I knew that the air humans breathe at sea level is about twenty-one percent oxygen. In polluted American cities such as New York and Los Angeles and Tokyo, the concentration can fall to eighteen percent. Man breathes in about eighteen cubic feet of air per hour, drawing the stuff deep into the sacs of the lungs, making his red blood cells glow as oxygen hits them, and, like a tree or a dog or a worm, returns carbon dioxide into the atmosphere. Fully a fifth of the oxygen we breathe is consumed by the brain. Not only do we need the stuff, we're made of it: sixty-two percent, by body weight. The lungs grow steadily in children, then quite rapidly during puberty, but also continue to grow after maximum height has been reached. In males, lung capacity may continue to increase up to the age of twenty-five. The greatest variable in maximum lung capacity is, as would be expected, the size of the person, and Jay's theoretical maximum lung capacity was probably about 680 milliliters. But in healthy people the limits of exertion are dictated by the limits of the circulation system, not by the lungs. This is why shorter people can outrun taller people and why Olympic athletes often train at high altitudes to increase their red blood cell concentrations and return to low altitude just prior to competition. For all people, however, lung capacity begins to fall after age thirty. The ability to absorb oxygen is, in fact, one of the medical definitions of aging. The downward curve in our capacity is slow, however, and, in the absence of disease, is usually gentle enough to carry a human being far into old age.

There was more. FEV, the thing Jay wanted so badly not to be obsessed with, stood for forced expiratory volume and was the ratio of an individual's lung capacity to his or her expected healthy lung capacity, given height, age, and sex. A normal FEV score is 85 or higher. The morbid effects of disease can be seen in a low FEV score. The average decline in FEV of long-term smokers, for example, when plotted against non-smokers, is quite dramatic. A heavy smoker in his fifties has often lost so much lung capacity that he or she has reached an FEV rating of 45 or 50, a score that a healthy nonsmoker would not reach until age one hundred, were he to live that long. But slowly smoking a mountain of beautifully poisonous cigarettes is not the only thing that causes a low FEV. Other causes include organic diseases such as severe asthma, cystic fibrosis, pulmonary fibrosis, and environmental irritants, including air pollution, asbestos, and exposure to toxins. These conditions can cause permanent loss of FEV by damaging the elasticity of the lungs and their ability to receive oxygen. They can also cause a reversible, mechanical loss of FEV by simply irritating the bronchial tubes, which both reduces the air that can get into the lungs and causes intense mucus secretion. Judging from the contents of his refrigerator, Jay was doing everything the books mentioned to marginally increase his breathing ability, dosing himself with steroids, bronchial dilators, and whatever else might increase his uptake and utilization of oxygen. His color, I reflected, was usually pretty good, which suggested his self-medication was successful. The inhalers, I read, reduced the sensitivity of lung tissue, and the prednisone actually shrank the tissue. Did he use these drugs constantly or just for intervention when his FEV was dropping? Put differently, what was his unmedicated capacity? That, I suspected, was pretty low—because of the enormous amount of oxygen Jay was using. An FEV below 60, in itself a very bad sign, requires supplemental inhaled oxygen, at least intermittently, and inhaled oxygen, as Jay no doubt knew, is a deal with the devil.

The more often you use inhaled oxygen, the longer you survive. People with low FEV scores on twenty-four-hour oxygen supplementation live longer than do people with the same FEV using oxygen only fifteen hours, and they in turn live longer than people using it only ten hours. And so on. But the more often one uses supplemental oxygen, the more addicted the body becomes to it, and the more constricted one's life. Clearly Jay was trying to avoid using the stuff, even in moments of high exertion—such as swinging a baseball bat, an activity that no doubt gave him pleasure and release and a sense of his former talents. This explained, perhaps, the shortness of his visits to Allison's apartment. It also begged the question of how he had sex with her. Swinging a baseball bat is a lot less rigorous than sex. Did Jay have on an oxygen mask when he was plugging Allison? That seemed unlikely. Freaky and sick, but unlikely. I kept reading. Jay probably needed a backup source of oxygen, and I wondered if the device in the rear of his truck that he used the night we moved the bulldozer might be what the books called an oxygen concentrator, a relatively inexpensive device that pulls oxygen from the atmosphere and stores it.

Because oxygen uptake tends to decrease at night, especially during REM sleep, he was probably using the oxygen tanks mostly then. The hyperbolic chamber, I learned, is used to saturate the tissues of the body with as much oxygen as possible. Its effectiveness occurs in the outer margins of measurable oxygen uptake but it does help prevent certain kinds of infection and stiffening of tissues. Jay was doing everything he could. But no matter what, the books said, FEV keeps dropping, and once it falls below a score of 11, then death is imminent. No wonder Jay was trying not to be obsessed with it.

Walking out of the library, I remembered the mail I'd shoved in my pocket and had a look at it. Marceno had discovered what was now my former address, perhaps through the New York Bar Association, and sent me a request for interrogatories, which is basically a questionnaire used to prepare for a deposition. I threw it in the trash and flipped through the rest of the mail. There was nothing coming to me that I might look forward to, so I didn't expect to see a postcard from Casole d'Elsa, a Tuscan hill town with lovely stone towers hundreds of years old. It was from my son, in his sloppy script:

Dear Dad, Mom doesn't love Robert anymore. She says we might fly to New York City. I know the difference between gelato and ice cream.
                                                                    Love, Timothy
P.S. Italian kids don't like baseball.

Never have I scrutinized a document like this one. Not when I was studying for the New York State bar, not when I was checking the final contracts for the sale of a $562 million office building in midtown. The fact that Judith had taken my address with her was at least somewhat interesting. What did Judith and Timothy say to each other about me? Did they talk about me, did she ask him if he missed me, did he ask her what I was doing? And how did he know she didn't love Robert anymore? Is this why he wrote the card? Timothy had addressed the card himself, which meant one of two things; that he'd discovered my address among Judith's things, her address book most likely, or whatever trendy little electronic gizmo she used, because he suspected or knew that his communication was forbidden, which meant that he had secreted a stamp and mailed the postcard on the sly, a complicated undertaking for a boy his age. The other possibility was that Judith had simply provided the address to him, which meant that she knew the card was being sent and may well have known its message. Which meant that she sanctioned its existence, which then was a message directly to the husband she'd dumped not so long ago: *Our son wants to communicate with you, and this is okay with me.* Who knew?

I had an idea. I hurried down to the great sporting goods store a few blocks away, near Grand Central Station, where fathers buy their children birthday presents before taking the train home from work. The store was open until eight. I bought a fielder's glove and a new Yankees cap and packed them, with the ball signed by the great Derek Jeter, five-time All-Star, owner of four World Series championship rings, in a box marked TIMOTHY WYETH, c/o JUDITH WYETH, AMERICAN TOURISTAS EN IL VILLAGGIO D'CASOLE D'ELSA, TUSCANA, ITALIA [POSTINO: PER FAVORE PORTARE. GRAZIE]. Close enough, and not bad for a guy who hadn't been to Italy since the Clinton administration. For a return address I taped one of my new business cards to the box. Judith would scrutinize the card, see if the address was a good one, inspect the quality of the paper. If the box arrived, that is. But I liked my chances. I've been to these little Tuscan hill towns. There's generally one post office, a public servant dutifully selling stamps, weighing packages. Nobody is in a hurry but everything gets done. The winter season is the slow time in Tuscany, very few foreign tourists. An American woman like Judith would stand out.

I took the box to an international overnight shipper.

"American tourists in a small Italian town?" said the clerk.

"Yes, the husband is an executive of an American company."

"He might be getting business mail from the States on a regular basis then?"

"Quite possibly, yes."

"Our guy over there might know who it is." He shrugged. "You never know."

Good enough. You have to shoot to score, you have to hunt to kill.

There's a nice hotel around the corner from the Public Library, the Bryant Park, and they had a room, the desk clerk said. Just the place to hide for a night or two. He asked about my luggage and I said I had none. "Late meeting at the office," I lied. "And a very early one tomorrow." He met this statement with a shrug. A few minutes later I stood at the window, watching the traffic. After my lunch with Dan Tuthill the option of going to the police about the destruction of my apartment seemed even less advisable. If he caught wind of it, Dan would rescind his job offer immediately. Lawyers breaking laws end up not practicing. No, I needed to surf and wriggle and duck my way through the problem. They'd found Poppy. Martha Hallock was coming into the city tomorrow. I'd meet her and take her to the steakhouse, try to talk to Allison again. As for Jay, I pulled out my cell phone and called. Nothing. The machine picked up the call, beeped with no message. I left my number. He could be anywhere. He could be with Allison, I realized. Maybe he was in the oxygen chamber and couldn't hear the call. Aside from his daily medications, though, he seemed to have no schedule, no routine I could anticipate, just circling around Sally Cowles. I recalled his fragment of a letter to her father about the cartilage in his own ear. Did he have a hearing problem? Did Sally? Not if she practiced the piano, not if—

I knew where I'd find Jay.

eight

I TRIED JAY'S PHONE fifty times over the next twelve hours, and if that sounds like harassment or stalking that's because it was. I was due to start a new job in a mere two days, and, standing at the window in my hotel room listening to the phone ring endlessly, I was keenly aware that if I could lay down several decent years in Dan Tuthill's new shop—and there was no reason to think I couldn't—then I'd have levered myself back into the game. With the gyrations in the economy, firms had shrunk and grown, splintered and recombined; no one would care what had happened to me a couple of years back. People forget, after all. (They *forget* that George W. Bush was once a dry-well oilman with a drinking problem, that Hillary Clinton once had a brown afro and snaggleteeth.) A few good years, that's all I needed. I could eat mountains of paper, I could clock monster hours. And maybe the firm would do well as a whole. Dan had private financing from his father-in-law if he needed it. And if he was walking the straight and narrow, he'd throw himself into the enterprise. So, my boat had come in and I needed to make sure I climbed aboard—not get caught in the riptide of Jay Rainey's strange life.

I called Allison, too, wondering where we stood, and reached her at the steakhouse.

"Well, look who it is," she said. "The man who called back."

"Of course I called back."

"They don't *always*, you know."

"About what happened—"

"I want you to know that, contrary to expectation and all previous behavior patterns, I am issuing an apology."

"You are?"

"I think I was a bit *brittle* the other morning."

"Well—"

"I had a headache."

I didn't ask why. "You're in a good mood now."

"Yes, I am."

"I was expecting crankiness and accusation."

"And until yesterday, you would have gotten it, too."

"What happened?"

"There was an arrival, a somewhat *unexpected* arrival."

"Who?" Had Jay shown up?

"Not a who, but a what."

"Fish?"

"Fish. It puts me in a good mood."

"You addicted to this stuff, Allison?"

"Only psychologically. Now then, are you coming to see me?"

"Yes, but I'm bringing a date."

"What?" came her shrill response.

"An older woman."

"How *much* older?"

"About fifty years."

"Who is it?"

"The woman who sold Jay's farm."

"This is still tangled up? There's still a problem?"

"Yes. Want to hear about it?"

"No, I don't. I want to dream about my *fish*."

I collected Martha Hallock at the corner of Forty-third and Third Avenue, which is where the luxury bus into Manhattan drops people from

Long Island's North Fork, and in the low light of a winter's day, she stepped down with her cane, looking more tired than I remembered. This was a great effort for her; I doubted she could walk without the cane. But she'd gone to the trouble, so something was at stake. I helped her into the hired car I'd arranged through the hotel and we drifted downtown.

"Things have changed." She looked out the window. "I came to the city so much when I was younger."

"See a lot of shoes?"

"Yes." She smiled, pleased that I remembered her terminology. The wrinkles around her eyes collapsed in upon themselves. "Many shoes, Mr. Wyeth. Big ones, small ones. Nice ones, rough ones. The city was good for that. I could come in and have an adventure and then disappear out into the country, and no one at home would know. Once met a man standing in line at the movies. He didn't know which movie to see and I told him to see the one I was watching."

"What was the movie?"

"Oh, for goodness' sake, I have no idea. I doubt I saw five minutes of it." She settled her purse in her lap. "I was like that. Some girls are, and most people condemn them for it."

We pulled up to the steakhouse a few minutes later and I helped her out of her door and down the steps, into the vault of mahogany and oil paintings. The door to the Havana Room, I noted, was closed.

"Wonderful!" Martha Hallock cried. "Still."

"Excuse me?"

"I ate here years and years ago!" she said, throwing her gaze toward the back of the room, then letting it come forward, over the white tablecloths and silverware, the pitchers of water sweating in the corners. "They used to say Frank Sinatra owned the place. It looks the same."

"Well, we probably changed the carpeting," said Allison, gliding up to us, carrying her clipboard. "Hi, I'm the manager."

Martha Hallock took Allison in. "What do you manage?"

"I manage people's expectations."

"She does more than that," I added.

Martha nodded skeptically. Allison showed us to Table 17.

"Need anything?" she asked. "A pillow, anything at all?"

"A drink. I'll take that."

"Bill?" said Allison. "What may I get for you today?"

"Nothing. I can wait for the waitress."

"Oh, there must be *something* you'd like?"

Martha Hallock looked up at Allison. "He's taken right now, honey. Sorry, all mine."

"Then I'll have to wait," she said. "Very nice to meet you." She met my eyes. "Hope you find your meal delicious, sir."

Martha watched Allison move away. "I'd say that you know her."

"Well, I eat here a lot."

"I repeat. I'd say you know her." The waiter appeared. "I'll have a gimlet, then your New York sirloin, well done."

"Yes, ma'am."

"I mean *burnt*, so well done the chef objects."

"Before we start," I said, "I want to make sure you understand the situation, *my* situation."

Martha considered me. How many messy problems had she dealt with in a life? City dwellers, especially New Yorkers, tend to underestimate the sophistication of country people. She gave me a humoring little nod. "Mr. Marceno thinks something untoward is buried on his land," she began, her voice confident and analytical, "based on the fact that local police discovered the former owner of the property, Jay Rainey, and his attorney, you, on that land hours after the deal was done. He is also suspicious because there appeared to be a lot of heavy bulldozer work done the afternoon of the closing."

"There's also—" I stopped. Better to listen first.

"Mr. Marceno is apparently *not* aware of the fact, not *yet* anyway, that Herschel Jones was found dead of a heart attack on his bulldozer that same night on the adjoining property. Mr. Jones was known to do work for Jay Rainey and his family for many years. He was a good man, loved by all. The police were called by another man—"

"Poppy," I said.

"Yes—"

"Who is your nephew."

That I knew this was a surprise to her. "I'm afraid that's true," she said after a moment's consideration. "Poppy called the police to report Herschel's death. He had a long history of heart disease, four heart attacks in the last few years, and the local doctor who signed the death certificate happened also to have seen him a few weeks earlier when he came into the emergency room with a scare, and had specifically warned him against heavy labor, or working in the cold. Herschel should've told Jay this. But Jay never should've sent him out into that cold."

"I don't think he did."

Martha held up her hand. "Because the body had been frozen solid, the family was advised to have him cremated, which they did. Am I right so far? Is this the topic under discussion?"

I nodded.

"The problem is that Jay is being hounded by Mr. Marceno?"

I wondered if I should tell her about H.J. and his friendly limo riders. Not necessarily. "Mr. Marceno is putting a lot of pressure on Jay and on me. I'm having trouble finding Jay. I don't want to talk to Marceno, not yet anyway. You yourself said on the phone that it didn't seem to be much trouble to dig up a bit of sand. But now you're ready to talk to me?"

"Yes."

"Do you know what's out there, what Herschel was covering up?"

"No."

"You're sure?"

"Positive."

"Then why're you here?"

"Because I realized that you and Jay have no idea what you're up against."

"A Chilean winemaker with deep pockets who wants to get a foothold on the fabulous North Fork of Long Island, no?"

"Yes, but also no."

"I don't get it, Martha."

She shook her head and appeared resigned to having to provide me a remedial education. She opened her bag and pulled out a tax survey map. "This is the area around Jay's land," she said. "These tracts aren't labeled or named but I know who owns them. Now look."

The map showed the land between Long Island Sound and the north road, and looked like this:

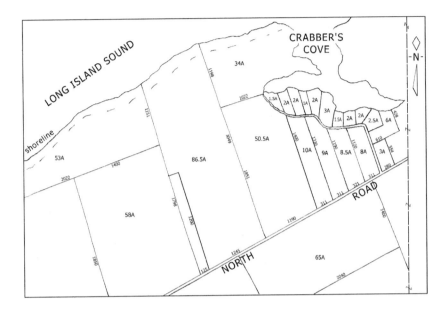

Then she labeled the lots, and it looked like this:

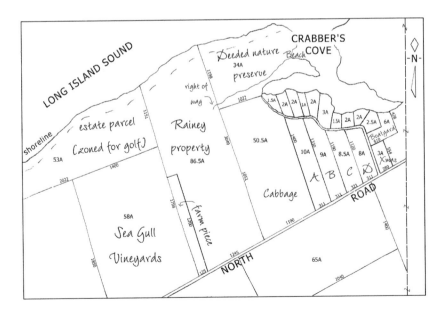

"Okay," she said, "let's talk about each of these properties. The old estate piece has some nice high bluffs, some roll to the land. It was once owned by the Reeves family, very nice people, and then they sold it. Not much has happened to it. In the sixties there was a commune there and they all lived in the old barn and tried to make goat cheese. Well, you know what happened."

"What?"

"All the girls got pregnant and the boys grew beards and they found out that the world doesn't need any more bad goat cheese."

I smiled. But Martha Hallock stared grimly at me. "Foolishness, Mr. Wyeth—the world runs on it. When it comes to real estate, foolishness makes things happen. More important than money, actually. Then the piece was bought by some fellow from North Carolina who said it was perfect for a golf course. He'd developed a dozen of them. Paid too much, but the development rights remained intact. I sold it to him. He had the surveys done, he got the approvals, which last ten years. Those ten years expire in eighteen months, by the way. As for him, he had trouble in the stock market, was in no position to develop. Okay, now, this large tract, Sea Gull Vineyards—terrible name for a vineyard, makes you think of bird poop in your wine—they, the Hoyts, planted one of the first vineyards out here, and their vines are now very good. Good vines with a bad name. Needs a new name. The development rights were sold to the county ten or fifteen years ago. You can only farm it. But Mrs. Hoyt got multiple sclerosis and her husband became depressed and the place started going downhill. Now then, next to it, to the east, is Jay's land. This little strip was a set-aside for the farm housing, separately deeded. You can see that it's a beautiful run, straight from the north road to the water. Mostly level, with a good well set back from the ocean, nice land. It was in his family a long time, came through the father's side. Remember it's in the middle of our map, it's the keystone property. Over here on the inlet is the preserve. It used to be part of the piece that was owned by Jay's family. It's beautiful but unfarmable. Marshes and lovely birds. You can catch crabs in a little rowboat. The land was deeded to New York State back in 1965 or '66. The way the deed was set up, the owner of the adjacent piece, Jay's piece, has a right-of-way along a dirt road from one property to the other. Remember that. Whoever owns

Jay's piece has sole legal access to the water through here. In other words, access to the marshes and so on, but also to—"

"There's probably a little beach."

"Yes, a beautiful little sandy beach just on the tip of the inlet. Very private. Backed by a stand of Norfolk pines planted a hundred years ago. One of the nicest beaches on the Sound, totally private."

"Jay never mentioned that."

"He probably didn't care much about it." She pointed to the little inlet called Crabber's Cove. "Surrounded by luxury houses. Serviced by one dead-end road. Large lots, mostly two acres. The subdivision was done in the early eighties and the lots sold for maybe ninety thousand back then."

"What would they be now?"

"Oh, at least four hundred thousand."

"Wow."

"That's the way it goes, Mr. Wyeth, up, sideways, then up again. Now, look here." She pointed at the property marked Boatyard. "This was owned by Kyle Lorton, who came home so dirty his wife made him wash off in the yard with a hose. Naked. You could see it from the road. His rear end looked like an old apple left out in the sun. So did his front end, for that matter. Kyle's business was lobster boats. That's what he did. He was no good with regular people. That's why lobstermen liked him. He was dirty and smelled and had black teeth and could fix anything."

"The lobsters are gone, though."

"That's right. Giuliani, your old mayor, who pretended he wasn't as bald as my knee, sprayed poison all over New York City for West Nile virus."

"Which turned out to be basically harmless."

"Yes, except for the old people and the lobsters. All that mosquito poison washed into Long Island Sound and killed our lobsters. They should have let the old people die and the lobsters live, if you ask me, which, as usual, no one did. Now the lobster business is dead and Kyle Lorton went bankrupt. It didn't help that he'd been dumping oil out back for twenty years and the DEC caught him. But that piece has a grandfathered commercial-marine-use zoning, which is now impossible to get, the only one on the inlet, by the way. It also has a nine-foot channel that Lorton used to dredge himself illegally, which means you can get a big boat in there."

"So all these pieces are in play?" I asked, studying the map. "It's a land assembly. Is that what you're saying?"

"Yes," Martha Hallock went on. "The cabbage farm also sold its development rights. I guess no one eats cabbage anymore. These little strips, A, B, C, D, maybe eight or ten acres each, are in contract now. They're used for sweet corn and potatoes. Actual potatoes, which you don't see very often anymore on the North Fork, except for the fingerlings. This is Christmas trees. This fellow's failing because too many people are selling Christmas trees and America is less and less a Christian country. We're pagans, Mr. Wyeth, every year more so, and I've been saying it for forty years." She sighed. "This is what Mr. Marceno has in mind, Mr. Wyeth."

She handed me an altered copy that looked like this:

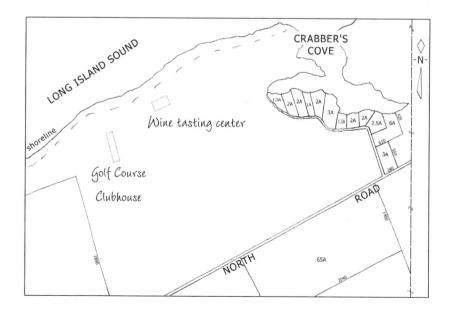

I studied it.

"Not just a vineyard, you see."

"A giant project," I said. "Have they bought all the pieces?"

"Everything except strip A, where he's holding out for a little more money, which he'll get. They own everything else or have it in contract."

A huge piece, being assembled. The key was to divide and conquer using stealth; to work through different brokers and to sequence the land buys in such a way as to avoid purchasing contiguous properties simultaneously, and to do it all as quickly as possible so prices didn't rise too much. Sometimes a matter of buying leases instead of land, it nonetheless was a common technique in developing property. The land under Rockefeller Center, for example, was assembled by gaining control over 229 deteriorating brownstones. Early in my career I helped put together an enormous lot in the East Sixties by buying nine little properties, one a mere sixteen feet wide. The firm sent me in because I looked young and guileless. I was thrilled, of course. The nine sellers sold to nine different legal entities, one with a Korean-sounding name, another with a Jewish name, and so on. If the sellers compared notes, they might not see the game. Of course, each buying entity was merely a stack of paper owned by our client, a Dutch bank.

"A big piece. Now I see it's, what, two hundred–plus acres?"

"Yes. There are a number of other sizable pieces on the North Fork, but very few of them are on the water, suitable for grapes, have proper zoning, come with their own private access preserve, have access to a sheltered inlet, and *also* are for sale."

"How much is involved here? I mean how much money?"

"The most expensive piece was the old estate piece, because it has the ocean frontage and the approval for the golf course. That was about six million. Sea Gull Poop Vineyards went for three million, owing to the quality of the vines."

I found myself remembering H.J.'s outrageous claim about the purchase price of Jay Rainey's property. The number was wildly high, but viewed in this new context, it made a kind of crazy sense. The locals must have figured something was afoot—seen the black Lincolns arriving, men in business suits standing in muddy fields, agate-type listings of real estate transfers in the weekly paper—and chattered among themselves, some of this talk reaching Mrs. Jones, and then H.J. himself, who, like Jay Rainey, was a native son. "But if you're talking putting in new vines, a golf course, and maybe building luxury housing, the total cost is moving up past, what, twenty, thirty million?"

She shook her head. "Forty-two million, Mr. Wyeth, in phases. A ten-year project. That includes a beautiful wine-tasting center right at the end of Jay's property. Golf and wine. Forty-two million." She leaned forward conspiratorially. "*They have the money.* A Latin American company buying prime oceanfront in the United States of America gets Latin American money very easily. These are smart, sophisticated people. They do business in eight or nine countries."

"What about all the local approvals, the zoning?"

"They have it. Or they will massage it through. All the property falls within the town of Riverhead, which is much easier. All those unemployed blacks in downtown Riverhead, frankly. Displaced by the Mexicans and Guatemalans who will work for less, live in a tent if we'd let them. Riverhead has huge social problems. The town has lost industry. One of the aerospace companies, Grumman, had a huge site but closed up, taking their tax dollars with them. The strip malls have sucked money out of Main Street. The town is addicted to new tax dollars, Mr. Wyeth. A project like this means jobs," she said proudly. "It won't be too hard to get through. Also they've hired a local person who knows all the right people. An old hand. Somebody who can fix things when they go wrong."

"Who?"

"Me."

Judging from the map, it looked like the wine-tasting building would be located in about the place where Herschel had been regrading the land. Did this account for Marceno's anxiety? I kept studying the map. "You could bring in private tour boats or small luxury cruisers in the inlet, have them dock at the boatyard and drive them straight to the golf course or the vineyards."

"Now you're starting to think like a real estate developer." Martha

Hallock smiled. "There's a local airport only five miles away. Private high-speed jet foil service to downtown Manhattan—a beautiful ride, by the way—takes forty-five minutes. You got a beach, a nature preserve, the whole thing."

"Why not do it on the South Fork, in the Hamptons, where there's more money and the famous beaches?"

"Because the Hamptons are too crowded, too built out, and you can't get pieces of land like this anymore. They just don't exist. All carved up. Plus, growing grapes on the South Fork isn't as feasible. The soil is different, the season is slightly shorter, and the zoning boards are controlled by ladies who lunch and run flower shops."

"You sound a little bitter."

"I'm sick of the Hamptons, Mr. Wyeth. Hate them. Snobs and bores. Silver spoons jammed into their brains. They've been looking down on the North Fork for fifty years. Believe me, I know. So now they've gone and ruined it and are looking around and want to gobble up the North Fork. All the big real estate agencies have opened offices, want to drive me out of business. Well, fine. But let them and anyone else who wants our fork *pay*. Let them make the old farmers and fishermen rich."

I jabbed at the map. "If it's all wrapped up, what's the problem?"

"I can help with the local officials," said Martha. "But if there's an environmental problem, then that involves the state of New York. I don't know anyone at that level. The state will take its own time, the state doesn't care that Mr. Marceno has money burning. Also, this deeded preserve piece has a section of wetland. It's on the maps. Wetland is federally protected. Any lobbying to change its designation would have to be done in Washington."

"You could lose five years."

"That's right. Easily. You see Jay's land dips to the east and drains into this section of wetland. They want to know what's under the ground before they dig it up, Mr. Wyeth. Once they dig it up, then they're locked into a sequence."

"And Jay knows what's buried there."

"*They* think so."

"Does Marceno know Poppy is familiar with the land?"

"He could find out easily enough. There's a lot of pressure on them. The next town board elections are in the fall and I'm pretty sure they want to railroad all this through before then."

She'd just wiggled past something. I said, "You're pretty sure, huh?"

"Yes."

"They're paying you to read the local weather patterns?"

"Well, yes."

"So you're telling them to get this pressed through before the local elections."

She looked at me.

"It seems, Martha, that you're being paid to make this happen and have guided them all along, and now you have a problem they expect you to solve."

"Well, that'd be one—"

"And that you weren't just thinking of Jay's better interests in all this."

"Mr. Wyeth," said Martha, "I'm here to *help*."

"I still don't understand why you don't talk to Jay directly."

She chewed a bit of steak in response, and it was hard for her. But she kept at it, just as she was doing with me.

"You do know about the accident?"

I shook my head. "Not really."

"Oh my. Well, so you don't understand a word of what I'm saying. One of the summer girls was just terribly enamored of Jay. And he of her. This was fifteen years ago, more or less. He wasn't even twenty. I think she was from a very wealthy family. British. They'd rented a big house on the water a few miles away. Girls like that would never look at local farmboys. But then Jay came along. She'd fallen in love with him, and her parents were closing up the house for the summer and the girl was frantic, you know, that was the way I heard it, anyway, and she called Jay's house and his father said he couldn't go out and—well, to make a long story short, he slipped out that night and on the way back he ran through the potato fields, his father's own fields, and someone had left a paraquat sprayer on. Use it on weeds, anything that grows. Terrible stuff. They found him in the morning, just about dead."

Martha looked straight through me. "The same night that happened,

Jay's parents had a terrible fight. I told you his father was a rotten man. His mother ran away. Never seen again, never contacted anyone. No one could believe it, except that her husband was so bad. They think she left the North Fork, could have gone anywhere. She was a good-looking woman and might have called a few men—who knows?

"And then Jay got better. He came out of it, after being in the hospital for weeks. It was terrible—a terrible blow for a boy. He was *still* a boy, nineteen. I call that a boy. His mother was gone and his father was no good. And Jay himself was—he was in a wheelchair for a month, too weak to walk. There was considerable lung damage. Permanent."

"Yes, I know."

"So, Mr. Wyeth, I'm trying to help Jay get free of that land. Get on with his life. What's wrong with that?"

"Can't blame you," I said.

"He left town after the accident. The family had blown apart. We didn't see him. I heard he went to Europe, ran chasing after that girl, still loved her. His father drove the farm into the ground just like I knew he would, finally leased it out, let the hands stay in one of the houses. He died a few years ago when his liver gave out and then the land passed to Jay and I guess he felt it was time to sell it."

She watched me as she finished her story, and it occurred to me that much as Martha Hallock had filled in Jay Rainey's biography, much as she had demonstrated the size of the operation arrayed against him, and me, she had not in any way helped solve the problem. In fact, I could even say that she was turning the screw—on *me*.

"Martha," I began, "what exactly is your fiduciary relationship with Marceno?"

"Well, I said I was helping a bit. Nothing more than that."

"I mean specifically. Contractually. Are you a consultant, fee-for-hire, an agent working on percentage, or a principal?"

"That's a ridiculous question, Mr. Wyeth, I'm an old woman who's only trying to—"

"Since you aren't answering me, I'll assume you're a principal. You have a stake in this thing. Which means, from a legal point of view, that you're Marceno's partner. Which means your interests are aligned, Martha. I might as well be talking to him directly."

She stared at me, eyes troubled.

"What's buried in the ground out there, Martha?"

She shook her head once, almost as if slapped. "Nothing."

"How do you know?"

"I don't," she hissed.

"Then how can you assert anything one way or another?"

"Nothing is in the ground that is going to *hurt* anything."

These were shavings of an answer. "Then why can't you tell your business partner that? Your interests are the same, are they not?"

"It's not like that."

"And while I'm on the topic, it sounds to me like you have a conflict of interest, Martha. You were the seller's broker. Your sign was out there in the weeds."

"That's not true."

"How else did I know to find you?"

She couldn't answer that.

"You were the seller's broker yet representing the buyer's interests. Does Jay realize this? And by the way, does Marceno know the man who found the dead body is your nephew?"

"I can't answer these questions, and even if I could, I wouldn't."

She started to rise. But I reached around the table and grabbed her cane. "Martha, you came into the city to put pressure on me, didn't you? Just like Marceno is putting pressure on *you*, now."

"No."

"He's suing me, you know, Jay as well."

"You don't say."

What kind of answer was this? "Marceno sent you."

"No."

"Told you to act like you were helping us."

"No, Mr. Wyeth!"

"And either you do know what is buried on that property and don't want anyone else to know, which means you're in a hell of a fix with Mr.

Marceno—I could tell him all this, by the way, or"—I stuttered for a moment, trying to understand—"or you actually *don't* know what's buried there and fear that something *is*. Something very *bad*. Like a barnload of arsenic or something. In either case, it seems to me, you are certain that Jay Rainey has no idea what it is. As am I! And yet you are letting Marceno attack him, and me. Isn't that right?"

"Give me my cane!"

But I didn't. "I just realized what you want, Martha, why you came into the city."

"I doubt that."

"No, I got it, I got the message."

"What?" she cried, seemingly more alarmed than ever.

"You wanted *me* to figure it out. This is all a big mistake. It was never supposed to happen. There *is* something buried there, and even if you don't know what it is, you want me to find out. Jay doesn't know, so he's of no use! Marceno doesn't know that *you* know either what's there *or* that Jay doesn't know. You want me to somehow figure it out—and if you do know, you're not telling me—and you want me *not* to inform Jay, but to inform Marceno, but not in such a way that it looks like you were coaching me to do so. Yes, you're in some kind of jam with *both* men, Martha, and you're dropping the pressure on *me!*"

I gently handed her the cane, and she stood to rise. The car was waiting for her outside. As she gathered her purse, a look passed into her face, and despite her advanced age, I glimpsed a shrewd businesswoman. "Pretty good, Mr. Wyeth," she allowed, "pretty good."

"Don't expect my cooperation, Martha."

"I won't. But you"—she put both of her wrinkled old hands on the cane and dared to lean forward, right into my face, so close I could see her stumpy teeth, the little hairs on her chin—"*you* should not expect Mr. Marceno to remain patient with you."

"With me?"

"With *you.*"

She stood back, quite confident of her position. I suddenly understood that Martha Hallock had been ahead of me at each step. "You told Marceno that I knew what was there?"

She didn't quite answer. But it was answer enough.

"And you told him Jay didn't know?"

Now she nodded.

"And if I find out and tell Jay?"

"Oh, Mr. Wyeth," she said, taking her first step toward the door, "I wouldn't do that."

The window said STEINWAY, and that evening I walked past milling parents and nervous children to confront a circular performance space, centered with an enormous grand piano and rows of chairs. Families of well-to-do people. I floated toward the rear, which receded very elegantly into a hallway that opened upon room after room of beautiful pianos, mahogany, ebony, cherry, some new, others reconditioned, each costing tens of thousands of dollars. I heard a round of applause and walked back to the performance space. A woman with ambitious hair stood before the group thanking the Steinway Company for lending them the space for the concert, and if any of the parents were interested in a piano, then a sales representative was there to assist them. The parents looked tired and determined, glad to be seeing their children perform, steeled against the effort of another event. And then I saw Jay, far off to one side, in a chair, holding a program. He was dressed, as at the basketball game, in a good suit, and appeared to be just another big, well-fed Wall Street trader or banker or corporate executive whiling away an hour, with whatever aloofness in his expression attributable to pressing worries over matters large and high-dollared.

Sally Cowles was the eleventh child to perform. Her interpretation of Beethoven's "Für Elise" was neither very good nor very bad—adequate, a bit of pedal work, the chords done well. But her determination was clear and she glared into her sheet music and then back at her hands, and the notes arrived more or less on time. Not that it mattered—she was sweet and spirited and were I her father I would tell myself that kid has no musical ability whatsoever but she's happy, she's going to be fine, she's one of life's winners.

I took this opportunity to check on Jay, and could see him in half profile staring at Sally Cowles. He sat dead still, hunched over like a diamond cutter, careful in his scrutiny, blinking from time to time. His face was filled with pain. Yes, it was pain on his face, a kind of uncomprehending suffering. When the girl had finished her performance she sprang up and gave a formal, nervous bow, charming in its artlessness. She hurried back to her seat and sat down with heavy relief next to a woman in her early thirties holding a baby boy on her lap. This was the woman I'd seen while looking through Allison's window. The girl shrugged at her stepmother's comment and giggled with a friend sitting next to her and then returned her attention to the next performance, which was being given by a fat little boy with red curls, and who was much better.

Jay looked down, as if to gather himself, and then back at Sally Cowles, who had no inkling of his interest. She was now giggling behind her program with her friend, rather rudely, in fact, and had slipped down on her seat. Her stepmother bent closely and said something sharp to her and the girl sat up obligatorily but returned to her secret communications with her friend. The fat little boy, meanwhile, sweetly filled the hall with Mozart. Sally Cowles was quite pretty but seemed still mostly unaware of it. Later, no doubt, it would complicate her life. Beauty always does.

I took a step back from the crowd then, and watched as Jay stood up during the enthusiastic applause over the boy and made his way through the audience, toward the row behind the girl. He smiled polite excuses as he moved past the clapping mothers and fathers and kids until he lingered behind Sally Cowles's head, staring down at the perfect part of her hair. He let his fingers linger on the back of her seat, perhaps incidentally touching her shoulder or long hair. Then he lifted his hand next to her head, as if to gently smooth his palm along her head. I felt suddenly alarmed. Did he mean her harm? Sally's stepmother noticed him and looked back in curiosity. Jay eased onward, crinkling his eyes and nodding and saying all the right things as he reached the end of the row and fled toward the entrance. I was ready for this and followed him from behind, but when I stepped out onto Fifty-seventh Street, I could see his wide back already down the block.

I ran and caught up. "Jay," I said. "Stop."

I took him by the arm.

"Bill? Hey. What a coincidence."

"It's nothing like that."

He smiled in false confusion and I had to remind myself that this was the same man I'd seen earlier sucking on adrenaline, smashing baseballs at the batting cage, a man who sat in an oxygen chamber penning unsent letters to Sally Cowles's father. I kept my arm on the sleeve of his coat. "You talk to me now, Jay, right now."

"What's the problem?"

It was a good try on his part, and if I hadn't known better I might have believed I'd made a terrible mistake. "You're good, Jay. You fooled Allison, and you fooled me for a while and who knows who else you've fooled, but—"

He shook my arm away. "You're out of your mind, Bill."

He stood there, squared off, daring me, and in some manner probably curious to see what I actually knew.

"The girl who just played the piano was Sally Cowles, Jay." I spoke slowly, trying to calm myself. "As you know, Sally Cowles is the daughter of David Cowles, your tenant on the fourth floor of the building on Reade Street. She was on the bench at the girls' basketball game a few nights ago. You wanted the building where Cowles worked. That building, that *specific* building, and no other. Marceno told me that, thought you were nuts. You negotiated a trade for the land. They looked into it and saw you were offering a fantastic deal. So they made it. And then there's Allison's apartment. This isn't all coincidence. I don't get all the connections, Jay, but what I do get is very weird, very sick."

Rainey considered me coldly, mouth a slit, like he might punch me in the face.

"And then there're your lungs."

He said nothing, but seemed to soften, even crumple before me.

"From the herbicide."

He blinked. "You found out?"

"Martha Hallock."

"She would know."

▪ ▪ ▪

He'd talk to me, Jay claimed, but he wanted to go back to Brooklyn to do it. At first this made no sense to me, as there were any number of bars and restaurants in Manhattan where we could have stopped, but then I realized he probably needed either medicine or oxygen.

"I'm not leaving you until I know the whole story," I said.

"Right." His head was bowed and I sensed he was already far from me.

"There are people looking for you, Jay, and they're making my life a fucking *misery.*"

"Right, right."

"No, *not* 'Right, right'! You're making it better, for me, *tonight,* Jay. You are going to tell me what I need to know to escape whatever fucked-up situation you're caught in."

We were quiet during the long cab ride, and who knows what the driver thought when he dropped off two grown men in front of a dark garage in the bowels of Brooklyn. Jay took out his keys as we climbed the steps. In the streetlight I could see the streaks on the risers from the oxygen tanks going up and down. "Somebody broke into my place yesterday," he said. "Didn't steal anything."

We stepped inside and he sat immediately on his small bed.

"Let me just do this," Jay said. He took what I thought was a clear plastic device off the table, fitted the mouthpiece between his lips, and blew hard. A red indicator jumped. He coughed mightily and spat a glob of mucus into the wastebasket. Then he studied the red indicator and leaned over to a chart and wrote it down. The device, I suspected, was a peak-flow meter, used to measure lung capacity.

"What was it?" I asked.

He didn't answer, so I picked up the device and looked at where the red indicator had stopped along the measuring line.

"Two hundred and thirty?" From the charts in the library, I remembered that a man of Rainey's size and age would have a lung capacity of well over six hundred milliliters. I did the math. His FEV was about 35— terrible. I was surprised he could stand.

Now he picked up an aerosol canister off the table, shook it, fitted it into the inhaler, and pressed it. I could hear the quick burst of medication go into his throat. He closed his eyes and held his breath. Finally he let it out. He was opening up the airway. Then he fit an oxygen mask over his face, punched a square red button, and breathed deeply. The oxygen machine hummed. His motions had the smooth unconsciousness of habit. Then he clicked on another machine that showed several readouts: pulse, blood pressure, respiration per minute, and percent oxygenation. They all read zero. Jay picked up a wire with a loop and a red light on the end, fit it over his finger, and the oxygenation number beeped on. It was eighty-nine percent.

"Even I know that's low."

He nodded. Lifted the mask. "I can go for a few hours with it low but no more."

"That night we drove back into the city?"

"I was close to passing out."

"You got some kind of oxygen tank in the back of your truck?"

"Yeah." He looked at the monitor. It had reached ninety-one. He poked through some pills on a dish, picked up several, and swallowed them dry. I realized that he lived on a cycle of medications, up and down, through the day, and from what I'd seen, he was a different man in each of the phases of the cycle: high and charismatic and exuberant when the steroids kicked in, despondent and nearly catatonic at the low.

"You just took a steroid?"

"Yes. Man, I'm sorry I got you into all this, Bill. I never expected it, okay? It wasn't the plan, I was just trying to get back . . . I've been, I've been way out, man. I'm feeling the oxygen."

He lay slack on the bed, eyes closed, a smile on his lips, and I felt like I was losing him.

"Who was your father?" I asked, for this is often a way into who a man is.

"My father? He was a bastard, a real hard-ass. He's the reason . . . he was just a bad farmer. Never should have been a farmer, but my mother loved the land, see. Potato farming was in his family, but potato farming on Long Island started to die in the sixties. He was frustrated. I accept that. A frustrated, bitter man. I don't think my mother was easy, either. They fought like hell. She once threw a pot of coffee at him. I loved her, though, I always did."

"You worked on the farm?"

"Sure, sure, I could drive a potato truck by the time I was eleven. Tractor, too."

"Your dad kept farming?"

"Even though there was no money in it, yeah. He broke even some years. We put some ornamental trees in, sold them to landscapers, that kind of thing."

"Who was the girl from England?"

Jay wasn't expecting my question, and his face fell into the same haunted melancholy I'd seen the first night I knew him, when he'd hugged Allison after the deal to buy the property on Reade Street.

"Her name was Eliza Carmody," he said. "Beautiful girl. Sassy as hell. It was June after my sophomore year in college. I was going to—I'd been—" He sighed, unable to say it.

I pointed at the yellow clipping on the wall. "The Yankees?"

He nodded and pressed his lips together and closed his eyes.

"Would you've made it?"

"Who knows? Maybe. They had a great farm system. I'd played well for two seasons in college."

"You had a shot."

"Yeah."

"You were a big kid from a farming town way out on Long Island, your family had no real money, your parents argued a lot, and you had a shot. You would've given it your everything," I thought aloud. "Is that fair to say?"

"Fair to say, yes," he agreed. "At this late date."

"So," I pressed him. "Eliza Carmody?"

"Yeah, it was the summer, I was working for my father. I'd had a bunch of girlfriends in college that year, you know, the usual sort of thing, no one special, nothing really serious, basically doing more fuck-ing than studying, playing ball and drinking beer, then I got signed, and they told me, Play out your season at college, finish the college playoffs, then we'll work you into the double A team in July. I had two or three weeks to kill, so I went home, worked out, threw the ball every day. I was just waiting for things to get started."

In that time he did a little work for his father, Jay said, delivering a truckload of privet hedges to a big shingled place on the water a few miles away, he and a couple of other sweaty, sunburned boys working for seven dollars an hour, more than the Mexicans got, simply because of the color of their skin, and they pulled the green farm truck up in the driveway and started unloading the bushes, each with a heavy ball of earth wrapped in burlap. That was when he saw a tall young woman of about twenty hitting a tennis ball against a backboard. She wore a pleated tennis dress that just reached her fanny and the boys on the crew watched her with hunger, watched not only her tanned thighs and shoulders but the way she drilled the ball with aggression, again and again, grunting each time she hit it.

"I just had to talk to her," Rainey said, adjusting his oxygen. "She was spectacular. I didn't care that I was some poor kid from a potato farm. Worse that could happen was she'd tell me to go to hell."

He threw down his shovel, he said, and stepped onto the court, suddenly awkward and out of place within the crisp white lines.

"Hello," she'd called, "those are not exactly tennis togs."

He'd looked at his work boots. "No."

She came over to him. "Can I help you with something?"

Was she amused by his presence? Her accent was British, he realized. He liked it. "No. Not really."

"You're not planning to serve it to me?"

"Excuse me?"

"Not planning to bang it at me?"

"No."

"Do you *play* tennis?"

"Not really."

"What good are you then?" She was standing quite close to him, considering they didn't know each other's names. "You have another sport?" she asked, squinting up into the sun.

"Baseball." He watched her eyes move from his face to his throat to his chest and then back again.

"I see," she said.

"You're British?" he ventured.

"Yes."

"I was watching you hit the ball."

"Yes, that was apparent."

She was a year or two older, he could tell, and decades more knowledgeable about the world. "You're visiting?"

"I'm just on holiday for a week with my mum and then it's back to London."

"You live there?"

"I do. You live here?"

"Jamesport."

"Where is that?"

"Here on the North Fork. Just a small town."

"So you may be accurately described as a small-town boy?"

He wasn't sure if she was teasing him or belittling him. But he also knew they'd be having sex soon, perhaps within the day.

"I guess."

"But a *big* small-town boy."

"I guess, yeah."

"You must play sports?"

"Baseball."

"Oh yes, you said that. Are you quite good?"

"Yes."

"You are?" She smiled to herself. "How good?"

It was his one piece of currency, he knew then and remembered now, his only one, and he had never used it before, at least not in this way, with someone from well outside his world, and he didn't know if she would find it valuable or even know what it meant.

"Well," he began, "I got signed by the Yankees."

"The New York City Yankees?"

"Yes, the New York Yankees is the name. Their farm system, I mean."

"The baseball team."

"Yeah," he said, a little frustrated, "the *Yankees*."

"They signed you up, then?"

"I play on their farm team first, then you eventually get your shot at the majors."

She had edged even closer, dragging her tennis racquet in the green clay. "Will you make it?"

He waited. "I don't know."

"What do you *think*?"

"I think I will. Yes."

And this twenty-year-old British girl, who later Jay was to discover had already enjoyed a number of lovers, ranging from an Oxford don to a banker colleague of her father's, saw in Jay, I suspect, what was really there. Strength and decency and confidence and pure talent. It was not just his size and animal health, it was the openness of his face, and enough of this had survived to attract Allison Sparks years later, I realized. She was embittered and amused and skeptical, but she still saw it in him. As I had, too. He had been, standing in the sun on that tennis court, a beautiful boy-man. Eliza Carmody had known such men before, but he was pure and this intrigued her. It was new.

"I think," Eliza Carmody said a little more softly, "that you should pick me up here tonight at seven o'clock."

"Okay," he said.

"You do want to, don't you?"

"Yes," he'd answered, and his look went through her. It had been simple between them five minutes prior but it was no longer.

Now Jay lifted the oxygen mask from its holder, fitted it against his mouth, and closed his eyes. The pulsometer atop the flow regulator blinked. I saw him inhale. He let the mask fall away.

"We had two weeks together. I was over there every night. I knew she was going to leave and I knew I was going to report to the farm team. Basically we just spent every night together. I was nineteen years old, man, I was at the top of my game, I was in love."

And then, he said. Their last night. Eliza called his house to say that her parents had decided to leave the next day, a change of plans. She had to see him that night, he had to sneak over. It was not far and he decided to run it, to keep in shape. His mother's car was an embarrassing little subcompact that only advertised how poor they were, and his father drove battered farm trucks and was possessive about them. So, better to run, and he did, slipping in past the tennis court, meeting her on the beach. She was ready with blankets and a picnic basket. They spent most of the night on the beach, and not for a moment did I not remember what it was like to be that age, to be torn by love and grief and desire, so I did not belittle this, I did not see it as any lesser than what happens to men and women later in their lives, which is heavier and filled with an awareness that one is not young anymore. Jay told me about that night and when I think of him with this young woman, I see them kiss agonizingly and then Jay force himself away. It's late. There's sunrise in a few hours. He must get home. He doesn't have a car, but no matter. His mind is full of the girl, and he feels strong. He knows he is strong enough to run the few miles from her house, after the sex and weeping and terrible parting. He knows this about himself without having to think about it. He is all arms and legs and lungs and he enjoys the sweat building on him, for he can walk the last quarter mile to his house and cool down. He pounds along the main road, enjoying the shadows, a bug catching in his mouth that he spits out, then turns the corner, nearing his father's field. He knows all the turns and dirt side roads, every one, and he sees the light of his house far across the field and wonders if he might be in trouble. Yes, he is probably in trouble. His father is expecting him to be up early, at 6 a.m., in fact. It's already well past two. Maybe he can get a few hours of sleep. So he will take a shortcut, striding over the rows of potato plants to save a few minutes, go directly. He feels the strength in his arms and legs, a pleasant cramp in his side, nothing he hasn't felt many times before during football practice, or running wind sprints on the basketball court. And the Yankees farm system coaches made him run for the physical, made him run the bases, run the outfield, and then a treadmill. They made him stand in against a practice pitcher throwing in the low nineties, they made him throw from a crouch from third to first to test his pure arm strength. He wants to play second base. Cal Ripken Jr. revolutionized the position. Ripken was six foot four. Second used to be for wiry little guys, now it can be big guys. He knows, however, that they might try to make him into a catcher. They've already told him this. He's got the size, especially in the legs. They put him on the leg press and he could stack seven hundred pounds and they said that's enough, you're still getting stronger, we know you played high school football, that's plenty enough, in fact. Pleased by it, writing the number down on their sheets. And they took him outside so he could put on the catcher's equipment and make the throw to second and he nailed it only two times out of ten. Not great. Sometimes the speed but not the accuracy, sometimes the accuracy but not the speed. Keep the arm up, come over the shoulder. Fucking bad habits, the old sidearm. And the equipment bothered him, the catcher's mask the most. The coaches didn't seem too worried. They knew he'd never played catcher, except back in Pony League. He had the size, they knew it. So he would agree to catcher but try to get some action at second. It occurred to him that he was thinking about baseball even though he'd just left her, which was a good sign. *I think I'm in love with her but if I have baseball I can stand it, can stand missing her.* They'd talked about him visiting her in London in the fall. Yes, she would wait. He worried that she would sleep with other men. He had already been with enough girls to know which ones were like that. But she had liked him, he could tell. And not too many other men would be playing pro baseball. At least there was that. Which did he love more? Baseball or Eliza? It was a stupid question. No it wasn't. They were different but they could be thought of in the same way. That was the thing. He saw it. His thing for her was as big as his thing for baseball. He needed both now. He thought it was just baseball but now it was her, too. Maybe she would come see him play. He would make the fucking team and send her a schedule, maybe a few clippings. Rainey goes 8 for 13 in three-game home stand. Fucking British with their cricket bats. She'd come over here and see American baseball. He pictured her in the stands. What's a fly ball? Why do they call it "fly"? That musical accent he loved. All those questions. He looked forward to the bus rides and the motel rooms. Of course it was tiring but it was exciting too. The best guys he'd ever played against and with. The best coaching, the best fields. Well, some of the university fields were pretty good. But the farm teams had their regular fans, the whole deal. It was good, good, good. A world away from the farm, from his parents. His father was a fucking bastard and his mother responded with open hatred, and Jay could escape them both by playing baseball. That was the beauty of it. *The better he played, the farther away he would be.* He kept the pace up as he turned onto his family's land. There'd be girls along the way. He didn't have to be faithful to Eliza yet. He loved her but there would be other girls. There had to be. It was too good. They'd done it twice that night, the second time much longer. He didn't worry about coming too soon. He'd learned to hold it. She'd been wet the first time and sort of sticky the second time, then got wet again as he was doing it. He reached down into his shorts and rubbed his finger against his groin, then brought it to his nose. That smell. You had to learn to like it and then you liked it a lot. He felt good. Stride was smooth, his shadow on the road rippling and synchronized, arm, leg, arm, leg, right through the rows of potatoes. The stitch in his side was gone. He had a tendency toward tightness in the calves but tonight they felt good, warm and loose.

And as he thinks this, he smells something, a metallic tingle in his nose, then his eyes sting. Blinking, suddenly tearing up. He slows his speed to rub his eyes; then he cannot breathe. He slows to a walk, then stops, leaning over. A sledgehammer is pounding his chest. His eyes burn. He lowers his head, realizing he smells herbicide. Someone left the paraquat sprayer on. He falls to the ground and crawls. *Which way is the wind blowing?* he thinks. Usually it comes out of the southwest. But it can wheel around. *Am I going farther into it or out the other side?* He can't open his eyes. He is coughing terribly. His lungs feel swollen, heavy. He had the whole night sky in his lungs one moment and then the next he's sucking life through a flaming straw. He can feel his head getting stupid. *I'm going to run as hard as I can in one direction, that's my only chance.* And so he does, somehow forcing himself to his feet and then, eyes closed, mouth tight, lungs burning, he runs through the night, stumbling and staggering over the low potato plants. Perhaps he runs fifteen seconds, thirty, no more. No one can run with lungs filled with paraquat, and then—and then Jay is on the ground, vomiting, nose bleeding, lips foaming, and if there is a benevolent God or a being or a higher power, then the wind would shift right then.

It doesn't.

When he is found the next morning by one of the farmworkers, a middle-aged black man named Herschel, Jay is lying in the dirt, barely alive. The wind has shifted, but only later. A boy of nineteen, in his prime, lying at the edge of a potato field. His fingernails have turned black.

You could think about that a long time, and I have, ever since Jay told me.

"When I woke up in the hospital, like three days later, they had an airway down me—" He lay back on his bed. I noticed that he was playing with the dial on the oxygen machine. He breathed through his nose, easily now. The oxygenation meter said ninety-six percent. "I asked about my mother. They told me she was gone. Drove off. She probably had no idea I was in the hospital. She and my father had a terrible fight that night. I think she was angry that he wouldn't let me use the truck. He probably hit her. He really might have. She had this little old shit car, a Toyota, and took off. Didn't pack. Just fucking took off. Later my father admitted he'd hit her."

"Where did she go?"

"I don't know. I always figured she went to live with her father, he was some oil guy in Texas."

"She never told you where she'd gone?"

Before answering my question, Jay did a strange thing. He reached into his drawer and pulled out what looked like a cigar. It *was* a cigar. He bit off the end.

"You going to smoke *that*?"

"I wish."

"You wish?"

"I love the taste of cigars. I light one maybe once a month. One puff and that's it."

I remembered the night I'd met Jay. "Is that the one Allison got for you in the Havana Room?"

"The very same, man. I saved it for a special occasion."

"Which is what?"

"I'm going to tell you something I've never told anyone. Hey, open the windows, would you?"

There were two, one facing the street, one over the stairs. I lifted them up and the cold night rushed in. Meanwhile Rainey went to the kitchen, ran the water, and returned with a glass nearly full. "Open the door, too."

I did. He pulled out an inhaler and gave himself several more shots, and when he pulled it away, the medicinal mist of the stuff floated from his mouth.

"Okay." He pulled the glass of water close, then lit the cigar. He blew air through it, making the tip glow, looked up at me, nodded, then puffed once, held the smoke in his mouth until his eyes widened, then released the smoke upward. It dissipated in the air from the windows and door so quickly I barely smelled anything.

"That's good." He dropped the cigar into the water, making a short hiss, then closed his eyes and seemed to redream the smell of the cigar. His face reddened. He coughed violently and shot himself with the inhaler again. "All right . . . I'm all right. There. Fucking stupid, fucking suicidal." He coughed deeply but laughed. "One half puff and I'm a"— he coughed—"a *mess*." He sucked hard on the oxygen. "Stupid, but I love it. Lung tissue reacts so quickly. That was it. My indulgence, Bill. Once a fucking month for Christ's sake, one half puff." He put away the lighter in his drawer, coughed again, hard, and spat a brown glob into the trash.

I got up to close the windows and door. "So, you were telling me—?"

"Right. My mother drove off that night and I never saw her again, man." He stopped, his eyes considering the enormity of this, the implausible strangeness of it. "I asked my father a million times where she'd gone, and he was so fucked up by everything, sometimes he said she must have a boyfriend, sometimes he didn't know, sometimes he said she must've gone back to Texas. He said he called information down there, in Houston. He took a trip one time and I figured he went looking for her. That he knew and didn't tell me. Maybe he'd seen her with another man. But I wasn't sure. He wasn't well. When he was dying, he made me promise to tell her that he was sorry, that he had always loved her, that he—shit, he was a mess, he was weeping, he was fucked up. It's bad to see your father like that. His life came to *nothing*, he was a drunk and a fuckup and he never got over how one day he had a beautiful wife and son who was, you know, maybe going to play in the majors, maybe—only maybe, and then the next he has no wife and a son who can't even blow out a match."

We sat there. I didn't have anything useful to say. I think it's possible to hate one's father yet also grieve for him, and this might have described how Jay felt. But I didn't give voice to the thought; instead I watched the compression device on the oxygen chamber rise and fall, while outside the room's tiny windows the Brooklyn night spun past.

But in time Jay began to remember again, and now he simply talked into the room toward the ceiling, his voice not confessional—for a confession requires not only wrongdoing but also a listener willing to make a moral judgment—but duller than that, as if giving testimony in a long and intricate case, the points of which he had mastered and yet which he knew was probably of slim interest to anyone else. There is only a little relief in simply letting such a collection of facts unspool from oneself, but we all of us were once chimps chattering in the trees, desperate to be heard and understood, to find a language particular to the self, and in this Jay was no different.

Within two months of his accident, he said, he'd regained the strength to get to England. His chances of playing professional baseball were now zero. The Yankees called after he hadn't reported, then received further details through his college coach. They sent a kind but brief letter wishing him well with his recuperation. Meanwhile he was spitting up buckets of phlegm every day, learning to use a nebulizer correctly. He could swing a bat weakly and he could throw off speed, but that was it. The shock was enormous, staggering. As was the fact that his mother had not yet come home. The only possible compensation would be to find Eliza Carmody. He'd written her, received one letter back. He did not tell her of the accident. He tried to call her, with no luck. So that fall he bought a ticket using the remains of his signing bonus money. He arrived at Paddington Station, rail thin, hair long, with almost no money, willing to live anywhere in London. He moved between neighborhoods and acquaintances, some benign, some not, the expectable grab bag of out-of-work models, would-be novelists, cannabis layabouts, abused seekers of truth, and piano-playing carpenters. That he did not understand the striations of English society meant that he was unencumbered by certain anxieties. And anyway, when you were an American in London, those things did not matter so much. The Brits liked the fact that you didn't understand, it was refreshing to them, or so they said. He found the London girls exciting and he wished he had more money with which to chase them. He found Eliza, he said. A house in Chelsea, on Tite Street. Ivy and black shutters. The parents were never home. Jay and Eliza were left alone. Her father was trying to rearrange the funding for the tunnel between London and Paris, the Chunnel. He was a little fat man with sausage fingers and almost no understanding of twenty-year-old girls. Jay saw him once at the end of the driveway and feared the man instantly.

Eliza didn't seem happy to see him. She didn't seem anything, really. Discouraged, or tired, actually. She played tennis with a friend on the soft clay court behind her house while he watched. But she wasn't well and in the middle of a point she went to the bushes and vomited matter-of-factly. He was in love with Eliza, and when she told him that she was pregnant he felt shock and a small sudden pride. Are you sure? he asked. Of course, yes, of course I am, she said. Mine? *My* baby? Yes *absolutely*, who do you bloody think I am? she said. They kept it secret for several weeks, but her mother, herself a former tall beauty, began to ask questions, and so with Jay present, Eliza told her mother. Instantly the parents were furious. They had plans for their daughter, plans that did not include a penniless, good-looking American who hung over park benches winded after a short walk.

There followed quite a fight, with Eliza defiant of her parents' disapproval yet noncommittal toward Jay himself. She was, after all, from a wealthy family, and had no intention of marrying someone with no money. None whatsoever, end of discussion, no romantic illusions ever suffered for a moment in this house, Mr. Raintree, or what*ever* your name is! Finally Eliza's mother burst into tears and fled up the stairs, leaving her father to glare coldly upward at Jay. He understood that he was an intruder, and said he'd come for Eliza the next day; when he did, pressing the buzzer on the big green door early in the morning, she was gone. I'm sorry, her mother said, lips pinched in resolution. I shan't discuss it. He called the house almost one hundred times over the next two days and there was no answer, and then a male voice answered and said if he called again they'd have him arrested and deported. They knew where his apartment was, they would make it difficult for him, maybe they would have a go at him—just so that he remembered what's what—Mr. Carmody's bank had security people. Finally, Jay stood outside the house with a small backpack of food for three more days, leaving his station only to use the men's room in a pub half a mile away. At length the maid took mercy on him and came out and told him that the family was overseas, where exactly she wouldn't say. He might as well give up.

He returned to his flat and continued his penniless existence in London. For a few months he helped tend a bar, other times he took the train to the sea, wandered around, and came back. In that year he returned to the big house with black shutters several times a week to check for activity. The grass was being mowed, the bushes clipped, the leaves raked from the gravel driveway. But no Eliza. In his disconsolate and random way, he began to see other girls, English, Irish, French, a new girl every few weeks or months, depending on a lot of things, including how his lungs felt, since they seemed to vary quite a bit, with the pollen in the air and how cold it was, many factors, all making his bronchial tubes unknowably fickle. He wasn't using any medicine with regularity—stupid, he knew, but he was resistant, for once you started you were dependent. At first the girls were understanding but in time they became irritated. He could still screw passably well but there were days he couldn't get out of bed. He arranged to have some inhalers stolen for him and for a time he was better. But the girls came and went. Fifteen years later he did not remember their faces or their names. "I still missed Eliza," Jay said, looking at his ceiling, "it was unfinished."

He continued monitoring her house, riding by several times a week on his bicycle, which he'd started to use to keep his lung capacity up. One day, nearly a year after Eliza had left, a taxi pulled into the driveway. Watching from across the street, he saw her mother emerge holding shopping bags from Harrods and other stores. The next day he called the father's London office and claimed to be a Mr. Williams from Citibank in New York. He made up a number with a 212 area code. The call would be returned within two days, he was told, Mr. Carmody was soon expected in town. And so it seemed the family had returned. When next Jay visited the house, he saw another young man with a flop of fine blond hair and a familiar manner around the yard. The young man stepped up to a porch, said something when inside, and then stepped out again holding a baby in the sun.

The sight of it was shattering.

He began to fall forward in a run across the grass but stopped himself, not yet believing what he already knew was true. The man took the baby inside, and Jay waited until Eliza stepped out of the doorway and saw him coming. "Stop!" she called. "Stop this!"

She hurried to the edge of the yard and, looking over her shoulder anxiously, agreed to meet him in Green Park, on a bench in sight of Buckingham Palace, two days later. He counted the hours and was there early. Eliza appeared along the path and was more composed this time. The baby slept in her pram. They didn't say much, they barely touched. Just fingertips—reluctantly on her part. The matter was simple: Eliza had married one of her old boyfriends, a man named Cowles, a few years older than Jay, much further along in his career, having been both well capitalized by family funds and a prodigy in business school, and they had spent much of the previous year in the south of France. I'm sorry, Eliza told Jay. That's all I can say. There was in her tone the message that she belonged to another man now, that no matter what had once briefly passed between them, that was done and gone, obliterated by four hundred straight days of another man—his eyes and hands, his voice, his cock, his family, his shoes and books and hairbrush. Does this guy know the baby—Sally, I mean—is not his? Jay asked. No, no, Eliza shook her head. That would hurt him too much. He will *never* know. There was the question of sex, the question of logistics. I don't understand, said Jay. How can he think he's the father if— I saw him once or twice last summer, Eliza interrupted, okay? He came over to visit me in America. You had sex? *Yes.* After you met me? No, she said firmly. Right before. But the baby is yours. Jay didn't understand. Why? Because I had my period just after. David and I had sex, then I got my period, he left for London, then you and I met and had sex and that was it. I guess I wasn't careful enough. All in about one week or ten days. Are you *sure*? Yes, Jay. But what about when you returned? Didn't you have sex with him when you got back? I did, she conceded, but not until later. I knew I was pregnant. You did? Yes. That's why I had sex with him as soon as I could when I got back. Because you knew—? How? You can feel it, she said. You feel it in your breasts and everywhere. The timing was close enough, she said, he just thought the baby was a few weeks early. Please don't lie to me, Jay said, please tell me whose baby Sally is.

She's yours, Eliza answered, I swear.

Jay looked at the infant girl. I want to hold her, he said, I've never held a baby. She helped lift the sleeping baby out of the pram and nestled her on Jay's shoulder. So light, so tiny. *Sally.* After my grandmother, Eliza said. Sally. The tiny eyes and nose, impossibly perfect. He had helped to *make* this child. He felt the warm weight of her go through him. He settled Sally in his arms and felt himself relax, let his chin fall to the fuzzy head, his own eyes drowsy with love. Eliza watched this and began to cry. After a few minutes, the baby woke, her lips puckering instinctively for a nipple, and Jay handed her to Eliza. She sat on the bench and nursed the baby. He saw Eliza's breast, enormous and full, and desire shot through him. A mother's wet raised nipple somehow was more erotic than usual, leaking life. She's really mine? Oh yes, Eliza said, I can prove it to you. Sally has your little horn. You mean the bump in my ear? She reached out and ran her fingers along the inside edge of the cartilage of Jay's ear, where a point sat hidden on the inner fold. It was more pronounced on his left ear than on his right and so he reached for Sally's left ear, and although it was impossibly soft, it had the same tiny, distinct bump. A horn, just like yours, Eliza smiled. What other proof could possibly be as good as that?

"My left ear," Jay said now, sitting up. "Feel it."

"You want me to touch your ear?" I said.

"Just go ahead."

So I did, tentatively, reaching out to pinch the cartilage at the end of his ear. The vein in his temple pointed to his eye like an arrow.

"Feel it? There's a bump."

"No."

He directed my fingers with his own. "There."

I felt exactly what he was talking about, a small triangular ridge, the tiniest of horns.

"Did you see the baby again?" I asked.

"No."

"No? What were you doing?"

He made, he told me, a point of cycling past the house every month or so, just to torture himself, or to remember, maybe both. And one April afternoon, he said, when he did this he saw that all the wooden trim had been painted a garish blue, a cerulean blue. The shutters and cornice and French doors. C'mon, he thought, why mess it up, it was something the newly arrived Turks or Arabs would do, someone with no understanding of—then he knew. The family was gone. This time for good. They'd sold the house and moved and that meant that something had happened. He turned the bike around and rode back the other way, slowly. Fuck it, he thought, I'm going to find out. He pulled over at the next house. A blond woman in her thirties was kneeling in one of the rose beds, turning fireplace ashes into the earth.

"Excuse me," said Jay.

The woman shaded her eyes. "Yes?"

"I'm an old friend of the Carmodys," he said. "Did they move?"

"Yes," she said. "Hated to see them go."

"But why?"

The woman stood, perhaps because of the naked misery of his voice. "They couldn't be here anymore." She brushed some earth off her trowel. "Business, I suppose."

He mumbled his acknowledgment. He sat there looking at the dusting of tree pollen on the road. Then he walked back to the woman.

"What about the little girl, the family?"

"With Mr. Cowles, you mean? I think they moved to Tokyo. Something about a branch office, I didn't quite follow it. A very good opportunity with the bank."

Thus did Jay lose contact with Eliza Carmody Cowles and his daughter, Sally Cowles.

"I tried to find them, calling, but it was no good. It was too far away."

"You think of following them?" I asked.

He touched the oxygen mask to his face. Shook his head.

"Too far?" I interpreted. "Too difficult and expensive."

He pulled the mask off. "I was a kid, you know? I didn't know anything. I didn't really know what it meant, either." He decided not to go back to America, he said, so he found a better job, not in a bar, where the smoke bothered him, but teaching American conversational English to Saudi princes located in London. A strange job, but not one he minded. All he had to do was talk. "They were very well educated," Jay said, "much better than me. Oxford, usually. Some had gone to school in the States. But they wanted to get the American idiom, the flavor." When one of the students, a young woman, saw him coughing and heard the story of his accident, she took him to her father, a doctor. The man put Jay on a course of steroids that changed his life. The steroids shrunk the swollen lung tissue and his coughing subsided. The chronic infections could clear and he began to gain back weight. Within three months he'd put on thirty pounds, and his color was better. Now a little older, back to nearly his full strength, much of his natural substantiality restored, and with a little money to spend, he began to explore London.

"I think there are women in the next part of the story," I said.

"Yes."

"You were feeling better, your mood was nihilistic, you didn't mind having a good time."

"Something like that," he said. "That's when I learned to like a good cigar, actually. Pubs. The young Brits, the traders and bankers, were giving up pipes and hitting the cigars."

A couple of years followed, Jay continued, in which he met dozens of young professional women in London, a few American, many European, and simply enjoyed himself. He dated two or three women at a time, sometimes seeing older women who were in unhappy marriages. So much money was washing around London that the collective euphoria rounded away the ends of these affairs. "It got a little crazy," he said.

"I got a little crazy. I was sometimes sleeping with three or four different women a week."

"You're lucky you didn't get anyone pregnant."

"I was very careful about that," Jay said. "There are tricks you can use."

"Besides a rubber?"

"You don't come."

"You pull out?"

"No, you just don't come. You teach yourself not to."

"You're a weird fucking guy, you know that?"

"You can have sex with a lot of women if you never come," Jay noted. "Or not often, at least."

"It sounds pretty hostile," I said, "a way of having control over women. Also a way to make sure you didn't have another child taken from you."

"Thank you, doctor."

"Shit, Jay, it's obvious."

"I know that. I mean, I know that *now*."

"Keep telling me," I said. "I want to hear about how you found Sally again."

London was a spinning carousel of money, he went on. "The boom happened there, too, just like in New York," he said, "and I got into a real estate firm that was relocating people into London. Offices, apartments, the whole thing. All you had to do was wear a suit."

"You met a lot of people. It was an education."

He nodded. "Five years. I ran some rehab jobs, I took a few architecture courses, that kind of thing. Learned the lingo. Everybody's a faker in this business. I was working the investment and sales side, in a very minor way. Little projects, nothing big, nothing where my complete lack of knowledge would show. Usually I hired some old boozed-out carpenter to run the site for me. I made some money, and I kept a little of it."

"Stayed in touch with the farm, with your father?"

"No. Not much."

"Your mother hadn't communicated."

"My father told me that he was pretty sure that she'd gone to Texas, because her father was from there. She'd always wanted to know him. I had to think whether I wanted to chase after my mother in Dallas or Houston or someplace or stay in London."

"You were waiting for Eliza to come back."

He was, he said, at least subconsciously. By now he had the business connections to track David Cowles, had even met a few of his associates socially. And then one day he heard that Cowles had moved back to London. "I found his office and followed him home. Sunglasses and a hat. Easy, right? He didn't know my face. There had been no direct communication and I'm sure Eliza never told him a thing. He had no idea. By then he owned a very nice house in the suburbs. High bushes, mansard roof, casement windows. He'd made a lot of money in Tokyo. I spied on him a bit. I saw Sally. She was almost seven now. A little Eliza. Looked just like her, the hair and eyes and legs. Of course, now, she *really* looks like Eliza at twenty. I mean, it's disturbing. But even then, it killed me to see her, Bill, it broke me up. That was my daughter. *My* daughter. Then—"

He stopped talking.

"What?"

"She died."

"Eliza?"

"In a car, with a man."

"An accident?"

"He was driving, driving too fast, and they rolled over, in a Jaguar. Roof collapsed."

Ripped from life. I wasn't sure what question to ask next.

"The guy lived," Jay narrated. "The fucker, though there's not much left of him."

"Who was he—?"

"They knew each other. Were driving at a high rate of speed to London from the country late in the afternoon. That's about all I could find out."

"Who was he?"

"Some guy, also in the financial community. I looked him up, he'd been in Japan the same time she'd been. Same age."

"An affair, hurrying back to town?"

"Yeah, maybe. Hard to say. She was capable of it. After all, that's how she got pregnant with Sally."

"People have secrets."

"Yes," Jay said. "Always. I couldn't go to the funeral, I couldn't do it. I should have. Fucking inexcusable. I was very messed up. It was on a Sunday afternoon, and I was passed out in some girl's apartment."

Jay stood, as if wanting to move away from his last thought, and walked to his refrigerator and opened the door. He shook three pills out of a bottle and swallowed them. "That was the beginning of the end," he muttered.

"What do you mean?"

He meant, he said, that he could no longer survive in London. Could not function. He lost his job and floated back to New York City. The boom was starting to age. He'd saved enough money to rent the apartment we sat in, and he found work rehabbing brownstones in the better neighborhoods of Brooklyn. And then the day came he woke one morning to find himself short of breath, not suffocating, just working harder than ever. "Your lung capacity is really dropping," the doctor told him. "And will keep on dropping."

So he told me about the oxygen. "I stayed off it as long as I could. Once you start, even a little, your body likes it, wants more of it. I'm okay most of the time. If I get tired, it gets harder. Like you saw out at the farm that night. I was really wasted that night."

As he reached thirty, his health began to fail. He felt it in the slightest of ways. He couldn't climb steps the way he used to do. His lips occasionally turned bluish and his fingertips hurt, he said. He had to think about breathing in a way he never had before. What this meant is that the natural decline of his lung capacity, which happens to everyone, was beginning to carry him into the zone of breathlessness. We are born with almost twice the lung capacity that we actually need. This is why people may survive on one lung and also why smokers dying from emphysema take so long to expire. As total lung capacity falls toward forty or thirty percent, problems set in. Breathing becomes labored, the lungs can't clear the mucus they make. In Jay's case, he said, he was told by the pulmonary specialist that he had the lung capacity of a man who'd been smoking sixty to seventy years, or, expressed differently, the lung capacity of a man who had never smoked and who had somehow lived to the age of one hundred and twenty.

His life span was now limited to the declining slope of his lung function; barring an accident, he'd die of gradual asphyxiation. The rate of decline was variable; it could speed up, it could slow, but it always moved in one direction. He had to have his lungs checked every six months, during which time the forced expiratory volume, the FEV, would be measured, the number always trickling downward. The disease was particularly cruel in that he could be stable for periods of time yet wake up with another percentage of his breath gone.

"And then somewhere in here, you found out that David Cowles had moved to New York?"

"Yes."

"How?"

"I got curious and called his London office. He'd gone to a new company. I called them. Got a forwarding number. I sweet-talked some people, said I had a deal for him to look at. You know, bullshitted the situation. I felt sorry for the guy. His wife had been killed and probably because she was sleeping with another guy. I admired him, to be honest. He'd pulled himself together, remarried. Had enough capital to relocate here."

"And once you knew he was in town?"

"Cold certainty."

I stared at him.

"About finding Sally."

"You bought his building."

"I did."

"Why?"

His eyes went hard. "Curiosity."

It was an unnerving answer, and I remembered Jay's ostensible friendliness when he'd been meeting Cowles in his office after buying the building. That performance was the height of fraudulence, I now realized, and furthermore, I remembered that Jay had allowed Cowles to negotiate for a lower rent.

"Did you tap Cowles's phone?" I asked. "In the basement?"

"That's what you would do? If you were me?"

"Yes," I confessed.

He nodded. "Sure. You splice into the phone box. Buy the hardware out of an electronics catalog."

"And?"

"It's boring stuff, mostly. But sometimes I hear Sally talking. Cowles and the new wife talk about the kids' schedules constantly, baby-sitter, birthday parties, school stuff, doctors' visits, you name it. The woman is a good mother, by the way. He married a good woman."

Hearing this made me think of my own lost life with Judith and Timothy, and so his words had a doubled sadness for me; both of us, it seemed, were pathetic, emptied of everything but yearning. Yet Rainey and I were different, too. I felt it. And saw it, in the bright urgency in his eyes. Some aspect of Rainey's character was eluding me, not anything having to do with the old farm and what might be buried there, but a more essential element that was concentrating his focus, pushing him to do risky things like shadow Sally Cowles at basketball games and piano concerts.

"So—that's why you bought the building, to listen to a few phone calls? I think it's more than that."

He didn't answer. He didn't want to answer.

"This isn't good, Jay."

"I know what I'm doing," he said obliquely. "I think out every move."

Ask another question, I thought, slide off the moment. "And Allison? This is why you started with her?"

"Man, you are *good*." Jay smiled, releasing tension, and if it was not a malevolent smile, then nonetheless it had a kind of coldness in it that worried me. "It wasn't too hard, really. I pretended to be a buyer two floors above. The real estate attorney showed me around. But the place was a little too high, you can't see right. But the second time I was there I saw the elevator man delivering the mail. I saw her last name. It was the right floor. So I had the last name and the floor. Her name is in the phone book. A. Sparks. No other name listed. Probably single. I sort of bet myself that if she was under fifty I had a shot."

"But you had to figure out who she was."

Rainey laughed, but it was at my expense. "Doorman. Hundred bucks."

"How'd he go for that?"

"Told him I was a cop. Said it wasn't her I was checking out, it was one of her friends."

"I have a feeling she's got a lot of guys going in and out of there, on an annual basis."

"That's what the doorman said, too. Once he told me that, I knew I could do it. I watched her, saw she has breakfast in the same place a lot. It was easy. A good suit, sit there with the newspaper. Not too hard."

"You two see each other a lot?"

"Afternoons, mostly."

Jay shrugged away the matter, and in his gesture I realized why Allison had fallen so easily for him; his indifference toward her was thrilling, somehow, and returned her to a more primitive part of herself, the position of a child with a stern father, perhaps. I wondered if she ate the fish with him as well, but this seemed unlikely, given how infrequently it was available.

"So your health now?" I ventured.

"You mean, how fast am I going?"

"I know how fast you're going."

"You do?"

"I guessed earlier you're at thirty-five percent FEV."

He smiled. "Pretty good."

I shrugged.

"But not good enough."

"What do you mean?"

"I'm at about twenty-four percent." He gave a little cough, as if to emphasize the point.

"You're supposed to be in an oxygen tent."

"Yeah, probably."

"Well?"

"I got things to do, Bill." He picked up the oxygen mask then, and, breathing its sweet stream, closed his eyes.

He was, I suddenly understood, preparing to contact his daughter. His desire to see her, if only occasionally, had become the desire to know her, which itself had become the desire to talk with her. It was the organizing principle, the gravitational pole. The more Jay knew about Sally, the more he wanted to know. To hear her talk on the phone with Cowles must have been an exquisite torture to him. It's in the nature of men to want what they cannot have, but it must have seemed to him, with his daughter's voice piping innocently in his ear, that if he had come this far, then all things were possible. And maybe they were. Only that same evening, in the Steinway store, Jay had stood behind his daughter, fingers grazing her shoulders, looking down on her shiny combed hair; it was a kind of triumph, actually, it proved that he was not utterly disconnected from his former self, proved that part of his youth and vigor and own innocence lived on. That Sally at fourteen genuinely resembled Eliza Carmody at twenty must have been further irresistible torment for him, to see the past and the future simultaneously in his daughter's face. The girl's mother was lost, but here she was, a perfect child without her natural parents. How could he turn away from this? How could he not be drawn closer and closer to look and then choose to look longer? To cut off the simple powerful truth of the matter would constitute a death in itself, one that followed the death of Eliza and presaged Jay's own. And who could do that, who could not look at his own child? Many times I had fought off the desire to hop on a plane to the West Coast and drive a rental car right up into Judith's new mansion, wherever the fuck it was, crash through the garage, and race along the hallways to Timothy's bedroom and crush him in my arms. That I did not do this was proof of my own damnable weakness, and I realized now that Jay was teaching me something, that very moment, about what might be necessary to hold on to one's child. You had to be a little crazy, you had to be insanely devoted to the idea of redemption. I felt my own frozen yearning crack apart; I needed to have Timothy back, I needed him like I needed air, and I would get him back, no matter what.

So I did not judge Jay harshly that evening, hearing his story, not at all. I was scared for him, but I admired the truthfulness of his intention.

All of his manipulations and lies, the maze of his own devising, were in pursuit of the one good thing he could yet imagine for himself, the recognition that passes between father and child.

"So," I ventured. "Where's all this go now?"

"Simple." Jay dropped the mask from his face and found my eyes. "I'm dying, man."

nine

"POTATOES!" Allison cried to me on the phone late the next morning. "All over the sidewalk in front of the steakhouse." I'd been lying in my hotel room bed, listening to the tape-hiss of my own head and wondering what to do about Jay, when her call came. "There's a huge green truck up on the sidewalk," she said. "A little old man is inside! And he won't come out. He says he knows Jay. He's drunk or something, says he has to talk to Jay right now. I told him I didn't know where he is, Bill!"

"Is the truck missing a front door?"

"I think so, yes."

It was Poppy. "Can you put the guy on the phone?"

"He won't get out of the truck. I'll take the phone to him."

Which she did. I heard her carrying it outside, the fuzz of the wind cutting across the mouthpiece. "Poppy?" I said when she handed it to him.

"Jay?"

"No, it's Bill, his lawyer. You remember me."

"I ain't talking to no shyster."

"I'll be down there in a few minutes." It was only about ten blocks away. "Don't go anywhere."

"You just bring Jay, just tell him I'm going to say what he don't want to hear, I can't take it no more . . ." His voice broke into a wretched sob. "I'm sorry, it was never, I'm—"

"Bill?" came Allison's voice. "He's *crying*."

"Don't let him go anywhere. Take the keys."

"Ha already did."

I told her I'd be there soon, then called Marceno's New York office. Miss Allana answered.

"Let me talk to Marceno," I told her.

"Mr. Wy-eth," came his voice almost immediately. "So you have responded to my inquiries?"

"Marceno, listen to me. Jay Rainey doesn't know what's buried on your land, and I don't, either. But I can tell you who does know, the little old man who worked on the farm."

"The fellow named Poppy?"

"Yes."

A dismissive grunt. "We already asked him."

"You personally?"

"One of my representatives."

"Who?"

"That is confidential, Mr. Wy-eth."

"If it was Martha Hallock, then I don't think you got the whole story." This bothered him, I could tell. "And why would that be?"

"Because they are related."

"Related?"

"Poppy is Martha Hallock's nephew."

"No one told me that."

"Why would they?"

"This man Poppy knows?"

"He's here in town, at the steakhouse where we did this deal in the first place. He's looking for Jay Rainey and he's not going to find him. But he says he has something to tell him. So I'm going there right now. I suggest you show up, too."

"I was expecting information to come from you or Jay Rainey."

I stood at my window and watched the taxis edge down Fifth Avenue. "Poppy is there now. Right now, a few minutes from your offices. It's the best I can do, Marceno."

"We will see."

"Hey, you're the one with forty two million bucks on the line, Marceno, not me."

I walked toward the steakhouse, listening to my phone ring in Jay's garage apartment. No answer. When we'd said goodbye the previous evening, he'd offered his hand to me in a gesture of friendship and apology and I had taken it willingly, sad for him, now that I understood the simple emotional logic behind his curious behaviors—all the man wanted was to find and know his daughter. On a Monday morning the city was busy, men and women climbing out of the subways ready to eat pressure and deadlines and phone calls. And the next day I'd be busy, too, finally. I'd report for work at Dan Tuthill's new firm, and from there I'd rent a new apartment—someplace with a real doorman who didn't let thugs up the stairs—and a few weeks later, Timothy would arrive, with Judith.

A block away from the steakhouse, I saw Poppy's half-ton truck bumped up onto the sidewalk of Thirty-third Street. He'd knocked one of the evergreens over. The enormous ceramic pot had broken into a dozen pieces and the tree itself lay on its side, roots exposed to the cold. Ha was out on the sidewalk, picking up potatoes and throwing them back into the truck. The wind lifted what gray hair was left on his head.

"Ha!" I called.

He looked up and nodded. "Miss Allison friend."

"Yes. She called me." I pointed at the truck. "You've got a little old man inside?"

"Every Monday, close for lunch," Ha muttered. "But Ha work anyway. The man is in that truck."

I saw a boot sticking out of the truck where the front door was supposed to be. The limp glove was still taped to the steering wheel. Poppy lay slumped across the front seat hugging a half-empty bottle of whiskey.

"Poppy, you don't look too good."

"I didn't tell them." He licked his lips in a daze. His face was swollen, as if he'd been punched a few times. "You see Jay, you say I didn't tell them."

Allison slipped out the front door of the steakhouse, arms huddled tight, eyes concerned.

"Who *is* he?"

"This is Poppy. He used to work on Jay's farm."

"Is he drunk?"

"Yeah, I'm fucking drunk." Poppy rolled onto his back, exposing a belly of gray hair. "I'm a *lot* of things, I'm a drunk and beat up and I also got coffee in me." He vomited into the well of the seat. "Christ," he moaned.

Allison stepped back from the truck. "What am I supposed to do here, call the police?"

"Don't."

"Why?"

"The night that we did the real estate deal, this was the guy who came to the restaurant."

She frowned. "I don't remember him, and believe me, I would."

"You were out with Jay celebrating. He needed Jay to drive east to his land. Remember you asked me to go out there? That night we found an old black guy dead on a bulldozer. He'd worked on Jay's farm for years. The bulldozer had gone off the edge of the cliff. Poppy and Jay and I hauled it back up using this truck, in fact. Jay thought the old guy had a heart attack."

"He *did*," bellowed Poppy. He pushed himself up and confronted us, his lips wet, nodding portentously, as if being questioned in a court of law. "He *did*, a fucking heart attack, plain and simple. I saw it with my own eyes. Nobody touched him."

I pulled on his arm to get him up. "You told us you *found* him."

"No, I saw him!" he growled. "I saw him die."

"You kill him, Poppy, did you kill him somehow?"

He seemed oddly fascinated by this question, distracted even, and didn't answer.

"Sir, we take deliveries on Monday," said Allison. "You're blocking our way here. You're going to have to move."

He didn't respond. I saw a bit of blood on his lip and bruising around his eye. "He needs to come inside, Allison. We can move the truck."

Poppy nodded at this suggestion as if he'd heard it from a great distance. "I'm sick," he muttered. "I'm sick of it."

Allison pulled me away from the cab. "Why didn't you tell me all this, Bill?"

"Jay's got a lot of problems, Allison."

She crossed her arms angrily. "Well, I figured *that* out."

"No, I don't think you did."

"You should have told me."

"Allison, you asked me to help Jay. Remember?"

She shrugged, holding herself tight.

"A guy is coming here soon, I hope," I went on. "Poppy's going to tell him something, and then at least part of this trouble will be finished."

"I don't understand."

"There's a problem with the land Jay sold," I told her. "The buyer wants to know what it is. He's been threatening Jay and me."

"You can't just drag all this into my steakhouse!"

"Allison, you dragged it into your steakhouse, not me. *You* told Jay he could finish his real estate deal in the Havana Room. You started this. You thought you attracted him, you let him work *you*."

"What do you mean?" She was figuring things quickly. "Is this about that woman named O, the woman he sees?"

I shook my head, stunned by how little she knew. "There is no woman named O. Jay picked you out, for something else."

"What?"

It was too late not to explain. "I'm sorry to tell you this, Allison. It's not what you want to hear—"

"Just *tell* me."

So I did. "Jay picked you out. He figured out exactly where you lived, the floor, everything."

"Why?"

"He wanted to look across the street."

She stared at me, not sure whether to be hurt or furious. "The living room window?"

I glanced at Poppy, then back at her.

"He was always at the window. We used to sit and talk. That's what we liked to do. It was sweet, you know?"

I nodded again, slowly.

"The girl?"

"Yes."

"Who is she?"

I checked Poppy again. He looked cold, a little out of it, munching his mouth in rumination.

"Who *is* she, Bill?"

I turned back to Allison. "His fourteen-year-old daughter."

She was a proud woman, Allison Sparks. She had a big job and an independent life, plenty of money, and a funny little drug habit, so basically she thought she knew the score, especially when it came to men, because, I supposed, she did not at heart trust them. And so here was proof that her vanity and passion had hidden the truth from her, which was that a man she'd liked a great deal had not found her attractive, but had let her think so, simply so that he could look out of her window. "Oh God," she muttered, dropping a hand against the hood of the truck. "He told you this?"

"I sort of figured it out, then he admitted it."

She stared dumbly at the windshield.

"Let's get Poppy inside, let's get this done with," I said.

She didn't have it in her to protest.

"All right, Poppy," I told him.

"Can you move this?" Allison asked Ha, pointing at the heavy, old truck.

Ha nodded. "I park it down the street."

Poppy let me lift him up. The bottle fell to the well of the truck, the liquor pouring out of it. He didn't notice. I wanted to get him inside until Marceno came, try to get him sobered up a bit so that Marceno would believe him. I took both of his arms as he stood and slipped a hand under him. He leaned heavily against me, and he smelled bad. But he made it over the pavement.

Allison opened the front door. We lurched into the foyer. Poppy leaned over the maître d's lectern.

"Gimme something to—wait, wait—" Poppy pointed to the Havana Room door. "In there, I want privacy."

I looked to Allison.

"Well, we're closed for lunch Mondays."

"But do you have staff coming in, to clean or whatever?"

"Not until much later, four o'clock. We open at six for dinner. It's just me and Ha here now. Of course, this is *exactly* what I was hoping to do on my only morning off!" She looked at her watch. "I mean, I didn't leave this place until one o'clock last night."

She unlocked the Havana Room door. "Can you make it down the steps?"

"Of course," Poppy groaned.

But he couldn't, not really, and I kept him up as he staggered down the stairs. The long room was dark and I smelled smoked-out cigars. I found a light. The enormous nude loomed over the bar, her dark eyes considering me. Poppy slumped into one of the booths, his head down. "Gimme something to write with."

"I think you need some coffee, maybe something to eat."

Poppy lifted his eyes. "Forget that. Give me a pen or something." He pulled an embossed HAVANA ROOM napkin from the holder. I turned on the sconce light near his head, leaning close enough to see the broken capillaries in his nose, then handed him my pen. He had trouble holding it, more trouble than the first time I'd seen him. He looked at his hand and couldn't seem to make a fist. "I mighta broke this."

"How?"

He looked up, eyes half closed. "I tried to fight back yesterday, for a minute. They found me. They knew right where I was."

"Who?"

"Some—" He looked at the pen and threw it aside. "I got no hands!" he bellowed wetly. "Come on, gimme something—"

Allison came down the stairs and turned the light on over the bar. She seemed to have regained her composure. I studied her back in the mirror, the curve of her shoulders, her neck. Despite myself, I remembered her curled up in her bed. "I have pens, pencils . . ."

"No!" Poppy cried, eyes almost shut, head bobbing a bit. I wondered if he was suffering from a concussion. Hard to say, with the whiskey in him.

Allison seemed to think the same thing. "He looks *bad*, Bill. Like he's half asleep or something. Maybe I should call an ambulance."

Poppy showed his rotten yellow teeth. "Don't call no one."

"Here, here." Allison fished in her purse and produced a gleaming gold tube of lipstick. She popped off the top and twisted up half an inch of the red stick.

"Wait," I said, "I want you to tell somebody else this, not us."

"I ain't got *time*." Poppy took the lipstick and leaned over the napkin like a tired but obedient child trying to do homework he didn't quite understand. "I'm leaving this for him, then getting out of here. I got money and coffee and I'm going for a little drive."

"Where?"

"Don't know. California, maybe. Florida's warm."

"In that truck?"

"Sure, sure. A little drive. Ain't been to Florida in years." Poppy made a quick upward stroke that left a line an inch long. This was followed by three more strokes—creating the four sides of an uneven rectangle. He coughed pensively. "I didn't tell them. No pity for a old man, neither. No class, just a bunch of lowlifes."

"Who?"

Poppy made three X's in a row on the napkin. The rectangle looked catty-corner to the last X, but I was too far away to see it well.

"Who?" I repeated.

"Them boys who done this to me." He examined his drawing with simian curiosity, then folded the napkin in half. "Oh yeah." He unfolded it. "Almost forgot." He looked at Allison plaintively.

"Yes?" she said.

"See there." He stabbed at the box. "I want you to write this for Jay so he will know."

"Sure. Where? Here?"

"Anywhere in there is fine!" He handed her the red lipstick. "First put C."

"Okay, C."

He rolled his head strangely, like he had water in his ear. "No, no, make it a K. It's a K!"

Allison made the correction.

"Then R, like ring-a-ding-a-bing."

"R, yes, okay."

He opened his eyes. "Then, uh, put O."

Allison caught my eye, her expression suggesting that we humor him. He seemed to be getting worse. "Okay, Poppy, you're doing very well. We have K, R, O. What's next?"

He shut his eyes again. "Put a W. Like *whiskey woman.* I knew a whiskey woman."

"That's it? KROW, like crow, the bird?"

"Now L-A," he insisted, eyes opening. "Just like the city."

"Pronounced *la* or *lay*?"

Poppy smiled at me malevolently. He seemed not just drunk but either crazy or brain-damaged. "I seen lawyers like you. I used to beat on guys like you."

"I'm sure you did." I leaned over to look at the napkin.

"Hey!" Poppy put his hand over it. "Take your eyeballs out of here, mister."

I leaned back. I'd see it later, I assumed. "That's it?" I asked. "The whole thing?"

"I said L-A, right?"

"KROW-lay? KROW-la?"

"Yes."

It sounded like the beginning of a Polish surname, something like Kowalski or Krawczyk, and I remembered that a number of Poles had settled in eastern Long Island in the early part of the twentieth century. Or maybe he had the spelling wrong and it was some other word, French perhaps. "What's it mean? Is it somebody's name?"

Poppy shook his head. "That's for Jay. I didn't come here to tell you."

"The word makes no sense," I told him. "Krow-lay?" How could we tell this to Marceno?

Poppy handed the napkin to Allison with tender formality. "Will you give it to him, miss?"

She nodded anxiously and tucked it into her purse.

"Allison," Ha called down the stairs. "Some men here to see you."

"Okay," she called, "send them down here."

We heard footsteps. "This is a guy named Marceno," I told her. "The man who bought Jay's land. Lucky Poppy's still here."

"But I'm going," Poppy announced. "Before they come."

Ha appeared inside the Havana Room, eyes wide open. "Miss Allison—" he began, then stumbled forward.

"Keep going, Buddha-boy."

H.J.'s two men followed Ha down the stairs, with guns pointing at the floor. They looked around, took in the room. I remembered the taller one as Denny. "Get back inside."

"Who are you?" Allison asked.

"You may call me Gabriel," said the other man, who wore a necktie and a rather good watch. "We are seekers of mislaid persons." He motioned with his gun. "I suggest you all have a sit in this lovely wee underground bar."

Denny pulled out a cell phone.

"Tell his greatness the fat one that his underpaid hoodlums are in the restaurant, that the great American artist named Wyeth is here and that he should come have a look."

Denny punched in a string of numerals.

"Lucky day," Gabriel said to me. "And thank *you*," he said to Poppy.

"For what?"

"You did just as we hoped, old man."

"I did?"

"You drove into Manhattan and found your friends, your intentional community." He pointed at me, then looked around. "One could make a lot of noise down here and no one would hear it."

We sat for ten minutes, saying nothing. I studied Gabriel and Denny, watched how fast they breathed. Normal, for the most part. Used to situations like this.

"I'm afraid that I have to use the bathroom," Allison said.

"Too bad."

"There's one at the end of the room."

"You'll need someone to go with you."

"All right," she sighed.

Gabriel followed her to the men's room, looked in, then let her inside. He kept the door open with his hand. "No, keep the door open there, too," he told her.

I heard some small voice of protest.

"I don't care about your bloody privacy." Gabriel stood, watching her. "That's it. Very tasteful underwear, miss, quite expensive I'd say. Victoria's Secret?"

"Is it?" called Denny, looking back and forth.

"Can't tell."

"How's her female equipment?"

"Standard. Working order." He followed Allison's actions. "Now the paper, hurry along, please."

A moment later Allison emerged. "Hope you enjoyed the show," she said.

"Sit next to Buddha-boy there," said Gabriel.

We heard a noise upstairs, a knocking. Maybe this would be Marceno.

"The boss?" said Gabriel. "Already?"

Denny stood and went upstairs. Then we heard footsteps coming down. A tall black man in a heavy coat entered, checked out the room, and stepped aside for H.J., who arrived with expectant aggression, face wrapped by sunglasses and roundly enormous, his head a thick ball of shaved flesh.

"Lamont, I like this place!" H.J. announced, looking around, teeth gleaming. "Very comfortable." He fixed on me. "The white dude lawyer! I told you to get my money, and you didn't and now you see we got a problem." He looked at Allison and lifted up his sunglasses. "Mmm, and who are you?"

"I'm the manager."

"You can manage *me*." He pointed at Ha. "Who's the old Chinese?"

"He works here," Allison said. "He has nothing to do with any of this."

"What's he do, clean the white man's toilets?"

"He's an excellent cook. A trained chef."

"That right? Got a specialty?" But he didn't wait for an answer, instead waving his hand at the room, enjoying his power. "All right, this is where we goin' to do business today. We goin' to get to the bottom of the whole damn thing. My uncle is sittin' in his little box of ashes waitin' for me to get this done. His ghost is tellin' me, Boy, make this right. Man works sixty-somethin' years, he ain't supposed to freeze to death. My aunt just sit at home and cry and say I got to do somethin' for the family. They puttin' a lot of pressure on me. Now I'm puttin' it on somebody else. My aunt say somethin' bad went down, somethin' ain't right. She don't like the explanation the police gave her. She say she got nobody but her nephew. So I got obligation in all this, y'all hear what I'm sayin'? I don't care how long it takes, I got the whole day. I'm goin' to Philadelphia later but right now I got the whole damn day." He looked at me again, smiled at my discomfort. "You remember me, right? Remember my anti-fuckin'-social tendencies?"

"Yes," I said.

"Good. So, where's your man at?"

"Rainey? I don't know."

"Well, call him."

"I could do that."

I pulled out my phone and dialed Jay.

H.J.'s newest man, Lamont, held his gun on Allison and Ha. Gabriel kept his on Poppy. The phone rang. No answer.

"Not there," I volunteered.

"You that Poppy I keep hearin' about?" asked H.J., pulling out a gold-plated automatic from the pocket of his coat.

Poppy shrugged. "I already told everything I got to say."

"You the man who killed my uncle Herschel?"

"It wasn't like that."

"My aunt say he was frozen to a bulldozer."

Poppy lifted his gaze. "I was working on the bulldozer. He came by and said what are you doing. He did some bulldozer work a week before. He thought I was messing it up. He thought I was doing something I wasn't supposed to be doing. I said nothing that's your business. And we had a big argument. He's bigger, got good hands. He jumped up on the Cat . . . I guess he got a shock and had his heart attack."

H.J. smiled hatefully. "That don't smell too good." He pointed the gun at me. "Lawyer-boy, you believe that?"

"He was driving by," moaned Poppy. "I already *told* this! He saw me and wanted to know what I was doing."

"That's why Herschel stopped?"

Poppy lay his head on the table. "Yes. I was adding some earth."

H.J. looked surprised. "Why?"

"Because I didn't want anyone to know what's down there."

"What *is* down there?" I asked.

Poppy's eyes closed. "I'm not telling you."

H.J. moved over to Poppy and put his gun directly into his ear. "My uncle Herschel see you diggin' around the field when he go drivin' by and then he stopped and got out and said stop doin' what you be doing?"

"Yes."

"Please don't shoot him!" exclaimed Allison.

H.J. jolted the gun deeper into Poppy's ear. "Why? Why he do that? On a cold and snowy day?"

Poppy started to lift his head but felt the gun. "'Cause I was messing up the field!"

"So he said let me get up there on the tractor? This ain't makin' any sense. I ain't getting any of this."

I remembered that the tractor had been found on the sea cliff set in reverse. "Poppy," I asked. "You let him get on the Cat?"

"I didn't let him do anything. He's bigger than me."

"He got on the Cat."

"Yeah."

H.J. removed the gun, interested in this sequence. "Then what?"

"He asked what I was doing and I was so mad I told him, I told him the truth."

"Then what?"

Poppy lifted his eyes. He was a sad guy, and he didn't have time for any more lies. "He had a heart attack. He grabbed his chest and fell back."

"You told him and he fuckin' had a heart attack?" H.J. shook his head at the seeming absurdity of this tale. "You gotta do *much* better than that, old man."

"Is it a straight shot from wherever you were working with the bull-dozer to the sea cliff?"

Poppy looked at me. "Yes, but—"

The problem, I realized, was that H.J. still did not know that the bulldozer and Herschel had been recovered from the sea cliff and moved to a barn on the adjoining property.

"Why you ask that?" said H.J. "They didn't find him in no field!"

But before I could answer, Poppy pushed himself to his feet. "I'm leaving," he announced. "I told you enough." He gestured at Allison. "Give that napkin to Jay. I can't do it."

"You ain't goin' nowhere!" said H.J. "Get back there." He waved at his bodyguard to stand in front of the door. "Lamont?"

"I'm going out to my truck—"

H.J. straightened out his arm, the gun three feet from Poppy. "You know who I am?"

"No, and I don't care," slurred Poppy. "I'm going to Florida."

"You're stayin' till I get my satisfaction."

"Nope."

"Sit down, Poppy," I warned. "These guys are serious."

"You got no reason to hurt me." Poppy held out his hands.

"Get back, old man!"

"I can't take no more," cried Poppy, unsteady on his feet. "I'm tired, my head hurts." He lurched toward the door. "I ain't been to Florida in—"

"Get back!"

"Come on, fuck you, I'm just—"

Lamont shoved Poppy backward. He hit the wall. It didn't appear to scare him, and he measured the distance to the doorway.

"Sit *down*, old man," said Lamont, sticking his gun out. "I don't want to hurt you."

"I'm walking out of here," said Poppy, and he did—or started to, when there was a terrible noise, and his neck exploded in blood. Allison screamed. Poppy fell over, head loose.

"Get back!" yelled Lamont, swinging the gun around at us.

Poppy lay hunched to the floor, blood spraying over the black-and-white tiles. His face grew pale, followed by a sucking sound from the neck wound, and then he went soft and died before us.

H.J. looked at his gun. It hadn't fired. He looked at Lamont, who was holding a pistol. "Shit, Lamont," said H.J. "What you do that for?"

"He was getting too close to you, boss."

"Oh God," moaned Allison as smoke drifted above us. "He's an old man! Do something."

But there was nothing to do. H.J. held us in place. "Y'all stand back," he ordered, looking around. "Fuck, Lamont! Now we got a *problem*, nigga!"

He certainly did, three people not his own—Allison, Ha, and me—who'd seen what his bodyguard had done. *We* were the problem. He looked at Allison. "You know where Rainey lives?"

Allison shook her head.

"You?" he asked me.

"Yes," I said. "But I doubt he's there. He didn't answer before."

"You know where he lives?" asked Allison.

H.J. looked at Ha and Allison. "Yo, people! You got to tell me what's goin' to get this guy to come here and give me my money, and tell me what I need to know, because otherwise we got a even *bigger* problem, you know what I'm sayin'?"

The room seemed hot, wheeled with a dark feeling. Four people could kill three easily enough. Things happened like this in the city from time to time. You read about it in the metro section of the paper with your coffee, shake your head at the strange carnage, then check the stock tables. The men could pull a truck up to the sidewalk doors and load out anything and no one would ever know.

"I want some answers to my question!" bellowed H.J. "I want to know what happened to my uncle and I want money for my aunt! We live in a fuckin' country where every college and university over a hundred and fifty years old, all those railroads and banks, got slave money in 'em, slave money built 'em up. Martin Luther King only got it *half* done. Jesse Jackson, he sold the fuck out, Clarence Thomas, he no good. White man *still* makin' money off the black man every day. Who owns those companies buildin' prisons, who owns the fuckin' NFL? It ain't my uncle, you see what I'm saying? Now I want to find out why he died, why he have a heart attack!"

I sat in the booth stunned, Ha next to me, his head bowed in submission.

"Boss," said Gabriel finally, his tone pacifying, "I think Lamont shot the man who could help you with that question."

H.J. told his men to clean up. Gabriel and Denny found some garbage bags and laid them out a few feet away from Poppy. Whatever had been in his lower intestines had started to seep out of him and we could smell it. They lifted him, feet and armpits, onto the bags in one motion. The blood had traveled to the grout between the tiles. Gabriel hunted around behind the bar and found some twine, which Denny used to bag up Poppy. Then the men laid him behind the bar. They found the closet behind the bar and wet-mopped the tiles. "Use the cleanser," ordered H.J., keeping his gun on me. "Not one speck. And clean the wall, too, clean it good."

They did. Fifteen minutes later, it was as if nothing had happened. The floor gleamed. Ha watched, his eyelids low, face without expression.

"What we going to do now?"

"We's goin' to think, is what we's goin' to do." H.J. straightened his shirt. "Hey," he asked me, "how we going to get this boy?"

"I really don't know."

Gabriel put his gun to Allison's head. "Talk to the man. Tell us how to find your boyfriend."

"He's not my boyfriend!"

"Whatever you call him, miss, your penile escort, I don't care, tell my boss where to find him!"

"I don't know, I don't know!"

Gabriel made a pinched face. "Nothing comes of nothing, miss."

"I don't *know*. He used to come over to my apartment in the afternoon."

"Sounds romantic," prompted Gabriel.

"It *was*," said Allison softly, to herself.

"Pity," noted Gabriel, voice droll. "Please continue with your emotionally charged testimony."

With that, Allison lifted her head, eyes angry, mood defiant. "So yes, he came over to—well, it certainly wasn't to be with *me*, I see that now, it was to see—" She glanced at me, including me in her fury. "Well, there's a girl who lives across—"

"Don't!" I yelled.

"—the street. She'll be walking home in forty-five minutes along Eighty-sixth Street. She comes home at 2 p.m. from school. That's why he used to meet me at my apartment! That's the time! His daughter. If you can get his daughter you can get him," said Allison. "She'll be wearing a blue-and-white school uniform and probably be carrying some kind of backpack. She's about fourteen or fifteen and dark-haired and *quite* pretty."

"That's wrong," I said quickly. "The girl's in basketball practice all afternoon."

Gabriel looked at H.J.

"See?" Allison said bitterly, pointing her finger at me. "He knows. He's in on it. *He* knows who she is."

"You?" said H.J.

I shook my head. "She's got nothing to do with all this. She's just some kid."

"Get her," said H.J. to Gabriel.

"I'll tell you where Rainey lives," I said. "That's better."

"We know where he lives," Gabriel said.

"You do?"

"Sure. Brooklyn, Seventeenth Street. We followed you. Watched it some. Broke in, fished around. Bit of a creepy setup, no?"

I was trying to think of a way to avoid involving Sally Cowles. "Did you find the box of cash he has?"

H.J. swung his gun at Gabriel suspiciously. "Answer the man."

"No, no, we didn't find a box of cash."

"He had cash there. You were inside."

"What?" said H.J., studying Gabriel. "What's the man talking about?"

"I helped Rainey with a deal," I said quickly, "there was cash. Two hundred and something thousand. He put it in a box and took it home. I know that. I was there a few days ago and the box was empty. Your guys just admitted they were inside. I guess they didn't tell you they found the cash—"

"That's a fucking lie, Mr. Wyeth, and I'll gladly shoot your face off to prove it," said Gabriel.

H.J. was inclined to believe Gabriel, I could see, but with a margin of doubt. Which was good, because I was lying. If I'd really led Denny and Gabriel to Jay's apartment, then they couldn't have been the cause of the empty cashbox I'd found. "You ever go in that building downtown, that place my aunt talked with him?" he asked his men.

"We did once," answered Denny.

H.J., I could see, was plainly worried. The crazed aggressor who'd confronted me in the hip-hop club was absent; this H.J. was taciturn and analytical, watching each of us, then studying his cell phone on the table before him, then watching us again. Was he expecting a call from someone? Did he need to make a call? Why he was forcing this game toward whatever conclusion awaited us was not clear to me. "No, get his daughter," he ordered, looking at his watch. "We got her, then we got him. Then he has to deal with me. He has to talk to me, he gots to give me my money. And if he don't have it, then you boys got a problem."

A minute later they had bundled me into the white limousine waiting outside. It was the same one as before, late model, spotless, smoked glass. Denny and Gabriel sat across from me, each with a gun drawn. The car rolled smoothly through traffic. The heater was on, the row of little floor lights elegant. I was worried about Ha and Allison, despite her betrayal of Sally Cowles.

"Stop thinking," Gabriel said.

"I'll try," I answered.

"If it was up to me," he announced, "I'd put a wee fucking bullet in your head right now."

I didn't doubt him. "You guys are insane for doing this," I said. "Just in case you didn't know that."

They didn't listen. The driver turned on a smooth jazz station. We glided up Sixth Avenue, past Bryant Park, past Forty-second Street, past the dense corporate cliff-dwellings, offices piled into the sky, every third person on the sidewalk talking into a phone, past Radio City Music Hall, then east at Central Park, past the Plaza Hotel, and on up toward the Upper East Side.

Where could Jay be, I wondered, dreading our arrival at Sally Cowles's school. If we could go to Jay directly, then we could bypass Sally Cowles. There was still time to turn around. Where *would* he be? Not in his sad apartment. What interested him most? Sally Cowles. But when she was in school what did he do? He didn't work. Did he hang around outside the school? Looking in the windows? That was not a good idea and probably didn't satisfy his needs. He needed to be near oxygen, of course, needed to have access to it. Yet he was secretive about this, too. There had to be an answer, but I didn't have it.

We slid up Park Avenue, drawing closer. I wondered if I could somehow jump to the door, scramble out. Not likely. Gabriel and Denny remembered the school from the basketball game and told the driver to pull over across from the main gate.

"She'll be coming out right here," Gabriel said.

So we waited. Several mothers congregated to one side, each dressed for the occasion, if not every occasion, their lipstick perfect, sunglasses darkly aloof, hair fabuloso. I was reminded of Judith, picking up Timothy from school.

"Couple of these yummy-mummies look insufficiently serviced," noted Gabriel.

Denny looked. "Think so?"

Gabriel nodded. "You can tell by the shoes. Women needing service tend to obsess about their shoes."

Denny smiled. "You're a sick fucker, Gabriel."

"Indeed."

Now a gaggle of girls in school uniforms left the school. Boys, too, in their coats and ties. Timothy could've been among them.

"How we going to tell which one?"

"Mr. Wyeth will advise us."

"No way," I said.

More girls were coming out of the school.

"Mr. Wyeth, recognize any?"

"Go fuck yourself."

"Well, if you don't look out of the window, then will you look at this?"

I looked. And was surprised. Gabriel was holding a picture of Sally Cowles, the one that had been on Jay's wall.

"Where did you—" I stopped myself.

"Thank you very much," said Gabriel. "That's excellent. Thank you. Yes, this is her," he said. "Figured."

He looked from the photo to the school to the photo. "No one is going to think twice about a limo pulled up outside of this school." And indeed there were other limos pulled up outside, and not a few of them.

"That's her," said Gabriel suddenly. He checked the picture, looked up again.

It was Sally, walking along Eighty-sixth Street with a friend.

"Ease along behind," Gabriel told the driver. "Stay back." The car pulled along slowly. "Say goodbye to your little friend, Sally," he narrated.

The two girls came to the corner.

"Don't turn, go straight," ordered Gabriel. "Make the light, make the light!" The limo jumped across the intersection. "Now slow, slow! We're ahead of her." He looked back through the rear window. "That's it. They're saying goodbye, very good, yes, see you tomorrow, pimples and all, that's it, right along here. She's coming—" He turned to me and stuck his gun in my face. "You say one word and I'll blow your nose off, right here, in the car."

"I know where to find Rainey," I told him. "I just figured it out. We can go there. He's in his building, he's—"

"Bullshit."

"No it's not. He's at 162 Reade Street."

"We looked there, do you think we're idiots?"

"You didn't look in the right place."

"We went through the boiler room."

"Did you go upstairs?"

"We knocked on a few doors."

"I know where he is, right now! You don't have to grab her!"

"Yes we do. That's our instruction," Denny said.

"You ready?" asked Gabriel.

"Yes."

Gabriel showed me his gun. "One word from you and you'll never play catch with your boy again—"

"My boy?"

"—and his lovely mother. In Italy now, right?"

I fell backward, cursing Jay Rainey, and myself. The car stopped. Gabriel threw open his door just as Sally Cowles passed by.

"Excuse me, miss," he called with theatrical friendliness, "we're rather lost."

"Oh," she said, with a bit of an English inflection.

"I'm looking for Sixth Avenue."

She came close to the car, reassured that it was a limousine. "Well, Sixth Avenue isn't nearby, really."

Gabriel stepped out of the car, leaving the door barely cracked open. I could see part of Sally's back. He showed her a New York City street map. "We're from out of town," he said apologetically.

"It's okay," came Sally's voice, cool and sophisticated for a fourteen-year-old, "it's sort of a complicated city."

I was about to yell. But Denny shoved his gun into my armpit, then reached around and rammed three fingers into my mouth.

"See, Fifth Avenue is here," explained Sally. "And Sixth—hey!"

Suddenly she was inside the car, backpack falling in front of her, Gabriel shoveling her forward, jumping in and slamming the door behind him. "Go!" he said to the driver, locking the door. "But easily. Roll forward."

"Hey! What *is* this!" cried Sally, her eyes angrily studying the men, then the windows and door locks, her distance from escape. "What're you doing?"

"Mind your manners, luv," Gabriel told her. He lifted his gun and flicked his tongue against the barrel, smiling with such frank sadism that Sally lowered her head in terror, knees locked together.

"Back downtown!" Gabriel ordered the driver. Then he turned to me. "All right, time to make good on your promises."

The limo headed south along Fifth Avenue. Sally dared to steal a glance at me. "Where are we *going*?"

Denny shook his finger. "Confidential, miss."

She ducked her head again, her hair curtaining her face, and a moment later I saw she'd started to tremble.

"Not a sound!" bellowed Gabriel. "Not a bloody whimper! Do you understand?"

She nodded, her back starting to heave.

Maybe there's still a way out of this, I thought, leaving her unharmed and not knowing about Jay.

"Where are you *taking* me?" Sally sobbed, face hidden.

"Why, Sally, lass," announced Gabriel, "we're taking you to your father."

We arrived at the building on Reade Street. Sally recognized it.

"He's upstairs. I know *exactly* where he is!" I said. "I'm sure of it!"

"Don't hurt my father!" cried Sally. "Please!"

"Out," Gabriel said to me. "Nothing funny or they drive away."

He stepped out first, a hand on my neck. "Thought you were clever with that box of money business."

"There's a pile of cash, I'm telling you."

"You better hope so."

I pondered this, the threat in it.

"You're thinking," Gabriel said. "I can feel it. Thinking about running, doing the quick squirrel."

"No."

"Don't do it, Billy-boy."

"I *could* do it."

"No you couldn't."

"I'd be down the street, I—"

"I'd get one clean shot. Might hit you, too. Might blow out your dream factory. Then your son wouldn't have a dad."

We got to the front door. Gabriel took out a set of keys. Stolen from Jay's apartment, I guessed. "Don't touch the buzzer, either."

He pulled open the door and pushed me inside. The same Chinese menus as before lay on the floor.

"Upstairs," I said. "Quietly."

On the fourth floor I stopped.

"Open that one," I said, pointing to the door opposite Cowles's.

Gabriel slipped a key into the lock. Tried another. It worked.

We stepped into an empty office suite. It needed paint. You could still see the indentations on the carpet where desk and chairs had been, a ghost layout. I saw papers on the floor. Some sort of e-commerce scam.

"Where is he, Bill?" asked Gabriel, pushing me forward.

In the next room I stepped past food wrappers, cans, bottles, and newspapers. Some clothes. Somebody had been living there. Spending a lot of time, anyway. A small oxygen bottle lay among the refuse. Bits of plaster had been tracked all over the carpeting.

Then, turning the corner to the next room, I saw a wide section of a party wall had been torn out, right where a heating duct rose from the floor below. The duct serviced both the office we were in and the one next door—Cowles's office—its vent set at a height of about eight feet. Plaster and old lathing and sheet metal lay strewn heavily over the floor. Jay had cut out his side of the heating duct, vent and all, and built a hooded observation structure in this torn-out space, about the size and height of a linesman's chair at a tennis tournament. The hood's black fabric, crudely attached with a staple gun, completely enclosed the chair so that no sunlight from the windows could penetrate within. In this high position, I understood instantly, Jay could peer through the vent that serviced Cowles's office. A second vent had been exposed six feet away, and several lipstick-sized cameras had been jammed into it, their cables feeding a computer humming on the floor. But that was not all. A phone cable, no doubt a secret splice off of Cowles's office line, hung down through a broken dropped-ceiling panel and split into two wires, one of which led to a phone sitting on the floor. The other arrived at the same computer that serviced the lipstick cameras. Jay was recording everything Cowles did in his office. Every gesture, every word, every breath.

I returned my attention to the large hooded chair and stepped closer to it. What was hidden behind the fabric? I lifted the flap a bit and saw a leg and a man's shoe dangling. I dropped the flap in surprise. Dead? A suicide? Maybe Jay had heard us coming, maybe—I pulled the flap back, ready for any murderous horror—and here Jay was, in the chair, wearing a jacket and tie, leaning forward against the wall, asleep, an oxygen bottle set in a crude cradle built for it, a tube rising toward his head. A plastic breathing mask covered his nose and mouth. For a younger man, he looked enormously tired, as he was of course, dragging himself everywhere with not enough air. His lungs took shallow, too-rapid breaths, like a child with a fever. How many hours had he silently peered through the vent—studying Cowles, watching him, living his life vicariously, studying the cameras' digital footage? What did this prove to him? The impossible distance that lay between him and his daughter, now captive downstairs? Was he studying the man who would care for her after he himself was gone? And, ridiculous as it sounded, was it for this reason that he'd bought the building in the first place, unable to resist further acts of voyeurism? Or had the idea lived in the shadows of his unconscious? It didn't matter. Here he was.

"Wake him up," Gabriel told me.

I put my fingers to my lips.

"If you want this done quietly, then let me do it," I whispered. "He's liable to react. If you make a big noise, you'll have more problems."

Gabriel conceded nothing, just motioned with the gun that I should wake Jay. I leaned forward and positioned one eye behind the vent.

There was Cowles, in his suit, talking on the phone. Papers on his desk.

"Yes," he said, "we'll get it over to you. Brilliant." He hung up. His assistant came in. Cowles handed him a piece of paper. "These are the numbers for the Martin thing."

"Okay."

"What's happening to the euro?"

"Up a bit."

"How big are the blocks?"

"Varies."

"Are the Japanese buying?"

"Can't tell."

"I'll come look."

Cowles followed his assistant out of the office, and I took this opportunity to wake Jay.

"Hey," I said softly. "Jay, wake up."

I would have expected him to be startled but he wasn't, instead opening his eyes slowly and lifting his head.

"You found me," he said softly, not seeming to mind.

"Wake up, guy."

He shifted in his chair.

"You need to come downstairs," I said, handing him his coat.

"Why?"

"They've got Sally."

"Sally?"

I nodded.

"I don't get it."

"You will."

That was Gabriel, stepping forward, gun up.

Outside, the limo door opened as we approached.

"Get in," said Gabriel, and Jay and I did as we were told.

Sally, pressed between Denny and Jay, looked at each of us, stricken. She didn't recognize me, or Jay, for that matter. "What's going on? What're you going to do with me?"

I answered, trying to sound as firm as possible. "Nothing is going to happen to you, Sally."

"Something already *did*." She began to cry again. "How does everyone know my name?"

"If anyone touches you," said Jay, "I'll kill him."

But this, I saw, didn't comfort her, just scared her further. She looked frantically from one man to another, lips tight, hands gathered tightly over her school blouse. "Are you—am I going to be—?"

"Okay, Gabriel," I said, "you can let her go now."

"We need money first."

"Jay?" I said. "The man needs his money. Where's the cash?"

No answer. He hadn't taken his eyes off of Sally. But for the moment he'd stood behind her at the Steinway hall, he hadn't been this close to her since she was an infant. "I want to talk with her."

This only scared Sally more. But I wondered if somewhere deep within her she might sense her connection to Jay. You could see him in her. You could see the fierceness in her eyebrows and her good shoulders. She was leggy and would be more so.

"Do it fast, then," said Gabriel.

Jay leaned toward Sally. She pulled backward, frightened by his scrutiny, turned her head to one side.

"Easy, Jay," I said.

"Are you happy?" Jay asked his daughter.

"Who *are* you?" she said.

He breathed heavily. "Are you happy?"

"Well, not *now*."

"No, I mean—" Jay coughed violently. "I mean—in life."

Even Sally understood the absurdity of the question, under the circumstances. "Yeah, sure."

"Very nice chitchat," interrupted Gabriel. "But we have to—"

Jay turned toward Gabriel. He wasn't afraid of Gabriel, and Gabriel saw this.

"A minute," Gabriel conceded.

Jay turned back to Sally. "You have a nice family?"

"Yes."

"You miss your mum?"

The girl looked at him, blinking. "Who *are* you?"

"I was an old friend of hers."

She was suspicious. "When?"

"Years ago."

"You knew her?"

"Sure." Jay smiled, painfully.

"I miss her," she admitted. "I think about her lots."

"You look like her, you know."

"Yeah. But it just makes me sad."

Jay nodded, gnawing his lip.

"Okay," called Gabriel. "That's it!"

"Listen," Jay said to Sally Cowles, his voice hoarse with sorrow. "I've got to ask you a little favor."

"What?" She looked around to check on the others. "Is this what all this is about?"

"Hurry up, Rainman," said Gabriel.

"I want to ask you if you'll let me feel the inside of your ear. Real quick."

"That's pretty gross."

"A little, yes," Jay agreed. "That's the last thing I'll ask you."

"Well, I *guess*." She flipped her hair back behind her ears and leaned forward a little.

Jay took a deep, troubled breath, then reached out with his right hand. His daughter jerked in surprise when he touched her. "Easy," he murmured. His fingers touched her ear in front of her long hair, and his thumb gently ran along the inside ridge of cartilage. She looked at him and at me.

"Duck your head down a bit," he instructed.

This she did, trying not to cry.

"It's okay," I said.

Jay rubbed his daughter's ear.

"Is this—" Sally began, pulling away.

"Don't move," Jay commanded. "There." He closed his eyes, remembering, measuring the time since he'd last touched his daughter. Thirteenodd years earlier, in a park in London, Eliza already married to Cowles, already stolen away. Jay let his fingers fall from Sally's ear.

"Yes?" I said gently.

He nodded in silence.

Sally hunched fearfully, cutting her eyes back and forth.

"Sally," Jay began, his voice grieving.

"Don't!" I said sharply. "Don't do it, Jay."

"Why?"

"Because there's no need." I matched his gaze. "It only amounts to cruelty."

Sally looked back and forth between us. "What's everyone talking about?"

"Nothing," I said. "Nothing you need to worry about."

"The money," Gabriel said.

"In a leather tool bag," answered Jay. He pulled a single key from his pocket. "Utility closet, first-floor hallway."

"Hold them here," Gabriel told Denny. He took the key and left the car.

We waited. I watched. I watched a father study his child. Jay's eyes traced the line of Sally's forehead, then her eyes, down her nose, across her lips, under her chin, caressing, holding, knowing her. "Your mother was a fine person," he said finally.

Sally didn't answer.

"And—" He coughed, then gathered something from deep within, a certainty, a will. "And, your father—your father loves you very much."

Jay had said it, had brought it forth out of himself.

"Thank you," Sally said, trying to sound cheerful and appreciative. "I love him, too."

Gabriel returned, carrying the bag. He was on the phone as well. "Bring him anyway? Fine. She can go?" He hung up.

"Miss," he said brusquely, "leave us immediately."

"I can go?" said Sally.

"Yes, get out of the car, now." He tossed Jay's keys into the car, hitting me in the head. He told me, "Here, put your fucking fingerprints all over these. Every one."

"Okay," Sally said, grabbing her backpack. "Actually, my dad works right here."

Gabriel looked to Jay and then me in confusion.

"Let her out," I said, taking the keys in my hand.

He opened the door. "Scram."

Sally leapt past him, landed on the sidewalk, and turned around to be sure she wasn't pursued. I could see that the whole episode baffled her. She'd been kidnapped for perhaps half an hour only to be delivered to her father's office. So it hadn't quite turned out like a kidnapping, really, just a bizarre episode. The anxiety drained out of her face, replaced by loveliness and curiosity. She actually bent at the waist and peered back into the car. I think she was looking for Jay, and he returned her gaze, his eyes sad.

Then the door shut and we were on our way.

Jay turned to his interrogators, coughing. "What do you need us for?"

"Boss wants a final word," answered Gabriel. "Every key," he said to me. Then he inspected the bag of cash. "Very beautiful, the sight of money," he said. "Causes optimism in human beings." He reached under his seat and slid out a leather case and nudged its lid open with his foot. Inside were small boxes of ammunition. He grabbed one and slipped it into his breast pocket. Then he noticed me watching.

Ten minutes later the car glided up to the restaurant. Gabriel had Denny make sure the heavy door was open. Lamont came out and hustled Jay and then me inside.

The main dining room was empty, all the places set perfectly, awaiting the roar of customers in a few hours. Would the restaurant's staff start to arrive as late as four, as Allison had said? Somebody had to put the wine in the cooler, start counting out steaks.

"Down the stairs, gentlemen," Gabriel directed, and we descended the nineteen marble steps.

In the Havana Room Jay confronted the sight of Allison and Ha in the far booth, H.J. waiting. Something passed between Allison and Jay that I didn't understand.

"All right," H.J. announced. "We are almost done. What time you got?"

"Two fifty-eight."

"What time your waiters start coming?" he asked Allison.

"Soon," she said. "Four."

"That's a long time. I'm hungry."

"Boss, we should just go," said Gabriel. "You should go. Denny and I will finish up here."

"Not until I get my answer about my uncle Herschel," said H.J. "I'm workin' off a debt here. That man visited me in prison like fifty times. Drove all the way upstate." He pointed at Jay. "Your man Poppy said my uncle had a heart—wait, wait, dag, I'm hungry. You got anything to eat, any decent food?"

"Boss," said Gabriel. "*Listen to me!*"

"I'm hungry. Can't think without calories. Brain uses the most, you know that? I'm fat but I'm dangerous, yo. America loves the fat black man, thinks he ain't dangerous."

"What?" said Lamont.

"Hey, George Foreman, he's fat and *rich*, you got Bill Cosby, you got Al Roker, the weatherman, you got Sinbad, you got that fat guy in the beer commercials." He looked at Allison expectantly. "All these black men *rich* because the white man ain't scared of a *fat* black man."

"We don't have much down here," said Allison. "We've got some bar food, nuts, pretzels, things like that."

"Fuckin' paste," said H.J. "No good for you."

Denny pointed. "There's a little kitchen behind the bar."

"Does the gentleman like fish?" asked Ha.

Allison stared at him. "I don't know," she said slowly, though the question had not been addressed to her.

"Fish? No shit. You got fish?" said H.J.

Ha looked dryly at Allison. "We have good fish here, very fresh."

H.J. pointed at Ha, head hung meekly. "You said he can cook?"

Allison glanced at Ha. "Yes, his specialty is fish."

"What, swordfish? Tuna steak?"

"What do you have, Ha?" asked Allison, her voice a confection of sincerity.

Ha nodded, as if in thought. "I have the special fish, very good delicacy. Makes sushi."

"You do? In a steakhouse?" asked H.J.

"Very good, yes. We have the fresh fish in the aquarium you see, behind bar, under shelf."

"I need to fill myself up," said H.J. "Fish ain't goin' do that."

Denny went around the bar. "It's here." He bent down for a moment and we couldn't see him. "Goddamned ugly fish!"

"But it's a specialty," said Allison. "Sort of Chinese sushi. Ha was Mao Tse-tung's chef, you know that?"

"I'm hungry, too," admitted Denny.

"The old Chinese guy, the emperor or some shit?"

Ha nodded humbly.

"Gimme that fish you used to make for the Chinese emperor," said H.J. "We'll get some burgers on the road." He pointed his gun at Jay. "Then I'm going to talk to this guy. 'Cause it ain't just about the fuckin' money." He looked back at Ha. "Get started."

"If you wish."

"Yeah, we're hungry here." H.J. smiled at Lamont. "Got to keep up the strength. We got a big party tonight."

Ha lowered his head. "I work very fast, you see."

He stood up from the table where he'd been sitting and shuffled under the bar bridge. He disconnected the bubbler in the tank and rolled back through the bar. Then he laid his table piece on top of it and retrieved the rolled white cloth filled with knives. "Before I open this," he said, "I have to tell you, these very sharp knives. I need these to prepare fish. Please do not shoot Ha. These knives just for fish."

Denny nodded impatiently. "We know. That's fine."

He trapped the fish in the tank, then speared it through the nose.

"So, I take this—" Ha deftly slit open the wriggling fish. "We were going to have this fish served for tonight," he said, setting out his little bowls for the different organs.

"People pay a lot for this fish," Allison said, "you'd be surprised."

"H.J.," Gabriel said, watching Ha's progress. "I've worked for you three years, okay? I've been loyal and true. I only argue when I think I should. I think we should go. You should go. You got a problem Denny and I got to deal with. These people saw everything."

H.J. shook his head. "We got ten minutes, maybe, we got time. Traffic's already bad. I'm going to get my fish first." He pointed at Jay. "Then I'ma deal with *you*, muthafucka."

At once a silence hung over us. I noticed that Jay was the only one in the room who seemed unafraid. The strangeness and danger of the room had no effect on him. Then again, he did not know about Poppy, who lay trussed and bagged and stiffening on the other side of the bar.

Jay looked at me. "They made you tell them about Sally?"

I glanced at Allison. "I made a terrible mistake," I said. "I told Allison."

"On the other hand, I wouldn't have met her," Jay said. "Not yet, anyway."

"I guess not."

"Your daughter?" asked Allison, voice subdued.

Jay regarded her. I could see that he lived still in the brief minutes he'd had with Sally. "Yes," he answered. "My daughter."

She wanted to be angry with him, Allison, she wanted to hate him, but instead tears came as she looked at Jay, then at me, then away, trying to hold on to her pride. "Why didn't you *tell* me?" she said, facing Jay. "Why?"

"I didn't think you'd like it."

"It wouldn't have *mattered*," she cried. "Don't you understand, don't you see how much I—?" She looked away, unable to say it.

"You what—?" Jay began.

She struggled to respond, not used to making statements of satisfaction and happiness. "It was *nice*."

Nice. A word that counted, after all. She withdrew the napkin from her purse and handed it to Jay.

"What's this?" he asked, taking it.

"Poppy drew that for you," I said. "He told Allison to write the word."

Jay took the napkin. It was small in his hand, already a little rumpled, and he studied it a moment, lips pressed together, eyes wincing. Confusion—then total recognition. Total shocked recognition. He dropped his head as if he'd been clubbed.

"What?"

Jay studied the napkin, folded it, and slipped it into the breast pocket of his jacket. He turned to me. "Sally's gone, right? She's okay?"

"Yes," I said, "but—?"

"How we comin' with my food!" announced H.J.

"Very fast," Ha narrated suddenly, with greater energy, "a little rice and seaweed, for the very good sushi . . . I cut this . . . and roll on the finger . . ." Within the minute he had prepared eight identical pieces of sushi. I watched his knife movements through and around the bowls of organs, where the poison was, but I could not be sure what he'd done. Eight pieces was more than the standard number of portions. Then again, as I recalled, there was plenty enough poison in the fish's organs for eight pieces.

"Who will be having some of this, please?" Ha asked.

H.J. pointed at his men. "We'll split it."

"I don't like fish," muttered Lamont.

"So, some for each? Two each?" said Ha, carefully laying out the plates and putting two pieces of fish on each one.

"Yeah, whatever," said Gabriel, reaching for the first plate.

"No, no, please," said Ha. "I am not done! But you will be first." He edged the plate back to himself and appeared to crimp the ends of the sushi a bit, give them an extra roll, and like a portrait artist, he sight-checked his subject, calculating, I guessed, Gabriel's weight and age, all in a glance, as meanwhile his small knife dipped softly into one of the organ bowls, then darted back to the plate, wiping the two pieces of sushi quickly while his other hand garnished the plate with a flowered carrot—a kind of magic act of misdirection and flourish. "There!" Ha said. "Now."

Gabriel slid the plate down the bar in front of himself, but seemed disinterested.

Meanwhile Ha decorated two more two-piece servings of Shao-tzou. I watched the knife dip into the organ bowls each time while the other hand manipulated seaweed and rice. Again the misdirection and fanning, the flickering fingers. He set the four pieces of sushi on two small plates and Denny picked them up, handed one plate to H.J., then quickly shoved a piece of fish into his mouth. "Good," he announced with his mouth full.

"Who will have left over?" Ha asked the room. "Two more pieces. Allison?"

"No thank you, Ha."

"Mr. Jay?" asked Ha.

"Sure. But I also want a cigar."

"A cigar?"

H.J. pointed at the wall of cigars with his gold-plated automatic. "Get the muthafucka a cigar, he been no trouble. Let him smoke it while I smoke *him*, smoke the goddamn *truth* out of him. You ready for my questions, boy? I got lots of questions, like how come nobody fuckin' knows what happened to my uncle."

Denny walked down to the wall of cigars, drew out one, replaced it, drew out another, then returned to Jay, handing him the cigar. "Montecristo," he advised. "Very good."

"I mean," H.J. continued, his face a righteous scowl, "what kind of man was this Poppy dude? He got them *worried* eyes, like he got something he always thinking about! How come I think he just some kind of lying cracker? Can you tell me that? Can anybody tell me that?"

No one could. Meanwhile Ha finished Jay's piece. I watched his knife. It seemed to do what it had done before. He placed the plate in front of Jay. "One piece left over. This is just right," he said to me. His hands were a blur, pinching the strip of flesh and rolling it up in rice, dipping a knife into one bowl then the next. "For you."

I must have looked startled as he put the plate before me.

"Do not worry, Mr. Wyeth." Ha's old eyes disappeared into amused slits but his gaze stayed fixed on mine. "Just enjoy. Ha is giving you very good fish today. You know this, you see this fish before, you must show the others it is very good to eat."

I took the piece of sushi, looked at it. Ha shuffled out from the bar and toward H.J. and Gabriel, who had not eaten any fish. "Please, it is very good. Protein. Very strong." Then he turned back to me. "Is it good?"

I watched Jay set his cigar on the table next to his plate. I saw Allison watch me. I popped the piece of fish in my mouth. I chewed.

"Hmm," I told them, "that *is* terrific."

"Yes."

"Are you sure there's no more?" I said. "I could eat a boatload of this stuff."

Ha bowed his head in apology.

Denny ate his second piece, Gabriel tasted his first. We needed a pause, a lag of a minute. I listened, and thought I heard the first footsteps of the staff arriving upstairs.

Allison looked at her watch.

"What's that?" demanded H.J.

"The restaurant is opening," she said. "I've got waiters and waitresses arriving, sous-chefs, busboys, everybody."

"Can't you close it?"

"No," said Allison. "I'd have to call thirty people."

We heard a vacuum cleaner start up.

"You lock that door at the top of the stairs?" asked H.J.

Gabriel nodded.

"Nobody can get down here?"

"No."

"What time will everybody leave?"

"Maybe one a.m.," said Allison. "That's a long time from now."

"Big night planned?" I said to Allison, trying to kill time. Jay was studying his cigar.

"Convention bookings, two waves. Insurance salesmen or something. They'll be there all night."

Ha busied himself with cleaning up. Now it seemed there was a lot of spit in my mouth. I glanced at Gabriel; he'd eaten his second piece, H.J. his first. Jay had lifted his piece, examining the skill of its creation.

"I'm feeling poorly," Denny announced. "Numb. My eyes don't move." He tried to grasp the bar but toppled over, heavily, right in front of me, gun loose in his hand.

"Denny?" Gabriel lifted his gun as he watched Denny's legs shake queerly. But then he himself was blinking rapidly and began to wave his hands around his head as if to stop a pestering fly, wetness spreading across his crotch. He fell down on one knee, pitched sideways.

"What the fuck?" cried H.J., mouth full. "Denny? Gabriel?"

Ha remained stooped over the bar, the portrait of servility. Mournful, almost. I wanted him to look up at me now, because of course I had eaten the fish in good faith, in all the faith that I had, and I needed—as I was feeling odd—I needed to know that I hadn't eaten too much, that Ha had only served me the *right* amount, just enough and no more. I felt oddly disconnected from my thoughts, unafraid, in fact, to reach down and take Denny's gun from his hand.

"Hey!" yelled Lamont, noticing. He pointed the gun at Ha, at Jay, at me.

"I'm sick," called H.J., lurching toward the doorway. "Get me out of here."

Lamont swung his gun at me.

I pointed Denny's gun at him and fired—

—then felt a kind of electric zipper running up the back of my throat. I wondered about my eyes, and I lifted my hand to touch them, but it was too heavy to lift. I fell sideways in my booth and the room broke into crooked planes. Maybe Ha wanted to kill all of us, maybe that was the truth. Jay had his piece of sushi in his fingers. About to put it in his mouth. "Fish," I coughed, pointing.

"What?"

But if he ate the fish or spat it out, or if H.J. made it up the stairs, or if Lamont was shot I didn't know, for I slumped in the corner of the booth, staring at the salt shaker. The roof of my mouth now itched terribly, and my toes and hands began to tingle and turn numb. I could not move or refocus my eyes. Perhaps they had closed, I didn't know. Some time may have passed . . . in the meantime I felt my breath within my chest, moist, my whole life in there, as it is with everyone's, and I felt a peacefulness at the thought of death, perhaps even a willingness to die, if it was really so easy as this, but then I either saw or imagined that I saw Jay bend forward coughing, at first violently and then weakly. Had he eaten the fish? Allison may have rushed to him. I became fascinated by her hair, a wig of translucent snakes that convulsed rhythmically above her head. Allison knelt to the floor, and I watched Jay get up or not. But whether this was dream or truth is lost to me now . . . a cascade of sparks froze against the surface of my face until it caramelized and cracked into distinct jigsaw shapes of numbness, and they fell out and away from my face piece by piece and it was then that I believed I heard—what sounded most distinctly like—another gunshot, and I saw or believed I saw the speeding bullet appear before me, the slo-mo rotation of the slug trailing an elegant thread of blue smoke, and just as the slug approached my face one of the melted jigsaw puzzle pieces fell away, and the bullet—still rotating to perfection—pierced it, making it shatter like glass, yet silently, and then continue into and through the empty place on my cheek. Of course this was impossible. I had the sensation of falling into myself, folding downward, heart collapsing into my lungs, lungs into my intestines. Then I went blind. It was not the sensation of darkness but of nothingness, like trying to see the world when one is asleep, and I felt something large twitch in my ear and it must have been my eardrum reacting to a loud human sound, and I sensed heat or, more accurately, smoke, some smoke or burnt vapor spiraled up my nose, familiar yet ominous, and there was a scream that seemed to take forever against the same eardrum, and only afterward did I understand it was a woman's scream, and who she was I did not know. You cannot know the usual things when you have eaten Shao-tzou fugu fish from China. You cannot know who people are, including yourself. You can only hope that there is still a breath in you somewhere, a faint glowing in the lungs, and perhaps too you know that you have fallen in dumb paralysis to the cold black-and-white tiles of the Havana Room, which would seem the first step toward being permanently dead.

ten

A CLATTERING WET DARKNESS, cold and filled with exhaust—this is where I awoke, a bulkily shifting weight atop me, hurting my back and legs and my head, my face pressed in lip-snarled compression against a leaking plastic mass. When I moved against this restraint, pain sparked down my neck, dwindling away as I fell limp again. I pushed off harder and this time the volume atop me settled to either side and the air was better. I was in what sounded like a truck going forty or fifty miles an hour. The top of my head seemed to flatten, then crater downward, then pop out to its original shape. I vomited, but I could not smell or feel what came out of me, and I was already so slick with refuse that I did not feel my own spew, whether it landed on me or away. I cannonballed myself to my hands and knees, only now beginning to hear a muffled shrieking in another language, tinny and incomprehensible—Chinese, coming from what sounded like a radio a few feet in front of me. A blast of music followed, then near silence. I took this opportunity to yell as loudly as I could.

The vehicle slowed, with much excited hollering of men's voices. The truck seemed to be executing one barrel roll after another, or perhaps that was me, tumbling sideways. I vomited again, upward, and this time I tasted myself, felt the stomach acid wash in my eyes. The van or truck accelerated and rocketed over bumps and stones and craters and thousand-foot pits and whatever else might break its tires, and then stopped, the bulky mass rocking forward, then settling back onto itself as the vehicle came to a dead stop. I vomited a third time. A bag fell against me. The engine stayed on. I heard the voices, a door open, then the voices come alongside the walls of the vehicle. The lock on the door was being opened. I lifted my head. A rectangle of light opened at one end of the space and two Chinese men in overalls and long rubber gloves stood before me. I hollered bloody murder again and they climbed into the garbage and hauled me out feetfirst, roughly, yelling as if I had betrayed them, and I fought them out of instinct, but they got their clammy gloves around my legs and pulled me roughly through the leaking garbage bags, then along the slick floor of the van. I fell straight to the ground, banging my shoulder on the bumper, and before they slammed the doors shut, one of the men picked up a fallen bag of eggshells and shrimp carcasses, a pause just long enough for me to look up and into the van—it *was* a van—and notice, or think that I noticed, a man's brown dress shoe resting in the refuse, a shoe not my own, since I had both of mine still on. I fell backward, stunned and weak, my lungs filled with exhaust as the van sped crazily over a rubbled wasteland, through a broken fence, then into the street. The sky above me was a cloudless infinity of blue. A seagull winged lazily past. My eyes hurt, my head felt too big, my back numb, legs stiff and weak. I rolled to my stomach, got one knee up, stood, staggered, vomited again, this time a thin, burning gruel, wiped my mouth with my sleeve, pulled a piece of limp lettuce from my hair, and saw now that I stood in an abandoned lot strewn with bricks and bottles. I was suddenly cold and dry-mouthed. The garbage had kept me warm. I felt my pockets and was pleased to discover my wallet, with all my identification as well. Plus a set of keys I didn't recognize. I studied them. They were Jay's. I had to give them back. I counted my cash, found I hadn't been robbed. No, that would have been a relief, in a way. I was being dumped, taken out with the garbage.

Dumped, as if they thought I was dead.

Like the other guy in the van.

In a bodega three blocks away I bought coffee, juice, three scrambled eggs, home fries, and a New York Giants sweatshirt off a kid delivering newspapers. I wasn't sure I'd be able to keep the food down, but I ordered it anyway. The cook, a big, authoritative man, told me I was in Queens. He let me use the bathroom, where I took off my reeking button-down oxford. I could barely move my arms, I was so stiff. A cockroach lay inside the sleeve. I washed my chest and armpits and face with paper towels, threw away the shirt, then put on the sweatshirt.

"You got jacked, right?" said the cook when I came out, rubbing a hand over his pear-shaped belly. He kept a pen behind his ear.

"Something." My head was a mess. Fourteen-odd hours later.

He set the ketchup in front of me. "No, no, let me tell you something, I'm telling you, you got *jacked*. You don't remember nothing, right? That lot, it's like, what, three, maybe four times a— Jimmy, how many times we see guys get dumped where the old paint factory used to be?"

A voice from a back room. "Howafuck I know?"

"Don't give him no never-mine," the cook told me. "His wife got mental-pause and it got him, too. Guys get fucking *jacked* and they throw them in that lot because it's just off the expressway. One guy, it was a hooker and she had him pull over his car and when she got his dick out there was another guy waiting, then another time this guy was left there, couple of sickos, they taped a dead cat against his head, fuckin'-unbelievable-tha'shit, trying-a scare him, and this other time they threw fucking toxic *waste* out there, the government came with all the white moon suits, you know, we sold like two hundred cups of coffee."

"They didn't get all of it!" came the voice behind the door.

"What? What's that, Jimmy?"

"They didn't get all the fucking toxic waste."

"What d'you mean?"

"They left *you*, didn't they?"

I looked at my watch. "What day is this?"

"What day?"

"It's uh, it's *Tues*day, guy."

"No, I mean the date."

"The date? Let me—what's the date, Jimmy?"

"Howafuck I know?"

The cook slicked his hand across his head and checked a spattered calendar next to the cash register. "It's the first," he declared, "first of the month."

March 1. The day I was to start work. I was due at work in three hours, showered, shaved, in a new tie—walking human capital. It took me another moment to remember I didn't live anywhere anymore. I checked the cash in my wallet.

"You guys do me one more favor?" I said.

"What. Anything, name it."

"I want you guys to call me a car into Manhattan."

"Can't."

"Why?"

"I'm driving you myself."

"No, no, that's all right."

"Come on, it's twenty minutes." The cook reached for his coat. "Jimmy, take the front." He pointed at the front door. "We're slow today, anyway. It's a slow week. Actually, the year's been pretty slow, matter of fact."

We drove in silence in an old Chevy Caprice that looked repainted. Maybe an old taxi. I was immensely grateful. I asked the cook to drop me in midtown.

"So, did you know these people who jacked you?" The cook turned his eyes onto me, and beneath their penetration, I couldn't lie. "Or was it just a surprise, wrong place-wrong time?"

"Basically I knew them," I said.

The cook nodded, as if he expected to hear this. "Let me tell you something," he said. "I used to be a cop. I retired. I got tired and I retired. But I seen a lot of things."

I went rigid. "All right."

"You want to go on, right, you want to avoid more trouble?"

Had I shot a gun? Did I remember doing that? "Absolutely."

"Don't try to get revenge."

"It's not like that."

He wheeled the car through Spanish Harlem. "Just listen to me. Don't try to get revenge, don't try to explain it to a bunch of people, don't tell nobody, don't tell the police for freaking sake, don't do nothing. And don't go back to those people, don't associate, don't talk about it."

"Okay." I realized I hadn't told him my name.

"You got out with your skin, right?"

"Yeah."

"You're lucky."

"Just go back to my old life, let time pass."

He nodded as he pulled the car to a stop. "Yeah. Go back to your regular life and stay there. Die old."

How do you walk into your hotel at eight o'clock smelling of garbage, have no change of clothes, then two hours later arrive at a new job looking great in a new suit? Answer: It can't quite be done. I hurried stiffly into the hotel, showered, shaved, cleaned up, then padded downstairs in pants and a hotel bathrobe, bought a ridiculous red sweatsuit in a gift shop on Fifth Avenue, returned to the room, changed, then took a cab to Macy's, which opens at nine, bought a suit off the rack, shirt, tie, belt, socks, shoes, dressing in the little changing cubicle, then took the subway to work—and arrived seventeen minutes late.

But it didn't matter. Dan was on the phone with someone—his new mistress, I learned later. That morning, after he had introduced me to the other principals (younger men and women straining on their leashes, eager for glory and promotions and big bucks) and the new assistants (three battle-hardened fiftyish women, attuned to health care benefits and flexible hours to see their grandchildren in school productions), and after I had inspected my office (decent, but nothing like my former one, which had a helicopter view of Lexington Avenue), after I had asked my assistant to order me stationery and a corporate American Express card, after I had established my new law firm e-mail account and signed the employment tax form, after I had done all these functional things and more, I slipped away to a pay phone on the street a few blocks away and dialed Allison, first at home. No answer. Then I dialed the restaurant. A recording came on, in her voice. The restaurant would be "closed for annual cleaning" the next three days, but would reopen on the weekend. Please call after 3 p.m. Friday to confirm or make reservations. And so on. I called Jay Rainey's number. I still had his keys. Nothing. I called Martha Hallock, but she hadn't heard from Jay. Neither had I, I said.

I returned to my office, pushed the little bit of paper that was on my desk, made phone calls using a voice that sounded like mine, then returned to the hotel at the end of the day. From there I called Judith's attorney and left my new work number.

Here, now, is where I begin to equivocate, to confess I told no one anything, to squirm my way free. A lawyer can be disbarred in ten minutes for being party to illegal activities, so naturally I considered going to the police, telling all that I knew and letting them sort everything out. But I didn't, really, know what might come of it, except trouble for myself. Poppy had been killed by Lamont, whom I might have shot. Gabriel and Denny, I suspected, were dead, given how violently they'd reacted to Ha's lovely pieces of sushi. Of course, these men had families somewhere. People would want to know what happened to them. But nothing I could say was bringing them back. Moreover, the matter with Marceno and the land was still unresolved. Poppy was dead, and whatever had been scrawled on the HAVANA ROOM napkin was with Jay Rainey. *Don't tell nobody, don't tell the police for freaking sake, don't do nothing.* This, I reflected, was good advice. Illegal, immoral, unethical, unlawyerly, selfish, cowardly, flat-out wrong, and utterly reprehensible. But excellent advice nonetheless, and I quietly reported for work each morning, eager to lose myself in the business at hand, waiting each hour for the time that Timothy would arrive in the city. Timothy, my boy, my own lost child.

The following Saturday, I saw a small item in the metro section of the *Times* about one Harold Jones, a New York City rap club owner found next to a Dumpster behind a McDonald's in Camden, New Jersey. This was H.J. He'd last been seen alive in his limousine in the Overbrook section of Philadelphia late the previous Tuesday. Some boys had stolen the limo and joy-ridden it around for several days, H.J. apparently dead in the back, and they were wanted for questioning. I bought the *Daily News* and the *Post* to get the whole story. They played it smaller than I expected, probably because he had died out of town and there were no good photos and H.J. wasn't well known, anyway, except among certain black kids who went to his club. He wasn't a musician, didn't produce records. So went the cultural logic. Just a small-time businessman, in fact. Just another fat black guy with a gold watch pretending to be richer than he was. I ended up walking to the newspaper shop at Grand Central Station and buying the Philadelphia papers. The reporting was more detailed, and between all four papers, I could get a lot of the story. But I read that his driver didn't remember him taking any drugs. The paper said toxicology reports were inconclusive. Who knew what he had in his bloodstream at any given time? He'd gotten in his limo after a meeting in midtown, carrying a leather bag, hollered something, and been driven to Philly. Fell asleep in the car, said the driver. The driver got stuck on the New Jersey Turnpike, finally reached Philly, the black neighborhood of Overbrook. Big house, big party. The driver said he'd opened the limo door, swore he saw H.J. sitting in the limo. Soon people were in the back with him. Talking, partying. The limo driver admitted he ended up in a back room for the rest of the night. The limousine itself was found parked on the football field of a high school in Chester, Pennsylvania, a dying industrial town hanging off the underbelly of Philadelphia. How Harold Jones ended up in Camden, New Jersey, and his car twenty miles away in Chester, Pennsylvania, was unknown. The police found "drug paraphernalia" in the backseat of the car as well as "an undisclosed amount of cash." This would have been whatever was left of the extra purchase money I had negotiated for Jay, money originally earned, when you thought about it, by Chilean vineyard laborers thousands of miles to the south. I was surprised any remained at all. One could picture the scene, people finding H.J., a fat bag of cash, loud music outside a house, confusion, hours passing, rumors of a dead man, move the car, yo, not on my property, gimme them keys, move his dead ass someplace else. Which they did.

I studied the papers, feeling odd, sickened all over again. You could say H.J. had brought all this on himself, but then again, he hadn't, for his original motivations were honorable; his grieving aunt had asked him to secure a death settlement for their family. I didn't expect to feel bad about H.J., yet I did.

On the next Monday I reached Allison at work.

"Bill?" she answered warily. "Where are you?"

"You know we have to talk, Allison."

She insisted we not meet at the restaurant, so instead we found each other at the southeast corner of Central Park, across from the Plaza Hotel, and walked down the path to the pond ringed with green benches with IN MEMORY OF plaques on them. She looked good, Allison, fingernails manicured, one black pump in front of the other as she walked, put together, not a care in the world—just as I expected.

"You saw about H.J.?"

She nodded.

"Probably the fish."

"I don't know," she said.

"What happened to Poppy? To his body?"

"I don't know."

"What happened to Denny and Gabriel?"

"Don't know."

"Did I shoot Lamont? I did, didn't I?"

"I couldn't tell. Honestly. I wasn't watching that. You might have just injured him."

"There was a second shot, I think. All that noise . . ."

"No one heard," she said. "Because of the vacuuming upstairs."

"Who took the second shot?"

"You didn't kill Lamont," she admitted. "He was just injured. He was waving his gun around."

"Someone else shot him? Who?"

She shrugged. I got a feeling.

"*You* shot him?"

She didn't answer.

"Jesus, Allison."

"It was horrible, that's all I'm going to say."

"Ha? What happened to him?"

"He's gone. Totally gone."

"Moved?"

"Disappeared. His little room at the top of the restaurant is cleaned out. He could be anywhere."

"If they come looking, then he draws the suspicion towards himself."

"Yes, I suppose so. He would think of that."

"What about all the videotapes of people going in and out of the steakhouse? You have all those cameras. Did Ha take the tapes with him?"

"No."

"So there's a record of everyone going into the place last Monday afternoon?"

Allison shook her head. She was composed. She had no worries. "The tapes get automatically erased with a magnet and reused every forty-eight hours. The machine does it by itself unless told not to."

"Days and days past. Erased three times over since then."

She nodded. "Has Jay called you?"

"No."

"I thought he might have."

"Did he leave after I passed out?"

"Yes," she said. "He left."

"I sort of remember him coughing."

"He was coughing."

"Did he say anything, about his daughter, before he left?"

"Not to me," she said, voice tight.

"He just left."

"Yes."

"He got up and walked out?"

"Yes."

"You saw this."

"Ha told me."

"What about H.J.?"

"He climbed the stairs and got out. The staff didn't see him go. Only a few people had showed up and they were in the kitchen. I think he had that limo waiting."

"What about Lamont? He was shot."

But she wasn't saying anything.

"What did you do, lock all the bodies in the Havana Room, open the restaurant like normal, then get rid of everybody after you closed?" I pictured the clientele arriving, the coat check girl collecting her tips, the waiters and cooks, the whole show, Allison coolly running the evening, while down in the Havana Room there were bodies on the floor, including mine.

"What do you mean?"

"How many bodies went out of there, Allison?" I remembered the man's shoes I'd glimpsed in the van.

She didn't answer.

"Did Ha think I was dead?"

"I don't know."

"He did, I bet. Did *you* think I was dead, Allison?"

She turned to me. "I did, yes. Well, I wasn't sure."

"You didn't bother to come over and feel for a pulse, to see if your old friend Bill Wyeth, who you'd dragged into this mess, was still barely breathing?"

"I was upset, Bill. Ha told me just to work upstairs. He stayed down in the Havana Room. I never went down there again that night, okay? He called some people, some Chinese men he knows, he said a van would come. I think they carried some of the bodies up the stairs, then down through the kitchen and up through the sidewalk doors. It would be easier that way. No one would see." She nodded. "Ha took care of everything. When I went downstairs to the Havana Room the next morning, it was clean, *really* clean."

"And Ha?"

"Like I said, then he was gone."

Allison was lying about something, but just what, I didn't know. I pretended a dull acceptance of all that she'd said, and casually got up to leave.

"Bill?"

"I'll come around the steakhouse, give me a little time."

Allison stared at me, then looked straight at the pond as if she didn't know I was still there, as if she had never known me.

If Jay had in fact walked out of the steakhouse, it would have been without his keys. Because I still had them. But certainly he had another set in his apartment. Had he moved his truck? Did it matter that my fingerprints were on the door handles and probably inside on the passenger side? Maybe not, but I didn't want to have to worry about it. And also, it was probably a good idea to see what was still in the truck. I caught the subway downtown to his building on Reade Street. It took me twenty minutes to find his truck three blocks away. A week had passed, and the windshield was plastered with three bright parking violation stickers threatening to tow the vehicle the next day. I found the right key on the ring, opened the passenger's door, keeping my gloves on, and removed the girls' basketball schedule I'd seen earlier. Had I not gone to that game, H.J. might never have found me. Nor would I have been hired by Dan Tuthill, for that matter. I tucked the schedule into my pocket. Anything else connected to Sally Cowles? I checked under and behind the seats, in the back, the glove compartment, behind the sun visors, everywhere. Nothing. I pulled out a handkerchief and rubbed hard over the passenger's dash, inside window, and handle. Then on the outside of the driver's door. Nobody saw, and nobody cared, anyway. I was just being paranoid, probably. I locked the door and slipped away, remembering to throw the handkerchief and the schedule in a trash basket a few blocks south.

The following evening, I made a point of walking down to Reade Street. Rainey's truck was gone, no doubt now sitting impounded in a city lot. I'd bought a handsaw and a box of heavy-duty garbage bags. I opened the building, took the stairs quietly, then opened the empty office adjacent to Cowles's. In a few minutes, I'd picked up the trash. Then I turned my attention to the strange hooded tennis-judge chair, cutting it apart and bagging the pieces. After that I took a hammer to the lipstick cameras and their computer, then tore out the secret phone wiring as far as I could trace it. An hour later the refuse was bundled onto the street, and the office looked marred by some incomplete repair. I spent another half an hour looking for anything else in the office that might be a problem, then checked the basement, finding nothing there.

I called Jay a few more times after that, halfheartedly, each time from a different pay phone, never leaving a message. Then, finally, I could not help myself, could not resist the temptation, and took the subway to Brooklyn two nights later and walked to his apartment. It was dark and there was no light on at the top of the garage stairs leading to his door. The glass had not been replaced in his door but someone had hammered a piece of plywood over the hole, from the inside. I had the keys. I cupped my hand against the glass and could see only Rainey's neat camp bed, the blinking light of the oxygen compressor. Was there anyone inside, was he dead on the kitchen floor? I found the right key, then checked behind me. Someone was standing on his stoop across the street, trying to light a cigarette. He hadn't necessarily seen me, but if I turned on the lights in the apartment, he'd know someone was inside. I'd made a mistake coming at night. I eased down the stairs, eased away.

In this mood of worried self-protection it occurred to me that I should probably get rid of my rotten walk-up apartment on Thirty-sixth Street. I called the super and said I'd like to pay for any necessary repairs, then break the lease. He laughed and told me don't bother, we rented it three days after you left. Have a nice life, mister. So I found a small sublet near my old neighborhood on the Upper East Side, one with an extra bedroom this time, and I moved in.

All this transpired in the ten days after I started work, long zombified hours during which time I was simultaneously aghast and relieved that the world remained unknowing of what was probably four murders in the private room of a Manhattan steakhouse one night the previous month, plus a possibly related death the next day, somewhere on the road to Philadelphia. Where were the bodies of Poppy, Gabriel, Denny,

Lamont? Where was Jay Rainey? Then, one morning, while I was shaving, looking in the mirror, my phone rang. I'd given my new, unlisted number to the people at the office but to no one else.

"William Wyeth?"

"Speaking."

It was a detective in Brooklyn, a man named McComber.

"You know a man called Jay Rainey?"

"Yes," I said, knowing I couldn't lie about this, what with witnesses, phone records, and my name on Rainey's documents. "I served as his lawyer for a recent real estate transaction."

"When was that?"

"About three weeks ago."

"When was the last time you saw Mr. Rainey?"

"It's been a little while, two weeks, I'd say."

"Mr. Rainey is deceased."

Was I surprised? I don't know. "What happened?"

His body had been found in the waters off Coney Island, McComber said, badly decomposed. Some kids on jet skis in wet suits found him floating, a swollen figure in sodden pants and shirt, and this being the world that it is, one of the kids had a waterproof cell phone and called the police. Jay's wallet was in the breast pocket of his coat, and my cell phone number was in it.

"But you called my new apartment line," I said.

"Yes."

"Oh."

"We like to know where people are," noted McComber. "Can you identify any immediate family members for us?" he went on.

"His father died a year or two ago, and he hasn't spoken to or seen his mother in more than a decade. I'm pretty sure there were no siblings."

"Was he married?"

"No."

"Children?"

"No," I said without hesitation.

"A girlfriend?"

"He didn't really discuss that part of his life with me."

"I see." The detective paused. "Well, we have a problem."

"Yes?"

"We need someone to identify and claim the body. We had to go ahead and do the autopsy, but we need to release the body."

"I don't know of any family members."

"Could you identify and claim?"

"Uh, I guess. I mean, I've never done it—"

"We need to release the body."

"Where do I go?"

He gave me the directions. I said I had some office business but could be there in three hours.

"Can I give you some advice?" asked the detective.

"Yes," I said, anxious that he meant some legal precaution.

"Don't eat lunch."

"Oh."

"I mean it."

"Okay. Thanks."

On the way to the medical examiner's office in Brooklyn I made a side stop at Jay's apartment, keeping my gloves on. This would be my last chance, I suspected, and I would take it. Inside I closed the door softly and turned on the light. Everything was as before. I had a plastic bag with me and removed sixteen unsent letters from Jay to Sally Cowles, including a few more I found in the oxygen chamber. But I knew there was more I should find. I took my time, I opened drawers, and the trunks under the bed. I found thirty-six different pieces of paper with references to his daughter. Plus some photos. Plus some more school schedules. Plus the handout from the recital. Plus his camera, which had exposed film in it that I removed. I also found a spare set of keys, both to Jay's truck and to the Reade Street property. The truck was gone now into bureaucratic infinity, eventually to be sold at auction. I slipped the Reade Street keys off their chain, checked around the apartment once more, set the door to lock, and pulled it shut behind me. Then I locked it from the outside as well. The whole operation took an extra twenty-five minutes. On the subway I stepped off at the Atlantic Avenue station, found a trash can that needed emptying, dropped everything but Jay's letters to Sally Cowles into it, then boarded the next train. I didn't want to have the letters on me in the presence of a police officer, so I stopped in a post office, bought an envelope, and mailed them to myself at home.

I met McComber in the hallway of the medical examiner's office. He was a small, tidy man. I shook his hand.

"You were his lawyer?"

"For one real estate transaction."

"How'd you meet?"

"We met and got to talking," I said, wanting to keep Allison out of it, if only for my sake. "I needed the work, so I said yes."

"Why'd he buy the building?"

I said it was a standard commercial investment but that the question was still a good one.

"Why is it a good question?" the detective responded.

"Because he was pretty sick."

"He was?"

"He had terrible breathing problems. Very bad."

McComber sucked at his cheeks, held my gaze. Of course, he had seen the autopsy report, which, I supposed, revealed the damaged lung tissue. "What do you mean?"

"He grew up on a potato farm on the North Fork of Long Island and was nearly killed in a herbicide accident."

"When was this?"

"I'm guessing fifteen years ago. It was degenerative. It caused a slow fibrosis in his lungs."

"How do *you* know all this?"

"He told me, but also I could see it. He had real difficulty sometimes."

"You guys got to know each other pretty well, I see."

"He told me a few things."

"But how well did you get to *know* each other, is what I'm really asking," pressed McComber.

"Not like that," I said.

"You're not married."

"Divorced."

"Children?"

"I have a son, yeah."

This relaxed him. "All right, so go on."

"He just had trouble breathing."

"You know where he lived?"

All the oxygen equipment, the black-market steroids and inhalers and bottles of pills were there, to be found by the police. "Here it is," I said, giving him the address. Seem to be helpful, I told myself, be the good citizen. "Can I also give you my work number in case anything turns up?"

"Yeah, yeah."

"Anything else?" I asked.

"Did he go to a doctor?"

"I don't think so, never mentioned it."

"He was sick but didn't go to the doctor?"

I said nothing, appearing reticent.

"Come on," McComber prompted. "We got a dead guy here, we're trying to figure it out."

"Okay," I said. "I got the impression Jay sort of experimented with his medications. He said his condition was only getting worse. He used to measure his lung capacity a lot. He was very worried about it. He always had pills and medicines for his lungs with him. Basically I think he treated himself. "

The detective nodded, and I sensed a tick of judgment and dismissal. *Lonely guy, sick, played with his drugs, knew he was going to die.*

Ten minutes later an assistant medical examiner pulled out the long refrigerated drawer three feet, and there was Jay Rainey, his head and wide chest, his skin a pearled gray, looking shrunken into the drawer, a long suture-tightened incision running from the bottom of his neck to his belly button. The medical examiner had cut him open, gutted him. It was goddamn sickening. I caught the bile in my throat, took a moment to swallow. As I slid closer I could see that his hair lay salt-thickened by the ocean, more salt dried in starry spots across his cheeks. His eyes were open but the eyes themselves were gone and I found myself remembering the heroic Roman sculptures in which the marble eyes are darkly hollowed, creating the strange sense of visionary blindness. Jay seemed similarly afflicted. You could look at him but he didn't see you. The attendant had stuffed some cotton wadding in his nostrils. Jay's mouth had fallen open, as if getting one last great breath, and I noticed that he was missing a number of back teeth, the effect, I supposed, of not having money for proper dentistry during all his lean years. His face was stubbled and he looked both younger and ancient.

"That him?"

I nodded. "Yes."

"You're sure."

"Positive."

"You'll sign the form?"

"Yes."

"No doubt?"

"None."

"You happen to know if he had a dentist?"

"I think he did, yes. But I'm positive this is Jay."

"Occasionally people make mistakes."

Yes, of course that was true. "Pull him all the way out," I said.

"Why?"

"Look at his calves."

"Why? He have a tattoo?"

"No."

"What?"

"Immensely muscled. Enormous calves."

The attendant pulled the drawer all the way out. It rolled smoothly, though I could see that the weight of Jay Rainey made the long drawer tilt ever so slightly. He was naked. Laid out, he looked larger, his true size. His chest hair was thick and tapered into an arrow toward his groin. His penis fell to one side. Jay Rainey's thick calves bulged inward toward each other from the pressure of the drawer bottom. The attendant nodded. Then he pulled out a tape measure. "Hmm."

"Yes, right?"

"Twenty-one inches. You usually maybe see that on someone who is grotesquely obese, but not someone with low body fat."

"Can I have a minute more?" I asked. "He was a friend of mine."

"That's fine. Just a minute."

Then I moved up to Jay Rainey's head and touched his ear, the left one, the one that matched Sally Cowles's. The distinct horn of cartilage was there, as before, except cold this time. Somehow it made me think of my son, how much I missed him, how I was still bound to him.

I let the palm of my hand rest on Jay's forehead for a moment, but of course that was for me, not for him.

"Okay," came the attendant's voice.

I stepped away from the drawer. The attendant handed me a clipboard. It was a declaration of identification. Under penalty of perjury, I swore that the human remains shown to me by the . . . yes. I signed.

"That's it," the attendant said. "You're free to go, thanks."

"No, he's not," came the detective's voice.

"No?"

"Don't you want somebody to claim the remains?" the detective asked the attendant.

"Sooner the better."

"You," McComber said. "You're going to claim the remains here. I got no family. But I got a lawyer."

"Wait, wait—"

"Nothing to it." McComber handed me a business card of a funeral home. "These guys are three blocks away, they'll take the body and keep it or embalm it or whatever. We need to clear the space. This is Brooklyn. People keep dying around here."

"All right," I said. "Fine."

"You'll call today?"

"Sure."

"Good. Then I can release the effects now."

He nodded at the attendant, who went to a separate drawer. He pulled out a cardboard box. "Here."

I looked inside. Clothes.

"Plus this," said the detective, and handed me a clear Ziploc bag. "Wallet and watch, book of soggy matches."

I looked at the clear bag. The matchbook was from the steakhouse, the watch ruined by seawater. Then the clothes. "These things kind of smell," I said.

"Yes, they do. That's why we like to get rid of them."

I remembered the last piece of sushi on the plate in front of Jay Rainey. "By the way, what did he actually die of?"

The detective handed me his clipboard, flipped over two pages, and stuck a finger at a long paragraph:

Decedent's lungs and stomach were filled with seawater but autopsy and further sectioning revealed severe and progressed disease of the lungs and airways. Diffuse, symmetrical alveolar disease noted. Indications of pulmonary collapse and consolidation. Probable bronchiectasis, although these tissue slides were not prepared. Obliterative or constrictive bronchiolitis noted, with characteristic plugs of organizing fibrous tissue accompanying similar changes in the alveoli. No indication of bronchial carcinoma. Reduced lung distensibility noted by digital examination. Airway was scarred, indicating multiple instances of mechanical ventilation. Indications of chronic arterial hypoxemia. Secondary breathing muscles in chest showed unusual compensatory development. Pedal discoloration was also noted, as is typical. Cause of death: asphyxiation secondary to chronic, degenerative airway disorder with diffuse pulmonary alveolitis or fibrosis of unknown etiology.

I handed back the clipboard.

"That means he couldn't breathe," said the detective.

I nodded.

"You'll call the funeral home?" he asked.

"Yes."

"Free to go then."

Free to go, perhaps, but not free. Not at all. I carried the box to the pocket park a block away and found a bench. I put the bag with the wallet and watch and matchbook in my coat, then examined the clothes in the sunlight. They looked familiar, and included the same tie Jay had been wearing the night I'd last seen him in the Havana Room. They had been thrown in a dryer and were stiff yet unwashed. Three homeless men watched me from across the park. First the shoes, size 12, larger than mine. These I set on the bench. Then the socks. I shot my hand into each one. Empty. I rolled them up as my mother had taught me when I was a boy and put them into one of the shoes. Next came the pants. They'd been scissored off of him and were useless. I slipped my fingers into every pocket. Nothing. These I set on the other side of me. Then the underwear. These had also been cut off. I noted the waist size, 38. Unstained, almost new. Then the shirt, also cut off. I checked the size. A 48 long, Brooks Brothers. Nothing in the breast pocket. I stood up and dropped the slit underwear, pants, and shirt into the municipal garbage can and returned to my bench.

The tie I kept. It was silk and quite nice and could be cleaned. I tucked it into my coat. Next came the jacket. It was discolored by salt and other liquids but intact. I slipped two fingers into the front breast pocket. The HAVANA ROOM napkin that Allison had handed him was still there, still folded into a tight square. I slipped it into my pocket. Next I checked the inside breast pocket and the side pockets. Nothing. I folded the jacket and set it by the shoes. Last was the heavy overcoat, a beauty. The label read Brentridge of London. I checked the side pockets. Nothing. I checked the inside breast pocket. Nothing.

"Hey," I called to the homeless guys. Then I pointed at the pile of clothes. "You want these?"

One of the men stood up, shambled over, poked disinterestedly at the pile, then picked up the whole bundle and shuffled away.

Now I drew the HAVANA ROOM napkin from my pocket, daring myself to unfold it. The marks on it, made in red lipstick, had nearly been bleached by the cold Atlantic. Nonetheless, unlike before, I could examine what had been drawn there. It was a small map, with the three X's and the box marked KROWLA.

Yes, a simple map. Of a small section of Jay Rainey's family farm, now owned by Marceno and his Chilean wine company. The scale was a little

HAVANA ROOM
XXX
KROWLA

off, but the three X's probably corresponded to the three ancient trees next to the driveway with the rectangle indicating that something might be found directly off from the third tree: KROWLA, in Allison's block letters.

I called Marceno that afternoon.

"This is William Wy-eth?"

"It's me. I have something for you," I said. "What you *wanted*."

"You are perhaps hoping to resolve the lawsuit, Mr. Wy-eth?"

"Why didn't you come to the restaurant that day?" I asked. "After I called you?"

"Simple."

"Simple?"

"I called Martha Hallock to see if you were telling the truth, that Poppy was her nephew."

"And?"

"She said he'd told her he was driving to Florida."

"But what about the nephew part?"

"She said in these old farm communities everybody's related to everybody else somehow. She also said he was an unreliable character, drank too much."

"Ah." This sounded like a fat lie. But I didn't have enough leverage on him to force out the truth, whatever it was.

"What is it you want?" Marceno said, his voice measured but not without threat in it.

"I have the information you wanted."

"I see. Why don't you send it to me?"

"No, I want to give it to you in person. I want you to have it. You caused enough grief and suffering that I really think you should have it."

"I will meet you tomorrow."

"You will meet me on Saturday morning and you and I will drive out to the old farm and then and only then will I give you the information," I told him. "Got that?"

He did. His chauffeured car glided up in front of my building at eight the next Saturday morning. The sun was out, spring not far away. The ride was smooth, if not particularly fast. The expressway is a nightmare, day and night. Weekends everybody is shopping. From time to time Marceno had a brief conversation on his phone in Spanish.

As we neared the old farm, Marceno said, "I am sorry for all of this trouble, Mr. Wy-eth."

I nodded.

"But you see, I had to press the issue, as you say."

"I understand that you panicked, yes."

"That depends on what we find." He consulted the palms of his hands. "Maybe my fears were well founded."

We reached the farm. The old barns had been demolished, and all that remained was a smoking pile of lumber.

"That will be where the winery goes," said Marceno, pointing across the field. "You are just in time. We decided to begin, we had to take a chance."

Across the fields, a dozen workers had just started to erect the parallel rows of grape trellises. The car traveled over a new gravel road. I noticed what looked to be a profusion of daffodils pushing through the earth at the edge of the field. When we reached the place where the barn had stood, we counted the three trees specified on the napkin. Rather, we counted two stumps and one old box elder tree that had been trimmed to a limbless trunk reaching into the sky like an immense bony finger, swollen at the joints. It was due to come down that day. Marceno told his driver to stop and we got out. The field was soft—spongy and wet, sucking at our shoes.

We walked to the tree. Marceno studied the napkin, then paced ten steps east toward the Atlantic Ocean and stuck a shovel in the earth. This, I realized, was a straight shot to the place where the bulldozer and Herschel atop it had gone over the sea cliff. Holding the napkin in his hand a different way, Marceno paced out from the tree again, arriving at more or less the same spot. "There." He dug with a shovel and a foot down revealed a thatch of browned grass. "This whole section was regraded," Marceno said. "A huge amount of topsoil was brought in." He pointed at the rotting grass. "That was the original elevation a few weeks ago." But he uttered this softly, as if not yet committed to the act that awaited him.

His men brought over their tools and sat on their haunches. The bulldozer swung around and dipped its cup into the earth, pawing away a few feet. The bulldozer—not the old rust-pocked one Herschel had died on, but another, shining red and twice as large—dug a long channel in the earth. The backhoe bucket dragged shallow scoops of topsoil, its operator skilled and meticulous. The patch of earth was about twenty feet by twenty feet. The work went quickly once he got through the topsoil into the sand beneath it.

"Like digging at the beach," Marceno noted.

Five minutes later the operator caught the teeth of the scoop on something, noticed, then cut the engine. "There," he hollered, pointing at the hole in the earth. "Look!"

At that moment I saw a car speeding along the new road, kicking up dust. It turned off the road, bumped over the field. Martha Hallock emerged from the door and stood uneasily ten feet away.

"Stop!" she screamed. "Stop!"

But Marceno didn't. And within a minute his men had scraped their shovels across a rusted flat piece of metal, which upon further digging curved downward at the edges. It was rusted through and the original paint had flaked away entirely. Then the men jumped down and dug until the curved ends of the metal became a chromed edge that then fell away to glass; we were looking at a buried vehicle of some sort.

"No, no!" cried Martha Hallock. "This, this—"

But the men kept digging, and whatever might be inside what now looked to be an old subcompact was obscured by the dirt on the windshield and a hanging forest of mushrooms inside. Marceno ran his thumb over the grille markings. Toyota Corolla. Or, spelled KROWLA, if you were semi-illiterate, drunk, and maybe suffering from a mild concussion. The men concentrated on digging away the dirt in front of the car to get access to the front axle, and after they did this, the bulldozer was able to haul the car up and out of the earth, the rotten and collapsed tires not spinning but dragging flabbily up the incline of dirt until the car lay perched over the lip of the hole. Then, with one more tug of the dozer, the car lurched forward ten more feet, prehistoric in its rusted ruin, yet all the same utterly recognizable as from our era, our modern time, the blurry then-and-now, a car that was once new and driven off a dealer's lot, used and lived in for the carrying of people and children and groceries and whatever else we use cars for, and the fact that the inside of it was dark, the windows smeared as I have said with earth on the outside and spores and molds on the inside made all of us stand back in sickened wonder.

"Open the door," Marceno ordered one of his men.

"No!" cried Martha Hallock. "No!"

"Open it this second!"

But the man, slope-shouldered and miserable as a dog that dares to disobey its master, just shook his head in meek defiance, whispering something fearful and worried. Marceno turned to another man, who agreed to touch the door with his shovel—experimentally, jabbing it like it might writhe in response, but this was all he could do.

"Don't," said Martha Hallock. "You mustn't. Enough is enough. I demand you stop."

I looked at Marceno and spoke in a low voice. "If you are decent, you will escort her away from this, no matter what is or isn't inside there. It's terrifying her."

"Yes," Marceno nodded. "Of course." And he signaled to his men to help Martha Hallock back into her car, where she sank into the cushioned seat and wept.

Then I turned to Marceno. "I'll do it," I said.

"You?"

"Yes," I told him. And I did.

I put my hand on the driver's-side door and pulled the handle. Nothing happened. I yanked, quite hard, and the door fell away, right off the car, hinges rusted to nothingness. I jumped backward. Inside the driver's side we saw an enormous mass of mushrooms crowding against each other, falling with thick abundance over the seat and floor and everywhere, covering like a thick blanket whatever might be below them, and I felt just strong enough to step forward and brush my hands against them, and what I saw made all of us understand that we were gazing not just into a buried car but a dripping, imperfectly sealed crypt—what I saw was a woman's watch and a curled brown athletic shoe and a rotten swath of a flowered material such as might be used to make a summer dress. What I saw was what remained of Jay Rainey's mother.

Yes, as the official tests would later prove—some remaining teeth, a bit of hair, the serial number in the car's engine block—this was what was left of Jay's mother, aged thirty-nine years old when she died, a woman who had *not* abandoned her only child, her strapping, beautiful son, but—judging from the position of the car in the field—had gone looking for him, perhaps catching a taint of herbicide floating on the night air, which meant that she found her death.

Marceno's men lay a section of plastic sheeting on the ground and on it they put what they found: one earring, a wedding ring, the running shoes, a necklace of semiprecious stone, and a small clay dog. Marceno examined it and handed it to me. It was heavy in the hand, and I wiped the dirt from it. The creature had a certain crude sweetness and had been glazed. I turned it over, my thumb finding the lettering on the belly: JAY R. 4TH GRADE.

We pried open the trunk of the car, and in it were the following items: a plastic gasoline can, a beach chair, an aluminum baseball bat, and rubber flip-flops. No suitcases, no items suggesting a flight from a bad marriage. I turned to Marceno. He and his men stood silently, understanding what the artifacts meant, tribally respectful of them and the earthen rituals of death.

Martha Hallock sat in her car, weeping fitfully. "My girl," she sobbed. "My sweet girl." How had I not figured out that she was Jay's grandmother?

Marceno and I walked away from the car toward the ocean.

"She sold me the land, you know," he said. "He owned it but she sold it to me."

"I think she knew somebody was buried here, feared it might be true."

"Who?"

"Her daughter, Jay Rainey's mother. Her nephew, Poppy, knew for sure, must have been the one to bury her. There was an accident with herbicide. The mother disappeared that same night, everyone thought she'd left the husband. But Martha knew, somewhere inside her."

Marceno ran his fingers through his hair, demoralized by the waste and stupidity of everything. "Poppy was just putting a little more earth on top of the car, that's all?"

"It looks that way."

"And this man Herschel happened along," confirmed Marceno. "Said what are you doing? And they got in a fight. That could cause a heart attack right there."

"Or Poppy told him what he was doing. Or Herschel figured it out. Or Herschel knew what had happened and was afraid it'd be discovered."

Marceno studied the rusted hulk of the Toyota.

"Poppy was desperate," I went on. "Once the vineyard was planted it would be a very long time, if ever, before the car would be discovered."

"He would be dead."

"More importantly, Jay Rainey would be dead."

"I don't understand."

"Poppy was probably the one who left the herbicide sprayer on. He killed Jay's mother. Found her, panicked, buried the car."

"Even if the ground was soft, that would still take hours."

"He had a bulldozer. He could've found her a few hours before dawn."

Marceno knelt down to touch the earth. "So he was trying to spare Jay Rainey from finding out?"

"I think he probably didn't want to face manslaughter charges. You could begin there."

"But *did* Rainey know?"

"I don't think so. At least not until recently," I said. "He found out in the Havana Room."

Marceno dusted off his suit and faced me, ever the tidy international businessman. "So, are we done then?"

"Not quite."

"Hmm?"

"I want to know why you didn't come to the steakhouse when I called and told you Poppy had arrived there."

He inspected his fingernails. "I didn't feel it was necessary, Mr. Wy-eth."

"But I had the information you wanted."

No answer. Marceno's silence felt cold. He adjusted his watch—stalling, I figured, preparing an explanation. "This man H.J. came to my office," he finally said. "Full of threats." He looked at me and shrugged, as if the rest of it was obvious.

"What happened?"

"We made an agreement. We were both looking for the same people. It wasn't supposed to—" He appeared to sense that I could still cause him enormous trouble. "I owe you an apology."

"It was just business for you," I muttered.

But this was not the way Marceno chose to understand himself, and his eyes found their way back to the rusted hulk sitting atop the earth, the blanket of mushrooms inside. "Men died for nothing. For money, for *wine*."

Not Jay, I thought.

I will tell now four more things. I will tell why I slept very poorly the next few days; I will tell what I did with Jay's estate, including his letters to his daughter, Sally Cowles; I will tell what I said to her about her true father; and I will tell what passed between me and Allison Sparks in our last conversation, during which we discussed the terrible events in the Havana Room.

Knowing only two things, that Jay lay in the field near death, and that his mother stopped her car before him, one can surmise the horror she felt as she saw her son fallen to the earth. She would naturally have wanted to open the door and rush to him. But did she pause? In an instinct of self-preservation, perhaps smelling or tasting the herbicide that had already come in through the window or air vents? Did she sense that she needed to back up in the soft earth and flee? And was Jay in any way aware of the headlights upon him, did he know it was his mother? Perhaps she called to him. Perhaps he knew that she was affected by the herbicide. In any case she must have looked upon him, seen him dying, and then known she was dying herself. These are the lost seconds of Jay Rainey's lost life. Seconds that yet tick forward unknown. And, I wondered, did Jay have any remembrance of the lights of his mother's car or her voice or perhaps even the sight of her slumped form against the dashboard, or even out the door, dying in the field? Had there been one molecule of this memory? Did he think that she had gone looking for him, that he had unknowingly drawn her to her death? That, too, was undiscoverable. One might infer from his pursuit of his lost daughter that the answer was yes—that there was within him a hidden call of the flesh, to find the flesh that was of him and of those from whom he'd come. These are the deep pressures of being human, and those of us who are parents feel the forwardness of our flesh even as we know our own is failing. The rhythmic scything away of the previous generation forces our attention to our children, for if we do not have our children, then, knowing ourselves to be doomed, we do not have anything. People who don't have children often take violent exception to the idea that their lives are in any way existentially different from the lives of those who do have children, and to this I only laugh darkly to myself and think, Well yes, you may think that, but you are already dead, my friend. I am also already dead, yet live on in my son, who will have his son or daughter when I am dispersed with the fluorocarbons, part of the mist of ozone cooking the earth. Yes, I will yet live. And I think this is in all of us. And in Jay Rainey, too. The will to live. To pursue life is always to flee death, including murders in which one is somehow complicit, and this pursuit of life is not only essential to the survival of the species but also a courageous pull from the terror of biological anonymity. We want to be known. We want someone to know us. And there is something more, which obtained in the case of Jay Rainey. If you are a man, you cannot live without women, whence men come. I don't mean that men cannot live without women sexually, which of course they can, but rather without the *fact* of them, in the man's past, as mother and sister, as mitigating influence against all that is the most awful in man's murderous endocrinological nature. Women, it should be admitted, often make men better than they otherwise would be, save them from themselves. Jay could find lovers, of course, but except for Martha Hallock, his grandmother, he had no female who knew him, no woman who had insight into his essence, no female blood. Is it unreasonable to think he hoped, if only instinctively, that his daughter might someday look upon him and know him as no other female might, with the knowledge of shared flesh? As daughter to him, her father? On this, the answer is not lost. The answer is yes.

And then there is the matter of Jay's letters to Sally and what she might know.

This was the hardest thing of all. I studied the question. I really did. She did not understand why she had been kidnapped. She had not been harmed, at least not physically. Not a hair. She had spent less than one hour of her life in the company of some strange men. If she was traumatized, perhaps her stepfather and stepmother had seen to it that she had a trip to Disney World or a ski trip, some distraction that melted and obscured that one strange hour. An hour in a girl's life, what might it mean?

It was a grave responsibility. I could give her those letters, either directly or through Cowles, whose whereabouts I knew. But in the end, I did not. She had not asked to be born to doomed parents, she had not asked to think that she might have been abandoned. It was enough already, I supposed, that she'd experienced her mother's death. We have a responsibility to be merciful, I think, to save not just a life but the best version of a life, if possible. I do not think that I can ever forgive myself for the death of young Wilson Doan, and all that resulted, but I believe that I decided rightly when I took Jay's letters and watched their torn little pieces float down the Hudson River, releasing his daughter from the life she did not need to have. If this damns me, then it will not be for the first time, but I trust it does not. I will never be at peace with myself—how could I?—but the sight of those letters floating along the water gave me some hope, some fleeting belief, that the past may leave our bodies as surely as we will leave the earth.

I thought that question was resolved. But then David Cowles called me, at my office.

"I have a few questions for you," he said. "It took me a long time to contact you. I had to go through the old Voodoo owners, then some man named Marceno, through his office."

"What can I do for you?"

"I can't seem to find Mr. Rainey, and—"

"He's dead," I said.

"Dead?"

"But let me try to answer your questions anyway."

An hour later, I climbed the stairs to Cowles's offices, wondering what he knew, what he wanted to know, what answers I'd provide him. He was waiting for me at the door, which he unlocked silently and locked again behind me. I followed him to his office. Sally was there.

"This is the man?" Cowles asked. "This man was there, too?"

She turned. For a moment she looked older, the woman she would become. "Yes." She nodded at Cowles. "He's the one who saved me."

He motioned for me to sit, which I did, with some apprehension.

"Naturally I want an explanation," said Cowles. "I want to know why my daughter was snatched on her way home from school and driven fifty blocks south." He drew a breath. "She's been terrorized. It took her three weeks to tell us. My wife and I were *shocked*. We are *this* close to calling the police. We see no reason not to bring the full fucking might of the law down on you, Wyeth!"

"Daddy, I wasn't gone *that* long. They brought me to *you*."

"You were taken!"

"It wasn't his fault, Daddy."

"I don't know that I believe that."

"Jay Rainey was not well," I began. "He had people after him."

"What does my daughter have to do with that?"

"He was—" I wanted to be careful. "He was unstable."

"What the hell did he think he could accomplish by kidnapping my daughter?" Cowles bellowed.

Oh pal, I thought, you should stop now.

"It's very hard for me to say what he was thinking."

"Sally," said Cowles. "I want you to leave my office so Mr. Wyeth and I can talk privately. But if you want to ask anything of Mr. Wyeth first, or tell him anything, then now is the time."

"Okay." She stood up. "I guess I want to know if it was dangerous to me. Being in the car, I mean. Was I in any real danger?"

"Yes." I nodded. "But how much I don't know."

"Why were you there?"

"I didn't want to be there."

"But why were you?"

"I was trying to get Jay Rainey out of the mess he was in."

"Did you?"

I waited for words to come to me.

"What happened, I mean?"

"He died, Sally." Your father died, I thought. You'll never know him now.

"That man? How?"

"Mr. Rainey had a breathing problem. He was ill."

"He was killed?"

"No. As I said, he had serious health problems."

"Was he a nice man?"

"He was a man who had been hurt," I answered. "He meant well."

"Did he want to hurt me?"

I looked at Cowles before I answered. "No. In no way did he wish to hurt you, Sally."

She heard this and something seemed to relax in her. "So it was more sort of a big mistake, kind of?"

I nodded. "A huge mistake, yes."

Sally shrugged. "Okay." She looked at Cowles. "Dad, I'm going to go check my e-mail, okay?"

"Sure, sure."

"Will you be long?" she asked.

"No, but why?"

"I was hoping we could go past the sports store on the way home."

"You got it," he said.

She left and Cowles closed the door and faced me, unable to contain his anger. "Which part of your sick story is bullshit?"

"What do you really want, Mr. Cowles?"

"I want to know why Rainey was obsessed with Sally."

"I'm not going to tell you."

"What?" He held his fists tight and I thought of Wilson Doan Sr., and how I'd been destroyed once already. "I can go to the fucking police, Wyeth. They'll—"

"I know. And then, unfortunately, I'd have to tell them."

"Unfortunately for *you*, you mean?"

I had an obligation here, an obligation to Wilson Doan and his wife, from whom I had taken a child, and I had an obligation to my son, whom I'd allowed to be taken from me, and I had an obligation to Jay Rainey, who, let it be remembered, never revealed himself to his daughter as her father, despite how painful it was for him not to do so. I also had an obligation to Cowles himself, and most importantly I had an obligation to Sally. I had an obligation to her because she was a child, still, and I was an adult, simple as that. My obligation to all of them and my obligation to myself was that I would never again be the agent that separated a child from a parent. Never, never again.

"Unfortunately for whom?" Cowles repeated angrily. "Who would be hurt if the truth got told?"

I looked at him and into him and stared down his fearful righteousness. He blinked several times, then looked away. "Those who love you very much," I finally said. "Those who need a loving father."

Cowles stopped at that. I don't think he quite understood. But he understood that he didn't understand. He knew he didn't need to know something. He slumped a bit, and sighed. "You're asking me to trust you," he said.

"I'm asking you to trust yourself. Trust in what you know."

He pondered this. Finally he nodded to himself.

"All right. My daughter seems okay. It helped her to ask those questions."

"It was wise of you to suggest that," I said.

He made a noncommittal humming noise. "I'm breaking my lease," he announced. "We're moving back to London."

"All right."

"Are you the executor of Rainey's estate?"

"I might be," I realized, "by default."

"You wouldn't be trying to enforce the lease."

"Of course not."

"You'll give me an address and number in case there are any further questions?"

"Yes."

"Let me just ask—"

"Sure."

"How long did you work for Mr. Rainey?"

"Just a few weeks."

"So you barely knew him."

"Barely."

"Did he have a wife?"

"No."

"No family?"

"No," I said. "He had absolutely no one."

He pondered this, his basic decency getting the better of him. "Bit of a sad story, then."

"Yes."

He stood and shook my hand. "I hope you understand I was scared—a father gets, you know—protective when—"

"You don't have to apologize for that."

I followed him out. Sally was sitting at one of the office's computers, typing away. She noticed me leaving and stood. She had Jay's wide shoulders, the dark eyes, his long legs. But Cowles didn't see it. "Bye," she called politely.

"Bye."

The office door closed behind me and I never saw David or Sally Cowles again. But I lingered behind the door and listened.

"Daddy!"

"What?"

"It's boring here!"

"You want to go home?" Cowles asked her.

"You said we could go get the new hockey stick!"

"We will. Let me just pull together my papers, sweetie, won't be a minute."

"Oh, Daddy!" Sally Cowles cried in exasperation. "I'm so bored!"

That was all I needed to hear, forever, so I slipped away down the steps and outside. The weather was getting warmer and I walked the streets for an hour feeling the strange emptiness of it all. *Jay*, I said to myself, *I did it to protect her.* She didn't need to know who her father was, because if she found out, it would crack her relationship with the man she thought was her father and because her own father was lost to her now. It was a truth within a lie or a lie within a truth—which, I wasn't sure. But I suspected I might have done the right thing. It didn't weigh on me. I'd lied on behalf of a greater good, and though it was not any-where close to bringing poor Wilson Doan back to life, it was a small of-fering of penance, one that might perhaps count.

In time I found myself walking by the steakhouse on Thirty-third Street, but not turning in. The second ceramic pot had been replaced, complete with evergreen. It needed to weather and didn't quite match. One night, finally, as the nights began to warm, I stepped inside the heavy door, past the gold lettering, and all was the same, the mahogany woodwork and oil paintings. As ever, as if nothing had happened. It was perhaps an hour before the dinner rush. I saw a busboy vacuuming at the far end of the dining room, the maître d' checking the reservation book. The door to the Havana Room hung open, I noticed, and before anyone could object, I darted through it and down the nineteen marble steps, expecting to see the painting of the black-eyed nude above the bar, the books on the shelves, the ancient barman wiping a glass, the dusty sconces above the wainscoting.

But the room had been painted an improbable yellow, cheery and harmless as a child's bedroom, with all of the paintings and old books removed. The tile floor had been carpeted over beautifully and the booths and men's room removed—torn out. Two long banquet tables had been set up, with folds of linen tablecloth, and each bore a printed placard that read: Women in Dialogue/Monthly Guest Speaker Dinner. On cue I heard voices coming in through the door and found myself confronted by fifteen or sixteen professional women eagerly taking their seats.

"I'd like three bottles of sparkling water at each table, please," one woman said to me. "Thank you."

I didn't bother to explain her mistake and instead slipped out the doorway and up the stairs into the main dining room. I walked straight through the kitchen looking for Allison. I saw cooks and busboys and waitresses, many of them familiar, but no Allison.

"Can I help you, sir?"

"I'm looking for Allison Sparks."

"She's here, somewhere."

"In her office?"

"I think she's in one of the lockers downstairs."

"Will you take me to her?"

"Is it—?"

"It's quite serious, yes."

I followed the waitress down the stairs and along a corridor hung with pipes until I saw the open door to the meat room.

"Allison?" called the waitress.

"Yes."

The waitress nodded at me and scurried away.

"Yes?" came Allison's voice, exasperated.

I stepped inside the room. As before, it was hung with perhaps fifty beef carcasses, each stamped and dated for aging. Allison stood examining her clipboard, back to me. She turned, and drew her breath. "Bill."

I nodded. "I almost called you."

"You should have."

"You painted the Havana Room," I said.

"I wouldn't use that exact word."

"No?"

"I *destroyed* the Havana Room, Bill."

"Scrubbed it away."

"I hate how it looks. *Hate* it."

There was an uncomfortable tension between us.

"Are you going to tell me?" I said.

"What?"

"What happened."

She shook her head. "I don't know. I told you before. Ha had some men come."

"Men in a van, I know that. I mean what happened to Jay."

Allison stared at me, something passing through her eyes.

"I mean, how did he die? You told me he walked out of there but I know he didn't. He didn't go to his truck, he didn't go to his apartment, he died in the very same clothes he was wearing that night."

"I really don't know what happened, Bill."

"Did he eat any fish?"

"I don't know."

"Did you *see* Jay eat any fish?"

"No."

"You saw him collapse?"

"No."

"Did you see him *after* he collapsed?"

"Yes."

"Did you see him after he died?"

She wouldn't answer.

"You *did*."

"Yes."

"Then you saw Ha's men take him away?"

Nothing.

"And me, too?"

Nothing.

"I was left for fucking dead, Allison!"

She'd been willing to let go of the chance that I might be saved, and I might have hated her for that, but here I was, after all. I'd been at fault like the others, in my own way, and the rope of mutual betrayal had been braided from the desires of all of us.

"Tell me how Jay really died, Allison."

"I don't know."

"Allison, *remember*. Ha made eight portions of fish. Denny and Gabriel had two each. H.J. had two. I had one. One was left. It was in front of Jay when I passed out. Did he eat it or not?"

"No."

"And he was fine?"

"Unsteady, but fine, I guess."

"What do you mean, unsteady?"

"He was bent over, like he got sometimes. Tired-looking."

I waited.

"I went upstairs to open the restaurant for the night. The cooks were there, the waitstaff, everybody. Ha came with me."

"Did Ha think he'd killed me?"

"Yes. By accident. He said he gave you too much of it. He said your brain was destroyed and that you would die in the van."

"Seems to me he got it just right," I said. "Where's Ha now?"

"I told you before, I don't know."

"Left?"

"Right away. That same night."

"Did you think about looking for him?"

Allison shook her head—sadly, I thought.

"Why not?"

"I have no idea where he could be, that's why."

"What's his complete name?" I said. "You could do a search for him by—"

"Don't know."

"You don't know? Is Ha his first name or his last?"

"Don't know."

"But you hired him."

"I paid him under the table. We never did any paperwork."

"Is Ha his real name?"

She smiled. "I don't know."

"No more funny Chinese fish."

"Nope."

"All right." I wanted to resume the sequence. "Where was Jay when you and Ha went upstairs to open the restaurant?"

"He had a cigar in his hand."

"You saw him light it?"

"No."

"That's the last time you saw him, saw him alive?"

Allison's eyes filled and she blinked.

"Come on!"

She nodded. "Yes. When we came back maybe, I don't know, maybe ten minutes later, he was dead. On the floor, dead. It was awful."

"Had he eaten the last piece of fish?"

"No. I didn't understand how—"

"Was a cigar there? Was it lit? Did it burn out?"

"I don't know. Maybe. I got kind of hysterical, actually."

She wasn't telling me something.

"I saw the girl the other day," Allison mused, eyes downcast. "I'd seen her in the neighborhood. She looks just like him."

I still wondered why I didn't believe Allison's story about Jay and the cigar. Or how I could believe it.

"You knew?" she asked. "That night we—?"

"I was figuring it out, yes."

"She lived right across from me." Allison was telling it to herself now. "He was trying to find her—"

"Wait," I said. "What happened to the last portion of fish?"

Allison slumped forward and fell against me. Despite myself I held her. "I kept looking at it," she said. "Then I ate it."

She wept against my chest. Yes, Allison Sparks, hard and tough and rotten, sobbed against my chest. "Jay was *dead*, I thought *you* were dead, you had foam in your mouth, and there was that Lamont guy, *he* was dead, too, and I panicked, Bill. I was so upset about the girl and I understood why Jay did it, why he—I wasn't angry with him anymore, it was just so sad, so terribly *sad*, and I wanted to just *die*, to die there with him."

"So you—?"

"I took the fish and ate it and Ha yelled at me and he dragged me down and stuck his fingers down my throat and I fought him and hit him and he wouldn't let me do it, Bill, he took the spoon and shoved it down my throat and made me vomit."

She collapsed against me again. I had eaten the fish of my own accord, but I had trusted that it was a benign portion. And it had not been, not quite—or just barely? But Jay's portion *had* been poisonous. Had Ha meant to kill him? Why? Because of his betrayal of Allison? For bringing trouble to the steakhouse? Or maybe a portion of the fish just right for a big man of Jay's size would have been lethal for Allison, and she'd realized this. I'd never know.

I left Allison there, collapsed against the wall in the meat locker, and found my way back upstairs, through the kitchen and out of the restaurant. I could not resist one more peek into the Havana Room, which, I now saw, had been renamed the Flower Lounge, and when I came to the door, I conjured the room for myself—the mahogany wainscoting, the black-and-white tiles, the volumes on the shelves—and there I stopped. I could hear the clever voices of the Women in Dialogue group and I realized it'd be best for me never to go down the stairs again.

I turned toward the exit, and it was at that moment that the elderly literary gentleman I'd seen twice before arrived, dressed in an excellent suit. Sober, he was quite the distinguished lion.

"I'm giving a talk," he announced, assuming I'd recognized him. "I'm expected."

I noted the haughty gray eyebrows, the lifelike teeth. "You're the guest speaker?" I asked.

He was in a hurry. "Yes."

I pointed at the Havana Room door. "You've been down there before."

"Yes," he answered, "and I see they finally abandoned their silly little charade."

I couldn't smile. My mood was not good. I pushed out through the heavy front door. If you live long enough in New York City, there are places you avoid, and now the entrance of that steakhouse is one of mine.

A week or two passed, and I was happy to be buried under paperwork at my new job. More than happy—relieved. Tuthill remained a stupendous rainmaker and the young men he'd hired thrived in the new business. He and I laughed a bit privately, older men knowing how younger men were going to make us rich. And we would be rich, or rather he already was and I would become so, because he told me that first I would be his partner and we'd build from there. It was a new cycle, a new season, a new chance—something that the city gives you from time to time. It was even better than that. Judith called to say she'd be coming to town with our son in the next month.

Meanwhile, Jay Rainey's estate would go into escrow. He had no registered will, so the court asked me, as his last lawyer of record, if I would dispose of the estate. This would be a lengthy process, and when I called Martha Hallock to ask her who his nearest living relative was, she said, "I am."

"What do you want me to do with the money?"

"I want you to sell that building."

"And the proceeds? How can I send them to you?"

She coughed. "I don't need the money. Give it to the land trust out here. They buy open spaces and preserve them. Several million bucks will go a long way."

I thought of Jay's boyhood out there, in those open spaces, and this seemed a kind of fitting memorial to him.

"Also give some to the family," Martha Hallock told me. "Give half."

"The family?"

"Herschel's widow," she said. "Take out your fee and give them half of the rest."

I called Mrs. Jones and explained that a very substantial sum was coming to her. She was gracious. "Our family lost one of our boys a little while back," she said.

"I'm very sorry," I replied. And I was. I could have told her that the reason H.J. was dead was that she had enlisted him in her effort to get compensation for Herschel's death, that her judgment had been wrong, but then again, her cause had been just, as had H.J.'s, and neither of them had imagined that his fate would come down to a piece of fish served in a steakhouse by an illegal Chinese immigrant. No one could have imagined that, and so I repeated my condolences and gently hung up.

I waited for the police to call. Try as I might, of course, I could not escape the fact that I knew how certain crimes and murders had been committed. I told myself that clearing up these cases wouldn't bring back any of the dead, would only endanger me and others. Yes, I absolutely was thinking of myself. I can't deny it. But I knew too that if I went to the police, one question would elicit ten others and within a few days Sally Cowles would be drawn into the investigation, and if that happened, she would know that the man who had touched her ear in the limousine had been her father and now was dead. And David Cowles, the man who had clothed and fed and cared for her as his own, would be revealed to himself, to the world, and to Sally as not her father. A child would lose her father, and a father would lose his child.

No, the police did not call, but I was not yet free. I felt infected by a splinter of dread, a nagging sense that one thing remained unresolved. And then, finally, I got it, I remembered.

In the plastic bag of Jay Rainey's effects, which I now kept in my office safe, there was the HAVANA ROOM matchbook. To the best of my knowledge, Jay had been in the room only twice, once when he did the real estate deal and the last time. I did not remember seeing him pick up a matchbook during the first visit, and except when I briefly left the room to read the contract, I was there every minute that he was.

Remembering all this, I opened my safe, the combination of which was Timothy's birth date, and retrieved the matchbook. It hadn't occurred to me before to open it, but now I did—

—and what was there was not proof, not exactly, but it will have to do. One match had been torn out of the book. Jay had lit a match and dropped the matchbook into his pocket. You could surmise that he looked around the Havana Room and saw three dead men and his own seemingly loyal lawyer unconscious (foaming at the mouth, eyes rolling) and wondered what lay in store for him. After all, he had just said good-bye to his daughter, presumably forever, and he had not told her who he was. This was an enormous blow, but it was followed by the crude map Poppy had drawn, which showed where his mother had been interred all those years ago—which told him that she had, in all likelihood, died the very death he had narrowly missed himself.

I assert that this is quite enough to kill a man, yank all hope from his heart, especially one who knows himself to be already doomed. Jay's long chase was over; there was only now the waiting for death, the slow sink toward asphyxiation. So he made a symbolic gesture, a grand one, even—except that no one saw it.

In the Havana Room, one could choose a Cuban cigar, and if the tobacco was excellent, the smoke thick and sweet and beguiling as it drifted past the mahogany wainscoting and oil paintings up to the pressed-tin ceiling, then it was also true that this particular act could kill a man such as Jay Rainey, especially if one brought the smoke in deep and held it, bit shut the mouth and squeezed tight the nose until the long-tormented and fragile bronchial tissue spasmed and swelled, so much that within thirty seconds or so it did not matter if Jay fell over, gasping freely, eyes bulging, throat ribboned in strain, face a red rictus of depletion. No, it did not matter by then. He dropped heavily to the floor; the cigar fell away to be unknowingly swept up later by Ha; he rolled, he gasped, and suffered there on the black-and-white tiles of the Havana Room. A human being with a very low FEV can drop into acute respiratory distress quite rapidly. Unconsciousness occurs as the oxygen content of the blood plummets, the heart pumps rapidly, trying to save itself, thereby consuming what oxygen is left, and all the bodily functions collapse. The linings of the lungs fall into what is termed "enzymatic cascade." Within five or six minutes the brain is saturated with waste chemicals and profoundly damaged; death ensues soon thereafter.

Yes, knowing what I know about my former client Jay Rainey, and considering that matchbook with one torn match stub, which I still possess, it is my opinion here and now and forever that he quickly took his own life before it was taken from him slowly, and I would be very hard pressed not to see his gesture as paradoxically self-affirmative, a certain gift to himself even, but no small tragedy for those few of us who knew the man, however briefly.

Judith had said she'd be staying in a midtown hotel, and would call when she and Timothy arrived. I tried not to expect anything but the worst. "It'd be nice to feel the city around me," she added, and I thought I heard a wistfulness in her voice. "Timothy wants to see you, so much."

When she got in, I waited for her call. I knew she'd be nervous, as would I. Finally, the phone rang in the evening.

"I want to see you," I told her.

Judith didn't respond to this directly. "So much has happened," she finally said.

I had to agree with that.

"So you're working these days?"

"I recently took a job with a new firm," I told her, making it appear more substantial than it was, and Judith made a sound of surprised appreciation.

"But it's not a situation where you end up with $852 million," I added.

"Yeah, well," she sighed. But she didn't elaborate.

I tried to think of something to say.

"You know, Bill," she began again, "basically I freaked out."

"Right."

"Are you seeing anyone?" she ventured.

I waited to answer this. "Yes," I finally said.

"Oh," she responded, a little flustered. "Do you mind—I mean, it's not my business, Bill—but do you mind telling me who you're seeing?"

"I don't mind."

"Well . . . who?"

"You," I said. "I'm seeing you. Tomorrow, at 3 p.m., in the tearoom of the Plaza Hotel."

Judith was pleased to hear this, I could tell. I still knew her, still heard everything in each breath. "Good . . . that's good," she answered, and I thought to myself that it might be very nice to see her, to look her in the eyes, to find her in the bustle and hurry of the city, to pick her out of the crowd and to stop in front of her—and embrace.

And I was right. There they were the next day, coming toward me. Judith walked resolutely, I could tell, and Timothy had a baseball glove on his hand, the one I'd sent him, and was tossing and catching a ball. I stood to greet them. Judith's body felt familiar. So did Timothy's, though he was much taller. I crushed him to my chest, as Judith watched. It'd be a matter of forgiveness, on all sides. Maybe it wasn't likely. Maybe it was beyond us. But maybe it also wasn't unthinkable. Things stranger than that have happened, after all, things much stranger than that.

ACKNOWLEDGMENTS

Each book brings me greater awareness that I have been helped by many people along the way. Their gifts vary—from time to thought to encouragement to unalloyed faith to rhubarb cake—and each gift, in its way, was crucial to the slow making of this book. I wish to thank: Lynn Buckley; Charles Church; Mark Costello; Jill Cross; Kris Dahl; Brian DeCubellis; Jim Dillon; Janet and Don Doughty; Jeremy Epstein; Nan Graham; Sloan Harris; Kathryn, Sarah, Walker, and Julia Harrison; Dan Healy; Mike Jones; Larry Joseph; Abby Kagan; Christopher Kent; Naomi Kristen; Sarah Knight; Al Kulik, M.D.; Jud Laghi; Susan Moldow; Spencer Nadler, M.D.; Aodaoin O'Floinn; Rich and Nancy Olsen-Harbich; Vince Passaro; Joyce and Rose Ravid; Tom Schindler; Lynn Schwartz; Earl Shorris; Charles Spicer; and Scott Wolven.

How an editor helps to bring forth a novel from a writer is intimate and mysterious. I am fortunate to work with one of the great editors in all of publishing, John Glusman. His questions were catalytic, his suggestions perfect, his reservations wise. John's gifts are in this book, too.

A NOTE ABOUT THE AUTHOR

Colin Harrison's previous novels are *Afterburn, Manhattan Nocturne, Bodies Electric,* and *Break and Enter,* which have been published in a dozen countries. He and his wife, the writer Kathryn Harrison, live with their three children in Brooklyn, New York.